E. H. Knatchbull-Hugessen

Crackers for Christmas

E. H. Knatchbull-Hugessen

Crackers for Christmas

ISBN/EAN: 9783743386815

Manufactured in Europe, USA, Canada, Australia, Japa

Cover: Foto ©Andreas Hilbeck / pixelio.de

Manufactured and distributed by brebook publishing software (www.brebook.com)

E. H. Knatchbull-Hugessen

Crackers for Christmas

CRACKERS FOR CHRISTMAS

More Stories

BY

THE RIGHT HON. E. H. KNATCHBULL-HUGESSEN

(Lord Brabourne)

AUTHOR OF 'STORIES FOR MY CHILDREN,' 'MOONSHINE,' ETC.

WITH ILLUSTRATIONS

New Edition

LONDON
GEORGE ROUTLEDGE AND SONS
BROADWAY, LUDGATE HILL
NEW YORK: 9, LAFAYETTE PLACE
1883

LORD BRABOURNE'S STORIES.

In Crown 8vo, cloth, 3s. 6d. each. With Illustrations:

———◇———

TALES AT TEA-TIME.

MOONSHINE.

CRACKERS FOR CHRISTMAS.

STORIES FOR MY CHILDREN.

QUEER FOLK.

UNCLE JOE'S STORIES.

OTHER STORIES.

THE MOUNTAIN SPRITE'S KINGDOM.

Her Royal Highness the Princess of Wales.

———◆◆———

Madam,

This volume is published at the request of many child-readers, and other lovers of magic lore. I did not venture to ask permission to dedicate a book to your Royal Highness until the kind reception accorded by the public to my first attempt emboldened me to hope that the second might not be deemed un-worthy of such an honour. It appears to me peculiarly appro-priate that stories, humbly framed after the model of the inimit-able Hans Andersen, should be dedicated to an Illustrious Lady who not only resembles that author in her Danish origin, but also in having won to herself the love of English hearts by a spell no less potent than that by which her great countryman has captivated the affections of countless English readers. It seems natural also that an author who ventures upon that field of Fairy literature, their mutual love of which constitutes one of the many ties of sympathy between the peoples of Denmark and England, should desire to dedicate his work to a Princess who represents in her own person the strongest and most popular tie which unites the two countries.

With the most profound respect,

I beg to subscribe myself,

Madam,

Your obedient, humble servant,

E. H. KNATCHBULL-HUGESSEN.

PREFACE.

I WISH to take this opportunity of thanking the numerous friendly reviewers of 'Stories for my Children,' and of alluding to one unfavourable criticism.

Certain tender-hearted people think that the domestic life of my Ogres and their cruel dealings with mankind are too vividly and graphically described, so as to alarm and disgust the youthful mind. But what was I to do?

It is a well-understood fact with regard to Ogres, that they do not, and never did, live upon strawberries and cream; and to paint them as pleasant, agreeable creatures would be contrary to all precedent. Seriously speaking, the Ogres and Dwarfs of Fairy literature are, in one point of view, intended to represent the evil of various sorts and degrees which surrounds mankind; and to describe them as otherwise than repulsive would be to destroy the whole force of the allegory. I hope, however, that the present volume may be found less liable to the imputed fault.

CONTENTS.

LIST OF ILLUSTRATIONS.

CRACKERS FOR CHRISTMAS.

———

I.

THE OGRE'S CAVE.

THERE was once a little boy named Cecil, who had blue eyes, light hair, a comfortable home, and an adventurous disposition. The two former were very good things to have, the third ought to have made him both happy and thankful, and the fourth was pretty sure to get him into trouble. And so it did. Instead of being happy and thankful in his comfortable home, Cecil was always wanting to see the world, and know more of its goings on. He was not content to sit still in the school-room and learn the lessons which boys and girls have to learn before they know enough to face the outer world, but he was too much inclined to think lessons altogether a bore, and to fancy that he could get on quite well without them. Poor little man! it was just like a child trying to run before he knows how to stand alone, or a little bird wishing to fly before he has proved and tried the strength of his young wings—both are pretty sure to have a tumble, and it is well indeed if no bones are broken. A spirit of in-

1

quiry is a good thing in a boy, but then it should be accompanied by a spirit of obedience to those who are set over him, and a desire to learn in the way and by the means provided for him. And the boy or girl who hates regular lessons and tries to learn only in his or her own way, and according to the fancy of the moment, is pretty sure to get into some scrape or another before long. So you will see it was with Master Cecil, and the story I am going to tell you will be a useful lesson to all young gentlemen who are of a self-willed and conceited spirit.

It happened that Cecil's papa and mamma had taken a house by the sea-side, that the children might have some bathing; and fine fun there was to be had, too, on the shore—picking up shells and building castles of sand and pebbles, and making trenches up to the castle, which the tide would wash away when it came in, and leave behind no more traces of them than old Time makes of the castles in the air which people are so fond of building, and which generally come to nothing after all. Cecil was very fond of playing on the sea-shore, and joining in games with the other children, but he also liked to steal off alone and play by himself; and although he had been told that he must never touch the boats which the sailors had left, drawn up high and dry on the beach, I am sorry to say that he paid no attention to what was said to him; but if there were no sailors near, he was pretty sure to climb into the first boat he could find, pull all the things about, and have a regular game all by himself. One day it happened that he had got a half-holiday given him—or taken one for himself, I am not sure which—and, as usual, he crept off to the beach as quickly and as

quietly as possible, and looked about him for amusement. There were several boats scattered about here
and there, but there was one, rather smaller than the
rest, not far from the edge of the water, and so tempting
to a mischievous boy, that, without thinking twice
about it, Cecil tumbled into it, and began to turn
everything topsy-turvy. Presently he jumped out
again, and seeing that the boat was fastened by a rope
to a post on the beach, nothing would serve him but to
try his new knife on the rope, and this he did to such
good purpose, that he cut it asunder in a very short
time. Then he climbed into the boat again, and
played till he was quite tired, and thought he would
make a bed of a sailor's great, rough coat which he
found in a corner of the boat, and play at going to bed.
His play, however, soon turned into real earnest, for in
a few moments he fell fast asleep, and slept as sound as
any little boy that ever was born. At last he woke up
with a start, and sat upright. Where was he ? Where,
indeed !

Whilst he slept the tide had come in, and the boat
had floated out to sea. I don't know what the sailors
could have been about to have left their boat so long,
so that it is not the slightest use to ask me. I only
know that out to sea the boat went, and carried Cecil
with it. And when he sat up and rubbed his eyes, he
was, as you may suppose, pretty considerably astonished to find that he was in such a condition. How long
he had been asleep he could not tell, but it must have
been for a long time, since not only was the beach out
of sight, but the boat was close in upon another shore,
and that, too, quite unlike the land which he had quitted. Great mountains sloped down close to the sea,

covered with palm-trees larger than any which Cecil had ever seen. On the narrow ridge of sand, between the foot of the mountains and the sea, huge masses of rock were scattered about as if they had been torn off at some time or other from the crags above, and hurled down with a mighty hand upon the place where they now lay. There was a barren, desolate look about the place, very different from the cheerful, friendly beach which he had left behind, and Cecil did not like the prospect at all. However, there was no help for it. The boat was slowly, but surely, drifting towards a point at which the foot of the mountain jutted out into the sea, and in another moment she would certainly be ashore. But as the boat almost touched the rock, the boy, who had crept to the further end, gave a little push against the rock, which turned her round, and she floated in another instant on the other side of the point, in a kind of small bay, which Cecil at once perceived. But this was not all he perceived. To his horror and astonishment, close to him, having waded into the water until it was as high as his knees, stood an enormous man. His large head, prominent and sharp teeth, hooked nose, cruel eyes, and general appearance, unmistakeably proclaimed the ogre, and Cecil, who had risen to his feet as the boat rounded the corner, sank upon his knees perfectly speechless with terror. It was useless, however, to think of escape: the monster was apparently waiting for the wretched boy, and making a short step forward, he drew the boat close to him, and exclaimed in a voice which sounded like the thunder at a distance, when you hear it muttering, miles off, over the hills,

'Break my shin-bone, if this isn't lucky! The brat

Capture of Cecil.—P. 4.

has come to the very spot I thought he would,' and
with a laugh so hideous that, as Cecil afterwards said,
it gave him a stomach-ache all over him, he stepped on
shore and drew the boat after him.   Then he stretched
forth his immense hand, and seizing the wretched
Cecil as if he had been a bird caught in a net, held
him out at arms length, and looked at him with a
terribly greedy look.   Then he put out his other hand
and felt the boy carefully all over, after which he
remarked, in a voice which, to other ogres would
probably have sounded cheery, but which filled the boy
with the utmost terror, 'Fat—decidedly fat—but
room for more meat here and there.   Good for a pie,
but hardly fit for a roast.   A week's keeping will do it,
though,' and here he broke into a low chuckle of
a fearful nature.

But at this moment Cecil found his tongue, and
burst into a loud roar.   'O-o-o-o-h !' he yelled.
'Mamma, mamma, take me away.   I *will* be good.
I'll never do it again!   O Mr Ogre, let me go;
please let me go.   I didn't mean it.   I won't do it
again.   Bo-o-o-o-o !'   And he ended in a burst of
tears, which appeared greatly to astonish the ogre.

'Cramp my knee-joints,' he exclaimed in an angry
tone, using an ogre expression which frightened Cecil
all the more because it was utterly unintelligible to him
or any other human boy.   'None of that noise, little
mortal.   Bone my carcase, but if you don't hold your
row this instant, I'll eat you raw !'

This terrible threat, and the extraordinary language
which accompanied it, so utterly paralyzed Cecil with
fear that he ceased crying in a moment, upon which
the ogre wrapped him carefully up in a red silk pocket-

handkerchief, which, as you would suppose of an ogre's pocket-handkerchief, was as big as an ordinary blanket, and putting him into the inside pocket of a large shooting-coat which he had on, walked off with enormous strides, chuckling as he went. You may imagine, though probably you can only do so to a small extent, having never been in a similar position, what were the feelings of the little boy in this new and terrible state of things. He tried to collect his thoughts, but they were so jumbled together by fright and shaking that this was quite impossible; added to which, the shooting-coat being loose, swung freely at each step which the ogre took, and caused the boy to experience a sensation somewhat similar to that which is caused by the motion of a steamer upon a rough sea. However, it did not last long, for after a short journey the monster stopped, and putting his great hand into his pocket, drew his victim out as if it had been a hare or a rabbit of which he was disburdening himself. He took the boy by the leg and threw him down, fortunately upon a lump of straw, so that he was not hurt, and was able to look round and see where he was. They had entered a vast cave which time or ogres had dug out of the seaside mountains, and which was evidently the giant's home. As far as Cecil could see it was a comfortable home enough for ogres, though a very unpleasant place for a mortal boy to find himself in. There was a thick matting on the floor of the room he was in, which seemed to be the hall, and was of considerable size, and the only light came through the large mouth of the cave by which they had entered. Cecil had little time to see more, for the ogre took him up again almost directly and placed him upon a shelf cut out of the solid rock on one side of the cave, about twenty feet from the ground, so that he could not jump down without standing a good chance of breaking a limb. The ogre made no observation as he put him up there, but smiled grimly to himself, as if he knew the prisoner was safe enough; and then walking to the end of the hall, pushed aside a heavy curtain which hung at the top of four stone steps, and passing behind it disappeared from sight. Cecil now began to look about him. He perceived several other shelves cut in the rock, and several large hooks in the wall, but there appeared to be nothing on them; although he could not help thinking that perhaps it was upon these that the ogre hung his game, and he trembled at the thought that before long he might himself be placed in that sad position. There was hardly any furniture in the hall. A large chair with a leathern back, a wooden footstool, and two or three huge walking-sticks, were all that he could see. Frightened as he was, Cecil, who had read and heard a good deal about ogres, but had never before seen one, felt very curious to see what sort of a place it was in which one of this species of beings really lived, and I think, if he could have got down from his shelf, he would have been almost tempted to try and peep behind the curtain at the top of the steps before leaving the cave. But it was quite impossible to get down, so all he could do was to stay quietly where he was, and think over his sad case and tremble at his leisure. He tried to remember all the stories of boys who had fallen into the power of ogres, and comforted himself with the reflection that they had generally managed to escape somehow or other. The ogre usually had a tender-hearted wife: but then, horrid thought, perhaps *this* ogre wasn't married! And when Cecil remembered the exceedingly shabby manner in which his enemy was dressed, and how he had noticed that the hand which seized him had no button on the wristband of its shirt, he feared that this was only too probable. Besides (and this recollection filled him with dismay), only the boys who had escaped from ogres could have told their stories; it was impossible to know how many boys had been caught, killed, and eaten, whose stories there was no one to tell. In short, there was very little comfort to be had from this sort of meditation, and Cecil was by no means in a cheerful frame of mind when the curtain was again pushed aside and the ogre reappeared, followed, however, by another person. This was a little old woman, not much more than four feet high, and exactly as broad as she was tall. She might have been mortal, and she might have been anything else. The thought crossed Cecil's mind directly that if she *was* mortal, and the ogre had never eaten *her*, perhaps there was a chance that he mightn't eat *him;* but a second glance prevented any further comparison between them. No ogre *could* have eaten that old woman. There was toughness in her very look; and so repulsively ugly was she, that to see her upon his plate would have deprived the hungriest cannibal of his appetite in a moment, and have probably rendered him exceedingly uncomfortable for the rest of the day. Her face was round, but wrinkled terribly; her nose was like the beak of a hawk; each of her eyes looked the wrong way; and she wore upon her head a paper cap, from each side of which a few straggling grey hairs peeped out. Altogether she was an object by no means pleasant to look upon; and Cecil felt that there was

little chance of help from *that* quarter, especially when
he discovered from their conversation that this was the
ogre's cook.

'That's him, is it?' she exclaimed in a voice as
harsh and scraping as if she had a dozen nutmeg-graters
at work in her throat at the same moment; 'a likely
young wretch he seems. Take him down, and let me
have a look at him, master.'

Without a word, the ogre stepped up to the shelf,
put out his hand, and taking hold of Cecil, set him
down close to the old woman, who looked at him first
with one eye, and then with the other, and then began
to punch him in the sides and feel his arms and legs, as
if he had been a prize bullock or a fat pig, whilst the
ogre stood gravely looking on.   Presently she leered up
into the latter's face and remarked, 'He'll be a wonderful deal better for a little fatting.   These growing chaps
run about so that they've scarcely time to get fat.   Let
me have him as kitchen-help for a week or ten days, and
you won't know him again.   Wouldn't you like to help
in the kitchen, chick-a-biddy?'   And here she gave
Cecil a playful punch in the ribs which nearly knocked
him over.

In trembling accents he replied, 'If you please,
ma'am, I'd rather go home to my mamma;' on which
the old woman burst out laughing.

'I dare say you would, little chap, but that won't
do.   Boys that sail away in boats all by themselves
can't expect to go back just when they please.   You'll
have to stop a bit with us, and then—'

With a horrible grin she here pointed to the ogre;
and Cecil felt a cold thrill go right through him, just as
if he had sat down suddenly in his bath on a winter's

morning without any warm water. He knew but too
well what the old woman meant, and he felt as he had
never felt before.   He did not dare say anything more ;
and as the old hag turned round and beckoned him to
follow her, he was just about to do so, when the ogre
demanded in a low voice, but one which the boy could
hear only too well, ' What is there for dinner to-night,
dame Mince-'em-all, and what cold meat have you in
the larder ? '

The old cook replied, after a moment's thought,
' Stuffed fisherman and seaweed sauce, and housemaid's
feet and ears to follow, for dinner.   Then there's a cold
loin of lawyer, an architect pie, and the head of that
member of parliament, only it has got no brains in it.
That's all you have.'

' Umph,' grunted the ogre ; ' then fat *him* as soon
as you can : ' and he pointed with his thumb to Cecil,
who hardly knew whether he was standing on his head
or his heels, so frightened was he by all that had occurred, and no wonder either.   He had now nothing to
do but to follow the old hag, who, passing behind the
curtain at the top of the steps, turned down a passage
to the left hand, cut out of the rock, which led to a
large room which, at a glance, Cecil saw was the
kitchen.   There was a large deal kitchen-table in the
middle of the room, dressers and shelves and everything
complete, and a large block in one corner for chopping
meat.   ' What meat ? ' thought Cecil with horror, and
fancied himself being chopped up by the cruel hands of
the old hag.   However, another object attracted his
attention directly—it was a boy ! Yes, another boy,
taller and thinner than himself ; and, in fact, so lean
and scraggy as to be nothing more than a very skeleton

of a boy. He was washing up some plates at the moment Cecil saw him, and Dame Mince-'em-all called out to him at once in a harsh voice, ' Now, Lazybones, look alive with your work; here's a mate for you, though probably not for long; so make the most of him while you've got him.' The boy turned round upon this; it was a miserable, wan, half-starved face that looked upon Cecil, but there was something in it that did not seem quite strange to him. He gazed earnestly at the boy for a moment. Was it? could it be? Yes, it certainly *was* Jack Browning, the boy in the village at home that they never *could* get to learn his catechism, and who *would* go bird's-nesting on a Sunday. This, then, was what he had come to, and a wretched fate it was; but why was he alive instead of having been long ago eaten by the ogre? This was more than Cecil could tell, or guess, and the boy said nothing, but evidently seemed by his look to know who it was that had been brought in by the cook. The latter now went to a cupboard, took out a large pot like a jam-pot, went to the fire-place, put something in a saucepan, and set it on the fire. In a few minutes she took it off and turned the contents into a soup-basin, after which she called to Cecil. ' Here, boy, you must be hungry after your sea-voyage; come and have some victuals.' Now, Cecil was by nature both a hungry boy and one that liked to eat when he was hungry. Frightened as he was, and mistrustful of the old woman, his appetite was very keen, and he thought if he was to be killed, it might as well be with a full stomach as not, so he walked up to the table and sat down on a wooden stool which Dame Mince-'em-all pointed out to him. She then proceeded to pour out

upon a soup-plate a mess of oatmeal porridge of a most
tempting appearance, over which she poured an abundance of gold-looking treacle, making altogether a dish
which no hungry boy could have easily refused. 'Fall
to, boy; fall to,' said the hag, with a grin, which she
meant to be encouraging, but which would have taken
away the appetite of most boys in a moment; 'fall to,
and eat like a man.' Cecil fixed his eyes upon the
porridge, and went at it with such good will that he
cleared the plate in a very few moments. 'That'll do,
that'll do; well done, boy!' chuckled the old woman.
'You're the right sort of feeder for me; no trouble to
make *you* eat;' and she burst into a laugh which made
Cecil think she must really be pleased with him.
'Now,' continued she, 'go and help Lazybones whilst
I go to the larder;' and she hobbled off through a side
door, leaving the boys alone. As soon as she was
gone Jack turned round to Cecil and said, in an earnest
but weak voice, 'What a fool you are to eat like that!
Why, you'll be fat in less than a week!'

'I can't help it,' replied Cecil; 'I was so awfully
hungry: but tell us, how did you come here, and what
sort of a place is it?'

Jack shook his head mournfully. 'Ah!' said he,
'you may well ask. It was all that Sunday bird's-
nesting that did it! The old cook, who is partly a
witch, can only leave this place on Sundays, and can
then do no harm excepting to people who are doing
what they ought not to do. She met me a month ago,
when I had got into the squire's shrubbery to have a
good bird's-nesting, when everybody else was at church,
and told me she knew of some sea-gull's eggs near the
shore. So I went with her, and she gave me some

jam to eat, and I fell asleep directly, and when I woke up I was here! I heard her tell the ogre she would soon fat me, so I have eaten next to nothing ever since. It is miserable work, and I don't know how it will end, I'm sure; but if you eat like you did that porridge just now, you'll be roasted before a week's out, mark my words!'

Cecil looked grave at this, and then said very slowly, 'I don't want to be roasted, and I don't want to be eaten, but I can't starve. Isn't there any chance of getting away?'

'I don't know *how*,' replied the other. 'The old woman is as sharp as a needle, and if we could deceive her there are other difficulties. There is an echo in the outer cave, which enables any one in the whole place to hear the lightest footstep, and the ogre himself is very wide-awake.'

'But,' said Cecil, 'doesn't he ever go out wa'king, or go to sleep? What can prevent our running away, then?'

'Ah!' rejoined his companion, 'you don't know everything yet. The ogre has servants who serve him well. Ten large crabs watch the mouth of the cave night and day. Terrible brutes they are, to be sure! I got out one morning. I really believe Mother Mince-'em-all let me go on purpose to show me how hopeless it was. As soon as I set foot outside the cave the crabs leaped out; one jumped up, and fastened on me behind, so that I could not help yelling, and the ogre was upon me in a moment. Moreover, he has a fearful dog, called Growler, whom he lets loose every evening, and also when he is away from home himself. This dog and the crabs he feeds with the broken meat which is left after his meals, and they are very faithful to him. Nothing can be done that I know of, and I sometimes feel inclined to put the ogre in a passion, so that he may kill me out of hand at once.'

Cecil thought for a moment, and then said very gravely, 'That wouldn't be much good. I don't like that plan. Ned always says " never give in," and Kate told me always to make the best of everything. That's what I shall do. And the best of everything just now was to eat that porridge, and the best of everything now is to keep a sharp look-out for a chance to get away.'

Just as Cecil finished, back came the old cook with some dishes, and set the boys both to work, washing sea-weed for the sauce for the ogre's dinner. So they could talk no more at that moment, but Cecil thought much over all that had been said, and determined to have a try for his life before he was fat enough to be cooked for the ogre's table. When night came, Dame Mince-'em-all told Jack Browning to show the other boy where to sleep. There were some steps out of a little passage at the end of the kitchen, which led up to several small rooms cut out in the rock, each of which was lighted by a small window looking out towards the sea. In one of these a lot of straw had been roughly thrown down, and some old railway rugs upon it—out of these materials the two boys had to make their bed as well as they could, and in a few moments Jack Browning, nearly worn out with fasting, fell sound asleep. But Cecil's mind was too much agitated for this. He had by no means given up hope like his miserable companion, and as he lay on his straw bed, he thought and thought again till sleep was further off than ever. He remembered everything that had happened for a long time past: all his faults seemed to

come up before him, one after the other, and he knew
better than ever that they *were* faults. He remembered
the times that he had been greedy, or selfish, or conceited, or self-willed. He recalled the times that he
had not given up to his sisters, but had been cross
to them, or disobedient to the governess, and even
to his own mamma. All these times · he recollected
very clearly, and he wished—oh, how he wished !—
that the time could all come over again, for then
he thought he would do very differently. But times
never do come over again, which is what everybody
ought to recollect when they are going to do anything which they feel not to be quite right. And
now that Cecil was in great trouble and danger, it was
no use wishing for that which could not happen, and
it was too late to be sorry, for it did not seem likely
that he would ever again see those to whom he would
like to have shown his sorrow. There he lay with a
heavy heart, and no pleasant thoughts, and quite envied
Jack Browning the heavy sleep into which the latter
had fallen. He tossed and turned about for some time,
vainly trying to sleep ; then he tried what keeping quite
still would do ; then he fidgeted again, then he laid still
again, and he was almost thinking he should go to
sleep out of very fatigue and sorrow presently, when he
fancied he heard a low murmuring noise. He sat up
and listened attentively for a few moments. Then he
was *sure* he heard a noise, like somebody singing, in a
very sweet but low voice, and it seemed as if the sound
came from outside the cave. Cecil got up very quietly,
and went to the window. It was only a small window,
with a strong bar of iron across it, so that no one could
possibly get in or out, but he could see through it quite

well, especially as the moon was bright and clear, shining on the rocky shore and the calm sea. And leaning upon the rocks, half in and half out of the sea, he saw, to his intense astonishment, several undeniable mermaids. Yes—with long hair hanging over their white shoulders, with beautiful faces and large tender eyes, singing to each other in tones more deliciously musical than you can imagine, and every now and then giving a playful flap in the water with their fish tails. These were mermaids beyond doubt. Cecil had heard some of the tales of these creatures which learned book-men have written—namely, that they try to tempt people down to the water by their sweet singing, and then drown them, or eat them, or do something disagreeable —he couldn't recollect what. But when he saw how pretty they looked, and how softly they sang, he thought that very likely these stories were not true after all, and, if they were, he quite settled in his own mind that, upon the whole, he would rather be destroyed by a mermaid than eaten by an ogre. But he determined to listen to their song, and try to discover what they really were in character and disposition. One mermaid had drawn herself almost entirely out of the sea on to a low rock, and as she reclined upon it in a graceful atti-tude, she wore a melancholy look upon her face, which seemed to have attracted the attention of one of her companions, who was floating on her back at a little distance from her, and from whom came these words in soft and musical accents—

' Gentle sister of the wave,
        Fellow-friend in joy and woe,
    Why so silent, sad, and grave?
        Fain the reason I would know !

'Softly on the rocky shore
  Ebbs and flows the ceaseless tide,
And the white foam evermore
  Sparkles on the ocean wide.

'Here, of old, for many a day,
  From the caverns of the main
Rising, 'mid the waves to play
  We have sang our tender strain.

''Mid the breakers and the rocks
  We have sported many a time ;
Girt with sea-weed crown our locks ;
  Woo'd the moon with plaintive rhyme ;

'Watch'd the glorious sun above
  Lighten up the depths below,
As the mighty power of Love
  Lights a Life with endless glow ;

'Watch'd the land and watch'd the sky
  From our ocean home so dear ;
Free from mortal misery,
  Free from mortal doubt and fear.

'Ever, in our sportive life,
  Foremost thou among the gay ;
What of sorrow or of strife
  Silences thy voice to-day ? '

And the other mermaid answered, in tones soft and
sweet as the sound of the evening chimes falling upon
the ear when it steals over the calm water upon a still
summer night—

'Truth thou singest, sister bright,
  Telling of the olden days,
When 'twas ever my delight
  In the song my voice to raise,

' From the depths to rise the first—
    Last to cease from sportive game ;
For those bygone hours I thirst—
    Would that I were still the same !

' Blame not silence, sister mine ;
    If I fail my tongue t' employ,
'Tis that all my thoughts incline
    To a theme which chases joy.

' Here we gaily sport and play ;
    But upon the island nigh,
We must witness, day by day,
    Ogre craft and cruelty.

There, within his darksome cave,
    Mortal children languish still ;
Can we not the babies save
    From the monster's cruel will ?

' Power is ours o'er rock and sea,
    Sea and rock the wretch detest ;
Oh! to set the captives free,
    Were a deed for ever blest!

Whilst the mermaid was singing, the other one
raised herself in the water, and listened attentively to
every word ; and as soon as her sister had ceased, she
again began :—

' Well thou knowest, sister dear,
    Rock and sea our power confess ;
If by these the way were clear,
    Mortal sorrow to redress ;

' But, bemoan it as we may,
    Though we rule o'er rock and wave,
Still the island owns the sway
    Of the ogre grim and grave.

' And within his island jail,
    Whilst he holds the children two,
Little can our might avail—
    What can gentle mermaids do?'

Cecil listened with the deepest attention to the singing of the mermaids, and with feelings divided between joy at finding friends so near, and regret at the limit to their power, which appeared likely to prevent them from setting him free. The other singer, however, answered the last words which he had heard in a manner which somewhat reassured him. Lashing the water with her tail in a meditative manner, and at the same time combing her long hair with a comb which sparkled so brightly in the moonlight that it seemed to Cecil as if it was made of gold or silver, she sang again, in her sweet and pleasant tones :—

' Freely, sister, must we own,
    That, alas ! which well we know ;
Mermaid power can ne'er alone
    Free the captives from the foe.

' Would they still remain alive,
    Nor be murder'd in the cave,
They themselves must boldly strive
    From their fate themselves to save.

' If they banish doubt and fear,
    Boldly dare and deeply plan,
Mermaid aid is ever near,
    To assist the child of man.

' Once if they shall touch the waves,
    Rippling on the rocky shore,
Mermaid help the children saves
    From the ogre evermore.'

Here the mermaid stopped, and Cecil could hear no more. He had, however, heard enough to convince him, in the first place, that there was a chance of escape if he could get to the beach; and, secondly, that he must think and act for himself, and try to help himself if he wished to be helped by the mermaids. And this is a very good lesson for boys and girls, and big people too, to learn,—that we cannot succeed in anything in life if we sit still and wait for some one else to bring success to us; but that, whilst we should be very thankful for aid and help which is offered, we should be up and doing for ourselves, and strive to do the work before us manfully and boldly. It is much more pleasant, too, to gain something honourably by our own exertions than to have it thrown down at our feet to pick up; and the boy who fairly wins a prize for which he has honestly worked, feels much happier in his own mind than one who has got it by accident or favour.

Cecil learned this useful lesson from the mermaid's words, and determined to lose no time in making some plan by which he might reach the beach and his friends. Escape from the window was perfectly hopeless, for it was too small to have enabled him to creep out easily, even if there had been no iron bar. His only chance, therefore, was either to coax Dame Mince-'em-all, or to evade her vigilance, and he determined to lose no opportunity of doing either the one or the other, according to circumstances. He was so much more comfortable in his mind after the song of the mermaids, and the determination to which he had come, that he actually dozed off to sleep while he was thinking matters over, and was only awakened by the noise of his companion getting up at the call of the old cook in the morning. The two boys descended together to the kitchen, and Cecil again partook cheerfully of porridge and treacle, while Jack Browning steadily refused it, though he looked with longing, hungry eyes at Cecil, whilst he devoured his portion as heartily as if he was at home in his own nursery. Dame Mince-'em-all was so evidently pleased with his manner of eating, instead of refusing, his breakfast, that Cecil thought he might as well take advantage of her good humour, and ask leave to take a stroll on the beach. He accordingly went boldly up to her, and said, in his most respectful tones, at the same time looking her in the face in the most innocent manner possible, 'If you please, ma'am, mayn't I take a walk some time to-day?'

On hearing this request, the old woman stopped short, turned round sharply upon Cecil, and looked at him for a full minute without speaking, during which time her face grew redder and redder, and she placed her arms akimbo, and panted as if overcome by some feeling which she found it difficult to repress. Then she went into a fit of laughter so violent that Cecil thought she would certainly have burst then and there. 'Ha, ha, ha,' she roared. 'Go for a walk, indeed! oh, you crafty little dodger! you cunning little Sly-boots! You want to steal off, do you? I should just think so! Go for a walk? and when would you walk back again, I should like to know? No, no, my boy, you can't come over Mother Mince-'em-all like that! No walk for *you* except round this kitchen table. Eat and drink, my little man, and make the most of your time, but don't think to get out, for you won't do it!' And the old hag roared again with laughter till the curtain was thrust aside, and the ogre put his head in to ask what was the matter, and, on being told, vented his feelings in a laugh which made the cave echo through and through with the sound. Cecil saw that it was clearly useless to hope anything from the good nature of either the ogre or his cook, and that he must try to discover some other plan by which to reach the outside of the cave. He therefore made no reply to the observations of the old woman, but busied himself about such work as she gave him to do, and ate his dinner with an appetite and satisfaction which astonished Jack Browning, and appeared to fill the old cook with the liveliest satisfaction. She herself set to work with a good appetite, and after she had eaten largely, and drank freely out of a huge bottle which she produced from a corner cupboard, seated herself in an arm-chair, put her feet upon the fender, and went into a sound sleep immediately. Cecil looked at Jack, and Jack shook his head sadly, for he knew what was passing through the other's mind.

'It's no use,' he said, 'not the least bit in the world. Just you try it on, that's all.'

'I think I shall,' replied Cecil, 'for one can't be *more* than killed and eaten, at the worst, and at all events I should like to know a little more about the cave.'

'Ah!' sighed Jack, 'you'll know soon enough if you go on eating as you do, and I am sure it is no good your trying to escape, but do as you please.'

Cecil accordingly walked very quietly out of the kitchen into the passage, and up to the curtain, through which he gently crept, and found himself in the hall. But the moment he set foot therein the sound of his footsteps gave an echo right through the cave, just as

Jack Browning had told him.   Dame Mince-'em-all
was so fast asleep that she never woke, and the ogre
was out for a walk; but Cecil hadn't gone half-a-dozen
steps before there rose up from a mat near the outer
door, where he had been sleeping, the most hideous
dog that the boy had ever seen.   His head was close
shaven like that of a bull-dog, but was twice as big as
any head that ever was set upon bull-dog shoulders.
His ears were close cropped, one of his eyes was out,
and the other glared with a fearfully savage expression ;
his colour was a dirty drab, his body was fat, his legs
short and thick, and as soon as he was quite awake he
gave vent to the most unpleasant growl that Cecil had
ever heard, and advanced slowly towards him, making
a hideous face at the same time, as if he was a mortal,
and a very ill-mannered one, too.   Cecil stood amazed
and aghast at this frightful animal, for whom he at
once saw he was no match if it came to a fight; but as
he had been told that if you run away from dogs they
are always more likely to bite you than if you look
them straight in the face, he chose the latter plan, and
stood his ground firmly.   The dog came up very close
to him and showed his teeth in a disagreeable manner.
Cecil, not quite knowing what to do next, put his
hand out gently, and, wishing to coax the animal, said
in his sweetest tones, ' Poor old fellow, poor Growler,'
for he remembered that Jack Browning had told him
that this was the dog's name.   But to his horror and
astonishment, no sooner had he uttered the words
' Poor Growler,' than the dog replied in a hoarse voice,
but in perfectly good English, ' Poor grandmother !
don't think to blarney *me*, you fool ; go back, or I'll
bite you ! '

Cecil was too much surprised at first to say anything; but, summoning up all his courage, he presently
rejoined,

'Really, Mr Dog, I meant no "blarney," and no
harm, but mayn't I take a look round?'

'No, you mayn't, and you know it,' replied the
dog, his one eye almost starting out of his head with
passion. 'None of your nonsense—it won't do. Nothing I should like better than to bite a piece out of
your leg, and I shall do so presently. Don't think I'll
let you go out of this cave! Go back!'

This speech opened so exceedingly unpleasant a
prospect to Cecil, that it made him feel more uncomfortable than anything which had yet happened, but he
thought civility could still do no harm, so he began
again to address the dog, saying,

'Pray, sir, do not be violent; I was not aware—'
but here the creature broke in with a sound between a
laugh and a growl,

'No more jaw, boy. Go back, go back!' and he
made a movement as if he would spring upon Cecil,
who slowly retreated backwards, whilst Growler followed, and pretended to snap at him, and to be about
to seize him, until he was fairly driven past the curtain
and into the kitchen, where he found matters much as
he had left them—Dame Mince-'em-all asleep, and the
miserable Jack Browning crouching sadly in a corner.
After awhile the old hag awoke, and the rest of the
day passed in much the same sort of way as the day
before, save that, after the old woman had been to see
the ogre when he came in from his walk, she took
Cecil by the shoulders and gave him a good shaking,
saying at the same time,

'So, you young villain, you thought to steal off when the poor old dame was asleep. Oh, you ungrateful vagabond! But it won't do, it won't do. Growler don't sleep, does he?' and she chuckled and grinned cruelly in the poor boy's face, who knew that Growler must have told all that had happened, and began to feel that escape was indeed likely to be difficult.

He laid awake again at night, and listened eagerly for the mermaid's song. For a long time he heard nothing, and then he heard a voice singing, the tones of which were so unlike the mermaid's that he couldn't understand it at all. Presently, however, he made out the words, and soon found that the singers were none other than the crabs, who were the friends and servants of the ogre, and of whom Jack Browning had told him, and this is what he heard them sing:

'Brother crab, brother crab, have you heard the good news?
 Two mortals are prisoners here;
I wouldn't for worlds have to stand in their shoes,
 For their fate is uncommonly near.

'The stock in Dame Mince-'em-all's larder is low,
 'Tis empty, I think, or almost;
So as for these boys, why, to pot they must go
 For the ogre to boil or to roast!'

And then came another voice, none the more pleasant to Cecil for that the singer seemed very cheerful over the business.

'Oh yes, I have heard the good news, brother crab,
 No need to inform me of *that;*
And the boy that the ogre did yesterday nab
 Is, they tell me, both lusty and fat.

'The other, they say, is an impudent ape,
　Who declines to get fat as he might ;
But I'll warrant the lads they shall neither escape,
　Though we keep on the watch the whole night.'

The other seemed to chuckle with joy, as he replied
directly,

"'Tis true, brother crab, no escape can be made
　By night or by day, though they try ;
And the ogre, our master, need ne'er be afraid
　That we'll let a mere mortal pass by.

'You remember, 'twas but t'other day, brother crab,
　A lad ventured out of the cave—
At the mouth of the cavern we gave him a grab—
　He'll remember the grab that we gave ! '

And both the crabs went off into a fit of laughter
at the remembrance of the way they had recaptured
Jack Browning on the memorable occasion which he had
mentioned to Cecil. All this was not near so pleasant
to the latter as the song of the mermaids, and he was
glad when the sounds died away, and all was again
silent.

No sweet mermaid's strain greeted his ears that
night, and it was with a somewhat heavy heart that he
rose next morning to hope against hope that some
opportunity of escape might yet present itself. He ate
his breakfast and dinner, but not with so good an
appetite as the day before, and the old cook grumbled,
as she perceived that he left some of the porridge, and
roughly told him that they couldn't keep two boys that
wouldn't eat ; and that, unless he went on as well as
he had began, the ogre would not wait till he was fat
before making a meal of him.

Cecil replied, as civilly as he could, that he had
a sincere wish to eat, and no intention of refusing
to get fat, but that, with every desire to comply with
Dame Mince-'em-all's request, and to consult the
ogre's convenience, he really could *not* eat unless he
was hungry, and hungry he could not be whilst air and
exercise were denied him. If he might but go out for
a walk now and then, he said, he felt sure that his
appetite would return, and he should be able to eat as
well as ever. But the old hag only gave him a sharp
pinch on the fleshy part of his arm (which hurt uncommonly), and said that he was a sharp young rogue, but
that it wouldn't do ; after which she got into her arm-
chair, and went fast asleep again.

Nothing daunted by yesterday's adventures, Cecil,
in spite of all Jack Browning could say, stole out of the
kitchen again ; but a peep behind the curtain showed
him Growler lying right across the entrance to the cave
from the shore, and evidently quite sure to be roused by
the echo of the hall if any one attempted to pass that
way. So he came back to the kitchen, and went into
the scullery and peered about. No means of getting
out could he see, and so once more sat down in the
kitchen to think matters over. Suddenly he recollected
the kitchen chimney. There was no fire, nor would
there be till the old woman woke up, which would in
all probability not be for half an hour or more at least,
and there seemed plenty of room for a boy to creep up.
No sooner thought of than tried. He slipped into the
fireplace and began to climb up at once. Up and up
he went, till he found himself quite close to the top, and
popped his head out cautiously to look around. The top
of the chimney was a mere hole in the rock, with no

chimney-pots or anything else to hinder a boy from
creeping out if he chose. But if he *did* choose, there
he was, some forty feet from the ground, on a rock so
steep that there was no climbing up or down, and all
he could do was to tumble to the bottom of the mountain with every probability of being broken to pieces
before he got there. In addition to this, he perceived
five of the crabs on the beach below, just where he would
fall if he chose to try a tumble, and, remembering Jack
Browning's experience, he thought that they would not
be precisely the most agreeable creatures to meet under
the circumstances. He looked up and saw nothing but
the steep side of the mountain, which it would be next
to impossible for him to climb, and as he had no rope
or anything by which he might break or lighten his fall,
he came to the conclusion that he could not escape that
way. However, he had got a good breath of fresh air,
for which he felt all the better, and he determined that
he would not yet despair. Slowly descending the
chimney, he found dame Mince-'em-all still snoring, and
Jack doing nothing as cleverly and miserably as usual.
He asked the latter to help him get the black off
him, for he was rather in a mess after his climb; but
the boy said he thought it was no use, for blacks
wouldn't come off by brushing; and whilst they were
talking about it the old woman woke up and saw by
Cecil's appearance what he had been about. She only
laughed, however, and told him he would spoil his clothes
for nothing if he played such tricks. However, she was
rather pleased at finding that he ate a better supper
after his airing, and muttered to herself that she thought
he wouldn't take long to fat after all. So passed
away the weary afternoon, and Cecil and Jack went off

as usual to their bed-room. As usual, too, Jack was soon asleep, whilst Cecil lay awake thinking and listening. Not long was it before he heard sounds as of soft music, and knew that it was the mermaids again. And thus ran the song :

> ' Sister dear, with me rejoice,
>   Since good news I have to tell ;
> Hither comes a cheerful voice,
>   Sure to break the ogre's spell.
>
> ' Comes a boat across the sea
>   Bearing welcome burden here ;
> Soon the captives shall be free
>   If no evil interfere.'

And the other mermaid sang back right merrily :

> ' Well I know these tidings bright.
>   O'er the sea a boat doth glide,
> To the boys a joyful sight,
>   Fatal to the ogre's pride.
>
> ' Yet the monster slumbers not.
>   Watchful must the captives be ;
> Careful in their plan and plot,
>   Would they home and safety see.'

Cecil listened with great interest to this conversation, and wondered what it could mean and who was coming to help him. He had not to wait long, however, for after a very short time he fancied he heard the dip of oars in the water, and instantly jumped up to look out of the window. Sure enough, there was a boat gliding quietly on the still sea towards the beach. In it sat the figure of a boy, but not dressed as an ordinary boy would have dressed himself for a boating expedition in the middle of the night. He had a blue-and-white jersey on, and a pair of thick corduroy trowsers ; a

leathern belt was strapped round his waist, and over
the jersey was a jacket composed entirely of rabbit
skins, whilst upon his hands were gloves of the same
material; and his hat was a wide-awake made of fern
twisted closely together, and an oak branch stuck in it
for a feather.   Cecil looked again and again, and it
was some time before he was convinced in his own mind
that this was really and actually his own dear brother
Ned come to his rescue.   The fact is that Ned (as will
be recollected by all those good and wise children who
have read 'Kate's Adventures' in 'Stories for my
Children') had once been befriended in his hour of
need by the Fern Fairy, and when he found that Cecil
had disappeared, and there was too much reason to fear
that he had fallen into bad hands, he directly went off to
see whether his old friend would again lend her assistance, with what result you will presently see.   Knowing
the dangers of the shore and the enemies which surrounded him, Cecil's first thought was, I am bound to
say, for his brother's safety, and he would have given
anything to have warned him of the crabs and Growler.
This, however, he could hardly do without making such
a noise as to run the risk of waking the ogre and Dame
Mince-'em-all, if, indeed, they were asleep.   Moreover,
he had great confidence in Ned, and felt sure that he
had come well prepared for anything that might happen.
He therefore contented himself with watching carefully
and eagerly, and you shall soon hear all that he saw.
Ned waited till the boat touched the beach, and then
quietly jumped out and made her fast to a rock hard by.
He then took off his hat, and drew from his belt a small
black cap which he put carefully on, and immediately
became invisible, by which Cecil knew that fairy

magic was at work, and cheered up accordingly. He
lay and listened in breathless anxiety, and had not long
to wait before he heard a low voice underneath, which
he knew to be that of his brother.

'Cis,' it said, 'where are you?'

'Here, Ned,' said the boy in a voice equally low;
'up in the bed-room.'

'Can you get out of the window?'

'No, it is too small, and there is a bar of iron across
it; but I could get out of the chimney when Mother
Mince-'em-all is asleep, only it is so far to fall—down
to the beach.'

'Ah, but we can't wait for that,' answered his
brother. 'Now, just do as I tell you. Put your right
hand on that iron bar, and your left hand exactly over
your heart. Have you done it?'

'Yes,' said Cecil, 'but the bar is as tight as
ever.'

'Never you mind,' said Ned. 'Now, just say these
words very slowly after me, and keep on steadily pushing at the bar as you say them:'

> 'He that trusts where trust is due,
>   He that loves the fairy race,
> Ne'er that trust and love shall rue,
>   Seeking aid in evil case.
>
> 'Now is come the trying hour;
>   Now the foe must we confound.
> Own the mighty magic power—
>   Bar of iron! drop to ground!'

And as Cecil finished the words the bar of iron gave
way easily to the pressure of his hand, and dropped
down on the beach below.

'Now, Cis,' said Ned, 'squeeze yourself through that hole and drop down at once.'

Without fear or hesitation, Cecil prepared to obey his brother's directions, when two circumstances occurred which caused him to pause. One was the awaking of Jack Browning, who sat upright in bed, startled from his sleep by the noise of the falling bar, and inquired in trembling tones what was the matter. Cecil told him that help was at hand, and begged him to keep quiet, and to follow him through the window, but before he made the attempt himself he thought it best to watch the other circumstance which had stopped his descent. This was nothing more nor less than the approach of two of the guardian crabs, who came lumbering up, one from each side of the beach, and the following dialogue ensued, each crab having heard, but neither being able to see, Ned.

'Brother crab, brother crab, there's a stranger on shore !
    Unseen though he be, yet his footsteps I hear.'
'So do I, brother crab ; 'tis a terrible bore,
    For he's certainly after some mischief, I fear.'

'Why, yes, brother crab ; yet he dare not attack,
    Or the power of the ogre and Growler defy ? '
'Oh, dear ! what is this ?   I am laid on my back,
    And I can't move a foot !'   'Brother crab, more can I.'

To explain these remarks it is necessary to observe that, as soon as Ned saw the crabs approaching, he quietly went up to them, and being invisible, was able to watch his opportunity and tilt them over, one after the other, on to their backs, where they lay helplessly, after the manner of crabs, quite unable to stir. He

then took off his cap and put it in his pocket, after
which he called Cecil again, who squeezed through the
window, and though it was some little way from the
ground, managed to drop down unhurt upon the
beach. Immediately afterwards appeared at the window the head of Jack Browning, who, in tearful
accents, implored them to wait for him, and began to
creep through the window in a cautious and timid
manner. And now occurred an incident which would
have been ludicrous in the extreme but for the perilous
position in which the boys stood, and the importance
to them of a speedy and quiet passage to the boat. Old
Dame Mince-'em-all, having probably dozed too long
and too heavily after dinner, had slept more lightly
than usual after retiring to rest. The noise of the
falling iron bar had aroused her; the voice of Jack
Browning asking the meaning of Cecil's standing at
the window had reached her ears; and most likely the
cry of the crabs, when suddenly turned upon their
backs, had also penetrated to the chamber of the half-
awakened old woman. At all events, from whatever
cause or causes, certain it is that she got up, left her
room, and quietly crawled to the chamber of the two
boys, to see that all was right. The moment she
entered it she saw that all was wrong : Cecil was gone,
so was the iron bar that had been fastened across the
window, and Jack Browning had already got his head
and half his body through the opening, and in another
moment would have been safe on the beach. The old
hag gave a yell, and made an instant rush at Jack,
who, hearing the noise, drew himself more hastily
through the window, but not so quickly but that the
enemy seized his ankle just upon the window-sill. So

far was he gone, however, that Dame Mince-'em-all
had only grabbed him by thrusting her head and
shoulders through the window after him, and the sight
which presented itself to Ned and Cecil was most
extraordinary,—Jack Browning hanging at full length
from the opening in the cliff, twisting, wriggling, and
yelling in the most terrible alarm and agony; whilst
the hag, pulled by his weight half-way through the
window, could apparently neither get forward nor back,
but retained her gripe upon the unhappy Jack, getting
every moment redder and redder in the face, and calling
for Growler as loudly as her uncomfortable position
would permit.   The moment was too serious for hesitation.   Seizing a large pebble in his hand, Ned threw
it with such good aim that it hit the old witch right in
the face.   In the pain and surprise she loosed her hold,
and Jack Browning dropped heavily on the beach.   As
he was quite unable to stand, the brothers helped him
along; and leaving Dame Mince-'em-all to her own
reflections, made the best of their way towards the
boat.   Before, however, they were half-way there, they
heard behind them a noise which caused Cecil and
Jack to turn pale with fear.   Growler was after them!
This wonderful animal, whether warned by his own
instinct, or aroused by the various noises of the night, I
cannot say, had somehow or other discovered that all
was not going on as he could wish; and issuing forth
from the cave to the beach, saw the three boys running
off, and immediately gave chase, coming along at full
cry like a foxhound, only that his cry was infinitely
more terrible and less melodious.

'O Ned!' cried Cecil, 'what shall we do?   Growler
is upon us, and we shall all be caught!'

Dame ' Mince-'em-'all ' seizes Jack Browning.—P. 34.

'Don't be afraid,' replied his brother; 'keep your heart up, and all will be right. The Fern fairy told me about this dog.'

'What *can* we do?' said Cecil.

'Do?' responded Ned. 'Why, what do clocks do when they've struck eight and three quarters?'

'Strike nine, I suppose,' answered Cecil.

'That's it,' said Ned; 'and it was some such word the fairy said when she gave me some stuff for Growler, and told me what to do if he attacked us. Stand hard, and you shall see.' So saying, Ned stopped, drew from his pocket a small paper parcel, unfolded it, and produced a piece of meat of appearance so tempting that no dog that ever was born could have resisted it. He then calmly awaited the coming of the enemy; and as Growler ran fiercely up, he accosted him, in a soft and pleasant tone—'Poor fellow, good dog!' and tossed the meat immediately before him. It so happened that Growler was particularly hungry that evening, and although it put him into a furious passion to be addressed like an ordinary dog, the sight of the meat was of itself almost too much for him, and the turn which his extraordinary talents took upon this occasion contributed to the results which I am about to relate. His first thought was, certainly, to neglect the meat and rush upon the boys; his second idea, however, was that he could catch them just as well without losing the tempting morsel; and it also flashed across his mind that, with so many crabs about, it was anything but safe to leave meat lying about on the beach. With a terrible sound, therefore, between a bark and a roar, he exclaimed, 'Fool that you are to think to bribe Growler! No, no, my boys; your meat first, and you

afterwards;' and with these words he snapt up the
meat in a moment.   Its effect was instantaneous.
Saturated with strychnine by the Fern fairy, and with
fairy strychnine, too, which is the most powerful poison
in the world, it was no sooner well within his mouth
than his fate was sealed, and he knew it.   One dreadful howl, one look of intense fury and hatred at the
boys, and the wretched dog dropped lifeless on the
beach.

'Now, then,' cried Ned, 'let us come on as quickly
as we can; there is no time to lose.' And he and Cecil
hurried forward, helping the miserable Jack along
as well as they could.

They reached the boat, laid Jack down in her, and
were just about to shove off, when they heard a tremendous outcry behind them, and, turning their heads,
beheld the ogre himself rushing down towards the sea.
There was indeed not a moment to be lost.   Off they
pushed, and Ned began to scull away as fast as he
could.

With his club in his hand, and with fury in
his countenance, onward came their gigantic enemy,
uttering cries loud and savage enough to have daunted
the courage of any man, woman, or child who heard
them.   Ned, however, knowing well that he had good
friends on his side, not only remained undaunted, but
cheered his brother up as well as he could, and urged
the boat quickly forward.

In another moment, crash came a large piece of
rock which the ogre hurled, and which, falling close to
the boat, made her shake fearfully, and a quantity of
water came in.

'Bale it out, Cis, as fast as you can, with my hat,'

said Ned, 'whilst I row,' and Cecil obeyed as well as he could manage.

Crash came another piece of rock, and as this fell rather shorter, and the boys were evidently making some progress, the infuriated ogre rushed right into the sea, and began to wade after them, uttering the most terrible threats.

'Stop, you vile thieves!' he cried, 'you murdering, dog-killing, house-breaking, abominable vagabonds! Turn back, turn back, or I'll crush you to atoms!' and he proceeded to indulge in language of a character which is better imagined than written. In fact, he called the boys all the bad names he could lay his tongue to, and used expressions of which no polite ogre would ever have been guilty for a moment. Worse, however, than his words were his deeds, for the boys perceived with terror that, over-weighted as was their little boat, he positively gained on her, and was coming so near, that unless some good fortune intervened, there was but too much likelihood that he would shortly overtake and recapture them. Still, however, Ned strove boldly, and bade Cecil be of good heart, for he was certain that if the Fern Fairy could help them she would not fail to do so.

And now occurred one of those remarkable incidents which appear so strange to those who read or hear of them, that they are sometimes disbelieved, although stranger things really happen in everyday life.

Calm, sweet, and clear, and perfectly audible to the boys, even in the midst of their anxiety and exertion, came floating across the water the musical voices of the friendly mermaids. And this was the burden of their song:

'Sister, sister, hasten here,
Surely we must interfere,
  For the ogre wadeth.
See, his knotted club in hand,
He hath left his cave and land,
  And the sea invadeth.

'Safe the fugitives should be,
Since they venture on the sea,
  On our aid reliant.
We, who love the briny main,
Must the ocean rules maintain,
  And oppose the giant.'

And the answer came back in tones equally strong and clear,

'Yes, sweet sister, since the knave
Insolently breasts the wave,
  And our rule defieth,
Come upon him! Nevermore
Must the wretch regain the shore:
  Forward, and he dieth!'

These welcome sounds prepared the boys for the arrival of speedy succour, and arrive it did. The ogre was within a few yards of their boat, and the water was up nearly to his shoulders, but appeared to rise no higher, and he was eagerly pressing forward, when all of a sudden—swish—came a mermaid's fish-tail bang across his face with such force as to make him howl with rage and agony. Brushing the spray off with his hand, he was still going on, when—whack—came another tail on the back of his head, whilst a voice melodiously chanted in his ear,

' Gentle ogre, come and prove
    How the mermaidens make love,
        Sporting on the billow.
    Come the pleasant waves below,
    Where the weeds and coral grow—
        They shall be thy pillow.'

And thwack across his face came another tail.
The ogre stopped, and the boys, having got their boat
a good bit in front of him, paused to look on. The
monster gave a fearful snort; and being confused and
half stunned by the last blow, had only sense enough to
know that, in the first place, he should never catch the
boat in the face of these marine opponents, and in the
second, that he had made a great mistake in venturing
out of his own territory. The water was now up to his
shoulders, and he turned as well as he could to retrace
his steps. Ah! how many of us there are who would
give anything in the world to retrace our steps—to
undo things that we have done—and to live over again
hours and days that have gone from us for ever. But
it is impossible for us, and so it was with the ogre.

Around him on all sides rose the mermaids with
their lovely faces, their splendid hair, and their arms
tossed gracefully and fantastically over their heads. They
swam close up to the ogre, and made believe to em-
brace him from time to time, and then suddenly
turned, and diving down, brought their tails with tremendous force upon his head. There was no escape
for the unhappy wretch, and his efforts to wade home
were all in vain. His sufferings were probably made
none the better by the sweet singing in which his tormentors indulged. The most delightful concert in the
world is no comfort—but rather the reverse—to a man

with a terribly bad headache; and it is more than probable that the ogre would just as soon have been without the music altogether. However that may be, he grew fainter and fainter; the flapping of the tails and the splashing around him, grew more fast and furious; and at last, with a kind of yell, which ended in a gurgling, choking sound, he sank beneath the waves, and the boys saw him no more. I do not know, to tell the truth, whether anybody ever saw him again, but they may have heard him, for there are strange tales told of that coast, which is the reason why, for the sake of the people who live there, I don't like to tell you its name. But it is a dangerous coast, and there are sudden and violent storms there; and when the storm is at its height, and the waves rage and swell like mad things, the sailor-men tell you that it is the old ogre struggling hard to get out of his prison below, where the mermaids have fastened him down to the coral-beds by ropes strongly plaited of their own long hair; and that, if the sea is rougher than usual, it is because he has succeeded in getting one arm or leg loose, and is struggling more fiercely than ever. And then, when the wind shrieks and moans round that rocky coast more wildly than usual, they say it is old Dame Mince-'em-all trying again to get through that window, where, for all that anybody knows, she is sticking fast to this very day. And when the wind goes down, and the lull and the calm follow, which are always so beautiful, and charm one's senses after a sea-storm, the wise sailor-men shake their wise heads and tell you that the old woman on shore has given it up as a bad job, and will be quiet for a while now, and that the mermaids have, as usual, mastered the old ogre again, and plaited another and a stronger hair-chain for the limb which had been loose.

Perhaps it is all true, and also the still prettier story they tell, that on the still summer evenings, when there is no storm, but the waves come rippling gently up to the shore, and tenderly bathe the pebbly beach at the foot of the great mountains, you may wander down, and if you are fortunate enough to hit on the right time, you may hear the low, sweet voices of the mermaids stealing over the water and falling with pleasant cadence on your ear; and may sometimes even catch a glimpse of one of the lovely creatures, combing her long hair on the rocks and singing to her sisters. It may, indeed, all be true, but I cannot say that I know it to be so. I have wandered there myself, and longed to see this lovely sight and hear those enchanting sounds. They never were seen or heard by me, however. All I saw was the rocks with the waves softly breaking upon them, and the great grand mountain, and the deep blue sea. But I heard a pleasant sound, too. The chimes of the evening bells from the little church on the mainland stole over the waters like the fabled song of the mermaids, and filled my heart with feelings both soft and sad. They carried me back to the days when I was a young child, and stood under the great beech trees that grew close to my old, happy home, and heard the chimes of the dear old bells of the home church sounding across meadow and woodland, and striking upon my boyish ears with sweet and touching melody. The home and the bells have ceased for me now. The light of the one has faded from my sight, and the sound of the other is no longer in my hearing, but their memory is ever with me, and good and holy thoughts, too often deadened and forgotten in the work and noise of the busy world around, rise up again as that memory is stirred to its depths by the soothing, loving sounds of other chimes. No doubt these bells, too, tell of home memories to other ears, and gladden other hearts as mine was gladdened of old; and they speak to others, too, of early days and early innocence which those are happy who have kept and cherished through their lives, and they bring thoughts of Love, and Hope, and Mercy, and Peace, tender plants springing from heavenly seed which the Father of all permits to grow in mortal hearts, and which hallow and bless the ground which fosters them. Chime on, then, sweet bells, chime on still with your soothing sound; for though indeed there are no ogres and witches to be dreaded or drowned, and your strains are not those of the friendly mermaids or the powerful fairy, yet there are worse enemies to be charmed away, in the sin and sorrow which haunt our mortal life, and ever you remind us that to work this mighty charm against these real enemies a greater than fairy power is ours to seek and to obtain, if rightly we read the lessons which you seem to teach, and lovingly cherish the tender memories which you gently waft back to us in the chastened cadence of your heart-softening music.

But I must not forget our boys. When the ogre had quite disappeared, which, as you may suppose, they did not much regret, Ned set to work to make the best of his way home, and as they went he told Cecil how his deliverance had all come about. He had gone, as I have already said, to seek assistance from the Fern Fairy, whom he had summoned to his aid by means of the old rhyme which had proved so useful to him in former days when seeking after Kate. He had not been quite sure, at first, whether this powerful friend had any authority near the sea-shore, so far from Barracks wood and her own country; but finding a bank some way inland upon which several ferns were growing, and observing some rabbits scampering about near the same spot, he determined to try at least; and remembering that the orders he had formerly received bade him rhyme to every case of the noun musa till the fairy came, he at once began—

'Musa musæ,
   I'm near the sea;
   Musæ musam,
   Young Cis, poor lamb,
   Musa musâ,
   Has strayed away.
   Musæ musarum,
   Harum scarum
   Musis musas,
   Ways he has;
   Musæ musis,
   Still, him we miss.'

And as the last words left his mouth, the Fern Fairy stood before him with her old bright look and pleasant smile.

'Well, Ned,' said she, 'so you have not forgotten your old friends. What is it that you want now?'

And Ned told her all the trouble there was at home about Cecil's disappearance, and how they were afraid that some witch or ogre had carried him off; and how Kate had ridden her pony Kitty all round the place in search of him without success; and Eva had ranged her 23 dolls in a row, and asked them all, one after the other, whether they knew where her brother had gone to, without getting a clear or satisfactory answer from a single one of them. Then the Fern Fairy smiled again upon Ned, and spoke to him in her sweet and friendly voice.

'Ned,' she said, 'Kate and Eva will not be able to find Cecil, and *you* will have some little trouble in doing so, and will have to run some little risk.'

'Why, where is he?' asked the boy anxiously, for he was fond of his little brother, and would have been frightened at the fairy's words but for her encouraging smile.

'Some of my rabbits in the sand-warren near the sea,' replied the fairy, 'saw him drifting off to sea in a boat yesterday, and by my directions the fern-owls sent a friendly seagull to watch and see what happened. He has been caught by one of the largest and fiercest ogres which trouble this part of the country and taken to his cave, where he will probably be kept until he is fit for the monster's table, unless he is rescued. Is he a boy likely to grow fat soon, so as to tempt the ogre?'

'Oh,' said Ned directly, 'Cecil is not so very fat, you know, but he is a One-r to eat. You should see him at the cake at tea-time! So perhaps he *will* get fat soon.'

'Then,' returned the fairy, 'no time must be lost.'

She accordingly proceeded to give Ned most particular instructions what to do, and provided him with the clothes and cap which, as we have seen, he wore, and the latter of which would make him invisible when it was necessary that he should be so. Ned left her with many thanks, proceeded immediately upon his journey, and met with the success of which I have told you. By the time Ned had told Cecil how all this had occurred the boat neared the shore, and in a short time the boys were with their friends again. You may easily suppose that there was great rejoicing over Cecil's escape; and they were so glad to get him back safe and sound, that nobody scolded him for having gone to play on the beach without leave. In fact, his papa and mamma thought he had had such a severe lesson in the ogre's cave that it would be rather hard to scold him under the circumstances, and they hoped he would profit by the experience he had undergone without their saying anything more about it. Kate and Eva, however, were full of questions, and made him tell them the whole story half-a-dozen times over; and Eva drew funny pictures of Dame Mince-'em-all sticking in the window, and the crabs lying helplessly on their backs. From this day forward, however, Cecil was an altered boy. He paid attention to what was said to him, never went off alone to play by himself without leave, and was so much improved in his general behaviour that everybody was pleased. As to Jack Browning, there was never such a change seen in mortal boy. Sunday or week-day, thenceforth he never even so much as looked at a bird's nest, or dreamed of trespassing in search of eggs. Twice to church did he regularly trudge in all weathers, and became so remarkable for his punctuality and attention, that upon the death of the old clerk he was unanimously elected to take his place. There he remains to this day, and woe betide the parish school-boy who fidgets in church or dares to go to sleep in the sermon-time when Jack Browning's eye is upon him. Still his past misfortunes have made him kind and gentle to all, and the only instance of harshness related of him is with regard to two mischievous young rascals

whom he caught jackdawing in Barracks wood one
Sunday afternoon, to whom he administered so terrible
a thrashing that they never ventured to appear there
again till next time. So now I have told you all that I
have ever heard about Cecil's adventures and the ogre's
cave. Perhaps you will want to know what became of the
crabs. Well, I really don't know ; and when I was
last in that neighbourhood, and questioned a highly
respectable lobster about the traditions of the coast,
thinking I might gather some news on this particular
point, he replied that *he* knew nothing either, and that
in fact he had always considered crabs as low and dis-
reputable creatures, about whom the less said the better.
So I gave the matter up in despair, and inquired no
further.   There is the story for you as far as I know it,
and if you want to know any more you must go down
to the shore yourselves and ask the mermaids. Perhaps
they will answer you in their sweet and tender strains,
and tell you all you want to know. Perhaps not. But
anyhow you will hear the murmur of the waves as they
break for ever and for ever upon that lonely shore ; and
if you stand close down by them, and look out over the
sea, and think and listen and try to understand what
they say, you will learn and know that they are ever
speaking of the Might of Him who made both them
and you, and reminding you that Time is creeping on
and on as steadily and as certainly as they are breaking,
wave after wave, at your feet, and that every hour is
bringing you nearer and nearer to the moment when
the things of the present will end for you, and the
wonderful future will begin ; when, if you have loved
and honoured Him in the hours of time, He will not
fail to love and cherish you in the ages of eternity.

II.

THE HISTORY OF A RABBIT.

I WAS born of honest and respectable parents, well-
to-do rabbits in the great warren in Hatch Park,
which, in those happy days, was generally known as
'the sand-pit,' an ancient and honourable name, which,
for aught I know, still belongs to the dear old place. I
can remember the sand-pit when there were not a great
many rabbit-holes in it, forty or fifty at most, and only
a fair quantity of our race, mostly relations, lived in it.
I believe that now the place is a perfect honeycomb;
hundreds upon hundreds of holes there are, from one
end of it to the other, and all along the bottom of the
park and in the beech plantation; and hundreds upon
hundreds of merry rabbits live there as gay and as
happy as I used to be in those early days. I have said
that my parents were respectable, and I was brought
up as well as any young rabbit in the place. Very
early in life I learned the mystery of scratching a hole
in the sand, and of making a pop-hole, so as to be able
to slip out easily upon the approach of an enemy. I
was also instructed in the art of nibbling off the green

shoots of the corn as they came up out of the ground, and of biting carefully round the tender ash plants whenever I had a chance of doing so. I could gambol, jump, and run with any rabbit in the place; and I well remember how I used to think and feel that I had the whole world before me, and that nothing was ever likely to go wrong with such a healthy, sprightly young rabbit as I was. I have lived to discover my mistake, but I thought so in those old days, and I dare say I was all the happier for it. But I must not forget to tell you about my dear little brothers and sisters. There were six of us, and a happy family we were. There had been seven, but one got accidentally smothered in his infancy, and he was never mentioned among us. The six of us who grew up and played together were Soft-skin, Tina, and Pussy, the girls; Fatty, Jollyboy, and Bunny, the boys. I was Bunny, and my two brothers and I rather lorded it over our sisters, I think, as boys sometimes *will* do, till time and absence from home teach them that sisters are things which people and rabbits can't be too fond of or too tender with, and that it is a great blessing to have them. They were gentle little things, my darling sisters. Softskin was so called because her dear little brown skin was as soft and smooth as velvet; Tina had white fore-feet, and a white spot on her breast; and Pussy was a lively, skittish little rabbit, the plaything and pet of the whole family. What games we had in that old sand-pit! Many and many a time, on a lovely summer's night, have we raced round and round the place, one after the other, dodging each other among the holes right merrily, squeaking with pleasure and excitement, with no thought of sorrow and no care for the future.

Many a time have we watched the keeper from a distance, as he crept nearer and nearer to the sand-pit, intending to secure a victim for his supper from amongst our merry crew. We would let him creep and creep until he got within a hundred yards or so, and then some old rabbit would give a violent stamp on the ground, as a signal for us all to know that danger was near, and down into our holes we all scrambled as fast as we could. Sometimes one of us, rather bolder than the rest, would only go a little way into the hole, keeping his head just above-ground until the keeper was almost near enough to shoot; then the head would go lower and lower, till only his ears were to be seen, and finally he would disappear altogether, just as the enemy was hesitating whether he should shoot at the ears on the chance of killing his victim by a stray shot. We seven were so well taught that we never trifled with danger like this, but were always off as fast as possible when we heard the first warning stamp of the friendly old rabbit. Then sometimes, late in the evenings, a company of us would go down together to the park fence, which was only a couple of hundred yards from the sand-pit, and creep under it into the fields beyond, where we could forage for fresh green food, and come back all the better for our journey. At last, however, I regret to say, the horrid men took to putting wire all along the fence, so that no rabbit could get through it, which was a great nuisance, and most unfair into the bargain, for why should the fields and the green crops belong more to men than to rabbits? I am sure we enjoy them quite as much as they do, and have every bit as much right as they have to our food and amusement. But it is no use to argue about men : they are the most selfish of animals, who believe that everything was made for *them,* and that they have nothing to do but to use other animals in the manner which suits them best.   Unfortunately for us, it happens to suit men best to roast rabbits, or put them in pies or puddings ; so, at least, I have been told by persons I could trust, and indeed it can be for no other reason that the cruel wretches wage such a ceaseless war upon our unhappy race.

Although my family and I had not suffered from these enemies at the early period of my life of which I am now writing, yet the traditions of the sand-pit were full of horrors relating to innocent rabbits who had fallen a prey to man at different times in the history of that famous place.   And, indeed, I was to know before long how much there is to dread for an honest rabbit who is disposed to look upon the rest of the world as friends, and to consider man as a respectable animal, as good as one of ourselves.

I was seated one day in a quiet nook in my father's earth, thinking of nothing particular, which is, or was, a favourite occupation of young rabbits, when I was roused from my dream by my dear brother Jolly-boy, who came scuffling along to where I was established, in a great state of excitement.

'O Bunny!' he cried, 'there's *such* a fuss in the earth! there's a strange animal come in, that the old ones say is a terrible beast, called a ferret, and we are all to get out of his way as fast as we can, or we shall certainly be killed!'

Being a rabbit of a cautious, if not timid, disposition, I needed no second warning, and began to follow

Jolly-boy through the mazes and windings of our abode. Presently we separated, and as I was stopping still to listen, I heard a prolonged squeak, as of a rabbit in pain, and thought I recognized the voice of an old neighbour of ours, called Bolter. Instinct impelled me to fly from the sound, but before I could do so Bolter himself came rushing past me, with his back bleeding, and quite bare in one place where the ferret had been scratching him. The poor creature gave a low squeak as he passed, and appeared nearly wild with fright; he dashed onward, as if determined to leave the earth and seek the open air, for in that direction he ran as fast as he could. He had not gone long before the horrible roar of a gun was heard over our heads; and as we never saw poor Bolter more, there is little doubt that he fell a victim to that deadly weapon in the hands of the cruel keeper or one of his friends. Whilst I was hesitating whether or no to follow my unhappy friend, I suddenly saw the ferret close upon me. He was quite white, but with villainous red eyes, and his mouth was closely tied up by a bit of string; this, I afterwards heard, is what men call 'coping' a ferret, and is done to prevent his killing the poor rabbits in their holes, which is not what his masters want. By tying up his mouth, and only leaving him his claws to fight with, they secure their wicked ends; for though he cannot easily kill, yet he can so scratch and worry the rabbit whom he catches, that the latter, like poor Bolter, is too glad to escape from him into the open air, where the wretches stand ready with their guns. Well, as I was saying, up comes Master Ferret to me, but very slowly, for his claws were filled with poor Bolter's fur, and he had to stop to clean them from time to time.

'Ha, young rabbit,' he said, as he came up, speaking in the rabbit language, but with a strong foreign accent, 'and pray how are you?'

I made him no answer, and stayed to hear no more, but cut away as hard as I could, and was fortunate enough to dodge the enemy, whom I did not see again, though several shots fired above told me but too surely that he was still at his vile trade. I remember we were all so frightened that night that none of us ventured out, and pretty hungry we were next morning in consequence. My mother assembled us six children together very early, and gave us a long lecture about ferrets, their nature and habits, and how necessary it was to avoid them if possible, which we all readily promised to do.

After this event nothing remarkable occurred for some time, until one day my father informed us that he should take us three boy rabbits up to the garden at the great house, where he had in old times had more than one merry feast. We were highly delighted at this prospect, and when the evening came we set off in capital spirits, our mother and sisters being, rather against their will, left behind. We crossed the bridge over the big pond (which, though I never saw a boat upon it, was called the boat-pond), and went along the park until we came to the foot of the hill on which the great house stood. This we skirted, turning to the left, and came up, past the stables and cow-yard, to a low stone wall, which, with a fence made of wires closely set together on the top of it, formed the boundary of the outer kitchen garden which it was our object to reach. Inside there was a large square kitchen garden, which it would have been delightful to enter, but the thing was quite impossible, for it was surrounded by a high brick wall, which no mortal rabbit could ever have climbed. But there was a good large space between this wall and the fence of which I have spoken. There was a fosse on the park side of the fence, but it was not hard for an active rabbit to run up the wall out of the fosse, provided there was a good gap in the fence for him to creep through afterwards. From the park, on the edge of the fosse, we could see quite easily through the fence into the garden, and a tempting prospect it was. There were rows and rows of gooseberry, currant, and raspberry trees; there were beds of asparagus; there were fruit trees against the wall beyond, and—oh, joy of joys! cabbages—glorious great cabbages met our gaze as we eagerly peered through the wires. My father carefully observed the fence as we walked along, but found that the wires were so close together, and so firmly set in the top stone of the wall that there was no place through which we could creep. At last—at the very end of the fence, or rather, where it turned at sharp angles to the right, he found what he wanted. A plantation came down near to the corner, but not quite close, and to fill up the gap between the end of the plantation and the corner of the fence, so as to divide the park from an enclosed meadow which was on the other side of the plantation, a high, stout post and rail fence had been placed. It was only, in reality, one large gate, but it had been fixed into the top of the stone wall firmly, and somewhat roughly; the wire had been there knocked away, the stone had crumbled, and there was just room enough for a rabbit of ordinary size to squeeze comfortably through. My father saw this at a glance, and calling us young ones up, we all scrambled through the hole, and found our-

selves in the desired place. Ah! it *was* a place! I can't
tell you half the delicacies which were there. We pitched
into the cabbages like fun—we revelled in carrots—we
nibbled parsley till we were tired of it, and then suddenly
came upon a bed of lettuces, which it makes my mouth
water to think of even now. When we had eaten till
we could eat no more, my father told us that we ought
to be going homewards, for it was no safe place by day-
time. Fatty, however, begged hard to stay, saying that he
was sure he should burst if he had to travel so soon after
supper. We other young ones were all very ready to
join in his request; and our dear father, being only too
good-natured, yielded to our persuasion. We crouched
down accordingly in a warm corner of the cabbage-bed,
and made ourselves as comfortable as possible for the
night. Very early in the morning we awoke, and
made a pleasant breakfast, after which our father told
us that, as we had stayed till daylight, and could not
now cross the park to the sand-pit unobserved, we might
as well remain where we were until the evening. We
readily agreed, but Fatty and Jolly-boy having expressed a great desire to visit the plantation outside the
fence, were permitted to do so, upon their promise that
they would return at night. Alas! how we make plans
in vain! The wisest rabbit that ever lived cannot tell
what is going to happen to him during the day, and in
this world of dogs and ferrets, traps and guns, no happiness is secure, no rabbit's existence certain for a moment. When my brothers had crept through the fence
and entered the plantation outside, my father and I
curled ourselves up in the cabbage-bed to pass the day
there as quietly as we could. He told me to go a little
further on than where he was, and if anything disturbed

us I was to be sure and run straight for the hole in the
ence as fast as ever I could.

Well—we lay there contented and warm for some
hours; the sun was shining brightly, and the flowers
were smelling sweetly, and the birds were singing
their pleasant songs, and I began to think that this
was a far nicer place to live in than an old sand-pit.
But I did not think so long. It might have been noon
—thereabouts I suppose, but I didn't wear a watch in
those days, and couldn't tell for certain, when we heard
a merry whistle, and a boy came along the garden path
which separated the cabbage-bed, where we were hiding,
from the raspberry-bed on the other side. I think he
was bound for the raspberries or currants himself, and
had he been alone all would have been well. But, alas!
he was accompanied by a black and tan terrier, who
ran by his side, now and then jumping up on him for
very joy, now and then darting playfully after a bird,
and barking merrily all the time.

When the boy came nearly to the cabbage-bed the
dog ran forward, and began to sniff about as if he smelt
something unusual there. 'What is it, Pincher?' said
his master. Hey in there! Fetch him out!' and,
thus encouraged, the dog came bursting headlong in
among the cabbages.

He was so close to us that there was no time to
be lost, and my father, being nearest to him, gave a
jump, and rushed out into the path. Whether from
fright, or, as I would rather believe, from affection for
me which prompted him to give me time to escape, he
did not run straight to the hole in the fence, but made
for the lettuce bed, somewhat higher up. I, obeying
his directions to the letter, darted straight off to the

hole, crept through it, and in another instant was safe in the plantation without having been observed by the enemy.   As soon as the boy saw my father he yelled out at the top of his voice, ' Here, Pincher, here, here! loo, loo, loo!' and the dog, by no means slow to obey the summons, rushed fiercely after his prey.   Oh, had it been in the park, with the friendly refuge of the sand-pit near, no dog could have approached thee, my gal-lant father; thy danger would but have shown thy strength and swiftness!   Here, however, the case was widely and sadly different.

Reaching the fence full a dozen yards before his foe, my father could but run along it, for there was but the one hole.   This the boy must have known, for, dart-ing across, he cut my poor parent off from his point, and forced him to run back out into the gooseberry bushes.   Pincher was close upon him.   He twisted and ~oubled, and so did the dog, who had ceased his sharp cries, and now ran with breathless excitement and fierce cunning.   It was a terrible race.   At last my father, making a successful double, ran direct to the hole at which we had entered.   He neared it; will he reach it ?   Oh, if I could help him !   He is close, but the dog is close, too; and within a yard of the safety which he sought, my dear, my doting father was seized by his cruel enemy, and with one squeak, yielded up his innocent life within sight of his unhappy child.   I saw the boy come up and take him from the dog, whom he patted and praised for his cruel deed.   I heard him, moreover, exclaim aloud, ' Hurrah for rabbit pie!'   And this was my father's epitaph !

The idea of one's father being made into a pie is under no circumstances one of a pleasant character, and the observation made me feel so exceedingly uncomfortable, that I was as near as possible fainting. Remembering, however, that danger was still near, and that my parent was past help of mortal rabbit, I thought that my best plan would be to find my brothers at once, and inform them of what had happened. I had no great difficulty in the matter, for the plantation was not large, and, in fact, they were both trembling with fear and anxiety under a neighbouring gorse-bush, having heard the shouts of the boy and the barking of the dog. We all shed bitter tears over the sad fate of our parent, and then resolved to follow his advice— remain quietly where we were for the rest of the day, and at nightfall seek our dear old sand-pit. Fearing, however, that the boy and his Pincher might take it into their murderous heads to come through the plant- ation, we determined to search for some earth into which we might creep so as to hide ourselves more securely. Accordingly, finding one hole, partially choked up with leaves, we scratched them away and entered it. Jolly-boy was first, and went blundering on in a reckless manner, when suddenly he gave a loud squeak of affright and pain, having run right up against an elderly hedgehog, who was fast asleep at the end of the hole.

'You impudent young scamp,' said she, as soon as she had fairly got her eyes open. 'What do you mean by coming in and disturbing honest people in their first nap like this? I wish the weasels had you, I do!' and much more language of the same kind she em- ployed towards us, so that we were glad to sneak out again as fast as we could, and seek some more hospit- able shelter. Such an one we found in a small earth,

with not more than ten or a dozen holes, in the bank
of the plantation. Pretty bluebells grew over this earth,
and there were holes in the wood side, and also in the
bank, so that a rabbit had a double chance of escape—
under the trees on one side, and up the dry ditch on
the other. Here we found a number of our own kind,
very friendly and very sorry for our misfortune. They
pressed us to stay with them for a couple of days, but
we declined, being very anxious to get back to our
mother, who, we knew, must be in a state of great
alarm at our non-appearance early in the morning. So
when evening came we thanked our kind friends, and
sallied forth on our homeward journey. We got safely
to the foot of the hill, crossed the park, and got over
the boat-pond all right. Then we struck across to the
sand-pit; and, when we got close to it, I remember we
all three sat down and cried bitterly before we went on
and faced our mother. It was a sad meeting, indeed,
and she was very much cut up about the affair, but it
was no use crying and moaning, and in a few days we
all began to get rather more cheerful.

However, it was not long before we had something
else to think of, for the cry went abroad through the
sand-pit that there was a weasel in the place! There
is nothing we rabbits so utterly and cordially detest as a
weasel. He can go wherever a rabbit can creep. He
is fierce, bloodthirsty, and ravenous. He hates us as
much as we hate him. He does not kill a rabbit by a
good honest bite, like a dog, or a fox, if hungry (for
foxes, if not pressed by hunger, are apt sometimes to
play with their victims, and thus aggravate their sufferings). No, his favourite plan is to fasten himself on a
poor rabbit's throat, and so draw away his life by slow

degrees, and as there is no one to tie up his mouth like the ferrets are tied by their masters, he is able to follow his own wicked inclination in hunting and killing; and, sneak as he is, it is wonderful what an immense amount of mischief one weasel can do in a rabbit-warren.

It may, therefore, be easily imagined that the greatest consternation was caused among all our tribe by the dreadful intelligence that there was a weasel in the sand-pit. There was no guessing how long he might stay, or what amount of misery he might cause. Few, save the oldest rabbits amongst us, could remember such an occurrence having taken place, although there was a tradition concerning a neighbouring earth, which told of one of these terrible creatures having established himself there, and wrought such destruction that, had he not been trapped by the keeper, the name of rabbit would have become extinct in that locality. No wonder, then, that we all trembled from head to tail, and looked at each other in sad dismay. There was nothing for it, however, but to take our chance with the rest, unless we were prepared to leave the home of our forefathers, which no well-disposed rabbit ever does if he can possibly help it. So we stayed, and for a day or two we only heard rumours of the dreadful foe, and reports of his having seized victims on the other side of the warren, for this sand-pit of ours was a large place, occupying perhaps three-quarters of an acre of ground; and although the holes were not then as numerous as they are now, nor did they all communicate as now, yet they were constantly increasing; and, being at some distance apart, it was quite possible that events might happen on one side which were not known to the inhabitants of the other side for several days afterwards. We knew, however, quite soon enough.

It was on a bright, lovely summer's morning—I shall never forget that morning—that we were all preparing ourselves for a pleasant stroll round the earth, and a breakfast off the young shoots of the grass, intending after breakfast to bask in the sun for a while, and vary that amusement by some of the many other pleasant ways with which we were accustomed to wile away the time. But we had hardly put our heads outside the hole, when, to our extreme horror, we saw the weasel trotting quietly across the sand-pit in our direction. There was no doubt of it—this was the wretch himself—his thin, long body; his keen eyes; his long brown coat, all betokened the villain; and we fled in every direction. Alas! it was but little use flying from such an enemy. Some strange fear seemed to paralyze us. We felt as if we could not run as fast as usual—as if our limbs would not obey us;—and, for my own part, I must confess that I never felt so queerly in my life. Run we did, however, into our earth, and scattered in every direction.

Ere long, the smell which accompanies this horrid animal told us that he was in the earth, and in hot pursuit. We had not long to wait. Several of us were crouching close together in the corner of our largest room, at the far end of one of the branch holes, when in came the monster, as cheerful as possible.

'Ha, little rabbits,' he cried, 'here you are! oh, how nice! I must make friends with some of you without delay,' and he ran up towards us. We squeaked with fright, and huddled still closer together, but it was of no avail. My poor brother Fatty was with us, and, unhappily for him, his food had always agreed with him so well that he was as fat and plump a young rabbit as you could wish to see.   The weasel *did* see him, and only too soon, for without any ceremony he rushed up and seized him by the throat.   Fatty uttered a piteous shriek, but his hour was come : the cruel grasp upon his innocent throat would never be relaxed while life was in him.   The eyes of the monster sparkled with delight as he tightened his hold, and we other poor rabbits, seeing our brother's case hopeless, turned and fled.   Not yet, however, could we make up our minds to leave our beloved home.   We fondly cherished the hope that our detestable enemy might be satisfied with one life, and might pass on to other earths and other victims.   Alas! we little knew him.   On the very next morning, whilst we were trembling together at the mouth of the principal hole of our warren, the destroyer was upon us again, and this time it was my little sister Tina whose young life was the sacrifice. Tender little Tina! she had never known sorrow, and never heard an unkind word, for she was a favourite with us all, but she had now fallen into hands which knew no mercy, and there was no escape for the poor child.   But why should I dwell longer upon so sad a scene ?   My mother having thus lost two of her children within so short a time after she had been deprived of the aid and comfort of my father's presence, was almost wild with despair.   She called us together with a melancholy squeak, and embraced us all tenderly.

'Come, my children,' said she, 'my tender Softskin and Pussy, and you, my Bunny and Jolly-boy, come around your poor mother and share her sorrow. We have lived here in peace and happiness hitherto,

but it is no longer a place for us. Come, let us leave
our home, let us hurry from scenes which will hence-
forth only remind us of those we have loved and lost,
and in which there is no longer either comfort or safety.'
So saying, our mother led the way up into the open
air, and, desiring us to follow her, passed over to the
beech plantation on the south side of the sand-pit. We
were sorry enough to leave the old place, but had been
too thoroughly frightened by the events of the two last
days to dream of raising any objection, and silently and
sadly we followed our parent. She stopped for a
moment at the edge of the plantation, and we all cast
a lingering look of regret back upon our old home. Ah
me! shall I ever see it again? I can see it now in my
mind's eye—just as it was that evening—with the
setting sun tinging the golden sand with a still brighter
hue—the mounds of sand which the rabbits had
scratched out in making their holes—the little heads
peering up here and there and looking around—and
two or three deer trotting away to the fern beyond,
startled by some one in the path which led by the sand-
pit to the white park gate below. Yes, I can see it
now, and I shall never forget that day and that hour.
We gazed but for a moment, and then went on through
the whole length of the beech plantation, and out on
the other side. Here was still a sandy soil, and many,
many rabbit holes. At some time or other men had
dug a very large trench across this place, hoping, I
suppose, to destroy our persecuted race more easily
thereby, but their efforts had been in vain, rabbits had
greatly multiplied, and the earth was a very large one.
Beyond, and almost close to it, a large extent of fern
spread from the park fence over many acres of ground :

we could not see any end to it from where we were on
coming out of the plantation.

'Hurrah!' cried Jolly-boy. 'Look, mother, what a
splendid place for playing hide-and-seek, and for nestling down warmly, too, in the cold weather.'

Our mother smiled and sighed at the same time.
'Yes, my child,' she answered, 'I hope you may have
many happy days there, as other little rabbits have had
before you. We must not, however, go beyond this
earth at present; it is here I hope to find rest and
shelter for the night, and to-morrow we will once more
set out on our travels.'

Accordingly she led us forward, and we found many
friendly rabbits seated about outside the warren, and at
the edge of the fern, who willingly received us and gave
us a hearty welcome, assuring us that there was plenty
of room, and that they would be very glad to give us a
night's lodging. We passed a quiet night there, and
the rest of the next day, till towards evening, when our
mother again led us forth, and brought us into the vast
tract of fern which we had seen from the edge of the
beech plantation. The fern was then green and high,
and afforded ample cover not only for rabbits but for
the deer, who made their lair therein, and sought shelter
from the flies; and the does hid their fawns there, and
came stalking timidly, but gracefully, out into the park
from time to time, as if to see that all was going on well
outside the fern, and darted back again at the sight of a
man or dog, stamping their pretty feet and giving a
little indignant snort before they fled. High and
green was the fern then, but, oh! the cruelty and bitter
hatred of man towards our harmless race! The better
to catch those unwary rabbits who might be tempted

to make their home among the fern, the wretches used
to mow down great tracks, leaving the fern standing
in large square pieces, more easily to be hunted by dogs
or crossed by keepers, as it got older and more beaten
down.   But of this I knew nothing then : my mother
and we four young ones journeyed on through the large
expanse of fern, bearing always rather to the right, until
we came to a large rabbit-earth upon the crest of a hill,
where the fern had been cut away year after year, until
it only grew very thinly, so that we could see down the
hill and have a good view of what was before us.   This
was my first sight of Barracks wood.   I have called it a
hill upon which we stood.   It was hardly that, but the
ground here sloped down southwards to the wood.
Immediately below the earth from which we were looking there were a number of high fir-trees, green and
beautiful, not growing very close together, but far enough
apart, generally speaking, for their branches to have
plenty of room, and here and there was a gap with no
tree for many yards; around and below these trees
grew more fern, thick or thin according as it grew
beneath the boughs, or where the bright rays of the sun
could reach and cherish it.   To our right, as we stood,
the fir-trees extended for about a hundred yards, then
some more open fern, and a beautiful large pond, with
a beech plantation running for a hundred yards or more
alongside of it to its further bank, met our view.   At
the east end of the pond grew a large number of high
reeds, on the edge of which we could see the moorhens
swimming about, and their harsh, homely crow continually greeted our ears.   Then a broad ditch ran from
the pond along the valley at the other side of the fir-
trees, from which the ground dipped again to the

ditch; beyond the ditch the ground, level for a short distance, rose abruptly in a hill, and beginning on the side of the hill and extending far beyond it was Barracks wood. Oh, the happy days which I have spent there! the very name has a charm for me, and as I talk of it I seem once more to be entering our grand old wood for the first time. There was no thick underwood, brambles and briars were unknown, at least upon that side of the wood, but it was full of large old pollard trees—oak and hornbeam—in which hundreds of jackdaws built their nests; and, where it was more open, large patches of fern occupied the ground, in which an honest rabbit might find secure shelter and plenty of companions. Squirrels bounded from tree to tree. Woodpeckers tapped and laughed all day long. The spring song of the cuckoo was heard here as early and as late as he sang at all. And, higher up in the woods, where the trees were younger and the shade less, the ground was carpeted with bluebells and primroses, and a million insects buzzed above and around us on a bright summer's day.

We did not stay gazing long, and what I am telling you has been gathered from many years' experience of the place. I did not take it all in at the first glance. But the view struck me at once as being singularly lovely, and I have never changed my opinion.

We passed beneath the fir-trees, and by the head of the ditch which I have mentioned, where the wood swooped down from the hill, and ran up to the first fir-tree, which stood just at the end of the ditch. There we came upon several rabbit-holes; and, indeed, we found that the members of our worthy race had taken up their abode all along the side of the hill, right up to the edge of the wood, close under the shadow of the old pollards.

'Here,' said my mother, 'shall we find a haven of rest. Beneath these old trees, in this romantic spot, surely care may be laid aside, and the heart of a rabbit may be allowed to beat in blissful tranquillity.'

It will be observed that my mother, being somewhat of a poetical turn of mind, occasionally used language which was rather beyond the comprehension of an ordinary rabbit. But, as we were used to it, we didn't mind, and received the words of our parent, as usual, with respectful attention. We were not long in finding a suitable hole. It was one which ran under the roots of a venerable oak pollard, one opening coming out in the hollow of the tree, where there was ample room for all our family. We made ourselves extremely comfortable here, and remained in our new home for some days without any adventure worth telling. At night we would sally forth to feast on the young grass at the edge of the wood, and during the day we would either remain in the tree, or would go out into the wood, and make ourselves nests in the fern, where it was very delightful to curl oneself up comfortably, and doze dreamily in our pleasant bed, half-asleep, half-awake, listening to the woodland sounds. So time slipped away, until the hot sun of summer had become cooler; the leaves had begun to fall off the trees, and the green of the fern had begun to turn into a deep brown. Then we used to creep out into the large squares of fern, and nestle there day and night while the weather was bright and dry. Many companions we had, and many friends we made, for our

race was very abundant in those parts.   But such happiness was too great to last.

It was on a fine October day, before the fern had
lost its uprightness and sank beneath the wind and
rain, but whilst it was daily becoming browner and
browner, and would soon cease to hold itself up against
the assaults of the weather, that my mother, Pussy, and
I went out for a ramble, leaving the other two at
home.   We had started very early, and after roaming
to and fro for some time, I established myself near the
corner of one square of fern, whilst my mother and
Pussy entered a square just beyond, and were lost to
my sight.   All of a sudden I heard the bark of a dog
and the shout of a man.   I sat up on my hind legs at
once, and listened attentively, with my ears pricked up
to their fullest extent, and my heart beating fast.
Presently came more barking and more shouts, and
then a sound which I had heard but too often at the
sand-pit—the report of a gun.   I crept into the square
of fern close to me, and lay there panting with fear.
Full well I knew that danger was abroad, and I should
have stolen back to the wood at once but for my dear
companions.   Again came the hideous howling ; again
the shouts of the men encouraging the dogs ; again
and again the guns resounded. Nearer and nearer they
seemed to come, and I longed for my mother and
Pussy to come back to me, but they came not, and
some instinct seemed to compel me to remain where I
was.   I could see across and along the track which
divided the square of fern in which I sat from that into
which my mother and sister had gone ; and before
I had waited very long, round the corner there stepped
a tall young man in a grey shooting-coat, with a gun in

his hand.   He stood in the corner of the other square of fern, which I heard the dogs enter, and almost immediately begin to give tongue, and no wonder that they did so, for I dare say there were a dozen or more innocent little rabbits in nearly every square.   I hardly knew the peculiar cry of those dogs at that time.   I learned afterwards to know it well.   It was the cry of the beagle, and presently I saw one, two, three of these little hounds come trotting round the corner and dive into the fern again.

'Hew in there, hew in there, good lads!' shouted the man.   'Hey, Countess, good lass; hark to Countess!   Hey, Ringwood, boy.   Fetch him out, Drummer.   Hey, roust him out, Singer;' and with such like cries he urged on the already too willing hounds.

There seemed to be a man stationed at each corner, at once to keep the dogs in one square at a time, and to shoot any unfortunate rabbit who tried to cross from that square to another.   I waited in terrible fear and excitement, which was greater than ever when I suddenly beheld Pussy, my own dear little Pussy, rush frantically out of the fern, pursued by the hound Singer.   The man at the corner raised his gun directly, but, fortunately for Pussy, Singer was so close to her that he dared not shoot.   The hound was old and very fat, but he was so near to Pussy when she broke cover, that she was obliged to dodge him and dart back again into the same square, which she thus entered two or three yards before the furious and howling foe, who followed her in hot pursuit.   I congratulated myself upon Pussy's escape, and was full of hope and confidence, if she would only keep inside the fern, when, lo! a new event froze my heart within my bosom.

The other hounds appeared to be hurrying up in full cry; true to the scent they ran, and nearer and nearer they came to the edge of the square which they were hunting. Suddenly, from out of that square bolted a rabbit at the top of its speed, and made for the square in which I lay. Barely had I time to recognize my beloved mother, when a bright flash issued from the corner of the square she had left, a puff of smoke followed, a loud report, and half-way across the track my parent fell head over heels, and lay lifeless upon her back, her elegant limbs quivering in death, her sorrows and sufferings over for ever. All this passed in an instant, quicker than I can tell it, and my mother could not have suffered a moment's pain,—there was no time for it. I felt stunned and bewildered, but had hardly time to think of myself or my feelings, for scarcely had I realized my loss, when a second flash and report showed me that another rabbit, at a little distance off, had experienced a similar fate; and at the same instant a third, in which I recognized my dear little sister, came darting across the track immediately where my mother had just attempted to cross. I gave her up for lost at once. Fancy my delight at hearing the man exclaim, in an angry voice—'Hang those rabbits—all bolting at once! I've got two out of the three, however; and if that little one had waited half a second longer, till I was loaded, I should have been ready for it, too.' He had not had time to load, and my sister was safe! But two of the hounds were close upon her track, and had they followed her into my square of fern, I don't know when I should have seen her again. Happily, they were under good command, and obeyed the man, who rated them well for

breaking cover, and sent them back into the square
they had left. I immediately followed my sister, and
was lucky enough to come up with her directly.
'Now, Pussy,' I said, 'there is only one thing to be
done; we must leave the fern instantly, before our
enemies enter this square.' Too weary and bewildered
to make any opposition, the little thing readily agreed
to what I said, and followed me whilst I crept quietly
through the square into the next and the next, never
stopping till we got to the fir-trees, under which we
passed, and soon reached our home. I was told by
some old rabbits afterwards that I had taken the
wisest, and, indeed, the only safe course under the
circumstances; and that, as the season advances, and
men and beagles more frequently visit the fern, it is
an understood rule among well-informed rabbits, that, if
they chance to be out on such occasions, they should
at once begin to steal off to their earths as soon as they
hear the fatal voices of the dreaded hounds in the
distance.

But the day had been a sad one for us. Here we
were—four little orphan rabbits, deprived for ever of
the counsel and advice which had so often supported us
in the hour of danger, and comforted us in sickness and
sorrow. Bitterly did we weep that day, and indeed it
was several weeks before we were ourselves again. Little
by little we became better able to manage without our
lost parent, and we received great kindness from our
neighbours, especially from one old black rabbit, who
paid great attention to my sister Soft-skin, and, being
possessed of much influence in the warren, proved of
considerable service to us. His language was sometimes extraordinary, but his heart was in the right

place, and we always found him a true friend.   I remember asking him, soon after my mother's death, whether he would advise us to leave our tree, and seek some larger earth, further from the scene where she had met with her sad end.

'Boil me with onions,' was his characteristic reply, 'if I can see any reason for your going!   You are well enough where you are; food is not scarce, friends are plenty.   No!   Eat me cold in a pie for breakfast if I think you ought to go!'

So we stayed, and for several weeks lived a life of great quietude and content, save for the recollections of the dear ones of whom cruel enemies had robbed us.

It may be thought, perhaps, that I am inventing dangers and magnifying the evils which beset our race, but I can assure you that such is not the case.   I make this remark because the events which now occurred were of a character which really gives rise to the idea that rabbits, and especially my unhappy family, are beyond all other animals persecuted and tormented by relentless enemies.   I do not know how this may be, but I *do* know that every word which I tell you is strictly true; and I verily believe that the enemies of our race are so many, that it might well happen to another rabbit to have encountered more of them, and to have undergone more and greater perils, than have even fallen to my lot.

I have said that we continued to reside in our tree at the edge of Barracks wood.   At the end of the great ditch, which I have mentioned as running from the Heron pond (for thus was the pond named), there was a large hole, which served as a kind of city of refuge to outlying rabbits when surprised by an enemy.   I mean that, as this was the hole nearest to the outside of the wood, any rabbit upon whom came a man, dog, or other foe whilst he was dozing under the fir-trees or in the fern beyond, and who was at all close pressed, always took refuge in this particular hole, where he stayed till the departure of the enemy allowed him to go to his own earth.

It was somewhere about the middle of November that our next great misfortune took place, in connection with this very hole. There were certain boys —who, you know, are a smaller kind of men, and generally twice as active in their attacks upon poor rabbits, though, until they are permitted to carry guns, they are not quite so destructive—I say there were certain boys, who lived at the great house in the park, who were never weary of roaming about in search of what they called 'sport.' They usually carried cross-bows in their hands, out of which they shot a wooden arrow, tipped with lead; and I have seen them kill unhappy squirrels with these, at a great distance off, and knock young rooks and jackdaws out of the trees with the same weapons. Terrible enemies they used to be to such creatures, and I have no doubt they would have served rabbits in the same way, but we were generally too sharp for them; and it was only now and then when they saw a rabbit sitting, who did *not* see them, that they managed to slay him with their lead arrows. But these boys almost always had with them two or three terriers, black and tan, and with these animals it was my ill fortune to come in contact more than once, as the course of my story will show. The worst of these, the most sly, cruel old animal that ever breathed, was named Vick. Her fame had spread over all the country round. She was said to have personally slain more rabbits than any terrier in the neighbourhood; her scent was keen, her sight good, her teeth sharp, her courage undaunted, her strength never-failing, and the rabbits throughout all the park were wont to tremble at her name. Her son Pincher was of a different mould. He had a white breast, and was rather larger than his mother, a handsome dog, who had the reputation of being remarkably good-natured; not so was he to rabbits, however, and by us he was little better loved than his hateful mother.

But to my story. It chanced upon one November day that Soft-skin and Jolly-boy had strolled out under the fir-trees for a game of play, and when they were tired, having roamed along towards the pond, they made two seats in the fern, a little way apart, and lay down to rest. They were aroused nearly at the same time by the short, sharp bark of a terrier. The boys and their dogs were upon them. Jolly-boy jumped up directly, and, being very near the edge of the hill whence we had taken our first view of Barracks wood, he rushed thither directly, and, being only pursued by a puppy, easily gained the earth, and ran into a hole safe and sound. Soft-skin was less fortunate. Up she sprang, poor little dear, distanced her pursuers in the first twenty yards, and then, following the zig-zag tracks in the fern at an easy canter, made for the hole at the head of the ditch where she knew she should be safe enough. Safe enough she would have been from any ordinary pursuer, but there was one behind her of a very different sort. As soon as ever Soft-skin sprang from her seat, Pincher followed directly on her track, running first in view, and then by scent, like an honest dog and straightforward foe as he was. Not so his abominable mother. With a cunning perfectly dreadful to think of, she paid no attention to sight or scent, but, taking the short cut, regardless of everything else, ran straight off to the hole, which long hunting experience had taught her to be the usual resort of rabbits upon such occasions. She hoped to arrive there before her victim, and so, indeed, she did! Breathless with her canter, but full of fancied security, dear little Softskin came quietly up to the hole of refuge, and ran right into the jaws of her expectant and exulting enemy! Short were her sufferings, poor thing! Vick's teeth were fastened in her throat before she knew where she was, and a savage shake or two stretched my tender sister lifeless on the ground, and robbed a once happy and united family of its fairest flower.

There was a terrible scene that night in the tree. To our bitter tears and agonizing squeaks of woe were added the heart-rending grunts of anguish which proceeded from the black rabbit, who turned out to have been engaged to Soft-skin for some time, and had built his hopes of future happiness upon her tender affection. It was terrible to hear his bitter words against dogs, boys, and men, and his utter recklessness as to his life thereafter. He wished himself in a pudding. He desired to be immediately roasted. Anybody that pleased might make him into a curry, or boil him down for soup, without a murmur on his part; and in fact he gave way so utterly to his grief, and behaved in so extravagant a manner, that we all thought he must be little better than a lunatic.

We three sand-pit rabbits who were left were now very miserable. Jolly-boy and I vied with each other in attention to our remaining sister, who was a dear, cheerful little soul as ever lived, and well deserved all the love and care which we could bestow upon her. We should have left the tree and the wood at once, I think, had it not been for the entreaties of the black rabbit, who was really so kind, and had evidently so set his heart upon our staying, that we put off our departure from time to time until we really began to doubt whether we ever should move at all. However, afflictions and trials were still before us, and it might have been better for us if we had moved when we first thought of doing so. We had somewhat enlarged the earth around our tree, keeping the hollow of the pollard as our principal room. We had made half-a-dozen different ways out, so that we could not be easily taken by surprise, and fancied ourselves tolerably secure from danger. But one day, whilst we three were all sitting together in our drawing-room, we heard low voices on the outside of our tree, and instantly suspected mischief. Jolly-boy and I laid our heads together, and, thinking the tree itself to be the safest place, we made our sweet little sister climb a little way up inside it, and seat herself on a ledge where there was just room for one rabbit to sit, and on which she could not be seen from below. We made her promise faithfully that, whatever happened, she would on no account stir from her post till all danger was certainly past, and then we silently waited and listened. Our suspense was, however, not long, for in a very few seconds we heard a scuffling and scraping sound, and a large white ferret entered our apartment for all the world as if it belonged to him. He made straight at us, and we, knowing what we had to expect, ran, one one way and one another, as fast as

we could, the ferret following with a cruel look.   I
rushed out at the nearest pop-hole at a great pace, little
knowing what was about to happen.   Over the hole,
loosely laid, but fastened by a string to a peg firmly
stuck in the ground, was a net, so made that, as soon
as an unlucky rabbit rushed into it as I did, he was en-
tangled in its meshes, worse and worse the more he
struggled, whilst the string drew up and encircled him
with the net as if it had been a bag.   The force with
which I ran was such that the string ran out directly,
and I rolled a helpless captive, confused and stunned,
and unable to move hand or foot.   Up rushed a boy
directly, seized me by the hind legs with one hand,
undid the net with the other, and took me carefully out.
I thought my last moment had come, for I was completely in my enemy's power, and never doubted that
my poor head would be knocked against a stick or
a tree the next moment.   But this was not my captor's
intention.

'Here, Daniel,' he said, to a little man who stood
by with a broad grin on his face and a sack in his
hands; and without more ado, the man opened the
mouth of the sack, and the boy popped me in, right on
the top of a couple more unfortunate rabbits, who lay
panting with terror in the corner.

Ere long time had elapsed, the sack was again
opened, and, to my surprise and grief, my brother was
the next comer.   He told me that he had waited in one
of the entrance passages to the tree until he actually
felt the ferret's claw upon his back, then he could stand
it no longer, but, rushing out as I had done, had ex- ·
perienced the same fate.   We had not the least idea
what was to become of us, and in fact our position was

not very favourable for the formation of ideas of any
kind, for the sack in which we had been put was placed
upon a little four-wheeled waggon, drawn by hand, and
hereon we were jolted along through the wood in the
greatest discomfort both of mind and body.   Now and
then the waggon stopped, and we knew the reason
pretty well, for again and again the sack was opened to
receive another victim, until it contained nine miserable
rabbits, more dead than alive with fright.

Too much frightened were we to speak to one
another; and though we were all wondering what on
earth was about to become of us, not a word was
uttered.

At last the man and boy left the wood, and the waggon was drawn on what appeared to us to be a never-
ending journey.   End it did, however, and we were
lifted up, the whole sackful of us, and taken into
a large building of some sort, the door of which was
shut, and the sack then opened.   Then followed a conversation which gave us some idea of what was about
to happen.

' It's too late to-night, Daniel,' said the boy.

' Yes, sir,' said the other; ' but they'll do very well
to-morrow, if we put them in one or two of the old
hutches.'

Then they began to talk of where the hutches
should be put, and whether we should be likely to feed
well, and I clearly made out that they intended to turn
us down on the next day for some kind of ' sport,' as
I suppose they would have termed it; but of its exact
nature I could not make myself sure.   At all events,
we were all taken out of the sack, and placed in two
hutches—five of us in one and four in the other.   My

brother Jolly-boy and I were in the same hutch, with
three other rabbits, and the lid being firmly shut down,
and we left alone, we all began to look at each other,
and to bewail our sad fate.   Very soon the door
re-opened, and the man came in with cabbages
and a little bran, some of which he placed in each
hutch, then fastened it down again, and left us.

Wild rabbits do not like to eat food under such
painful circumstances as those in which we found ourselves placed, and for some time none of us even so
much as looked at the food which had been thus put
before us.   We crouched moodily down in the corners
of our hutch, and sadly meditated upon the happy
past, and the gloomy and doubtful future.   Little rest
or sleep fell to our lot that night, and morning found
us as miserable and uncomfortable as when we had first
been deposited in our unaccustomed habitation.   But
as the light came shining in more and more strongly
through the windows of the stable, and it was evident
that before long we should again be roused from our
state of torpor, and made, in some way or other, to
minister to the pleasures of our tyrant captors, I began
to think to myself that, whatever might be the fate for
which we were destined, it was probable that it would
be better to encounter it with a full rather than with an
empty stomach.   Accordingly, I roused myself from my
quiet state of lazy terror, and stole gently to the cabbages and bran.   Then I nudged my brother, and he,
encouraged by my example, came with me to the food,
and we nibbled together at that which might be, for all we
knew, our last meal.   Our appetites were not so good
as usual, but we ate from a sense of duty, and felt all
the better for it. Our companions would not follow our

example. Depressed with grief and terror, they appeared to have abandoned themselves to despair, and none of them would touch a mouthful.

We remained as we were till the sun had risen for some hours, and then, whilst we were wondering what would become of us, the door of the stable opened, and we could tell by the voices that several men and boys were entering the place together. Our hutch was opened. We were taken carefully out, and again put into a sack, and then carried off, amid the talking and laughing of our tormentors. After walking for a quarter of an hour or so (though it seemed an hour or more to us), the party stopped, and our sack was thrown upon the ground.

With a horrible dread we now heard dogs come running up, and sniff at the sack, whining meanwhile in an unpleasant manner, as if they well knew what was inside, and longed to be at us.

What was about to happen? We had all of us heard terrible stories of rabbits destroyed by terriers, and some of us, as the readers of this true history well know, had had sad experience of the same, still it seemed strange that we should have been brought so far merely in order to be handed over to these monsters, and we could not imagine what was to be done with us. Soon, however, the conversation of our tyrants showed us their intentions. We were to be coursed by these dogs for their sport, and the only doubt was whether all the dogs should be allowed to run at once, and whether one rabbit at a time, or more, should be turned down before them.

An eager discussion took place, which we could only partially hear or understand, but it did not last long; and then, the mouth of the sack being opened, a hand was thrust in, a rabbit was seized, and the sack was refastened and left on the ground. We who were left in it heard presently an eager shout, a barking of dogs, and a tumult of cries, which lasted for a few minutes, and then the party seemed to have again gathered round the sack.

'He ran well,' said a voice close above us.

'Yes,' replied another; 'but not so well as if he had been turned down yesterday. He had been cramped in the sack, and I dare say hadn't eaten his food. No wonder that Pincher caught him so soon.'

And from this we collected that our poor companion had perished.

Presently in came the hand again. Out was drawn another rabbit, and the sack tied once more. Then came the same shouts and barking, and we heard a voice say,

'He won't move, poor brute; he's stiff, and tired, and frightened. Go and stir him up, some one.'

And some one went and tried, I supposed, but apparently without success, for we heard the men grumbling because the poor wretch had been unable to run and show the sport which they had expected.

Next time the hand came in I found myself seized by the head, and dragged forcibly out. The sight which met my eyes was not particularly pleasant, or re-assuring. Several men and boys stood about, three of whom were holding back three eager terriers, among whom, at a glance, I recognized Vick and Pincher. I had not much time for observation, but I saw that we were in a grass field, and that the park fence—though it was a part of it which I had never seen before—was right opposite to us, about a hundred or a hundred and fifty yards off. The man who had taken me out of the sack advanced in front of those who were holding the dogs for about eight or ten yards, and then stopped.

' Go on further, Tom,' shouted a voice from behind ; ' let us give this one more " law." He'll run better if he has more time, and that last course was no fun at all.'

Thus directed, Tom moved several yards further on, and then put me down upon the ground. Now it was that my wisdom in having eaten some of the food in the hutch became apparent. Had I been faint with hunger, I could no more have run than have flown; and, indeed, the confinement in the sack had so cramped my legs that, even as it was, I was in no very good condition for a race. But I knew full well that it would be a race for life. My breakfast, not too hearty to prevent my running, had given me fresh strength, and having in very early life been taught to make the best of any position in which I might be placed, I at once determined to spare no effort to get out of the scrape in which I now found myself. The instant, therefore, that Tom put me down on the ground, and let me loose, I started off directly, and made straight for the park fence at the top of my speed. I heard a loud out-cry behind, which told me that the dogs were after me, but I had no time to turn round and see how near they were. I perceived a few trees near the fence, rather to the left of the spot where I had been turned down, and I bore towards them. I was close to them—within a dozen yards of the fence, when the cry of the foremost dog sounded close to me. I had but little time to think : there was no hole in the fence immediately before me, and I saw I should have to run along it for some dis-

6

tance, perhaps, until I could find one. This would
give my pursuers a terrible advantage, and would in all
probability prove fatal to my chance of escape. Therefore, whilst still a dozen yards from the fence, I bore
away suddenly to the left, so suddenly, that my foremost
pursuer, who was none other than the dog Pincher,
overran himself, and lost several yards by so doing.
This gave me time to see two things; first, that
two other dogs who were after me were ten yards or
more behind, and, secondly, that there was a ditch
under the trees, a little way before me, which, according to the general plan of ditches, was almost sure to
end at the fence either in a hole through the fence, or,
better still, a drain under the road. This, then, was
evidently my best chance of escape, and this must be
my object. The thought flashed through my mind
more quickly than I can tell it, and I had not a moment to lose. Pincher recovered himself directly, was
before the other dogs again, and so close upon me that
I almost gave myself up for lost. But there was a tree
—a blessed tree—between me and the ditch I have
mentioned, and when I came up to it, instead of rushing straight on, I suddenly turned round it and lay
down. The eager Pincher rushed past me without
being able to stop, and in an instant I darted into the
ditch. So quick, however, was the dog in recovering
himself, that I was as nearly as possible caught—and, in
fact, had the other dogs been a few yards nearer, or
had there been no way out of the ditch, nothing could
have saved me,—but, by the greatest piece of good luck,
at the end of the ditch was a drain, the mouth of which
was open, and I darted at it immediately. So close
was my enemy, that in my momentary pause to enter

Escape of 'Bunny.'—P. 83

the hole I felt his warm breath upon me, and actually heard his jaws snap not half an inch behind my tail as it disappeared from his eager eyes. Disappear it luckily did, and I scrambled along several yards in the drain before I lay down, panting and breathless, but, at all events, safe for the present. Never, I suppose, had rabbit a more narrow escape, and certainly never was I so near bringing my life and adventures to a sudden end. But luck was on my side to-day. I do not know what the men and boys thought of it, or why they did not put a ferret into the drain after me at once. Perhaps they had no ferret with them; perhaps they thought it better fun to finish their coursing with the six rabbits still in the sack; perhaps they were inspired with a more generous sentiment, and considered that it was but fair to leave alone a poor rabbit who had struggled so hard for his life against such fearful odds. How this may be I cannot tell; but the result, happily for me, was that no one disturbed me in my drain, which was a common stone drain running underneath the road, with only one outlet at each end. I laid there for a long, long time, before I dared move, and it was not until quite the evening that I ventured to creep out the other side into a dry ditch corresponding with that through which I had entered my place of safety. I crept quietly up the bank, and found myself in a small green field with a plantation at the further end of it, some hundred yards or so from the road. Slowly and sadly I moved along over the grass until I came to the wood hedge, and there I sat down to think upon the best course to pursue. I had but little doubt that my poor brother and the other Barracks wood rabbits had fallen victims to their cruel enemies, who would be

sure to have given them less 'start' after my fortunate
escape.   I would have willingly returned to the scene
of the coursing if by so doing I had been at all likely to
discover what had become of my friends, but I knew
only too well that there could have been but one end
to the affair, and there was nothing to be gained by re-
entering the park.   I therefore crept through the wood
hedge, and finding a small earth on a bank not many
yards from it, I entered one of the holes, and found
two or three rabbits at home, who gave me a civil welcome, and listened with much attention to my account
of all that had happened.   I remained in this quiet
abode for several days, and had some difficulty in
making up my mind what to do.   I had not the heart
to go back alone to Barracks wood.   To me it would
be full of sad memories; and although I sometimes felt
a great longing to see my sister Pussy again, somehow
or other I could not bear to return.   My new friends
were very kind, but I did not like to trespass too long
upon their hospitality, and therefore determined to go
forth and find myself a new home elsewhere.   Accordingly, one evening I left the plantation, and went down
the road by the park in the contrary direction to Barracks wood; following the line of the park fence until
it ended at a little narrow slip of an ash plantation, the
other side of which was a private road leading into the
park, which was entered by a large white gate, close to
which stood a lodge, built at the edge of the aforesaid
ash plantation.   I crept through the latter, past the
lodge, under the gate, and found myself in a wood full
of old pollards, much the same as my dear old Barracks
wood.   Yes! there were the trees, the fern, and everything to remind me of home, and I sat down and wept

at the thought. As I sat and wept I was roused by a light tap on the shoulder, and, looking round, perceived one of my own race, of pleasant appearance, and wearing a friendly look.

'What is the matter, brother?' said he, and at the word, which brought up thoughts of my beloved Jollyboy, I burst out into a fresh flood of tears.

The new-comer consoled me as best he could, informed me that his own name was Burrower, and that, like myself, he was at present a travelling rabbit, loving change of place and scenery. He told me, moreover, that we were then in Bockhanger wood, and invited me to come with him down to Quillet's pond, where there was a noted spring, whose waters were delicious. I went with him, and found him so amusing and good-humoured as a companion, that I agreed to continue my travels in his company. We stayed two or three days in Bockhanger, and then spent a pleasant week in Spring wood adjoining, where was much thick grass, and a famous place for hiding. After this we crossed some meadows below, through which flowed a narrow stream, and on the other side of which was a farm called by the name of Quarrington, close to a wood of the same name, which I think was one of the most pleasant places I ever inhabited. Sunny banks, plenty of sand to scratch in, plenty of fern to use for resting-places by day, and dry earths in which to take refuge when too cold for out-door amusements. Pheasants and hares abounded in this wood, and I think all animals seemed to thrive there. But, as usual, hateful man was the ruin of animal happiness. We had stayed there some little while, and had taken up our abode in an earth upon the further side of the wood.

One day we thought we would go and have a quiet nibble in a nice field of corn close by; out we went, and Burrower happened to go first. He trotted along to the wood hedge, and then crept through one of the 'runs' by which rabbits daily passed into the field beyond. Suddenly I, who was following close behind, heard him give a faint squeak, and roll over as if struggling with some invisible enemy, and, rushing up, I saw in an instant what had happened. Some wretch in human form had been setting wires along the hedge, so that as soon as my poor friend had put his head down to creep through the run, the thin wire which had been set there closed round his neck, and, being in a slip knot, clasped him the tighter as he struggled, and the weight of his own body, as he kicked himself down into the ditch, made matters still worse. The poor fellow struggled manfully, but it was of no avail. Faintly he murmured, 'Fly, Bunny, fly!' and then, as he kicked and rolled over, the cruel wire tightened and tightened until my unhappy friend was absolutely strangled, and in a few moments lay there a murdered rabbit.

Distracted by this new misfortune, I scarcely seemed to care what became of me. I sought the open fields, and lived for some time in hedges and ditches, maintaining myself upon turnip-tops, or any other casual food upon which I could light.

After the lapse of some time I made for a large wood, at no great distance from my last abode. Naccult was its name, and in the very midst of it was a strange-looking tower, which could be seen for miles around, and at which I have often sat and gazed with awe and reverence, wondering what could possibly have

induced any one ever to build it there.   But the wood,
though not so sunny and pleasant as Quarrington, had
its advantages.   The soil was clay, and therefore damp
and cold for sitting out, but the underwood was very
thick and close; and a rabbit of discretion, who kept
his ears and eyes open, could dodge his enemies with
tolerable ease.   I lived there many months, during
which time beagles invaded the wood several times;
horrible guns were fired, and still more horrible men
stalked through the wood as if it was their own.   But
by this time I had become aware of the fact that the
enemies of a rabbit are to be found everywhere, and
that it is useless to hope to escape them by hurrying
from place to place.

One day I had been sitting out in some low springs,
nibbling the tender shoots, and enjoying myself greatly,
when I saw a remarkably-pretty little light-coloured
rabbit tripping merrily along.   I went up, and made
my politest bow at once, asking her if I could be of
any service to her.   She replied, with a blush which I
thought became her very well, that she was a Foreland
wood rabbit out for a holiday.   It was a mild spring
morning, I recollect, and I felt myself attracted to her
in an instant.   There it was that we began an acquaint-
ance which ended in her becoming my loving and
affectionate wife.   Her name was Fairy, and fairy-like indeed she was in all her graceful ways.   She asked me to
visit her in Foreland wood; and having done so, I pre-
ferred it so much to Naccult, that I went and lived
there.   We were married with very little delay, and
took up our abode in Foreland wood, having a winter
residence in Chute's wood hard by.   I may say that
our life was one of unmixed happiness; and as our

tender children grew up around us, my experience proved of the greatest service in warning them against the dangers which surround the existence of a rabbit in this wicked world.

Time passed away, and no extraordinary adventure disturbed the even course of our life: grey hairs began to show themselves upon me, my whiskers grew more bristling and lengthy, and I felt that I was no longer the young and sprightly Bunny of former times. Looking back upon the past, and thinking of old days, a strong desire seized me to revisit the scenes of my youth, and I proposed the plan to my dear Fairy. Always ready to obey my wishes like a dutiful wife, she consented at once, and we set out on our journey, taking with us two of our children, Pet and Pearly. We travelled the first night to Bircholt wood, a regular half-way house for rabbits travelling towards Hatch Park from the woods under the great chalk hills. Here we found a party of rabbits, assembled in an earth of moderate size, and complaining that the wood was quite spoiled, owing to the hares being preserved. There were, they said, as many as thirty or forty hares in that small wood, and the proud, overbearing disposition of these animals is hateful to any rabbit of a well-regulated mind. We were sorry to hear that matters were not going on quite pleasantly in this respect, but, as it was no business of ours to interfere, we did not attempt to do so.

We proceeded on our journey the next evening, and having passed through several large fields, came to a rushy meadow, which was situate immediately at the bottom of the park. Having crossed it, and crept under the old fence, we were at the edge of that great

tract of fern of which I have before spoken, and which
my mother, my brothers and sisters, and I had all
entered upon the day following our eventful flight from
the sand-pit.   With a heart full of sad and tender
memories, I led the way into the fern, and we slowly
marched from square to square until we reached that
self-same earth upon the edge of the sloping ground
from which I had taken my first view of Barracks
wood.   There it was, quiet and grand as ever; the old
pond sparkling in the distance, the beech-plantation just
as I had first seen it, the reeds still the same, and the
moor-hens sailing about as they had done ever since I
first knew the place.   The old fir-trees were there, too,
—the ditch, the bank, and the old pollarded trees
beyond; but where were the gentle voices and loving
hearts which had been with me on my first visit to
that charming spot?   Alas! the thought was too painful to bear, and although my wife laid her tender paw
upon my shoulder with a loving look, well knowing
the sad memories which were passing through my
mind, I could not at the moment overcome my grief.
But at this instant my attention was attracted by a
rabbit, apparently about my own age, who was sitting,
almost alone, outside the earth, and gazing, with an
air of quiet contentment and repose, upon the happy
scene before him.   Something in his appearance struck
me, and I drew a few steps nearer to him; then I
stamped my foot, and gave a sneeze; he turned his
head to see who it was who thus disturbed his medita-
tions, and as his countenance was thus brought to my
view, I started back with joy and surprise.   Could it
be? was it possible?   Yes!   It certainly was none
other than my lost brother Jolly-boy.   He knew me in

a moment, and with a loud squeak of joy, we rushed into each other's paws. Then we asked each other a thousand questions, each having firmly believed the other to have been dead for years, although, as Jolly-boy afterwards told me, he had been surprised at not seeing my body, with that of the other dead rabbits, when he was taken out of the sack. Eagerly I asked him how he had managed to escape.

It was little short of a miracle. It seems that, after they had coursed and lost me, the boys and men turned down the two next rabbits with more success, both being speedily caught and killed. It then entered their heads to vary the amusement by turning out two rabbits at a time, and this they accordingly did, giving them some dozen yards start. As soon as the two rabbits felt themselves at liberty, they took somewhat different courses. Jolly-boy, who was one of them, set off to the left hand, whilst the other rabbit, bewildered and frightened, ran right back into the teeth of his enemies. The dogs, of which there were three, being astonished at the novel sight of a rabbit running straight towards them, turned all their attention to him; he saw his fatal mistake when too late, and dodged off to the right, the three dogs yelling and snapping in close pursuit. The poor wretch was doubtless slain before long, but this my brother could not positively say. All he knew was that his companion dodged the dogs at first, and that, whilst they were occupied with him, Jolly-boy kept on at best pace, and got such a start that he had time to collect his thoughts, and get his breath; he heard the men and boys calling the dogs to pursue him, but being out of sight of the latter in a short time, they did not quickly take up the scent; and, in fact, he never saw them again.   After running for several hundred yards, he came to a plantation, which he recognized as the very same one in which he, Fatty, and I had taken refuge after our father's death.   Hope instantly revived in his breast, for he knew exactly where to run to now, and accordingly made the best of his way to the earth in which we had been lodged upon that sad day.   Here he found some of our old friends, with whom he passed a couple of days, bewailing my loss, and believing himself to be the last male descendant of our illustrious family.   He determined to return to Barracks wood, and accordingly did so, where he found our sister Pussy safe and sound, and consoled for our long absence by the tender attentions of the black rabbit. The latter had transferred his affections from the lost Soft-skin to Pussy; they were shortly afterwards married, and Jolly-boy told me that they were now blessed with a numerous family, and were occupying a large earth higher up in the old wood.

Delighted with this news, I introduced my brother to my wife and daughters, and we all proceeded to the earth, where I was told I should find my sister and her family.   There they were sure enough, although at first I could scarcely recognize the playful Pussy of my younger days in the respectable, motherly old rabbit whom I saw before me.   Tender, however, was our greeting; and the black rabbit (who had become far more grey than I) was right glad to see me again, being a rabbit of a kindly and jovial disposition.   He and my sister both urged us strongly to give up any idea of returning to Foreland wood, and to take up our abode in Barracks.   At first my wife expressed some reluctance at the idea of leaving a locality where she had lived so long and so happily, and where several of her children were left behind her. But seeing what a healthy and beautiful spot we had in Barracks wood, and what protection from enemies was afforded both by the largeness of the earths and the roots of the trees under which they had been made, she gradually came to the conclusion that we had better consent to my sister's proposal. So we took up our lodging in that large earth. Do not, however, let it be supposed that we forgot our dear children. We were not so unnatural; but having secured the services of a friendly jackdaw, we sent word to Foreland wood of the change in our plans, and invited our dear ones to join us; nor were they slow in obeying the summons. They had frequently heard me speak of the beauties and pleasures of Barracks wood, and were eager to partake thereof. Sons and daughters soon joined us; and though it was always a subject of boast on the part of Pet and Pearly that they had been the first of our children who had seen Barracks wood, yet I must in fairness say that the boast was always made in a friendly and pleasant way, and that I had every reason to rejoice at the family love and unity which prevailed in our home circle. So it is in every family of rabbits or children where happiness is to be found. To be fond of each other, to do little kindnesses for each other, to give up one's own little pleasures to make another happy, is the surest way for either a child or a rabbit to be happy, and nothing is so pretty a sight as to see brothers and sisters living together in loving and tender unity. This has always, I am happy to say, been the case with us. As I sit out now, in the pleasant summer evenings, with my children, grandchildren, and great-grandchildren around me, they come, often and often, as they have done to-night, to ask for a story. I tell them the story of my past life and adventures, and I love to see their dear little faces as they listen with so much attention. And when they feel inclined to cry over the fate of Fatty and Tina and Soft-skin, and the tears come into my own eyes as I tell the tale, I can honestly tell them that it is a great source of happiness to me that I am able to look back upon my early days, and remember nothing but love and kindness between those dear departed rabbits and myself. We knew no ill-feeling, we had no quarrels. I am an old, grey, worn-out rabbit now. Unless they boiled me for a very long time, I should be too tough a morsel now for the sharpest human tooth, and I am long past the age for roasting or being baked in a pie. But my heart is soft and tender still. The love which I cherished for the dear relations of my early youth has been transferred, in an amplified and intensified form, to those who have proved the support of my middle age and the consolation of my declining years. In my beloved Fairy I have found the partner of my joys, the soother of my sorrows. In my darling children have been reproduced the sweet companions of my earlier days; and I shall leave this world in the happy consciousness of having lived a harmless and I trust a useful life, secure in the affections of those to whose love I have always looked for my chief happiness, and whose affection I have ever returned with sincere devotion.

III.

THE ROBBER-BAND.

ONCE upon a time there was a very large forest. I do not know in what part of the world it was, and therefore it is not the slightest use asking me. All I *do* know is, that the people, all through my story, will be found to talk English, so nobody will be able to pretend that they do not understand it; and if anybody doesn't believe every word of it, it won't matter the least bit in the world. Wherever the country was, it was one of those countries of which robbers are so fond. I suppose there were no such things there as policemen, or, if there were, they always took care to be just where the robbers were *not,* which at once shows that the country couldn't be England; for *there* we know that a robber can't show his face anywhere without a police-man being down upon him in a moment. On each side of this forest there was a large town, at some considerable distance, and the shortest road from one town to the other lay through the forest; but it was a very dangerous road, and people had so often been robbed whilst travelling along it, that few of them cared to do so, and would rather go a long way round in order to be sure of arriving at the end of their journey with their purses in their pockets, and their heads on their shoulders. For you must know that several persons who had entered the forest had never been heard of again; and the friends of one young man, Marley by name, had been written to in a strange way, to say that if fifty pounds were not left at a certain place on a certain day, his head would be sent home without his body; and, as they thought the affair was a hoax, and took no notice, his head did actually arrive, neatly packed in straw, in a hamper, and directed to his house, 'This side uppermost—with care.' When it was opened, it so terrified an old aunt who lived in the house, that she lost her senses directly; whilst a fat old butler, who had known him from a child, went into a fit on the spot with horror, and died miserably. You may well believe that such things as this filled the whole neighbourhood with dread, and all kinds of reports were spread abroad as to the number and cruelty of the robber-band who lived in the forest.

One bright day, when summer was flaring up with his last heat before autumn came to cool him down, and strip him of his fine green leaves, two men were seated upon a bank by the side of the road which led through the forest. One of these was a man apparently about forty years of age; he had a small close-fitting black velvet cap on his head, with a long tassel; a dress, which seemed to be made of leather, with a belt of the same material, in which two or three pistols appeared, carelessly stuck in, and alongside of them a dagger. He had in his hands a gun, which he balanced on his knees, and his face was bronzed by exposure to the wind and sun; although a deep scar, extending from his brow down one side of his face to his chin, told that it must also have been exposed to something else at some time or other. As he sat talking to his companion, he glanced constantly round with a suspicious look, and seemed never off his guard for a moment. The other man could scarcely have reached the age of twenty-five; he had light curling hair, dark eyes, and an open expression of countenance, with a certain stern look about the mouth, which seemed to show that there was plenty of resolution in him if occasion required. The elder of the two had just asked him a question to which he was replying.

'Come far?' he said. 'Yes, I have; a long, long way, with nothing in my pocket, and only good fortune to trust to. There is no humbug about me. I want to join the robber-band, if I only knew how to do it; for, in spite of all that folks may say, I believe they are a brave set of fellows, living a merry life; and I, at least, have no ill word to say of them!'

'That's right,' replied the other. 'You take a just view of the case. These poor robbers have done *you* no harm, and why should you abuse them? "Let us speak of a man as we find him,"—that's my motto.'

'Yes,' rejoined the other, 'and a good one, too; but suppose you *don't* find him, which is my case as regards the robber-band?'

'Why, then, don't speak of him at all—so *that* question's easily settled,' growled the elder man; and then, looking very closely at the other, he added, 'Do you really want to become one of the band, young man?'

'Of course I do,' said he, 'or why am I here at all?'

'Then you have a good opportunity of carrying out your intentions,' said his companion, 'for here you are right in the midst of them!' and with these words he put a whistle to his mouth—a regular good, old-fashioned robber whistle,—and blew a shrill blast upon it, which was followed by the instant appearance of four men, each of whom carried a gun, and were plainly enough members of the robber-band. They came jumping out of the bushes, and ran up at once to where these two men were sitting.

'What is it, Captain Blackcap?' asked the fore-most, a tall, dark, savage-looking man.

'Why,' answered the other, 'here is a young chap who wants to join the robber-band; there are scarce twenty of us now, and another will be useful, if he turns out to be of the right sort; but search him first, and see if his account of himself be true, and that he has nothing in his pockets.'

The young man was immediately seized by the robbers, and carefully searched, but nothing was found upon him except a lead pencil, a corkscrew, and two cigars wrapped carefully up in a sheet of last month's 'Bradshaw.' This seemed satisfactory to the robber captain, who then said to the young man,

'My friend, you shall have your wish. I am captain of the robber-band, and you shall become one of them. Here are four of those who will be your future companions, Jim, Pedro, Bouncer, and Gentleman Joe. You will now come with us, and be made acquainted with our mode of life.'

So saying, he rose from his seat on the bank, and sauntered slowly down the road for some distance, followed by the young man and the four robbers. The tall one, who had first accosted the captain, and who was called Pedro, asked the new recruit what his name was, to which he replied 'Johnson,' and told the same story which he had already told Captain Blackcap. The latter, after walking some half-mile along the road, turned sharply aside into the forest, and after making his way through the thick bushes for a few yards, struck into an old track, apparently but little used, and proceeded along it silently for some distance, until he approached an old ruined castle which stood in the middle of the forest.

Few people had ever seen this castle, and no one knew by whom it had been erected or to whom it had originally belonged. It was very large, and the huge stones of which it was built were covered with moss and ivy, the growth of many years. Vast masses of rock lay around, as if they had at some former period formed part of a building, destroyed by earthquake or by the wasting hand of man, but within the circle round which they were to be seen rose the castle itself, of which sufficient was still standing to have accommodated a goodly number of inhabitants. On the side at which the party now approached it, picking their way through the scattered masses of rock, the ground was level with the foot of the wall, but it fell away right and left, so that a broad chasm, perhaps a moat at some distant period, separated the other side of the castle from the forest, and in this chasm the brakes and brambles, with a number of evergreens of great age, formed a natural and dense rampart which neither man nor beast could have easily surmounted.

Down a very narrow path, close to the wall of the castle, the robber captain led the way; presently the path turned with the wall of the castle, and at the foot of the wall, close before him, appeared steps, which he descended with his attendants. A low door was at the bottom of these steps, three raps upon which were followed by a scuffling sound, and it was presently thrown open by a wild-looking man whose face was almost entirely covered with grisly red hair, whilst a long beard of the same colour hung down nearly to his waist. He greeted the captain with respect; and the latter, addressing him by the name of Griper, told him of the newcomer, and asked if supper was ready.

'Yes,' answered Griper. 'Mother Jack has been wondering for some time why you were not home before.'

'Better late than never,' said Captain Blackcap, while the thought crossed Johnson's mind that it was just possible that a visit to that place might be better paid 'never' than either 'late,' or at any other time, for the room and the company both looked queer enough. However, he was in for it now, and on he must go.

The robbers passed along this vault, and then ascended some steps, which led into the large hall of the old castle. This was their living room, and a fine one it was for the purpose. When they entered, an old and remarkably ugly woman was standing by the fire, watching some meat roasting, whilst several other men were seated in different parts of the room, yawning and stretching, and evidently quite ready for the meal.

'I've brought you a new brother, men,' said the captain, and then they all began to question Johnson, and push him about here and there, to see, as they said, what he was made of. He bore all their free-and-easy ways with great good humour, and tried to make himself as much at home as possible, but was not sorry when it was announced by the old woman that supper was ready, and fell to with the rest in a manner which showed that his appetite was all that could be desired. After supper pipes were lighted, and drink poured out, and a merry evening the party had of it, till the captain ordered lights to be put out, and every man to turn into bed. Bed consisted of a quantity of clean straw in three separate corners of the room, upon which the robbers threw themselves just as they were, and went fast asleep. Johnson followed their example, Pedro and another lying down in the same corner as he did; and the former, warning him that as he had yet to prove his truth as well as his courage, he would not be allowed to leave his bed or the room until the captain gave orders as to his future life. This gave Johnson no sort of uneasiness, and he remarked that had he wished to escape he had no notion how to set about it or where to go to. He therefore slept as happily as possible until the morning, and was quite prepared for anything when the robber captain called his band together at an early hour. Captain Blackcap then informed Johnson that, unless they knew of some party of travellers being about to approach for whose capture the whole band might be required, their practice was to sally forth in two bands of four, five, or six each, leaving the others at home to look after the castle. Until they knew more of Johnson, he would not be allowed to join the party who went forth to rob, but would stay at home with Mother Jack and two others, who on this first day chanced to be Pedro and Jim. Johnson of course agreed, for he could do nothing else, and made himself as useful and

agreeable as he could during the day. Towards night one
party of the robbers returned without any booty ; they
were Griper and five of the others who had been at home
when the captain brought Johnson in. The captain's
party had been more fortunate, for they brought in a
burly butcher, whom they had caught as he was driving
his cart home from the market of one of the neighbouring towns. They came laughing and shouting into the
hall, driving the man before them, who strove to make
a joke of it too, but to very little purpose. Captain
Blackcap seated himself in a chair near the fire-place,
and ordered the prisoner to be brought before him.

'So you are the butcher, I hear, who is not afraid
of the robber-band ?'

'Oh sir,' replied the man, 'I am sure I never meant
any disrespect, I only meant to say that people needn't
be so timid about coming into the forest, for that the
robber-band were not so terrible as was often said.'

'Liar !' exclaimed Blackcap, 'I have means of
knowing what you say of which you have little idea.
You have lately said that *you* were not afraid of the
robber-band, and were as good a man as their captain,
whoever he might be. Now you shall learn your mistake,' and drawing a pistol from his girdle, he deliberately shot the unhappy butcher through the head,
and directed some of the band to throw the body out
of the window into the chasm below. He then divided
the money which they had taken from the victim, after
which the robbers sat down and made as hearty a supper as if nothing unusual had occurred. Johnson made
no remark upon what he had seen, having resolved to
take everything as a matter of course, and for the next
few days nothing extraordinary took place. Meanwhile

he seemed to be gradually gaining the confidence of the
robbers by the manner in which he performed the duties
imposed upon him, and at length the captain told him
that he might now take his turn with the others in
going out on the robbing expeditions.   Armed with a
gun, a knife, and a brace of pistols, and accompanied
by Pedro, Jim, and a robber called Nosey (principally
from having no nose, that useful organ having been cut
off in a brawl with a friend), he started off on his first
trial.   The four men proceeded along the road for some
way, and then, choosing a spot where the trees were
large and thick, each concealed himself as best he could
in the bushes, one of them mounting a tree so as to be
able to command the road for some distance.   They
waited for a long time without any one passing but a
working man, whom they judged to be not worth robbing, and they were beginning to despair of getting any
booty that day, when the man on the look-out gave the
signal, and descending the tree, told them that a cart
was approaching.   As it drew nearer it became clear
that there were two people in it, one a stoutish man of
some fifty or sixty years of age, and the other somewhat younger.   On they came until they were exactly
opposite the place where the robbers were concealed.
All four fired at once, and the horse fell dead, whilst
one of the men jumped bolt upright in the cart, clapped
his hand to his side, and dropped with a groan.   The
robbers rushed out, and were received with two pistol-
shots from the elderly man, one of which grazed Jim's
arm, whilst the other carried off Johnson's hat.   The
man, however, was seized and dragged out of the cart,
struggling fiercely, and as Johnson came up with his
hat off, he cried out, ' I know you, George; 'tis *you*

who are one of these vile robbers, are you?' He might have said more, but Jim, infuriated at the wound he had received, sent a bullet through his head which stopped his tongue for ever. Then the robbers searched the two dead men and took their watches and money, and all their clothes that were of any value. After which they put back the bodies in the cart, and pushed it along the road a little way until they came to a deep chalk-pit, overhung with bushes and brambles, and dark with the same below, down which they overturned the cart and its contents, merely drawing the dead horse aside into the bushes near which he had fallen. Little chance was there of any traces of the murdered men being ever found in that pit. As they left it, Pedro remarked—

'Johnson, what did that fat fool mean by calling you George? do you know him? and who is he?'

'I don't know,' replied Johnson. 'He must have mistaken me for somebody else, for I never saw him before; I am not even sure that he meant *me* when he spoke; one thing is, he won't have the chance of seeing me again!'

Johnson spoke in a careless tone, but there was something about his manner which aroused the suspicions of Pedro, who looked at him attentively, and thought gravely for a little while, but said no more.

Upon their arrival at the castle, the four robbers handed over their booty to be divided amongst the band by Captain Blackcap, who asked Pedro how the new recruit had behaved. Pedro could say nothing against Johnson, for he had fired his gun, rushed in with the rest, and willingly aided in throwing the bodies and the cart down the chalk-pit, but there was evidently some suspicion lurking in the man's mind, and a dislike which Johnson had unaccountably taken to him at first, was increased by his evident want of trust in him.

Next day it was Johnson's turn to remain at home, and having finished his work about the place, cleaning the guns, sharpening the knives, and aiding the other men who were left in their various duties, he thought he would try to make friends with old Mother Jack, who was knitting away in one of the old windows, and as she knitted kept by her side a certain black bottle of which she was uncommonly fond, and from which she took a hearty pull from time to time. She was not generally given to much civility, and the treatment and language which she received from the robbers was not always of the most polite description, but Johnson had taken care to be as civil and obliging as possible, and she had once or twice showed somewhat of a friendly feeling towards him. Drawing near her he began to talk of the weather, the old castle, the forest, and various other things, till at last the conversation turned on the success which the robbers had lately had.

'Ay,' said the old woman, 'that butcher was a queer customer. Drat the fellows, I wish they'd be killed outside like Christians, and not go blundering into the captain's hands and be caught alive. I don't care for having them killed inside the house, especially since they cut off that poor young chap's head some months ago because they couldn't get their fifty pound ransom for him.'

'How was that?' asked Johnson eagerly.

'Why,' replied the old woman, 'it was a fine young man they caught, and wanted him to join the band, but nothing could persuade him to do so; then they sent a letter to his friends to say that if they didn't send fifty pounds for his ransom, his head should be cut off and sent home. No fifty pounds ever came, and I dare say the friends thought it was only an empty threat. So thought most of the band, I fancy; at least they were for letting the young fellow off, but Pedro got hold of the captain and persuaded him that if they didn't do as they had said, people would leave off being afraid of the robber-band, so those who were for mercy had to give in, and Pedro and Griper together killed the poor chap, and his head was sent in to his friends. Oh, he's a rare cool hand, that Pedro.'

And then the old hag went on to talk of other things till it was time to go to work again, and their conversation ended. This kind of life continued for several weeks: sometimes the robbers were without booty for many days together, and sometimes they would sally forth into the country and bring in sheep or oxen or anything upon which they could lay their hands. Johnson regularly went out in his turn and took his share with the rest, although some of them now and then jeered him for not appearing anxious to take part in the killing of any prisoner who happened to be caught. He laughed it off always, however, saying that he thought robbing better fun than killing, and as the latter amusement gave Pedro and Griper such pleasure, it was a pity to deprive them of any of it. So time passed on, until the events happened which I am now about to relate.

There was a certain old nobleman who lived in a fine palace in one of the two towns which I have mentioned. He had an only daughter of whom he was very fond, and she was also very fond of him. How-

ever, as her heart was too big for this love alone, she
was also very fond of a young gentleman named Ferdinando, who belonged to the town on the other side of
the forest, and to whom she was engaged to be married
as soon as her old father could make up his mind to
part with her.   Now, about this time it happened that
the old baron had agreed to pay Ferdinando a visit,
and to bring the lovely Rosalie with him.   There had
been some doubt as to the road they should take, but
the young lady did not like the idea of delay, and was
all for the shorter cut through the forest.   Her father
did not much fancy it, as the deeds of the robber-band
had become so daring, but he yielded to his daughter's
persuasion, and, after all, thought he, 'the villains
would never dare attack a nobleman's carriage, well
protected as mine will be.'   So the lumbering old coach
was taken out and packed, and off they went.   Inside
were the baron and his daughter, together with the
latter's lady's-maid, and as the carriage was roomy,
they were comfortable enough.   They were drawn by
four horses, driven by two postillions; two footmen,
well armed, sat behind the coach, and it was followed
by two men on horseback, also armed, so that there
might be no fear of attack.   Off they set, and travelled
without interruption until they reached the forest.
Rosalie was in high spirits, and talked to her father
about the visit they were going to pay, and about her
dear Ferdinando, and how long it would be before they
should see him; to which the old baron replied, half in
jest and half in earnest—

'If we meet no robber band, oh !
   Soon you'll see your Ferdinando.'

But he little thought how much meaning his words

had. They entered the forest, where, the road not being very good, they could proceed but slowly, and they did so for some distance without accident. But after a sudden turn of the road, they came suddenly upon a number of large branches of trees thrown across the road in such a manner as to prevent a carriage from passing, and the postillions accordingly stopped their horses. The very moment they did so a volley was poured in by the concealed robbers, and fifteen or sixteen men rushed out upon the travellers; for, having discovered the approach of so considerable a party, Captain Blackcap had taken out all his band but two, Griper and Johnson, whom he had left at the castle, thinking that he would thus be able to make sure of a valuable prize. The robbers' volley killed one of the postillions and two of the horses. The other postillion jumped from his horse. The two footmen were down in a moment, and the two armed horsemen were close at hand, but, even with the old baron, they were but six against more than double that number, and did not know how many more enemies might be at hand; in fact, they had but little chance unless their skill and courage had been great, and I am afraid it was not, for the postillion scuttled off and hid in the bushes as quickly as he could. After a short scuffle, one of the footmen, having slightly wounded Bouncer, was himself slain, and the other captured, whilst the horsemen, after firing to no purpose, clapped spurs to their horses, and galloped away as fast as they could. The brave old baron resisted manfully, and killed one of the robbers with a pistol-shot; but his valour was in vain. He, his daughter, and the maid, were dragged from the carriage; their trunks and boxes were stripped of their contents, and, in spite of all the baron's rage and threats, his hands were rudely tied behind him, and he, with the other captives, was driven through the forest, most of the valuables being strapped on to two of the horses, whilst the bodies of the other two horses were dragged out of the road into the bushes and there left.

It was a sad sight to see the poor young lady driven before the robbers along the narrow path, and after they had gone a little way, it was so clear that she could hardly walk, that the captain desired two of the band to carry her, and in this way the whole party arrived at the old castle. They did not all enter at once, but whilst the captain and several of the band conducted the captives by the same way that Johnson had entered the castle, the others remained outside till they had taken the booty from the horses into the vaults below, and the poor animals were then taken round and slaughtered on the other side, so that their bodies might be thrown into the chasm, and no chance be left of discovery.

When he found himself within the castle walls, the old baron again began to abuse his captors violently, and asked who was their captain, who presumed to treat a man of his rank in that manner?

He was not long in receiving his answer, for Captain Blackcap stood forward and told him that, if he couldn't keep a civil tongue in his head, he would have it cut out in about another minute, and as his looks plainly showed that he was in earnest, the baron thought that he had better, upon the whole, remain silent.

He was dragged off, away from his daughter, to a separate room at some little distance from the robbers'

Capture of the Baron.—P. 108.

hall, and poor Rosalie, bathed in tears and reduced to
the depths of despair, was placed in a small chamber
up-stairs, the window of which looked out upon the
chasm, which interposed on that side between the castle
and the forest.   Here she was left alone for a time
to ponder upon her sad fate, and to think with bitter,
but unavailing regret, upon her own foolish fancy,
which had led her to persuade her father to take the
shorter road through the forest, instead of the longer
but safer route through the open plain.   If she could but
have lived the last few days over again, how differently
she would have acted!   But, unfortunately, people
never *can* live days over again, however much and
however often they may desire to do so, and Rosalie
had therefore nothing for it but to make the best of
a bad business.

She walked to the window and looked out.   It was a
lovely evening; the red rays of the setting sun were
tinging with fiery gold the green boughs of the forest
trees, and the soft south wind fanned her cheek as she
sorrowfully gazed upon the peaceful face of Nature,
which seemed to contrast so strangely with the sorrow
and fear which were distracting her young heart.   She
was aroused from her occupation by the sudden entrance of no less a personage than old Mother Jack,
who came to bring her some food, and perhaps also for
the purpose of having a good stare at the young baron-
ess.   The sight, however, of one of her own sex inspired Rosalie with hope, and she turned at once to the
old woman, and addressed her in tearful accents.

'Oh, where is my dear father?   Why have they
taken him away from me, and where are we?   Pray,
pray tell me, and help us if you can!'

'Hoity-toity,' replied the old woman with a laugh, 'I'll tell ye where you are fast enough, my dainty damsel! You're in the robbers' castle, and there you're likely to be, as far as I know, till the captain makes up his mind what is to be done with you. And as for the old gentleman, he's safe enough, I'll warrant you! safe till he pays up like a trump—gives his gold and saves his carcase—that's good robber-law, my girl, and you fine gentlefolks will know it soon enough.'

'Oh, *do* help us—cannot you help us to escape?' said the poor girl.

'Escape?' replied Mother Jack. 'Like enough you are to escape from a place like this, poor tender bird, and like enough I am to offend the robber-band by helping you. Why, they'd make mincemeat of me in no time. No, no, my fine lady, make up your mind about *that*, the sooner the better. Folks don't escape *here*, I can tell ye.'

Poor Rosalie, thus repulsed, spoke no more to the old woman, but, when the latter had left the room, threw herself on the floor, and bitterly bewailed the sad fate which had befallen her. Not long, however, was she allowed to remain undisturbed, for hasty steps were heard ascending the stairs; her door was rudely thrown open, and two of the band appeared, who, taking her one by each arm, dragged her down to the room below, where sat the robber-band round a table, Captain Blackcap at their head, and the other prisoners standing bound before him.

'Here comes the girl,' said he as Rosalie was brought in. 'And now, my masters, to settle what is best to be done with the prisoners. Has any one a plan to propose?'

'Kill 'em,' said a gruff voice, without any hesitation, at which a roar of laughter burst from the robbers.

'Just like old Griper, always for killing,' remarked one of the number; and then half-a-dozen began to speak at once, some suggesting one thing and some another. At last Pedro stepped forward; and when the captain had ordered silence, he suggested that the footman and maid should be killed at once, and the baron and his daughter be kept till a ransom should be received for them. At this the maid set up a scream, which caused the nearest robber to stuff a remarkably dirty napkin into her mouth in so rough a fashion as greatly to amuse the merry company, and to effectually stop her utterance of further sounds for the present. Order, however, having been restored, Captain Black-cap again spoke.

'My men,' said he, 'I have a plan to propose to you; but before doing so let us ask the chief prisoner a question or two, which may, perhaps, assist us in our decision.' Then, turning to the prisoners, 'Baron,' said he,—'for this I find is your title,—you have been fairly taken captive, and are now in the hands of the robber-band. What ransom are you prepared to pay for yourself, your daughter, and your two servants, that you may again be set free?'

'Villain,' answered the enraged baron, who, bound as he was, was still unsubdued in spirit, 'you have violently and unlawfully taken me prisoner, slain my servants, and robbed me of my property. Not one farthing will I pay you; and for any injury you do me and mine, I warn you that a fearful vengeance shall be taken!'

'Say you so, my proud old cock?' retorted the

robber; 'thou shalt crow less loudly before thou quittest this castle!' and then, turning again to his band, 'Now, boys,' said he, 'you know that although this old fool talks so big, a little gentle pressure and a few days of short commons will make him alter his tone. The difficulty is, how to communicate most safely with his friends, so that the ransom which they are sure to pay may be received. This has been a difficulty before, but I think I see a way out of it this time. Suppose we spare the footman's life, binding him to secrecy by a solemn oath, and let him take such message as we shall dictate to the baron's friends. Meanwhile we will keep the baron and the women; and if the footman prove false, or any attempt at rescue be made, kill them instantly.'

A murmur of approval ran round the room at this proposal, when Pedro again stood forward and addressed the captain.

'It is rather dangerous,' he said, 'to let this man go, although he may be very sure that if he *does* play us false, revenge will be executed upon him. But I should propose that he himself should bring back the ransom upon which we may agree, and that he should understand the consequences of his not doing so. I vote that we settle now, and let the prisoners know, that if the ransom is not brought back within two clear days after the messenger leaves this castle, on the third day we shall roast the maid, on the fourth boil the young lady, and on the fifth turn the old baron loose in the forest with his hands and feet cut off.'

This idea seemed to amuse the robbers vastly, and, after some further discussion, it was resolved to let the footman go, as the captain had proposed, upon the full understanding that if he did not return within the time allowed, the prisoners would be put to death.

This having been settled, and the footman fully warned of the consequences which would certainly follow his disobedience to the orders given him, the baron, Rosalie, and her maid, were led off to their respective places of confinement, to await the events of the next few days in no little anxiety. It was, indeed, a case in which it was impossible not to feel anxious. Was the footman to be trusted, or, having once got out of the forest with a whole skin, was it not probable that he would either be afraid to return, or, if he received the money for the baron's ransom, be tempted to make off with it instead of coming back to the robbers' castle? Then, a thousand things might happen to prevent his return within the prescribed time. He might meet with an accident, he might fall ill, he might lose his way in the forest, and thus be delayed; or even such a trifle as slipping and spraining his ankle might retard his progress, and cause him to be too late to save the lives of the prisoners. All these thoughts passed through the mind of poor Rosalie as she sat at her window and gazed out over the forest scenery; and then came the sad thought of the probable result if the footman was actually stopped by some of the above-mentioned causes. Would the robbers really kill her father, her maid, and her? or was it only a threat to terrify them, and to make sure of a ransom? And, if she *was* killed, what would Ferdinando do? How miserable he would be! and perhaps he would never know what had actually become of her! O Ferdinando, Ferdinando, if you could but be with your poor Rosalie at this moment! As

8

she sat and thought, and the tears stole down her
beautiful cheeks, her attention was suddenly attracted
by a slight noise which appeared to proceed from the
window of the room in which she was confined.   She
looked eagerly round and listened ;—the moon was
now shining through the window with its calm, clear,
holy light, and all was still and silent in the solemn
grandeur of the old forest.   Rosalie approached the
window, and again she heard a sound as of something
gently striking the wall.   The bars of the casement
were sufficiently far apart to allow of her putting her
head between them, and she was about to do so, when
a hand suddenly appeared, grasping firmly one of the
aforesaid bars, and at the same moment a voice said, in
a low tone, ' Don't be afraid, lady; friends are near
you.'

Now, to be told that friends are near you is always
a cheerful thing, provided that you believe the person
who tells you so, and have no reason to think that he
has any object in deceiving you.   But when young
ladies have been carried away to robbers' castles, have
heard threats of a remarkably unpleasant character as
to their future fate, and find themselves shut up in a
lonely room, as had happened to poor Rosalie, they do
not feel ready to take everybody for a friend who
chooses to call himself one.   Nor is the sight of a
hand at your window, or the sound of a strange voice,
calculated to inspire with confidence or delight a young
lady under these unfortunate circumstances.   Poor
Rosalie, therefore, started back in alarm at the unexpected sight and sound, and though she did not
scream, having sense enough to know that it *could* do
no good, and *might* do much harm, yet she felt any-

thing but secure that the new-comer, whoever he might be, was what he evidently wished to appear, and her first thought was to retreat hastily from the window. But she remembered that, after all, she could hardly be worse off than she was, and that she might be throwing away a chance of safety if she declined to hold any communication with her mysterious visitor. She therefore answered, in low and trembling accents, 'If you are a friend, take me out of this dreadful place.'

'That is my wish and hope,' replied the voice; 'but I come now to beg of you to trust me, and to give me some token by which your friends may know that I am to be trusted.'

'But who or what are you?' said Rosalie, and timidly drew near to the window as she spoke. There she perceived a young man, dangling from a rope which was fastened above, and which he grasped firmly with one hand, whilst with the other he clung to the bar of the window, supporting himself as well as he could upon a stone which projected from the wall.

'Lady,' he said, 'I should hardly dare expect that you would trust me, did I not know that your position must appear so desperate to you that you may be disposed to clutch at a straw like a drowning man, and to place your confidence in one who *may* be a friend, and, if a foe, can hardly bring you to a worse pass than that in which you are.'

Rosalie started, as she thought how exactly the speaker's words reflected the thought which had passed through her own mind. 'But your name?' she said; 'and how came you here?'

'Lady,' replied the young man, 'my name matters

not, but I am here supposed to be one of the band who
have captured you and yours; *they* know me as Johnson.   You could ruin me with them by merely telling
them of this visit.   Thus I place myself in your power;
but my only object is to serve you.   I can communicate
with your friends, but it is necessary that they should
know that I came from you, and should believe that
which I tell them.   There is no time for delay.   If
you can make up your mind, tell me at once, and give
me a token; if not, let me know, and I bid you fare-
well directly.'

Rosalie doubted still, but, like a wise girl, knowing
that she could lose nothing by trusting her visitor,
determined to do so.   'Here,' said she, hurriedly taking
from her finger an opal ring and handing it to Johnson.
'If my Ferdinando could but see this ring, he would
know at once that the person who has it in his
possession has received it from his poor Rosalie.   But
stay, you do not know who Ferdinando is.'

Johnson smiled.   'Lady,' he replied, 'be easy upon
that score.   Your confidence is not misplaced, and you
have only now to put your trust in Providence, and
keep up your courage with the thought that friends are
at work for you.'

At this moment Rosalie heard footsteps approaching her door, and, making a signal to that effect to her
strange visitor, hastily retreated from the window.
The footsteps, however, passed on, and she again
looked out, but Johnson had disappeared, and she
could gain no more information from that quarter.

It is time, however, that we heard something of the
part which was being played by other actors in this
veracious drama.   Fortunately for his master, the foot-

man was an honest fellow, and made the best of his
way home with the full intention of obtaining and
returning with the ransom. He arrived without any
accident at the baron's palace, and found all uproar
and confusion. The two mounted men who had fled
from the forest, had spread the report that the baron's
carriage had been attacked by at least two hundred
robbers, that they had performed prodigies of valour in
his defence, and had barely escaped with their lives
from such an overwhelming force, whilst the rest of
the party had certainly been slain or captured. On
hearing this sad news, the old nobleman's household
was thrown into a terrible state of alarm and uncertainty. Nobody knew what to do, and therefore
nobody did anything until the next day, when old
Puzzle-brains, the house-steward, bethought himself of
sending off two messengers,—one to inform the baron's
brother, who lived a few miles off in the country, and
another to lay the matter before the mayor of the
town. The latter immediately summoned the town
council, laid the business before them, and, after a
lengthy discussion, prevailed upon them to call a
special meeting for that day three weeks, when, the
whole affair being by that time well over and settled,
they came to the conclusion of doubling their police-
force, which had hitherto consisted of the town-sergeant
and two elderly constables of more weight than vigour
or activity.

The baron's brother, however, did not await the
action of the local authorities, but immediately hurried
to the palace with some dozen of his people, and was
actually there when the footman arrived with the message from the robbers. The ransom demanded was

considerable, but there could be no doubt that it must
be forthcoming, and that speedily.   Moreover, as the
brother was a worthy man, he felt all the more anxious
about the matter, because in the event of the baron and
Rosalie being killed by the robbers, the palace and property would become his own, and therefore hesitation
or delay upon his part might be attributed to covetous
motives, by which he was far from being inspired.
Therefore the ransom was prepared, and the footman
sent off in the afternoon of the second day, with two
men to assist him in carrying the money.   But, resolved that the matter should not end thus, the baron's
brother, with thirty picked men, followed at some distance, with the full intention of falling upon the band
as soon as he should be well assured of the safety of his
relations.   Meanwhile the castle of the robbers had
been in a state of some excitement.   Owing to the revelry which followed so great a success as the capture of
the baron's party, discipline had been somewhat relaxed,
and instead of the band being all gathered together in
the one large room in which they usually slept, they
had been scattered about here and there during the
night following the capture, and only met at an early
hour upon the next morning.   It was thus that Johnson
had been enabled to communicate, as we have seen,
with the Lady Rosalie.   He had fastened a strong rope
to the iron bars of the window of an uninhabited room
above that in which she was imprisoned, and had boldly
let himself down. With a calculation which proved his
talent, he had reckoned upon being able to re-enter the
castle by one of the passage windows beyond the lady's
room, by crawling upon the stone ledge below her window for a few yards.   Then he intended to have re-

ascended to the room from which he had let down the
rope, to have drawn it in again, and thus destroyed all
traces of his adventure.   His calculations, however,
were destroyed by a circumstance which he could not
have foreseen, and which might have been entirely fatal
both to him and to the captives.   Although most of
the robbers were overcome with liquor and fatigue, and
slumbered soundly, such was not the case with the
wily Pedro.   No amount of fatigue or liquor appeared
to affect this remarkable personage, and the state of the
rest of the band only made him doubly vigilant.   His
suspicions of Johnson had, as we have seen, been
already awakened, and he was not satisfied when he
perceived that the young man was not among the latest
and deepest drinkers on this eventful evening.   He said
nothing, but, when the rest of the band had scattered,
and most of them lay in heavy sleep either in the supper-
room or wherever their inclination led them, Pedro arose
and commenced a stealthy journey all over the castle.
He saw nothing of Johnson, and found no suspicious
circumstance until he arrived at the uninhabited room
above mentioned, and there his attention was immediately
attracted by the rope fastened to the bars of the window.
He crept up and looked out, but could see nothing,
owing to the thick branches of some of the tops of the
trees which touched the castle at this point, and through
which Johnson had made his way, rope in hand, as he
descended.   But Pedro knew well enough that the rope
was there for no good, and that it betokened mischief.
He hesitated for a moment.   Should he await the
ascent of the person who had thus gone down, and
whom he rightly suspected to be Johnson?   Was he
sure that the man either would or could return by the

same way ?   If he did so, was he sure of being able to
master him ?   As he hesitated, the rope moved violently,
which was caused by Johnson's action in suddenly leaving hold of it in order to crawl on to the stone ledge.
Pedro's mind was instantly made up, and he did that
which, a few seconds sooner, would certainly have destroyed the other.   He drew his dagger and deliberately
cut the rope close to the iron bar.   It took him a few
moments to do this effectually, and then he eagerly
thrust his head out of the window and listened.   The
rope fell heavily down through the branches of the
trees, but no other sound, and no cry of pain or distress,
followed its fall.   Pedro listened with intense anxiety
for a full minute, little dreaming that every second was
worth its weight in gold (if anybody can tell me what
the weight of a second is) to Johnson, who was meanwhile crawling carefully along the ledge, his fate depend-
ing upon his safe re-entry into the castle.   He reached
the passage window, two bars of which he had observed
to be wanting, raised himself gently up, and crept into
the passage.   Softly he stole towards the turreted staircase which led to the rooms above, when suddenly he
heard a hasty footstep overhead which changed all his
intentions; for although he did not absolutely feel certain that it was Pedro, he felt assured that it must be
one of the band, more sober than the rest, and that
whoever it was had probably entered the room overhead and discovered the rope.   His resolution was taken
in an instant.   Turning round and retracing his steps
as quietly as possible, he descended a small stone staircase which led down to a part of the castle which,
being more in ruins than the rest, was made little use
of by the robber-band.   He stopped close to an open

window, the bars of which had long since disappeared, and through which a man could easily pass. Here he waited for a moment, until, as he had thought likely, Pedro had passed by the staircase, hurrying on to continue his search elsewhere. Then Johnson boldly sprang through the window into the branches of a huge sycamore tree which almost touched the walls of the castle. He quickly descended this tree, and stood in the forest, or rather, a few yards within the tangled mass of bushes, brambles, and evergreens which protected that side of the castle. Stealthily as a fox he crept through these, and then darted forward at great speed. It was towards midnight, and all was still in the forest. Any one who was unaccustomed to the place might well have felt fear, but Johnson appeared to have no such feeling. He hurried onward as if every inch of the place was known to him, and in some three quarters of an hour came to the outskirts of the forest, quite the other side from that on which the baron had entered. Still on and on he pressed, until he reached the first of a few straggling huts, in which dwelt the shepherds and goat-keepers of the country, a rude set of men, but too poor to be plundered by the robbers, who generally confined themselves to the plunder of richer travellers, and in any case did not care to interfere with such near neighbours, who might be dangerous if trifled with and rendered active enemies. At the door of the hut Johnson hastily knocked. It was presently opened by a tall, dark man with a large slouching hat, and a dried sheep-skin cloak carelessly flung over his shoulders.

'Who is it?' he asked in a rough tone.

''Tis I, 'tis I,' answered Johnson hurriedly. 'The

pony, the pony, as quick as you can, Bertram! The doom is near, but time is gold!'

The man did not hesitate for an instant, but running to a neighbouring shed, brought out in a few seconds a shaggy pony with a large clumsy saddle, which he led up to Johnson. The latter jumped upon it in an instant, but before he started he turned in his saddle and held up Rosalie's ring before the eyes of the other. 'This,' said he, 'will be the token. The haunted oak the day after to-morrow, at midnight. Tell them all to remember the oath and follow the token.'

With these words he dashed off as fast as the pony could go over the wild country, and it was marvellous to see the rate at which the little animal got over the ground. It was within two hours of Johnson's leaving the castle that he cantered into the court-yard of a large building at the very entrance of a town which must have been at least ten miles from the forest. Here he rang loudly at a bell, the rope of which hung from the wall at one corner of the building, and receiving no answer, he repeated the summons immediately. A window was thrown open, and a voice, in lazy tones, demanded who was there.

'A messenger for Don Ferdinando, on matter of life and death,' was the reply.

Then came a shuffling and scuffling down-stairs, a drawing back of bolts, and the grumbling of a man's voice, after which a small door in the wall was thrown open, and an elderly man appeared who had evidently been awakened from a pleasant sleep, and didn't above half like it.

'Now, then,' he began, 'what's your business, young man?'

'Sir,' replied Johnson, 'you will bitterly repent one moment's delay. Haste directly to your master; tell him that the Lady Rosalie is in danger, and requires instant aid, and pray him to see me directly.'

The servant was about to reply, when a voice from above exclaimed in accents of command, 'What is that? Do I hear the Lady Rosalie's name? Who is it that speaks? Bring him hither at once.'

Without delay the old servant now admitted Johnson, who, ascending the stairs, saw before him the figure of a young and handsome man, evidently just aroused from sleep, with a dressing-gown thrown loosely around him, and with a look of dignity about him of which his half-dressed state could not deprive him.

He beckoned Johnson to him, strode into a room into which the latter followed, and impatiently demanded the reason of his visit. In as few words as possible Johnson told him all that had occurred, and produced the opal ring which was to be the proof of his good faith. What more he told Ferdinando I cannot here relate, but the upshot was that the young count was to come as soon as possible to the rescue of his betrothed, and that passing through the shepherds' country he was to summon them to his aid by the display of the opal ring, and the magic words, 'The doom is near. Follow the token;' and to be guided by them to a spot whence they might, so Johnson said, best direct their operations against the enemy. Ferdinando pressed Johnson to remain himself, and guide the attacking force. This, however, the young man steadily refused. 'Already,' he said, 'it is near two o'clock; the robber-band will be about early, and if I am missed, and do not appear to give an account of myself, sus-

picion of treachery may be aroused, and it will go hard
with the prisoners.' So saying, Johnson took one
crust of bread and a draught of wine, and remounting
his pony galloped as hard as he could back to the forest,
leaving the little animal at the outskirts, whence doubtless it soon found its way back to its master's hut.

It must be confessed that it was not altogether
without some apprehension that the young man re-entered
the forest, and found himself again at the foot of the
sycamore tree which he had previously descended. If
Pedro had discovered his absence and had aroused the
band, the consequences might be serious; and if he
was seen re-entering the place, awkward inquiries would
certainly be made as to his manner of passing the night.
There was nothing for it, however, but to face matters
out, and to remember that fortune favours the bold.
So he climbed again up the sycamore tree, and with no
great difficulty entered the castle by the same window
through which he had left it; then descending the
stone steps, after taking a couple of hours' rest at the
foot, he moved slowly along the passage and sought the
large room where were several of the robbers, mostly
still asleep.

It was not till some time later that Pedro entered,
accompanied by Captain Blackcap, and, looking suspiciously at Johnson, asked him where he had passed
the night. Johnson answered that he had wandered
down to the ruined part of the castle after supper, fallen
asleep there, and not awoke till it was nearly daylight,
when he had come to the room where he then was.
Pedro was dissatisfied with this answer, but, not having
searched that part of the castle, could say nothing.
His only regret was that he had not at once roused

Captain Blackcap when he had found and cut the rope, so that the whole band might have been summoned, and the missing traitor—if traitor there was—discovered. However, he had neglected to do this for reasons best known to himself, and it was too late now. The whole band were present at breakfast, and the day passed off without any particular occurrence. The robbers amused themselves in speculating as to whether or no the footman would be back at the appointed time, and if not, whether the captain would really follow out Pedro's plan about the captives, or give any longer time in the hopes of getting the ransom. The captives passed by no means a pleasant day, although Rosalie had great hopes in her messenger. The baron remained as furious as ever, and would have eaten nothing at all if he had not discovered that this course would be far more disagreeable to himself than to the robbers; therefore, exercising a wise philosophy, he ate when he was hungry, and only declined to do so when he did not happen to be in that condition.

During the whole of this day Johnson was very careful to do nothing which might excite suspicion in the minds of the rest of the band, and at night he slept in the large room, taking heed, however, to watch Pedro, whom he thought quite likely to do him some mischief if opportunity offered. The second day passed in much the same manner, and there was no appearance of footman or ransom when the day was well-nigh over. Then the robbers began to murmur, and to think they had been foolish to let the man go. They had the captives, however, and began to talk freely of how they would serve them. The lady's maid was so terribly afraid of being roasted, that she afforded the greatest amusement to the more merrily-disposed of the band, who told her that her only chance of escape would be by marrying Griper, and frightened her dreadfully with stories of his cruelty. However, Pedro's plan did not come to be put in force, if indeed it had been seriously intended, for towards sunset the scouts reported that three men bearing sacks, which probably contained the ransom, were slowly approaching the castle. This was in truth the worthy footman and his two followers. The baron's brother had halted a mile off from the wood, lest his presence should be discovered, and the ransom was brought safely in. Captain Blackcap ordered the money and the bearers to be safely lodged in a room in the castle, and declared that on the morning of the next day the former should be counted, and, if correct, the latter sent safely home with the baron and his party.

This night, in honour of the arrival of the ransom, there was a great supper, and much noise and merriment in the robbers' castle. After supper, when the band had drunk their fill of good liquor, the subject of the captives was again discussed, and Pedro openly declared his opinion that they ought not to be allowed to return next day unless pardon to the band could be secured from the authorities, and they could be assured that no attack should be made upon the castle to revenge the capture of so great a man as the baron. Several other robbers agreed with this, and it was proposed to bring down the old nobleman and acquaint him with their determination. Accordingly, he was taken from his room in spite of all his objections, and, some time after midnight, was ushered into the presence of his gaolers, who were most of them much elated by the revelry of the evening. Then they told him that even if the ransom were found to be all right, he must not depart without a solemn pledge that neither he nor his friends would try to avenge his capture; and that he would do all in his power to prevent any other person from attempting the same. The old baron declared that he would give no such pledge whatever; the ransom they had asked they had received, and they were now bound to let him go according to the arrangement. Then they threatened the old man with torture, and declared again that they would boil Rosalie before his face; but he remained as obstinate as a mule, and all the more so, as he saw that there was some difference of opinion among the men, some of them holding the old-fashioned notion that they ought to keep their word, and let him go now that they had got the ransom which they had demanded. The dispute rose high, and Captain Blackcap was endeavouring to the best of his ability to put an end to it, and restore order, when suddenly the door was thrown open and Mother Jack appeared, shouting at the top of her voice, 'Fly, boys, fly—you are betrayed—there's enemies upon you !'

This news stopped the dispute instantly, and at the same moment a loud shout from outside the castle showed the robbers that their retreat was discovered, and sobered them in an instant.

Captain Blackcap sprang at once to the nearest window, at which he had scarcely shown himself when a bullet whistled over his head, and a loud voice from below was heard to exclaim, 'This way, lads, this way—follow the token.' And it was evident that the enemy was at hand. Without a moment's hesitation, Blackcap passed through the door at the end of the banqueting-room, and directing his men to follow, led the way to a room beyond, in which, for safety's sake, he usually ordered all fire-arms to be deposited upon nights when a long and merry supper was likely to heat the blood of his band, and render pistols dangerous weapons to carry. Here he seized upon arms for himself, and told his men to provide for themselves as best they could. They had followed him in haste from the banqueting-room, but Griper dealt the unhappy baron a blow as he passed which stretched the old nobleman on the floor, whilst the robber savagely remarked that the old fool's babbling would now be stopped for ever, and that he had been longing to stop it for a good while.

Having armed themselves as well and as quickly as they could, the robbers had now two courses before them—to fly for their lives, or to try and defend the castle. Being taken by surprise, and not knowing the number of the attacking party, an organized system of defence was almost impossible; but Blackcap, who had long foreseen the chance of some such attack, was not altogether unprepared. Gathering his men for a rush, he crossed the inner court-yard of the castle even as the enemy entered it, and boldly retreated to the more ruined side of the building. Here were three chances in his favour. First, every hole and corner being known to the robbers, and not to their pursuers, the difficulty of the latter in an assault would be increased; secondly, the tangled thicket which there touched the walls would afford a good chance of escape if the band were finally driven from their stronghold by superior force; thirdly, the captives were there confined, and terms might be made, if the worst came to the worst, by

threats of putting Rosalie to death. There was, however, little time to think. Including Johnson, there
were but twenty robbers, who were followed by more
than double their number as they crossed the court-yard.
Pedro sullenly brought up the rear, and as he entered
the gap in the opposite wall through which Blackcap
had led his men, he turned and fired a pistol at the
nearest pursuer, which brought him to the earth. But
with loud shouts of vengeance his companions followed,
and all disappeared within the interior of the castle.
But only nineteen of the robbers had entered the gap.
As soon as they rushed into the court-yard Johnson
threw himself flat upon the ground, and, watching
eagerly for a moment, rushed after the pursuers until
he overtook one of them who was silently advancing
across the court.

'This way, my lord,' he said, 'this way to Lady
Rosalie's room—'tis her best chance.' And without
pausing for a reply, he darted across to another point,
where the wall had crumbled away, and through its
ruins was an opening on to the stone staircase down
which Johnson had passed on the previous night.

He had rightly calculated that Blackcap would
ascend by the other and main staircase, at the top of
which was a ruined gallery, which, full of deep recesses
and broken marble pillars, and having a floor which time
had rendered insecure except in particular places, would
form a refuge to the band if they could succeed in
reaching it, and enable them to fire down upon their em-
barrassed pursuers; whilst it could at the same time be
quitted, should the robbers be hard-pressed, by means
of the passage which led out of it round to the rooms
of the captives, from which latter passage the stone

9

staircase was the back means of descent. With the greatest haste Johnson ascended this staircase, closely followed by the stranger, whom my readers will have had no difficulty in recognizing as Ferdinando. They reached Rosalie's door—it was fastened. 'Open, lady; open to the opal ring,' said Johnson; and in another moment the bolt was drawn back with a trembling hand, and the lovers were in each other's arms.

'My lord, my lord!' cried Johnson, 'this is no time for dallying! Vengeance to-day, love to-morrow; let us get the lady out of the castle, and then to our work.'

Ferdinando tore himself away from the lady of his love, and only just in time, for, before they could quit the room, footsteps were heard in the passage; and hardly had Ferdinando and Rosalie passed the door and hurried towards the staircase, when Johnson, who was following them, was stopped by the whistle of a bullet within an inch of his head, and a voice, which yelled in his ear in terrible accents, 'Treacherous villain, die in your treason!'

Pedro was upon him. Whether he had intended to murder Rosalie I do not know, but having reached the old gallery, he had not paused to defend it with the others, but had hurried at once towards the lady's room.

Johnson faced him boldly. 'Villain in thy teeth!' he shouted, 'and cowardly murderer to boot;' and they grappled together in a moment. The wiry, sinewy frame of Pedro writhed and twisted, and so great was his strength that Johnson would have doubted the result had he not felt that within him which gave him the strength of ten men,—the earnest thirst for venge-

ance which had caused him to be where he was, and
the sense of right and justice struggling against law-
lessness and crime.

In vain Pedro strove to stab the young man with
his knife, or to hurl him to the ground, whilst he
uttered the most furious language against him as well
as his breath would permit. They met but a step from
the chamber which Rosalie had left, and into this they
struggled and fought, with none to separate them. At
last Pedro's strength began to give way, and slowly he
sank upon the floor, still in the grasp of his enraged
opponent. 'Wretch!' said the latter, as the robber
relaxed his efforts, and he felt that his life was at his
mercy. 'Wretch! your hour is come!'

'Let it come, then,' growled Pedro through his
clenched teeth; 'and may you receive a traitor's reward for the same!'

'Traitor, indeed!' replied Johnson. 'Come it will,
and die you shall, but not before you know that it is
your own vile cruelty which has destroyed you. Know,
detestable wretch, that I am George Marly, brother of
him whom you so basely and savagely murdered!'

A savage smile lighted up the face of the conquered
robber. 'Is it so?' he grimly said. 'Ay, I killed
him,—a timid coward that wouldn't join the band;
then I have my revenge before I die. I rejoice at the
deed, traitor; do you hear? I would have tortured
him if they would have let me. Ha! ha!' and he
uttered a wild and horrible laugh as Johnson, or
Marly, as we must now call him, drove the dagger
into his heart.

Meanwhile Blackcap and his men had made a gallant defence in the gallery. They had shot several of

their assailants, and would probably have made good their retreat, but for an unforeseen circumstance, namely, the arrival of the baron's brother and his thirty men, who, having approached the forest at night, in order to be ready for an assault upon the castle at an early hour the next morning, if the safety of the captives was secured, were alarmed by the sound of the firing, and, directed thereby, hurried to the castle at a critical moment.

Escape was now the best that the robbers could hope for. Their pursuers being well assured of their own superiority in numbers, spread everywhere over the castle in search of the enemy, and resistance was no longer possible. The shepherds, who partly composed the party of Ferdinando, were almost as fierce as the robbers themselves, and followed them closely from corner to corner. At last only Captain Blackcap, Nosey, Gentleman Joe, and Griper were left alive. Begrimed with smoke, blood, and dirt, these four made their way to the lower part of the ruins, where they were followed by their relentless pursuers with an evident determination to make an end of them once and for all. Having seen Rosalie in a place of safety, Ferdinando was himself foremost in the pursuit, and at last brought Blackcap to bay. With his back against the wall, the robber captain defended himself right valiantly for some minutes, until a skilful thrust of Ferdinando, who was one of the best swordsmen of his day, deprived him of his weapon. In an instant he had drawn his dagger, and, in spite of the efforts of his antagonist to prevent it, plunged it into his own throat, and fell lifeless to the ground. This really ended the affair. Nosey and Gentleman Joe, both wounded and both exhausted, were captured by the victorious enemy, who now assembled in the court-yard, having satisfactorily accomplished the object of their expedition. Sixteen bodies of the robbers were collected and brought down into the yard, where they were laid in a row, and nine of the attacking party had also fallen. Diligent search was then made all over the castle, and the servants and ransom were discovered, the first released and the second restored to its owners. Then some one began to ask after the baron, and Marly told what he had witnessed in the banqueting-room. There they accordingly repaired, in the melancholy expectation of having to pay the last sad tribute of affection to the venerable nobleman. Far from this, however; they found the old boy alive and kicking. Indeed, he was kicking violently, if the truth must be told. The blow which Griper had dealt him had been severe indeed, but had not inflicted the slightest wound. But striking him exactly in the middle of the belt, just above the waist, the edge of the dagger had been turned indeed by the said belt, but had had the remarkably unpleasant effect of taking away the old gentleman's breath, and doubling him up in agony, which caused him to roll on the floor. His arms being strapped to his sides, he had been unable to rise, and had sat with his stout body propped up against the wall, listening with painful anxiety to the battle, and longing to know what it all meant. They got him up and brought him into the court-yard, where he viewed with extreme satisfaction the bodies of his slain enemies, and embraced his daughter with great delight. He was, however, in such a furious passion at what had occurred, and the indignities to which he had been subjected, that nothing would serve him but the imme-

diate execution of Nosey and Gentleman Joe, who
were accordingly hung from the dead branch of a neighbouring oak, in spite of all their prayers for mercy and
promises never to do it again. Eighteen of the band
were thus destroyed ; and although Griper could not be
found, he was known to have been wounded, and it
was supposed he had crawled into some corner to die
quietly. Only one personage remained, and that was
old Mother Jack. Brought before the baron, she began
to scold at such a furious rate, that it was hopeless to
stop her. ' *She* didn't know anything about robbers
and robbings, not she. Who were they who had come
and broken up her quiet home in the forest and killed
all her masters. Call himself a baron, did he ? a proud,
red-faced, fat old porpoise of a turkey-cock—a pretty ·
sort of baron indeed—' and so she went on until half
the party roared with laughter, and half were frightened
at her audacity. But Marly put in a good word for
her, and begged that her life might be spared, and so it
was. What became of her afterwards I never heard
for certain, though at one time there were strong reports current that she had been seen in the temporary
situation of nurse in a London workhouse. But of this
I have never felt assured. Then Ferdinando presented
George Marly to the baron as the man to whom they
owed their lives and safety. The young man came
modestly forward and told his story, at the baron's
request.

He and his brother Henry had been brought up at
a farmhouse, not far from the forest upon Ferdinando's
side. They were the children of a gentleman who lived
in the town, which in fact mostly belonged to the count;
but, for the sake of their health, had been sent into the

country, where constant exercise in rural pursuits had
rendered both of the young men as healthy and robust
as could be desired by their friends. Meanwhile they
had become great friends with the rough, wild shepherds of the district, whom they constantly visited, and
towards whom they had performed many little acts of
kindness, which entirely won the heart of these simple
people, who regarded the two brothers with the deepest
affection. During their long residence in that neighbourhood they had constantly explored that side of the
forest, with which they were perfectly familiar, although,
as their visits had been made either as boys searching
for birds' nests, or with the shepherds after stray goats
or sheep, they had never come in contact or made ac-
quaintance with the robber-band.

They had returned to their father's house for a
couple of years or so, when Henry Marly had been
seized with a desire, not only to revisit his old haunts,
but to explore the other side of the forest. His brother,
for some reason or another, had not accompanied him ;
and, wandering through the forest alone and unarmed,
he had been captured by the robber-band, and had met
with the fate which has been described.

The brothers had been tenderly attached; and from
the hour that Henry's death was known to him George
had vowed vengeance upon the murderers. His first idea
was to rouse the shepherds, and lead them to the attack,
as he knew they would follow him to a man. But,
being uncertain of the number of the robbers and the
strength of their position, he thought that success would
be more probably attained by the stratagem which he
adopted. First, however, he took the precaution of
visiting his shepherd friends, of raising their indignation

against the slayers of his brother, and of arranging with
them for the rendering him speedy assistance, in case of
any such occasion arising as did actually happen.   He
impressed these simple-minded men with the idea that
he carried with him the doom of the robber-band, and
he bound them to silence and secrecy until the hour of
doom arrived, and then to prompt action in support of
his undertaking.   All had answered well.   His courage
and caution had been crowned with success; his brother's memory had been avenged, and the robber-band
rooted out.

So he told his story to the baron, and received in a
proper manner the thanks which he and his daughter
hastened to bestow.   Thanks, however, were not sufficient to express their gratitude, or to reward his merits.
Nothing would satisfy the baron but that the young
man should accompany the party home, and remain
with them until the wedding of Rosalie with Ferdinando
should be duly celebrated. Anxious as he was to return
to his own family, Marly knew not how to resist their
entreaties, and accordingly he accompanied the party in
their homeward journey.   Before they left, however,
the bodies of the slain were decently interred, and everything of any value in the place was divided among the
shepherds and the retainers of the baron and count.

There was some talk of blowing up the castle
altogether, lest it should again become the hiding-place
of another robber-band; but Rosalie declared that it
would be a thousand pities to destroy such a fine old
ruin, and that, as everything had ended so happily, it
might as well remain, as a remembrance of the events
they had gone through. The baron said that he felt by
no means so sure that everything had ended so happily,

for he greatly doubted whether his appetite or digestion would ever be quite the same as it was before that blow which had been given him in the banqueting-room. However, I have reason to believe that no real difference in this particular was ever discovered by lookers-on; and, at all events, he was not proof against the entreaties of his daughter, and the castle was spared.

Homeward journeyed the cavalcade, and, on arriving at the gate of their town, were met by the mayor in his robes of office, the councillors walking two and two behind him, and the body of town-police, properly armed with staves, drawn up in formidable array opposite the great pump in the principal square. Then the mayor came forward, and solemnly congratulated the baron upon his safe return and happy escape from danger. The baron told him that he was a pompous old fool, and would have sallied forth to aid him at once if he had been worth twopence, with which reply the mayor was just as well pleased as if it had been highly complimentary; and the town newspaper declared next day that the worthy baron had received the congratulations of the chief magistrate of the town, with his usual kindness and condescension. Then they went on to the palace, where all was merriment and rejoicing for several days, until the time came when the wedding was to be celebrated. Oh, what a wedding it was! First of all, I must tell you that Rosalie was one of the nicest, dearest girls that ever was born. I can't describe her beauty, because beauty is very much according to the eyes that look at it, but Ferdinando thought her lovely, so I suppose she was. Then she had twelve bridesmaids, which always seemed to me to be a great many more than are necessary, but I suppose it was all

right. They wore—oh, what *did* they wear? I know
Rosalie had a tremendous great lace veil, that cost ever
so much money, and everybody said it was the hand-
somest veil they had ever seen. But I am not quite
sure about the bridesmaids' dresses. I know that Ferdinando gave each of them a locket, though—a diamond
locket, with a ruby fly upon it—lovely lockets they
were, such as London and Ryder never had in their
shop, and Hunt and Roskill never even thought of, but
Ferdinando found them out somewhere or other. The
bridesmaids were all pretty, too, and they all agreed
that George Marly, who was ' best man,' was the best-
looking young gentleman they had seen for a long time.
However that might be, everything went off very nicely,
except that Puzzle-brains, the steward, in throwing an
old shoe after the carriage in which the bride and bride-
groom went off, unfortunately hit the baron's brother
in the eye, and the lady's-maid was so much affected by
all that she had gone through, that she fainted in the
arms of the honest footman as soon as it was all over.

Ferdinando and Rosalie were to spend the honey-
moon at a neighbouring watering-place, and then return
for a few days to the baron's Palace, after which the
count would take his wife home, and had earnestly re-
quested Marly to accept the vacant position of land-
steward and manager of his extensive property. Not
without some pressure, the young man consented; for,
as his father's property was very small, and a profession
was necessary to him, this offer was tempting, although
he had previously resolved to seek his fortune in some
country in which he would not be so constantly re-
minded of the fate of his beloved brother. However,
having made up his mind to accept the offer, he returned

to his father's house; and after making all the necessary arrangements, he met the count and countess on their return home, and was formally installed in his new office. His duties took him constantly from the castle, but this was to be his home, at least for the present; and as he lived on terms of equality with Ferdinando and Rosalie, his position was really one of great comfort, and the best and most friendly feeling existed between him and his employers.

It was on his return from one of his visits to a distant part of the country, that, as he was riding quietly through the avenue which led to the court-yard of the count's castle, he saw two persons—a man and woman —hastily separate, as if startled by his approach. The woman entered the building, whilst the man advanced down the avenue, but kept close to the trees, so that their shadow prevented his being clearly seen, the more especially as the evening was closing in. Marly wished him 'Good-night' as he passed, to which the other grunted out something in a gruff voice, the tones of which did not seem quite strange to the young steward; but he could not remember where he had heard them, nor could he in that light distinguish the man's face. He thought little of the circumstance, but on entering the court-yard, asked who was the woman who had just entered the house, and was told that it was the lady's-maid, who had been out for a walk. A day or two passed by, and again George Marly saw the two together, and was satisfied, by the way in which the man retreated into the shrubbery, that he wished to avoid him. Suspecting that all was not right, he spoke to the woman, who with tears and blushes assured him that it was only the young man to whom she was en-

gaged to be married, and hoped there was nothing
wrong in her meeting and speaking to him.   Marly
could of course say nothing against so reasonable a
proceeding, and thought no more of the matter.

· Not many days afterwards Marly had again occasion
to leave the castle for some days.   Upon his return he
was welcomed, as usual, by Ferdinando and Rosalie, and
upon the same evening they all three dined together in
the large dining-room opening upon a balcony from
which could be obtained a lovely view over the country,
stretching out from and beyond the foot of the hill
upon which the castle was built.   As they passed into
the room, Marly casually glanced at the row of servants
drawn up on one side of the door, and at once recognized a new face.   Somehow or other, it was a face
which he felt he did not then see for the first time, but
how, when, and where he had seen it before he could
not for the life of him recollect.   It was a face with an
expression to which at once he took a dislike, and during dinner he thought of it several times, but without
being able to recall it to his memory.   After dinner the
three strolled out upon the balcony, and gazed down
upon the flower-garden at their feet, the low stone wall
by which it was bounded, and the distant view beyond.
Suddenly, from behind the wall there arose the figure
of a man, who, without a moment's hesitation, raised a
gun to his shoulder and fired upon the three gazers.
The bullet grazed Marly's shoulder, and shattered to
pieces one of the large panes in the window behind
him.   To rush down-stairs was the work of an instant.
The servants were summoned, and a strict search for
the would-be assassin was immediately set on foot;
but, unfortunately, without success.   The servants

themselves were closely questioned, as it was next to impossible that any one could have ascended the hill to the castle upon that side without observation from some of the numerous household, and it was still less likely that he should have approached by the avenue and skirted the garden, without being seen by any one. However, no clue to the villain could be discovered, and the evening closed with a vague sense of insecurity, which was really worse than the certain presence of a known danger.

On the next day the count and Marly rode out during most of the day, and the evening was already approaching when they returned to the castle. No occurrence took place to alarm them; and being fatigued with their ride, they retired to rest at an early hour. Somehow or other, however, Marly found it impossible to sleep. I cannot say whether or no his mind was excited by the adventure of the preceding night, or whether there was present to it some foreboding of coming ill, but he lay awake for some time, unable to prevent himself from thinking over all the stirring events in which he had lately played so active a part. Suddenly he heard a low whisper in the gallery into which his room door opened, and very gently the handle was turned. In an instant Marly slipped out the other side of the bed, close to the wall, and hid himself behind the curtain. Some one entered—stealthily as a cat creeping after a mouse, and Marly held his breath as he heard the low breathing of his visitor drawing nearer and nearer to his bed. It was dark—profoundly dark, and whilst Marly could not therefore see his enemy, the latter could not discover that the bed was empty. Close to it did he creep, and the next moment a dagger was plunged into the place where Marly's body had lain not five minutes before, whilst a low, savage whisper was heard at the same moment hissing through the room these words—'Die, traitor.' Upon that instant it flashed through the brain of Marly that the face he had seen in the avenue and among the servants the day before, the voice he had heard from the lady's maid's friend, and that which he now heard, belonged to one and the same man, and that Griper was upon him. But there was no time for thought; action, immediate action, was the only chance for him under the circumstances in which he now found himself, unarmed as he was in the presence of a merciless ruffian. Without the loss of a second, he sprang upon the robber, who had buried his dagger in the mattress, and was for the instant overbalanced by the force of his own blow; and as he closed with him the young steward shouted loudly for help. A shrill scream from the gallery answered his appeal, but he had no leisure for listening; for Griper having recovered himself, though, fortunately, he had left his dagger in the bed, grappled furiously with his adversary. Both were strong men; and whilst Marly had the advantage of youth, his opponent's chances were brought pretty nearly equal by the fact of his being dressed and armed, and fighting, as he knew he did, with a halter round his neck. They rolled over together on the floor, and Griper made the most desperate efforts to release himself from Marly's hold, and to draw a weapon. Fortunately, however, the young steward was able to prevent this, and in a few moments more Ferdinando, half-dressed, and with his sword in his hand, rushed into the room, followed by several servants. The assassin was securely bound, and great

was the delight of the count to find that the valuable
life of his faithful steward had been saved from such
great danger.   The lady's maid was found fainting in
the passage, and when she recovered vowed that she
knew nothing of her sweetheart's intention, and begged and prayed that she might not be punished for it.
As Ferdinando partially believed her, she only received
a month's wages and was sent off next morning without a character, which was a great deal better fate than
she deserved.   Griper was placed in a strong room, and
left there bound until the next morning, when Ferdinando would determine upon his fate.   He was, however, spared the trouble, for the wretched man succeeded in getting one of his hands loose, and, finding escape
impossible, frustrated the unpleasant death which probably awaited him, by plunging a knife into his own
breast, and there he perished, and with him the last of
the forest-robbers.   I cannot tell you any more at present about the other personages of my story, save that
they all lived happy and died respected.   Rosalie made
Ferdinando a wife as good as she was beautiful.   Ferdi-
dinando was as tender as a husband as he was brave as a
man ; and as to George Marly, I do not at this moment
recollect whether he ever married or not, but I know that
he was generally considered to be a careful steward and
an excellent man, and that everybody in that part of
the world felt very much obliged to him for the determined part which he had taken in breaking up and
destroying the notorious robber-band.

IV.

THE BATTLE OF THE STOATS AND RATS.

For many years past the relations existing between the two great families of stoats and rats had been the reverse of friendly. Tradition told of many members of the latter race brutally assassinated by the former, whilst the stoat literature was full of accounts of injuries suffered by their people at the hands of plundering rats. The fortress of the latter race, famed in the history of the glorious past, sung by ancient bards, and chronicled by grey-bearded writers of the olden time, was situate in the back premises of a certain noble mansion, inhabited by mere men and women, and was familiarly termed 'the rat-place.' The stoats held their principal habitation in Bockhanger wood, scarcely more than a mile distant from the stronghold of their enemies. There might be found old pollard trees in abundance, containing many a sly hole and corner in which an honest stoat might make his comfortable home. There, too, were far-stretching rabbit earths—grand hunting-ground for the sportsman stoat,—whilst the fern which grew so thickly wherever there was open space enough for it to thrive, sheltered the innocent victims upon whom these crafty little animals delight to prey. Many a hare, crouching in her woodland form, and dreaming lazily of the young and tender shoots of the green grass, and the sweet-tasting clover in the field by the side of the wood, had been rudely awakened by the cruel fangs of the eager stoat fastened in her luckless throat, and starting madly from her quiet resting-place, in her headlong flight had carried with her the relentless foe, who, having once seized upon his prey, never relinquished his hold until the poor victim sank fainting on the ground, her strength exhausted, and her life forfeited to his wily craft. Many a rabbit, too, nestling in the fern, or curled up in the tufts of grass, had been startled from his fancied security by the approach of his dreaded enemy; and, rushing off hastily at first, had become palsied and paralyzed with fear, as the stoat gradually, but surely, followed him, and had yielded up his life with a parting squeak of despair. Oh, it was a fine place for stoats when the boys were at school, and their terriers shut up, and right proud were the little animals of their grand old wood and its beauties.

So far as any one can tell, there was no earthly reason why these two great families of stoats and rats should ever have fallen out, for there was no necessity at all for their interests clashing. They did not live so near to each other as to make their constant meeting a matter of certainty; and, indeed, as stoats do not generally approach nearer than they can help to the dwellings of mankind, there did not exist any apparent cause why they should see much of the tribe of rats, who always made their abode as near as they conveniently could to a kitchen, and found it both comfortable and advantageous to profit by the broken victuals, crusts, and offal which, to a far greater extent than was proper, the scullery-maids continually threw out into the back yard and the rat-place. Indeed, the two races did really meet so seldom, that possibly their smothered dislike would never have broken out into open hostility, had it not been for an unfortunate event which took place close to the rats' territory, and which rendered impossible any further peace between the two.

It happened that a stoat of advanced age and great respectability, having wandered out upon a hunting expedition somewhat further than was his wont, and having reached, indeed, the other side of the park in his rambles, became exceedingly weary towards evening; and, fearful of being benighted, took a short cut through the plantation, near the great house, which obliged him to pass quite close to the rat-place. The name of this stoat, which was Chumper, might or might not have been known to the rats as that of a person supposed to be hostile to their nation. At all events, he was not upon the war-path, and had no intention of interfering, in the slightest degree, with anybody. Having, however, been seen by a sentinel rat, he was, upon his approaching the rat-place, set upon by a dozen or more of the largest and strongest rats, and, in spite of all his cries and remonstrances, bitten and torn so cruelly, that he could only just drag himself to the edge of the beloved wood before he yielded up his life, with his last breath commending his cause to the stoats around him, and imploring that his blood might be avenged upon the cowardly villains who had so basely murdered him. There were only three stoats present to receive his last words, who had met him dragging himself with difficulty towards the wood of his forefathers; but these three soon imparted the news to the whole community of stoats. The names of the witnesses of Chumper's end were Bird-slayer, Nest-finder, and Teaser, and each gave a somewhat different account of the victim's last utterances. All three, however, agreed that he had accused the rats of being his murderers, and the news ran like wild-fire through the wood.

Indignation filled the breast of every stoat, and the scene was visited by nearly every one of them in the wood. The body of the murdered Chumper was placed upon dry leaves, and stoat after stoat dipped in his blood the sharpened bit of stick or stem of a fern plant, which he had fashioned into a sword, and swore bravely to wash out the stain in the heart's blood of a caitiff rat.

They carried the old warrior to his grave, which they made in a hole inhabited by a hedgehog, who mightily objected to the plan; but being only laughed at, left the place in a passion, and used language which no educated hedgehog would have thought of for a moment.

Having thus paid the last tribute of affection and respect to their lost friend, the stoats—one and all—felt that it was absolutely necessary that steps should be taken to avenge him. Accordingly, they determined to summon a council, and to adopt such measures as, after full consultation, should be deemed most expedient. It was not to be tolerated that such an insult to the stoat nation should be passed over, and there could be little doubt that the council would be quite unanimous in this opinion. And so, indeed, it proved. Vengeance was in every mouth, rage in every eye; and it was determined that an attack upon the rat-place should be made without delay.

The old king, Brock, who well knew the craft and cruelty which characterized the rat nation, wished to send scouts out to ascertain the state of defence of the enemy's fortress before taking further proceedings ; but the eagerness of his people admitted of no delay, and he was obliged to consent that an attack should be made upon the very next night.

During the whole of that day the wood resounded with preparations. From tree to tree and from hole to hole the warlike little animals hurried, rousing the slothful, encouraging the timid, and comparing the different weapons with which each had armed himself for the coming battle. Not less than one hundred and fifty stoats responded to the call of King Brock, even upon that short notice; and although they might be somewhat deficient in the drill of regular soldiers, still there was no lack of courage amongst them, and the rats might well dread the coming of so fierce and resolute an army.

Towards the evening of the day for which the assault had been fixed, King Brock reviewed his warriors, and informed the chief stoats of the plan of attack which he had arranged. One band of fifty stoats, under the command of the famous chief, Kill-game, was to advance by the side of the hill upon which the great house stood, and enter the rat-place by a drain which passed under the wall not far from the door leading into the kitchen yard. A second detachment of fifty, entering the plantation upon the park side, were to creep stealthily up to the edge of the rat-place, await a signal which would be given by the first party as soon as half their number had passed the drain, and then rush

boldly upon the enemy.   Meanwhile, King Brock himself, with a reserve of fifty picked stoats, would pass
through the shrubbery, which was on the other side of
the rat-place, from which it was separated by a low
wall; and when the battle was at its height would scale
the wall, and, if possible, attack the rats in the rear, and
carry confusion into their ranks.

This plan having been carefully explained to the
captains and other officers who were to lead the different divisions, the army set out, moving stealthily and
quietly in the direction of the enemy's territory.   But
the rats were not easily to be caught asleep.   They
knew full well that the cruel murder which they had
perpetrated upon the luckless Chumper would awake
the indignation of the stoats, and they determined not
to lose a moment in preparing for the conflict which
was probably near at hand.   The very morning after
the murder, having procured the body of a stoat from
the branches of an oak tree whereon it had been hung
by the keeper, they deliberately skinned it, and having
carefully disguised in it a large and particularly cunning
rat, named Wily, sent him off as a spy into the enemy's
camp.   In the bustle and confusion of their warlike
preparation, the stoats never discovered the presence of
the spy, who was able to note all that went on, and to
ascertain the plan of attack which was settled.   This
done, he slipped quietly off to his home, and told his
friends what they had to expect.   Now Spandor, the
rat-king, was a crafty and experienced rat.   Although
his subjects were very numerous, and he could summon
to the field nearly three hundred rats, he knew full well
that it was to cunning, and not to force, that he must
trust in order to gain a victory over so powerful an

enemy as the stoats. Upon hearing, therefore, that they were certainly about to attack his people, he at once set about making preparations for resistance. His first act was to have the drain under the wall carefully stopped with bits of brick and mud, so that not more than one stoat could possibly pass at a time, and that only with difficulty. He next caused a trench to be dug across from one side of the rat-place to the other on the plantation side, too wide for any animal to jump, so that any stoat advancing from the plantation must descend one side of the trench and creep up the other before he found his way into the rats' territory. He then caused the skin of the dead stoat which had served Wily so well to be stuffed by the cleverest stuffer among the rats, and hung from a laurel branch over the low wall between the rat-place and the shrubbery in such a manner as to be easily seen by any one approaching from the shrubbery side. Having completed his arrangements, and briefly addressed his principal rats upon the importance of attending to his directions, Spandor now awaited the coming of the enemy with tolerable calmness.

He had not long to wait. The moon rose cold and clear that night, and by her light there might have been seen a long line of stoats creeping stealthily over the grass hill, past the great house, straight to the wall under which they were to creep into the enemy's camp. There was but little hesitation in their ranks, and all were eagerly rushing forward to the drain, when the wary Kill-game restrained them, reminding the ardent warriors that silence and caution were necessary, and that they had better enter one at a time, and he himself, going as the twenty-fifth stoat, would give the signal which was to summon the plantation band as soon as he was through.

After some doubt as to who should be the first into the drain, the post of honour was given to one Hare's-foe, a cousin of the murdered Chumper, who claimed it by right of his relationship to him whose death had caused the expedition. Boldly he entered the drain, followed by several gallant stoats, eager for the fray. It was but a short distance they had to pass; but when Hare's-foe reached the other end, he found the mouth of the drain almost entirely choked with mud and bits of brick plastered together, so that he had to push somewhat hard with his head before he could get it through one corner, so as to creep into the rat-place.

But now occurred a strange event. Scarcely had Hare's-foe's head been pushed through the opening than the next stoat in the line became conscious of a violent movement in the body before him,—the hind legs seemed at first to fix themselves firmly in the ground, then they jumped suddenly forward, the whole body appeared to quiver violently, and then to dart through the hole in a manner almost too quick to be natural. The fact was, that the crafty Spandor had arranged a noose with a running knot, placed very carefully over the only hole through which a stoat could push his head. The string was held by several of the strongest rats; and the very instant that Hare's-foe's head was in the noose, they pulled all together, and with such hearty good will, that they dragged the body of the unhappy stoat through the hole, and strangled him before he knew where he was. The stoat who followed him was rather surprised at the sudden manner in which Hare's-foe disappeared, but being pressed on by those behind, and having but little

time for consideration, he pushed boldly forward.
Scarcely, however, had he managed with difficulty to
insinuate his head through the hole at the end of the
drain, when a blow from a sharp stone stunned him,
and he was speedily slain by the rats who stood by.
The next stoat was received in a similar manner, but
was fortunate enough to be able to withdraw his head
only partially stunned, and great confusion now ensued
among the stoats in the drain.   Those who were behind
kept pushing on, whilst those who were in front wanted
to get back, and the noise and dismay were equally great.

Meanwhile the detachment of stoats who had advanced by the side of the plantation, marched in good
order until they came within a few yards of the rat-
place, and then anxiously awaited the signal which was
to be given by those who were to have entered by the
drain.   They waited and waited until their impatience
was beyond all bounds; and hearing at last the noise
which proceeded from the drain, they could bear it no
longer, but charged boldly forward.   Presently they
came upon the trench which Spandor had caused to be
dug, and here they were forced to slacken their pace, in
order to pass the unexpected obstacle.   But scarcely
had they begun to descend one side of the trench,
which they did in a somewhat tumultuous and dis-
orderly manner, than they became aware of the serious
nature of their position.

The king of the rats had here posted the flower of
his army, under the command of his son Spandee and
Pick-bones, a renowned old warrior among his people.
With one hundred and fifty picked rats, these leaders
held the sides of the trench; and as soon as several of
the stoats had descended one side and prepared to creep

up the other, their enemies showed themselves, and rained down upon them a perfect shower of stones and sticks, which had been previously piled up close to the trench.   This division of stoats, however, led by an ancient chieftain named Pilus, and having amongst their number the celebrated Bird-slayer, with the other two witnesses of Chumper's end, bore themselves bravely in the fight, and charged boldly through the trench against the gallant defenders of the rat-place.

If at this crisis Brock could have led his reserve force through the shrubbery, according to his original plan, their timely arrival would in all probability have settled the fate of the battle.   But although the surprise was well and craftily planned, Spandor had been able to counteract its effects owing to the information which he had so cunningly obtained.   In case the stoat detachment should succeed in scaling the wall, he had placed a vast quantity of broken bottles and sharp bits of glass beneath it, on the rat-place side, and had posted seventy rats to watch the result.   But he had great hopes that the wall would *not* be scaled, and the event even exceeded his expectations.   The stoats stole stealthily through the shrubbery, not without some apprehension of the terriers and cats which lurked about the stables not very far from the scene of action.   Arrived at the dark corner of the shrubbery, which joined up to the rat-place, Brock sent forward a stoat named Egg-sucker, with ten companions, to advance through the shade of the laurels, which spread out to the wall, and to form the first scaling party.   Cautiously and quietly they advanced; and Egg-sucker, mounting on the stem of a strong ivy plant, crept slowly up it on to the wall, the others following behind him in line.

It so happened, however, that the leading stoat
had selected the very spot at which Spandor had
caused the body before-mentioned to be hung; and
scarcely had he gained the top of the wall, when he
perceived the body, as he supposed, of one of his comrades swinging close before his nose. He never stopped
to consider that there had hardly been time for any one
of the attacking party to be killed and hung up in that
position. The surprise, the dusky light, the melancholy
appearance of his dead fellow-countryman, the dreari-
ness of the place altogether,—had such an effect upon
him that, with a shrill cry of affright and dismay, he fell
backward off the wall, knocking over the stoat who was
clambering up next behind him, and throwing all the line
into inextricable confusion. To make matters worse,
whilst they tumbled over one another without knowing
what was the matter, and therefore being much more
frightened than they would otherwise have been, the short
sharp bark of a terrier dog at the stables sounded full in
their ears. Already unnerved and disconcerted, this
seemed to them a confirmation of their fears,—the sure
sign of an attack from a foe whom they could not hope
to resist. Without a thought of further advance upon
the rat-place, they fled in the greatest confusion. In
vain did Brock throw himself in the way of the retreating squadron,—his influence was gone; he might as well
have spoken to the winds. ‘Every one for himself’ was
the motto of each stoat, and they scattered through the
shrubbery in their homeward flight with only one thought
and one desire—namely, to reach Bockhanger wood as
fast as possible. The brave king shed bitter tears of
shame and mortification, as he thought of his valiant
soldiers in the other detachments, left unsupported to

face the whole power of the rats. He could, however, do nothing. To scale the wall alone would have been worse than useless, and probably a simple act of yielding himself a prisoner to the enemy. He could not join the other detachments in time to be of service, and there was nothing for it but to follow his retreating band.

Meanwhile the battle waxed sore in the rat-place. The stoats in the drain extricated themselves with difficulty, and the rats at once filled up and securely stopped the hole at their end of the drain, and hurried to join the defenders of the trench, whilst the stoats, confused and disarranged, hesitated what to do, and therefore at first did nothing; and then, whilst a few sought to join their friends in the plantation, the rest scattered away in the direction of Bockhanger. But at the trench the fight was furious. One or two stoats had been speedily slain at the first onset, but their leaders boldly urged them forward. Pilferer, a young rat nearly connected with the Royal family, dealt a furious blow at the veteran Pilus as he charged up the bank, but the stoat avoided it, and disdaining arms, seized the rat by the throat, dragged him back into the trench, and made an end of him in a moment. Nor less did the valiant Bird-slayer strike terror into the heart of the rats. He had extracted the longest and sharpest of Chumper's teeth, fastened it into the thighbone of the largest mouse he could procure, and vowed to dye it deep in the blood of Chumper's murderers. Fear-cat, a rat of some notoriety in his day, was the first to feel the effects of this novel weapon, for Bird-slayer struck him a blow on the head therewith which fairly cracked his skull. Then the brave stoat rushed boldly up the bank and flew at no less a personage than Spandee, the king's son, whom he slightly wounded at the first blow by striking off a toenail from his left foot. But Pick-bones, armed with a rusty nail fastened in the handle of an old tooth-brush, kept the stoat at bay till the number of rats who poured down upon him obliged him slowly to retreat, though not before 'Timid,' a rat of tender years, fell a victim to his weapon.

This, however, was one of the last rats who died upon that eventful day. For, re-inforced by the arrival of the numerous warriors who had been freed from the defence of the drain, the rat army now charged in overwhelming force upon the stoats, filling the air with shrill notes of mingled rage and triumph. The terrible Pick-bones, a rat of enormously long bristles and ferocious aspect, encouraged his followers with fiery words, and bore down all before him. In vain did the outnumbered stoats attempt to rally. The unhappy Nest-finder was caught by Pick-bones in the trench, half-stunned by a blow with the flat side of the tooth-brush, and miserably destroyed by the teeth of the countless rats who jumped down upon him. Sundry other stoats perished in the trench; and several, whilst endeavouring to climb up the sides, were dragged back by their remorseless enemies, and either slain or captured. Among the latter was the luckless 'Teaser,' whom Spandee and his immediate followers succeeded in taking alive and leaving fast bound in the trench.

Panic seized upon the remaining stoats. Disheartened and outnumbered, they wavered on the edge of the trench, and it was in vain that their leaders endeavoured to cheer their drooping spirits. The rat king now ordered the trumpets to be sounded for a general charge, and a mighty phalanx of rats hurled themselves upon the already half-discomfited foe. The effect was such as might have been looked for. The stoats broke and fled down the plantation at the top of their speed, pursued with exulting cries by their victorious enemies.

But at this juncture the bearing of the gallant chiefs, Pilus and Bird-slayer, was such as has never been forgotten by the chroniclers of stoat history. Side by side, with only some half-dozen of devoted followers, the two warriors slowly retreated, ever and anon turning round and presenting to their clamorous foes an undaunted front which deterred them from the attack. Retreat was unavoidable, but at least *their* retreat was honourable. Seeing their steadiness and courage, and perhaps respecting those qualities even in an enemy, King Spandor gave orders that they should not be molested, and they left the scene of conflict without loss of life or limb.

Had every stoat borne himself as these two, the result would doubtless have been different. But, as it was, the most terrible defeat had that day been experienced by the forces of King Brock. It was impossible to discover the extent of his losses that night, which the king passed in sleepless rage and anguish. But early on the following morning he issued summonses for a council and general assembly, being most anxious to ascertain the nature and extent of the disaster which had befallen his people. Of the fifty stoats whom he had himself led to the combat, none indeed had been slain or captured ; but Egg-sucker and ten of his companions had become so dreadfully ashamed of themselves, that, instead of appearing in answer to the king's summons, they quietly decamped, left the wood secretly, and are believed to have fled to foreign parts.

Of the fifty stoats led to the drain by Kill-game nine were missing, including Hare's-foe and the next stoat to him, who had been killed at the mouth of the drain; the other seven had probably joined the plantation detachment which, practically, had sustained the whole brunt of the fight. Of this detachment of fifty only twenty-seven presented themselves before the king, and of these several bore unmistakeable marks of the conflict in which they had been engaged. Twenty-three were missing; and, as was afterwards discovered, seventeen of these lay dead in and about the trench, three had never got beyond the plantation, and three were prisoners in the hands of the victorious enemy.

Brock found, besides, that several stoats who had gone forth to battle absented themselves from the assembly; and altogether, out of his army of a hundred and fifty soldiers, only ninety-four appeared before him in answer to his summons. These ninety-four, however, were warriors good and true; and most of them were unwounded and unhurt save in spirit, for the spirit of every stoat was roused to the greatest indignation by the defeat which they had suffered at the hands of an enemy whom, upon equal terms, they so entirely despised. Brock gazed upon his friends and followers with a sad and mournful look, and then proceeded to address them with as much fortitude as he could muster.

'My brother stoats,' he said, 'we are beaten, but not disgraced; or, if disgraced in any sort, we shall have, I promise you, an opportunity of wiping out that disgrace, and of proving our superiority to the wretched foe, who, by cunning rather than by valour, has for the moment got the better of us.'

He then proceeded to tell them the causes of their defeat, which he had collected from the reports of the several chiefs and leaders, and to point out the mistakes which had been committed, and the errors into which they had fallen. He spoke with tears in his eyes of the death of so many of their dear companions, and his whiskers bristled with pride as he recounted the bravery and true courage of Pilus and Bird-slayer, and held up the conduct of these two noble stoats as an example worthy of imitation, and as something which went far to redeem the misfortune into which their army had come. He said he was sure that no stoat worthy of the name would sit tamely down, and allow the rats to boast of their victory, without an attempt to reverse the fortune of war; and he invited the advice of the great leaders around him as to the course which should be pursued. The opinions given were many and various. Some stoats thought that another attack upon the rat-place should be made without delay; others that the rats should be insulted as much as possible, and tempted to invade Bockhanger, whilst others were for carrying on a different kind of warfare, and appointing stoats to watch the rat-place constantly, and kill every rat who could be caught alone, so that the place might be in a perpetual state of siege, and every rat's life made a burden to him.

Before, however, the matter could be finally settled, Brock said that there was another question which they were bound to consider, namely, whether they should take any, or what, course with respect to the liberation of those stoats who were known to be in the hands of the

enemy.   True it was that they had no rat-prisoners to
offer in exchange, but, according to the usages of war,
a ransom might fairly be offered and taken ; and it was
beneath the dignity and contrary to the feelings of a
king to allow his subjects to remain prisoners without
making some effort to effect their release.   Whilst they
were discussing this question, and debating whether it
would be prudent and proper to send a herald to the
rat-place upon such an errand, the matter was decided
in a manner which none of them had expected, and
which changed the whole current of their thoughts.

A little bustle was visible among the stoats on the
outside of the circle which surrounded Brock, excited cries
of rage and astonishment were heard, a passage was
cleared, and an animal rushed into the inner circle, and
threw himself at the feet of the king.   Could it be—was
it possible that it could be—yes, it certainly was—
Teaser, but different, indeed, from the Teaser who had
sallied forth the previous evening in the troop of Pilus,
full of martial ardour, a gallant warrior in a just cause.
His ears were cropped close to his head, his tail was
cut off, one of his eyes was out, his head and body
were close shaven, and the latter bore marks of stripes
and bruises which betokened that the unhappy stoat
had undergone no gentle treatment.

Overcome with pain, fatigue, and grief, the miserable Teaser allowed some moments to elapse before he
could answer the inquiries of the king as to what had
occurred, and the cause of his wretched condition.   At
last, amid groans and sobs, he related his story ; but as
I can hardly give it in his very words, I had better endeavour to tell in my own way the events which immediately followed upon the repulse of the stoats, and

the return of the triumphant rats to their stronghold.
Their victory had not been obtained entirely without
loss to themselves, for fourteen rats had been slain, and
nine disabled in the trench, where Pilus and Bird-slayer
had attacked so vigorously.   But this loss was of small
moment to Spandor, in comparison with the important
results which had been obtained by the defeat of so
powerful an enemy; and the bodies of friend and foe
having been speedily buried out of the way, universal
rejoicings took place in the rat-place.   A long proces-
sion of rats, tossing their tails wildly in the air, and
carrying lighted lucifer matches in their mouths, marched
four abreast past the king, squeaking triumphantly;
whilst the minstrels sang the famous rat ballad at the
top of their voices :

> ' Hail to thee, Spandor, great lord of the rats,
>   Monarch of rat-place and all it contains ;
> Let them attack thee with dogs and with cats,
>   Death and defeat shall they get for their pains.
>
> ' Rich in the love of the drain-loving race,
>   Proudly above thee thy banneret floats ;
> Joy to thy friends, to thy foemen disgrace,
>   Death and defeat to unsavoury stoats.
>
> ' Hail to thee, Spandor ! the danger is o'er ;
>   Well have we battled with teeth and with claws.
> Stoats shall invade the old rat-place no more,
>   Victory smiles on the rats and their cause ! '

and the squeaking was tremendous.   Then the proces-
sion broke up into an irregular tumult of shrieking
rats, mad with joy at their victory, and excited beyond
measure by the events of the day.

Suddenly a small detachment was seen advancing,
bringing with them Teaser and the two other stoats

who had been captured in the trench. These were about to be conveyed before the king, but the furious crowd broke in upon them with squeaks of rage, and in spite of all remonstrances, miserably destroyed Teaser's two companions, bound and helpless as they were. With the greatest difficulty, Pick-bones, a rat of high courage and of an honourable disposition, preserved Teaser from so sad a fate, and succeeded in bringing him before Spandor. His bearing was gallant, and such as might have touched the heart of an enemy, for he boldly confronted the king, and demanded to be treated as a prisoner of war, protesting against the foul and shameful treatment which his companions had experienced. But, whether Spandor was himself somewhat under the influence of the general excitement, or whether he feared to oppose the will of his people upon such an occasion and at such a moment, I cannot say; certain it is, that neither mercy nor courtesy fell to the lot of the wretched Teaser. Seized by several gigantic rats, he was subjected to the most cruel treatment—his war-garments torn from him, blows and kicks, bites and scratches, freely bestowed upon him on every side; and, finally, when more dead than alive, the rat-king's chief barber was called forward, who with sharpened bits of glass shaved him closely, severed his tail from his body, and cropped his ears in the most degrading and uncomfortable manner. Then, being again brought before Spandor, amid the jeers and scoffs of the surrounding rats, the miserable stoat had scarce voice enough left to complain of the injuries which had been inflicted upon him. Bold, however, to the last, he told the king that vengeance should follow such rascally behaviour as he had permitted, and begged him to finish the matter by killing him outright. This, however, did not appear to meet the views of the rat monarch. He did not, indeed, condescend to join in the scoffs and gibes which his courtiers vented upon the helpless captive, but told him that his life should, indeed, be spared, but that he might return to the stoats, his brethren, with the message that his fate would be the fate of all those who ventured, as he had done, to enter the rat-place in a hostile manner.

Poor Teaser could make no further reply. He would, indeed, have bristled with rage, but there were no hairs left upon his body to bristle. His ears would have stood erect with excitement, but his ears were gone; and the melancholy satisfaction of shaking his tail in defiance had been taken from him by the cruelty which had deprived him of that natural ornament.

Slowly and sadly he dragged himself away from the scene of his barbarous usage, and had barely strength to reach a patch of fern at a short distance from the rat-place, before he fainted away in a dead swoon. How long he lay thus he could not tell, but as soon as he came to himself he made the best of his way to Bockhanger wood, and arrived, as we have seen, at the critical moment when Brock was holding his council.

When Teaser had finished his story, which he told with difficulty, pausing for breath repeatedly, the stoats burst forth in one cry of indignant rage. Had such an event ever before been heard of? A prisoner of war, taken in fair fight, had every claim to be treated as an honourable foe, and by an honourable foe he would so have been treated. But here was not only a gross cruelty practised upon an unhappy person, but a wanton and abominable insult offered to the whole stoat nation, and every law broken which the common usage of civilized animals had long established.   There could be no excuse for such an outrage, and every stoat felt himself wounded in his tenderest feelings by that which had occurred.   Cries of vengeance rent the air, and the excitement among his followers was for some minutes so great that Brock could not make his voice heard.   When order had at length been restored, the brave old king stood forward in the front of his people, bristling with suppressed rage and emotion.

'My children,' he said, 'vengeance must now be our watchword, and no stoat must rest or taste the flesh of rabbit until this terrible wrong has been redressed.   But I implore you to restrain your feelings, and trust to your king and his chiefs, who will lose no time in making the necessary arrangements for prompt and decisive action.'

Thus implored, the angry stoats suffered their excitement to calm down.   The injured Teaser was wrapped at once in the skin of a newly-slaughtered rabbit, and conducted to the public hospital, which was situated in the roots of a very old oak-tree, and was presided over by a venerable stoat of the name of Cure-all, assisted by Pill-take and Mix-draught, two well-known medical practitioners among the stoat nation.

Meanwhile Brock held deep counsel with his best statesmen, and in a short time messengers were hurrying forth in every direction, to make known the event which had just taken place, and to summon stoats from all parts of the country, to join in a crusade against those enemies who in their treatment of the prisoners of war had so terribly outraged the usages of civilized animals. To Barracks wood a herald flew, and the Quarrington stoats were also quickly summoned. Old Strong-scent, the Naccult stoat, received a special message, whilst Hampton, Foreland, Combe, and Brook woods resounded with the herald's trumpet. Within four-and-twenty hours it was known in Bockhanger that the summons would be obeyed. Sneaker, the Quarrington stoat, was the first to appear with his band of followers; Love-chicken, from Barracks wood, came hurrying next; and although the cruel efforts of the west Brabourne keepers rendered the assistance which came from Combe and Foreland but slight in comparison with others, yet old Strong-scent brought full five-and-twenty brave Naccult stoats, which had lived securely in that well-known covert for many years past.

It was towards the evening of the second day after the return of poor Teaser that Brock found himself at the head of nearly two hundred stoats, burning for the fray and thirsting for vengeance. He then announced his plans to the assembled chiefs, having first carefully ascertained that no traitor was present. He did not intend to advance, as before, against the rat-place at first, but to occupy a strong position as near it as possible, annoying and harassing the enemy in every way, tempting them to sally forth if possible; but if, as he supposed, they proved too wary for this, he meant to approach by slow degrees, to starve them out as much as he could, and finally carry the place by general assault. The whole force of the stoats, therefore, marched off together, full of confidence and hope of the result. They skirted the foot of the hill on which stood the great house, and arrived at the further end of the plantation beyond the rat-place. Here was a wide and broad ditch, with rushes growing in and around it, and on the park side a small

patch of fern, and several young trees enclosed in upright
post and rail fences, to keep off the deer and sheep.
On this side Brock had determined to encamp, having
the ditch between his army and the plantation, there
being no fence on either side of the ditch, which ran
up to the wall between the plantation and the main
shrubbery.   Beyond the fern and rushes the ground was
rough and full of ruts, in front was the ditch, on the
upper side, being on the slope of a hill, there was a carriage road within some twenty yards, and on the lower
side the open park.   It was a position of some natural
strength—water could be obtained from the ditch, and
at a little distance off were several rabbits' earths, from
which supplies could be drawn,—one actually within the
rat-place plantation; one in the bank of an ice-house
built of brick, but deeply covered over with earth and
surrounded by a plantation of which rabbits had long
taken forcible possession; and one just beyond this, being
all within a hundred yards or so of the spot which Brock
had selected for his camp.   On arriving, his first act
was to post sentinels, so as to guard against any surprise.
He then apportioned a part of the camp to each of those
chiefs to whom he intended to give a command, keeping
as much as possible under the same leader those stoats
who came from the same woods, and had been used to
fight together. He himself occupied a lump of fern in the
patch before-mentioned, flanked by a young tree, and
not far from the ditch.   Before retiring to rest he went
round to all the sentinels, and made every provision for
his army's safety, having arranged with Bird-slayer, Pilus,
Strong-scent, and two or three other of the principal
stoats, that one or other of them should constantly visit
the outposts, and see that all was right.

Meanwhile it is time to return to the rat-place, and discover what the recent victors were about.   Although Spandor had found it necessary to yield to the popular clamour with regard to the captive stoats, he well knew the folly and impolicy of the act, and that he was certain to arouse against his nation a spirit of bitterness, which might have most unpleasant results.   Accordingly, as soon as the rejoicings after the victory were over, he summoned his chiefs together, and arranged with them that the fortifications of the rat-place should be at once thoroughly repaired, the wounded soldiers well cared for, and better arms provided for their future use.   By means of a well-managed treaty with the mice, he obtained from the latter a considerable number of pins which they had been able from time to time to steal from the nursery and to pick up from the floors of various rooms in which they had been dropped by the housemaids.   By this means he found himself able to arm some seventy rats with an effective weapon, with which he hoped that much execution would be done in any hand to hand conflict.   Then he had the drain under the wall carefully and completely stopped, the trench at the head of the plantation dug deeper and wider, and several wooden bridges provided, over which his soldiers might cross, if necessary to pass beyond the limits of the rat-place. The top of the shrubbery wall was also well covered with bits of broken glass bottles, and the whole place rendered as strong as rat-craft could make it.   About stores he had little anxiety, as nothing could stop the daily supply from the kitchen and scullery of the great house, and the large hog-wash tub in one corner of the yard was always something to fall back upon in case of necessity.

Spandor was speedily informed of the coming of the stoat army. Indeed, it was impossible that so large a body of troops should move without attracting attention; and their arrival at the end of the plantation was very soon known to every rat in the place.

A council was immediately held. It was found that three hundred and fourteen rats capable of bearing arms were at that moment in and about the rat-place, and with such a force it was thought that the fortress might be held against all comers. But great difference of opinion arose upon the question of defence or attack. Old Pick-bones was strongly of opinion that the true policy was for the king and his forces to remain where they were, content with the glory which the nation had gained in the recent battle, and leave it to the enemy to make the first move.

On the other hand, young Spandee, at the head of a number of impetuous youths, was greatly in favour of attacking the stoat camp forthwith.

'They are tired,' he said; 'they are disheartened by their late defeat; they do not expect that we should dream of attacking them. Let us take them by surprise, let us make a general onslaught at once; and depend upon it, the result will be such as to establish for ever our superiority in war, and the security of our beloved home.'

These sentiments met with approval from no inconsiderable portion of the inhabitants of the rat-place. Elated with their late victory, they were rather inclined to despise the enemy, and it cannot be denied that there was some wisdom in the idea of attacking the latter before they should have time to entrench themselves in their camp. Spandor, however, knew pretty well that a stoat is generally a stronger animal than a rat; and

considering how much was at stake, he hardly liked to
run the risk of a defeat which might be followed by consequences so serious to his kingdom and his people. He
therefore did his best to restrain the ardour of his son ;
but the feeling of the younger rats was so strong, that
he was obliged to yield to it in some degree.   But by
this means the rats were led into that mistake which is
often made by people who take half of one man's advice
and half of another's, forgetting that the value of each
probably depends upon it being taken as a whole, and
that part only of a good plan may turn out to be a very
bad one.   Spandor promised that an attack should be
made upon the stoats, but he waited to strengthen his
fortress and to watch a favourable opportunity, and by
this means he let the moment go by in which he would
have found his foe unprepared.

The day after the rat council passed away without
movement on either side, save that, whilst the defences
of the rat-place were somewhat improved, Brock was
hard at work in rendering his camp strong against any
surprise, and also in drilling the younger stoats, and
finally arranging his divisions.

Kill-game, in consequence of his former failure, was
upon this occasion condemned to fight in the ranks.
To Pilus was given the command of fifty stoats, whose
duty it was to guard the half of the big ditch above the
king's tent, whilst the other half was confided to the
care of Strong-scent, with fifty followers, and Brock
himself held a reserve of twenty-five picked stoats in
the centre of the camp.   Three bodies of twenty stoats,
under the command of Bird-slayer, Love-chicken, and
a stoat named Cheat-keeper, who came from Hampton,
respectively guarded the right, left, and rear of the

camp. These arrangements having been completed, Brock next turned his attention to providing supplies. He had brought with his army several large waggons of preserved game, potted hare, and rabbit lozenges, but desired to keep these stores against a time when it might be difficult or impossible to provision his army; and therefore determined to get fresh supplies whilst he could. A detachment of ten stoats was therefore sent over to the ice-house, where they met with tolerable success, and returned with several rabbits. Brock thought it better not to try the earth in the rat-place plantation, which he might have to fall back upon afterwards.

Nevertheless, upon the second day three stoats, Flip, Flap, and Flumper, belonging to the Naccult force, issued from the camp early in the morning, and, without orders, advanced upon the earth in question.

Now, it happened that upon that morning Spandee had with difficulty obtained his father's leave to head a party of skirmishing rats, and to ascertain what the enemy was about. He chose thirty young soldiers, with old Sly, a venerable warrior of great craft, and advanced down the centre of the plantation, throwing out skirmishers on either side, to provide against a surprise.

The rabbits' earth was some thirty yards from the ditch, and less than a hundred yards from the rat-place trench; and Spandee had proceeded with great caution as far as this spot, when he perceived one stoat with a rabbit in his clutches just upon the rat-place side of the earth, and another just behind him. Comprehending the situation at once, he sent ten rats to cut off the enemy's retreat, and charged at once with the rest of his follow-

ers.   Flip and Flap, the two stoats outside the earth,
fled at once, but within a. dozen yards of the ditch
were overtaken by the ten foremost rats.   Flip lost one
ear, and Flap was only saved by a flank movement of
Strong-scent, who threw fifteen stoats into the plantation
in such a manner that the rats would have been taken
in rear, and cut to pieces, had they not immediately retreated.   However, Flumper, emerging from the earth
at this instant, was surrounded and slain by Spandee's
party, who returned to the rat-place with triumphant
squeaks, carrying the head of the slaughtered stoat
fixed upon the end of a rusty nail, and waving aloft his
tail with proud and disdainful gestures.

Brock lost not a moment in enforcing the discipline
of his camp.   Within an hour Flip and Flap, tried and
condemned by court-martial, were hung from a branch
of the nearest tree, confessing their sentence to be just.
The result, however, was not unfavourable to the stoats.
So delighted and puffed up with this new success were
the rats, that nothing could now restrain them from the
attack upon the enemy's position.

Still doubtful of this policy, Spandor appealed once
more to his council, but the more ardent spirits were in
the ascendant, and it was resolved that the attack
should be made.   At the earnest request of Pick-bones,
who, in fact, made it a condition of his undertaking to
accompany the advancing party, Spandor consented to
remain in the rat-place with some sixty soldiers.   Two
hundred and fifty rats, meanwhile, formed the attacking
party; and on a pleasant morning, when Nature wore
her loveliest appearance, and seemed to speak of love
and peace and tenderness, these fierce warriors marched
out to the scene of blood and war.   Spandee was in

command, and with a hundred rats he took the lower
side; Pick-bones, with another hundred, held the upper
side of the plantation, and advanced alongside of
the wall; whilst old Sly kept the reserve of fifty in the
centre. So they advanced, slowly and quietly, until
they appeared close in front of the large ditch, and perceived at once the difficulties before them.

To descend the ditch upon one side, and creep up
the other, would have been no difficult task to a rat
under ordinary circumstances, but to do so in the face
of an enemy was a different matter altogether, and no
commander would be justified in so exposing his men.
On the other hand, if the army were to separate, and
endeavour to enter the stoats' camp by the right and
left sides, leaving the ditch unguarded, nothing would
be easier to the enemy than to throw over a force which
might operate injuriously upon their flank, and, in case
of a repulse, cut off, or at least seriously impede, their retreat to the rat-place. Therefore, after some delibera-
tion, Spandee resolved to attack in the following manner. He and his hundred, bearing to the left, would
pass below the ditch, and attack the camp from the
open park side, leaving the ditch close upon their right.
Pick-bones would take his force along the wall, through
the white swing-gate of the coach road, close at the
head of the ditch, and thus assault the upper side of
the camp, whilst old Sly would guard the ditch with his
reserve. Thus the stoats would be exposed to a double
attack, whilst any attempt on their part to cross the
ditch would be at once discovered, and probably
checked. But the fault of Spandee's plan was two-fold,
by thus dividing his forces, neither could his party aid
Pick-bones, nor could the latter succour him, if the

day went against either of the two, whilst the fifty reserve rats were rendered idle and useless, unless the
enemy chanced to make a particular movement.

The wary old soldier Brock saw the error at once,
and was not slow to take advantage of it. He ordered
a few of his men only to the front, so as to show the
enemy that the ditch was well protected, and deter Sly
from any possible attempt to cross. Meanwhile he
strengthened his wings right and left, and every stoat
stood to his guns manfully.

Round the end of the ditch marched Spandee, and
without sound or signal, hurled his men boldly against
the position of the enemy. Bravely they advanced over
the ruts up to the small patches of fern, from which the
stoats maintained a galling fire with pea-shooters.
These, however, were soon silenced as the rats poured
in, and a terrific hand to hand fight ensued. Bird-
slayer and his twenty held the outposts, Strong-scent
having brought his men up to the end of the ditch,
where Spandee fought in person.

The outposts were soon driven in, but Bird-slayer
held his position on a large ant-hill with fern on each
side, and resisted every effort to dislodge him. Waving
over his head his now celebrated weapon, he encouraged his party by voice and gesture.

'Think on Chumper' was his constant cry, and
full bravely did he sustain his great reputation. But
Spandee at first bore all before him, killing with his own
hand Hen-plunderer and Shun-trap, two Naccult
stoats, who first came in his way, and cheering his men
forward right gallantly. In fact, so impetuous was his
assault, that the line of stoats wavered, and would
probably have been broken, and the camp entered at

once, had not Brock been able to support and strengthen it with his reserve force, and with ten stoats taken from the rearguard

Strong-scent, however, never lost confidence. He had with infinite pains manufactured a terrible weapon out of the leg of an old cock pheasant, who had during his life-time possessed a tremendous spur. This being very strong and sharp, was a most powerful engine of attack in the hands of a strong and resolute stoat, and great was ·the execution done by it. Moreover, the Combe stoats, who also fought in this quarter, were armed with woodcocks' bills, sharpened to a point and fixed in handles of hardened mud, which they managed right cleverly, and which in a great measure counteracted the effects of Spandor's pin-armed rats, most of whom were in personal attendance upon his son, and fought in his regiment. The battle had waxed more and more furious, and many had fallen on each side, when at last Spandee and Strong-scent approached each other. A blow from the latter's weapon had slain a young rat of the name of Steal-cheese, and it was over his body that a conflict took place which has been the subject of song and sermon among stoats and rats for time beyond the memory of man. The rats had gathered round the body of their friend, as determined to rescue, as Strong-scent was resolved to drag it within the camp. Slippery, an active young rat, held Strong-scent at bay with a pin-weapon for some time, and had just retired with a broken shoulder when Spandee came to the rescue. He warded off a tremendous blow from the Naccult chieftain, and grazed his shoulder by a skilful lounge at his throat. Then each dropped his weapon, one seized the head and the other the tail of the dead rat, and each pulled fiercely his own way, amid the maddening shouts of eager friends.

Strange it is, as showing the extraordinary differences which exist among even the most veracious historians, and moreover as evincing the curious fact that matters comparatively small often occupy so much larger a share of thought and attention than more serious points; strange it is, I say, that one-half of the controversy respecting this combat, the results of which were of such enormous importance, has turned upon the question, which it was, the stoat or the rat, who had hold of Steal-cheese by the head, and which by the tail?

True-song, the great historian of Bockhanger wood, uses these words in his narration : 'Then did the famous Strong-scent, with one hand on each ear of his dead enemy, strive manfully with the royal rat for possession of the worthless carcase;' whilst, on the other hand, 'Sly's narrative' (a little work which has had an enormous circulation among rats) distinctly states that Spandee 'held fast by the head of Steal-cheese;' whilst in the old rat-place ballad, 'The Ancient Song of Spandor's Fame,' these lines certainly occur :—

> 'The stoat with many cruel blows
>   Our Spandee did assail,
> Who held dead Steal-cheese by the nose,
>   While Strong-scent tugged his tail.'

The point, however, is scarcely of sufficient importance to debate upon, and I cannot solve the doubt. Certain it is, however, that after severe pulling on either side, the matter was settled by the tail suddenly coming out, and both combatants falling backwards in consequence. Recovering themselves, however, and regaining their weapons, they rushed upon each other with redoubled vigour, and their efforts were fearful.

Meanwhile, we must not forget the other wing of the rat army, which, under the command of the renowned Pick-bones, was advancing to the attack at the upper side of the camp. Pick-bones himself kept close to the wall, which brought him to the head of the ditch between which and the wall there was just room for two rats to pass abreast. Cheat-keeper, who had the command of the twenty stoats on the upper side, here opposed the rats' advance, Pilus, with his fifty, advancing upwards to support him. But Pick-bones, whose promptness in action was as famous as his wisdom in council, saw at once that the passage must at all hazards be secured, or his wing of the army would be taken at great disadvantage. He therefore sprang with haste and fury upon Cheat-keeper, parried a blow which the stoat aimed at him, and with a fearful answer, drove his rusty nail into the head of the foe with such force that he rolled over lifeless into the ditch, never more to deceive the guardians of the game. Without an instant's delay, Pick-bones struck down the next stoat, one Stump-dweller, and in this manner gained a footing on the opposite bank of the ditch. Here he firmly planted himself, and kept the enemy at bay, until his men had poured over after him in such numbers as to enable him to assume the offensive, and, being on higher ground, steadily to press back the stoats upon the centre of their camp, and down by the side of the ditch. For some time they slowly but surely gave way. Brave and resolute as they were, there seemed something strange about the gaunt old rat which terrified the stoutest heart amongst them ; whilst his followers,

Combat of Pilus and Pickbones.—P. 177.

inspired with confidence, and filled with courage as they witnessed the bravery of their great leader, pressed boldly forward as if sure of victory.

At last, however, the only man in the stoat-camp who was at all his equal in military reputation encountered the fine old warrior. Amid the squeaks and cheers of his friends, the noble Pilus came slowly to the front, armed with a sharpened splinter from the horn of a buck, full of courage and boiling with rage at the hesitation of his countrymen to face the foe. No hesitation had Pilus, and he knew not fear. As he drew near, he raised his voice, and spoke out clear and strong to his advancing enemy: 'Rat,' he cried, 'why come so foolishly against thy betters? Fly, wretch, fly, ere thy doom come upon thee!'

Pick-bones smiled grimly. 'What! is it thou, old stoat?' he replied. ' Hast thou mustered up courage to face Pick-bones? Come hither, and meet thy fate!' and on came the two champions, whilst their followers on either side paused in breathless expectation.

' Have at thee, rat,' shouted Pilus, and struck fiercely at his foe. Receiving the blow upon the back of his tooth-brush, Pick-bones aimed one in return, under which the stoat fairly staggered, but recovering himself in a moment, he flew like a tiger upon the rat, and a furious struggle ensued, each giving and taking blows without a word on either side. At last they neared the edge of the ditch, from the other side of which Sly and his men seeing the combat uttered loud shouts of encouragement to Pick-bones, and abuse to Pilus. Still the two fought on, bleeding from many wounds, yet would neither yield or leave off from the battle upon which so much depended. At last a clever stroke from the horn-sword of the stoat fractured the hind leg of the veteran Pick-bones, who felt that he could no longer stand firmly or wield his deadly weapon with effect. His resolution, however, was so great, and his courage so undaunted, that even at this moment neither failed him. With a tremendous bound, receiving a fearful wound in his side as he sprang, he broke through the stoat's guard, inflicted an equally severe wound with his trusty sword, and fastened his teeth firmly in the throat of his enemy. The two warriors rolled over on the ground; even then none dared approach them. They struggled furiously for another moment, and then, locked closely together in the fatal hug, they rolled slowly down the bank into the ditch, exactly into a place where there happened to be water still standing. A dull, heavy splash followed, and the warriors were seen no more by the contending armies. But, when the heat of the summer had dried up that ditch, weeks afterwards, the bodies of the stoat and the rat were found together, the teeth of the one still fastened in the other's throat, and their paws closely locked, each round the other's body. So died these two great leaders, whose names will never be forgotten as long as martial skill and warlike courage continue to be respected by the two great nations of stoats and rats. The death of Pick-bones struck the rats with terror and dismay. They had so long looked up to him as one who could not be conquered, and to whom every one might look for aid and advice, that his loss was to them beyond everything terrible. Nothing prevented their instant and total rout save the action of one young rat, who first became famous upon that memorable day.

Nibble-meat, a distant cousin of Spandor's, and

nephew of Pick-bones, had long admired his renowned uncle, had served upon his staff, had eagerly received his instructions, and profited by his experience and example. As soon as he perceived that his beloved relative had fallen, his first thought was of the course which the departed warrior would have followed under the like circumstances. Nor did he hesitate long. Seizing the well-known weapon of Pick-bones, which the latter had dropped in his last rush, he waved it over his head, and cheered his men on, striking down a particularly stout stoat of the name of Fat-sides, who, to tell the truth, had kept close behind Pilus all day, and was now endeavouring to retreat quietly. But although his action was seen, and applauded by his followers, they were too much disheartened by the death of Pick-bones to be capable of the exertions necessary to carry the position of the enemy. They rallied, indeed, and not a rat showed signs of flinching; but there was no dash, no life, no eagerness to advance, such as they had recently shown. All that Nibble-meat could do was to keep them steady, and check any advance on the part of the enemy. To do this, however, was by no means easy.

Love-chicken, with his Barracks wood contingent, was foremost on the stoat side; and as these stoats were by no means so well acquainted with Pilus as was every rat with Pick-bones, the death of the stoat champion had no such considerable effect upon the army of his nation.

The hero of Barracks wood was a stoat of a rough-and-ready character. Brandishing the drum-stick of a Cochin-China fowl in his paw, to this and to his own sharp teeth he trusted, as he urged his followers forward against the attacking rats. Firmly they stood, taking advantage of every lump of fern, and holding their ground manfully. No great progress was made by either side; and although the skirmishes were frequent, the fight was less general and fierce. The one party could not penetrate further into the camp of the other; nor could these, on their part, dislodge the foe, and drive him from the camp altogether.

But at length, after some considerable time had elapsed, a whisper ran through both armies, which had very great effect upon the movement of the rats, and the ultimate fortunes of the day. How the rumour got abroad no one could say, but a report flew from one end of the fight to the other like wild-fire, that Spandee was killed. Nor, indeed, was the report without foundation. When the severance of the tail of Steal-cheese from his body had parted the two chiefs who had been so fiercely fighting over the dead, short time elapsed before they renewed the combat, and both strove hard for victory. The eager bravery of the youthful prince was well matched by the cool craft of the veteran chief, and for some time it appeared doubtful to which side victory would incline.

Strong-scent had narrowly escaped from a blow which lopped off his left ear, and Spandee had lost half his whiskers in a similar manner. Yet each stood his ground firmly; and it is uncertain what might have been the issue of the contest, had not a stoat of the name of Fawner, a toady and hanger-on of Strong-scent, stolen treacherously round, and dealt Spandee a foul blow with the scull of a rabbit fastened to the end of a dried fern-root; and whilst the noble rat staggered for a moment under the blow, the terrible weapon of

Strong-scent descended with fatal force upon his devoted head.

From that moment the battle was lost to the rats.
A desperate charge was made by the immediate friends
and followers of the prince, to rescue him from the
stoats, but the latter pressed boldly forward, and,
whether or no he would have recovered from the blow of
the Naccult warrior can never be known, for amid the
furious battle which followed, his body was pierced
with wounds innumerable, and then and there the
brave young prince met his fate. Drain-lover and
Dish-licker, two young rats of noble family, hurled
themselves recklessly into the fray, dragged Strong-
scent from the body of their beloved prince, and inflicted upon him injuries from which he never completely recovered. For years afterwards a miserable
cripple wandered about the Naccult lanes, pointed out
to younger stoats as the once famous Strong-scent.
But Dish-licker lost his own life in the struggle, and
Drain-lover was severely wounded.   Moreover, at this
moment there resounded through the air the terrible
cry of Bird-slayer, 'Think on Chumper,' and that determined stoat having, by a desperate sally, repulsed
the rats who were attacking his position, executed at
this moment a brilliant flank movement, and fell upon
the rear of Spandee's detachment with terrible effect.
The rats broke, and fled in every direction.   The attempt to rally them was hopeless.   Out of the hundred
who had followed the rat-prince to the assault, only
fifty-three left the camp of the stoats; and the latter,
flushed with victory, followed them fiercely in hot pursuit. Had Pick-bones lived, and had Sly done his

duty, even now might the result have been different. As is always the fashion with the historians of a defeated nation, the rat-writers love to point out how this battle ought to have been won, and really *was* won as far as superiority in warlike skill may be said to constitute a victory.

Had Pick-bones succeeded, as, say they, he was actually succeeding, in driving in the stoats on the upper side, the stoats on the lower side of the camp, even had they still been victorious, could not have followed up their victory, whilst it is even probable that their beaten comrades, being driven in upon them, would have so confused their ranks, that the triumphant Pick-bones would have carried all before him. Again, had Sly brought up his reserves at the critical moment, Bird-slayer would have been taken in the rear; and even had the reserves been brought round, after the death of Spandee and repulse of his forces, the defeat might have been attended with less disastrous results, and the pursuit checked.

The stoats, of course, have their reply to this; but it is in vain to speculate upon what might have been, though people always *will* do so as long as the world lasts. The facts alone can be told by the true chronicler of history, and the facts were different from those which the wishes of the rats would have made them. Bird-slayer led a large number of stoats in close pursuit of the flying enemy. Brock, as soon as he saw that on the lower side his troops were successful, drew off all the forces he could draw to the upper side, and reinforced the brave Love-chicken with considerable aid and some little effect. For, when Nibble-meat found that a fresh force of stoats was upon him, and that his followers, already dispirited by the fall of Pick-bones, were rapidly becoming demoralized by the rumours of Spandee's death, he began to devote all his efforts towards securing a calm, orderly, and safe retreat. All might still have been well had it not been for the inexplicable conduct of Sly. Whether this old rat had any cause of grudge against the royal family; whether he was so much attached to Spandee, as to care for nothing after he was gone; or whether, as some have surmised, he really thought that the glory of the rat-place was gone for ever, and that no safety there was possible, I cannot tell. Certain it is that, instead of helping either the right or the left wing, as soon as he was assured of the death of the young prince, he drew off his reserve towards the wall, and, addressing them a few words, told them that the cause was now hopeless, that Spandor's family could no longer rule them to their advantage, and that nothing could prevent the rat-place from falling into the hands of the stoats. He therefore announced his intention of retiring at once, over the wall, to the cow-yard, which was distant about a couple of hundred yards beyond the coach-road, and invited those who agreed with him to follow him there, and seek a new, a safer, and a happier home.

This speech at first caused some consternation among his band, but I regret to say that no less than thirty-three of them agreed to follow the traitor, and accordingly scaled the wall with him, and retreated through the shrubbery. The remaining seventeen, scorning such a base action as to desert their countrymen in the hour of danger, fell back upon Nibble-meat's band in time sufficient to materially aid that gallant rat in the retreat upon which he was now bent. Had the whole reserve joined him, they would have done inestimable service; as it was, slowly and sadly he gave way before a superior foe, and with diminished forces drew back to the very end of the ditch. Here, however, the backward passage was next to impossible without a terrible sacrifice of life. Reluctantly, therefore, he fell back into the coach-road, and sixty-three rats, the remnant of the gallant hundred, whom Pick-bones had led to his last battle, crept beneath the white iron swing-gate, and slowly retreated through the shrubbery. The stoats were anxious to pursue; but Brock, fearful of an ambush, and not knowing the country sufficiently well, restrained them as well as he could, and contented himself with following, on the wall and inside the plantation, so as to prevent Nibble-meat's forces from reaching and re-inforcing the rat-place. This he was the better able to do, as the broken glass bottles on the top of the wall, nearer the fortress, prevented either rat or stoat from crossing, and therefore Nibble-meat and his band were entirely cut off from their friends, and could only take up the best position they could find in the brambles in the shrubbery, on the other side of the wall, where at least they were tolerably safe from pursuit.

Meanwhile, Bird-slayer rushed furiously on, followed by nearly a hundred stoats, mad with rage and intoxicated with success. The unhappy rats could offer no resistance: they were overtaken and slain one after the other, and scarce twenty out of Spandee's hundred reached the rat-place. These, too, were so closely followed by their savage enemies that they actually entered the place together, and a scene of consternation and carnage followed which baffles description. Span-

dor had remained with his sixty rats under arms, ready
to defend his stronghold to the last. But the first rat
who reached the fortress in his headlong flight told the
king, in broken accents, of the defeat of his army, and
the death of his beloved son. Unnerved by the sud-
denness and severity of the blow, the old monarch's
reason gave way under the shock. Uttering a piteous
cry of despair, he staggered back, dropped his arms,
threw up his fore-paws in agony and terror, and, fling-
ing himself headlong into the large hog-wash tub, then
and there perished miserably.

There was no one left to maintain discipline or to
defend the place. Brock and his stoats now came in
from the wall, the furious Bird-slayer crossed the trench
without opposition at the head of his victorious band,
and no mercy was shown to the unhappy garrison.
Squeaks of despair, pain, and rage were heard in every
direction, and the place was covered with the carcases
of murdered rats. The most accurate returns which I
have been able to obtain lead me to believe that out of
the three hundred and fourteen rats whom Spandor had
reviewed on the previous day, the number slain was
one hundred and eighty-six. Of the hundred who had
followed Spandee only thirteen survived. Of the hundred and fifty who had composed the band of Pick-bones
and the reserve, sixty-three were saved with Nibble-meat
and thirty-three fled with Sly, whilst of the sixty who
had remained with Spandor, only nineteen escaped from
the massacre in the rat-place. Indeed, it is impossible
to say whether any rat would have been alive within the
fortress to tell the tale, had it not been that a strange
and unexpected occurrence now interposed between the
rats and utter ruin. The door between the rat-place

and the kitchen-yard was suddenly thrown open, and a boy entered, accompanied by a couple of terriers. The moment he saw the stoats running hither and thither, pursuing and killing the unhappy rats, he burst out with a loud halloo—

' Here, Pincher ; here, Boxer, boy, seize 'em, old lad,' and rushed forward with a stick in his hand.

The dogs were ready enough to obey, and rushed eagerly upon the stoats, seizing and shaking them with blind rage. The stoats were so eager in their vengeance upon the rats, that all order and discipline was lost among them, and it is a wonder that they did not all fall victims to this sudden assault of so powerful an enemy. However, in the confusion and hurry, the dogs hardly knew what to do and whom to seize ; and Brock, being a wary and sagacious old fellow, sounded a retreat upon a penny whistle which he always carried with him, and dashed off as quickly as he could into the plantation. The boy, however, encouraging his dogs and dealing a round of awful blows with his stick, did sad execution among the victors, no less than seventeen of whom were then and there slaughtered in the very moment of their triumph. Some, who had not even entered the rat-place at all, quietly retreated back to their camp, and others hid in the rats' holes, the rats being far too few and too timid to face or oppose them in any way.

After a little while, the boy, having killed more stoats than he had ever seen together before, and not dreaming of the number which were so near, and which, had he hunted the plantation, must have fallen into his power, called in his dogs and went to fetch some men and maids from the kitchen and servants' hall, who came eagerly running to see such an unusual sight. The bodies of the slain were removed, and the inhabitants of the great house talked for a long time to come of the wonderful invasion of stoats and the number which had been killed, little knowing that, had the boy and his dogs not interfered, the rats, which had so long and so greatly annoyed the inhabitants of the house by their thievish ways, would have been totally destroyed.

So the shades of evening closed in, and silence reigned throughout the rat-place and the country round. Then did Brock return to his camp from the rabbits' earth, to which he and a number of his friends had fled, and began to make inquiries as to the condition of his army. Of the number of stoats whom he had led to battle many were then missing; but scouts having been sent out, and those who had taken refuge in the rat-place having gradually crept back to camp, he was enabled during the next few hours to ascertain the exact extent of his losses. Upon the side which Pick-bones had so boldly and so skilfully attacked, nineteen stoats had been killed, and a number more severely wounded. Spandee's rats had also done their share; and, the battle having been more confused in that quarter, twenty-three stoats had fallen. These, added to the seventeen killed by the boy and the dogs, and three who had perished by the hands of dying rats in the rat-place itself, made a total of sixty-two stoats who had that day lost their lives, and of the gallant band which Brock had led forth, there were less than a hundred and ten who were now assembled around him. Pilus, Cheat-keeper, and other gallant leaders were among the dead, and Strong-scent was past hope of recovery.

Nor must I forget to chronicle the fate of the valiant

Bird-slayer.   Foremost in the assault upon the rat-place, he was dealing death around with savage fury, when the boy and the dogs came, so unfortunately for the stoats, upon the scene of action.   He scorned to fly, nor indeed had he time to do so before he was seized by Boxer.   The bold and savage stoat turned fiercely upon the dog, seized him by the lip, and hung there with a firm grip.   But what could he do against an animal of five times his size and weight?   Infuriated with pain, the dog shook Bird-slayer with a force which soon de- prived him of sense and motion; and though he only relaxed his hold with life, it was but a second before he lay dead at the feet of his enemy, having to the last maintained his character for brave and determined ac- tion.   Love-chicken was more fortunate—Pincher was close upon him, but he ran up the ivy which grew against the wall between the rat-place and the shrubbery, and the eager dog turned upon another victim, and allowed him to escape.   Sneaker, the Quarrington wood stoat, de- sperately tried to run up the leg of the boy's trousers; but the boy was too much for him, and dropped his stick upon him with such effect that he never spoke again. Brock himself was without a scratch ; and although he gnashed his teeth with rage at the loss of his brave stoats, and at having failed to secure the head of the rat-king, which he had resolved to carry back to Bockhanger if he could possibly do so, yet was he well satisfied with the general result, and the enormous loss which he had inflicted upon the foe.

No prisoners had been taken on either side ; and as it was evident that, whilst the power of the rats had re- ceived a terrible and probably a fatal blow, yet the rat- place was not a fortress which it was desirable that stoats

should occupy, the stoat king found that there was nothing more to be done than to lead back his forces to
the wood and rest upon his laurels. So, early in the
morning, when the sun had scarcely risen, the little army
once more set out, skirted the foot of the hill, crossed
the intervening space of park, and marched bravely into
their dear old wood. Many of them carried the ears,
tails, and some even the heads of rats, mostly, of course,
of those which had fallen in the attack upon the camp,
and they entered Bockhanger with songs and squeaks
of joy which made the old wood re-echo again and
again.

Foremost before the army danced the minstrel stoats,
Squeaker and Symphony; and although their voices were
not what mortals might have deemed sweet, their en-
thusiasm was great, and they were welcomed with
clamorous shouts by all their friends. As they danced,
they loudly sang; and adopting new words to the popular stoat melody, 'O Susannah,' thus did they carry
the glad tidings of victory to the inhabitants of their
ancient wood.

> 'We've seen the rat-place once again,
>   And made the foe turn tail;
> And now to all we've made it plain
>   That stoatdom must prevail.
>   Oh, poor Chumper! won't we cry to you,
>   The fight is won—the rats are done,
>   And beaten black and blue?
>
> 'We've fought as only stoats can fight—
>   With these no foeman copes.
> We've put the caitiff rats to flight,
>   And crushed the rat-place hopes.
>   Oh, poor Chumper, &c.

'Bold Pilus marched to victory
 His country for to save ;
And blest by stoatdom will he be,
 Tho' sunk in wat'ry grave.
  Oh, poor Chumper.

'For Pick-bones, that detested foe,
 He valorously slew :
And Spandor's head at length lies low,
 And youthful Spandee too.
  Oh, poor Chumper.

Three cheers for Bockhanger we'll give,
 And all the stoatish stock ;
Long, long may stoats in triumph live—
 And now, three cheers for Brock !
  Oh, poor Chumper.'

The triumphant army, cheering this song to the echo, marched up to the hospital oak to carry the news to Teaser. They were but just in time : the earless, tailless, enfeebled stoat had ill borne his enforced absence from the stirring scenes of action to which his countrymen had marched. Sick at heart and suffering in body, he had grown gradually worse since the departure of the army, and on this very morning the attendant stoats had brought him out and seated him in an arm-chair of plaited rushes, in which he might once more breathe the fresh air of his native wood, and bask in the bright sunshine probably for the last time. When the shouts of joy told of the approach of the returning warriors, the whole frame of the injured stoat quivered with emotion. Louder and louder the cries reached his ears —or rather, the place where his ears had been—and at last, as well as his dim and weakened vision would permit, he saw the crowd drawing nearer and nearer, and gathered from the words of the minstrel-song the great and joyful tidings of which they were the bearers.   The great revulsion of feeling was too much for the noble-minded stoat.   He staggered wildly to his hind legs, threw out his fore paws with such sudden vehemence and unexpected strength, that he knocked Pill-take and Mix-draught clean off their legs, and exclaiming in a sepulchral voice, 'Then I die happy and avenged,' fell lifeless upon the ground, his heart actually broken by the strength of his feelings.

They buried him in the moss beneath a neighbouring tree, and his grave is still pointed out to youthful stoats by antiquarian teachers as the resting-place of a patriot-martyr.

What more need I tell of the rejoicings which followed upon the victory, and from which the death of Teaser took but little of the spirit and happiness?

Brock gave a great feast, at which the usual loyal toasts were given, and 'confusion to the rats' drank, until the whole stoat company became so confused themselves, that they hardly knew whether they were standing on their heads or their heels.   The power of King Brock was more firmly than ever established after these events.   The history of Bockhanger tells of his glory and greatness, and I suppose that no stoat-king was ever more famous.   He lived to a good old age, generally respected and beloved, and his name has been handed down in the literature of the stoat nation as among the wisest and bravest of its monarchs.

Meanwhile it will be well to relate what occurred in the rat-place after the sad battle of which I have had to tell.   The surviving rats kept very quiet in holes and corners during all the next day, and no signs of life were to be seen till towards the evening.   Then a few miserable wretches began to peep out, and to wander about the rat-place, with a melancholy idea of trying to find out whether any of their friends were left alive.

Little by little they got together, and began to inquire of each other how things had happened, and each to explain his own conduct and criticise that of others. I must freely say that, if every one's account of his own doings was to be believed, such a race of heroes as those survivors had never before existed; and it is little less than a miracle how the rats could ever have been defeated! However, rats—like men—are sometimes apt to exaggerate a little, and, perhaps, occasionally to magnify their own meritorious deeds. At all events, they could not deny that a defeat had been experienced; and out of those who re-appeared from the holes and corners of the rat-place, no chief or leader could be found.

Pick-bones would have been naturally looked to, after the death of Spandor and Spandee, but Pick-bones also had gone the way of all rats, and all was doubt and uncertainty. But towards evening things took a new turn, and the first ray of light and spark of hope for the future shone upon the disheartened nation.

Slowly and sadly, but with firm and martial bearing, the valiant Nibble-meat came marching in at the head of his heroic band of sixty-three, all of whom were loud in his praises. He had, indeed, done wonders, and to his skill and courage alone was due the fact that this detachment of the original army returned safe and sound to the old rat-place. Alas! this detachment now comprised more than half of the inhabitants of the fortress capable of bearing arms. There could be no doubt as to the course which should be pursued. The direct line of Spandor being extinct, Nibble-meat was elected king by acclamation, and invested with the royal robes and crown. How long and how wisely he reigned I cannot here relate. There were many rats who wished that he should form an alliance with some other nation, and seek vengeance upon the victorious stoats. But many reasons prevented this course of action. In the first place, the rats, had they been united and agreed, were not popular animals, and it would have been difficult to find any nation to join with them whose alliance was worth having. Then, alas! they were far from being united: the treachery of Sly was not forgotten, and indeed from that day to this a feeling of intense bitterness and hostility has existed between the old, loyal rat-place rats and their descendants, and the followers and children of Sly and his thirty-three, which has more than once broken out into positive civil war, and which at this very hour renders it unsafe for a cow-yard rat to visit the rat-place, or for one of the inhabitants of the latter to approach the cow-yard territory. And, moreover, the deeds of that fatal day struck such terror into the hearts of the rat nation generally, that from thenceforward these animals have thought it no shame to fly before the face of a stoat, and thus tacitly to acknowledge the superior strength and courage of the woodland animals. Perhaps this is right and just, and according to the laws of nature. However it may be, considering the habits, character, and ferocity of the two nations, and the propensity of both to consider man as their common enemy, and to plunder him accordingly, I cannot but consider it as a subject of rejoicing that so dire a feud should exist between the two, and that an alliance—offensive and defensive—

between them, which must inevitably have resulted in the establishment of a state of things most injurious to the interests of mankind in general, should have been prevented (as I trust for ever) by the course of events which I have endeavoured truly to describe in this wonderful and interesting history of ' The battle of the stoats and rats.'

V.

THE MOUSE TRAVELLER.

DID you ever lie awake listening to a mouse? It is not a particularly agreeable occupation, and can hardly be called an amusement, but sometimes one has to do it. There are two sorts of mice, I think, which inhabit houses, or else a mouse's disposition, like that of a human being, changes at different times and seasons. However that may be, the noises which mice make are very different at different times. There is your nibbling mouse, who keeps on biting and tearing away at some piece of paper or plaster in the wall to which he has apparently taken a fancy, and which seems to afford him considerable pleasure and occupation. Sometimes he moves on quietly and stealthily, and if your fire is still alight, and happens to be blazing a little, you may even see his small sharp-nosed head and bright black eyes peeping out of the little hole from which he sallies forth into that which is the outer world to him. Then there is your noisy, blustering, rampaging mouse, who is for ever running up and down behind the wainscot, making such a prodigious row, that you declare to yourself, over and over again, that it *must* be a rat, and wish him a thousand miles off from the bottom of your heart.

This kind of mouse is a rackety, unpleasant neighbour, who makes you feel hostile to mice generally, and inspires you with a sudden and earnest affection for cats, mouse-traps, and toasted cheese. The other mouse excites no such violent animosity towards himself or his race. If you rap the wall, he frequently ceases his noise and troubles you no more, and it is possible to become quite accustomed to his ways, and at last even to consider him as a companion and friend. Such a mouse it is who will be the hero of my present tale, and a highly respectable mouse he was. Do not think the worse of him because he lived in London. Very good people, as well as very bad ones, live there, all the year round, generally because they have nowhere else to live. And although we have all read of the simple, honest, country mouse, who, after a short stay in town, was frightened at the first danger he met, and went back declaring that he liked his dry country crust, eaten in safety, better than all the town delicacies which were obtained with so much risk, yet, if the truth were known, there are mice in London just as simple and honest as those in the country, and just as contented with a bit of bread and cheese as their neighbours. At any rate, the mouse of whom I am going to tell you was as worthy a little fellow as ever entered a wainscot. He lived in a house which was situated in one of the most fashionable parts of London, but I will not tell you the name of the street, for fear the mouse newspapers might get hold of it, and find fault with the poor little fellow for having told me his story, since mice are not permitted to speak to people if they can possibly avoid it, but are ordered by the laws of mousedom to run away as fast as they can if a man, woman, or child, comes towards them or speaks to them. So it would clearly be wrong if I was to expose my little friend to unpleasant consequences by telling his name or that of the street in which he lived. It is enough for you to know as much as I have already told you, and I must beg that none of you will try to find out any more. This little mouse was of a contented disposition : he kept quietly behind the wainscot all the day, only treating himself to an occasional peep into any of the rooms which appeared to be unusually quiet. Then, as night came on, he was in the habit of creeping out of the hole in the corner of the room, and foraging about for provisions. A few crumbs of bread from the dining-room floor contented him ; a bit of hard biscuit gave him great pleasure, and a morsel of cheese delighted him beyond all bounds. So you see our town mouse was not so very dainty, nor was he accustomed to live upon delicacies, and consume the fat of the land. One day he had crept out rather earlier than was his usual custom ; and as he was watching the dining-room table with hungry eyes, his attention was drawn to the conversation of two gentlemen who were sitting over their wine and cracking their jokes and their walnuts together. They were telling each other of the curious things which they had seen in foreign countries, of the difference of the people who inhabited them, their various languages, those of their habits and customs which seemed strange to visitors from other lands, and, in short, of the many remarkable lessons which might be learnt by people who travelled abroad.

Then one of the gentlemen began to say how odd it was that so many persons went abroad to see strange sights and scenes, and never visited half the beautiful places in their own country, or discovered the curiosities and amusing things which were very often close to them when they were at home.

The mouse was much struck by this remark, with which the other gentlemen appeared perfectly to agree. So when the dessert was over, and the dining-room was left empty, although the little mouse crept out and enjoyed himself mightily with the scraps which he found on the floor, somehow or other he found it impossible to get the conversation which he had heard out of his head.

'Here am I,' thought he to himself, 'one of those very stay-at-home folks of whom the gentlemen were talking. I cannot go to those foreign countries of which I heard them speak, but there must be many strange sights within my reach which I have never seen, or even taken the trouble to look after. I really feel that I am doing myself an injustice by refusing to make use of the opportunities before me, and I must seriously consider the matter.'

So thought and so talked the mouse for several days, until at last he quite made up his mind to take a voyage of discovery, and to see all that was to be seen in the neighbourhood of the house in which his lot had been cast.

Accordingly, the very next evening he set to work; and creeping up the curtain, and out on to the window-sill, he found that, by passing along the gutter at the edge of the roof, he could easily find his way into the

next house, and, indeed, could traverse the whole street
if he pleased in the same manner.

Into the next house he crept, under the eaves; and
after creeping and crawling as only mice and courtiers know how to creep and crawl, he found himself in
a strange wainscot, along which he travelled until he
came upon a little hole in the corner, from which he
peeped out into a room that was quite new to him.   It
was evidently the nursery, for there upon the floor sat
three little girls and a little boy playing with some dolls,
whom they were making believe to be real people, and
talking to them and answering for them as gravely and
seriously as possible.

'Now, Gertrude,' said the eldest little girl to one of
her sisters, 'you and Mary shall put your dolls to bed,
and Johnny and I will make our dolls the nurses, and
rub their feet and tuck them in quite snugly.'

'Yes, Emily dear,' said the other, 'that will be very
nice; and then one of them shall have a cold, and
Mary shall be the nursery-maid, and bring her some
bran tea.'

'With lemon and lots of honey in it,' said Mary.

'Yes,' said Emily; 'and then she must have her
bed warmed, you know, and I will be the mamma,
and come in the last thing to see that the little ones
are all safe in bed.'

So they began to undress the dolls, and talk to them
all the time, as if they were real children.   One they
called Julia—she was a large wax doll with very red
cheeks and very black eyes; another was Lucy Jane—
she was also a wax doll, but not quite so large as Julia,
and with flaxen hair; then there was Amelia, who was

still smaller, but very smartly dressed in white with a crimson sash and crimson bows on her shoulders; and there were several other dolls whose names I do not happen to remember just at this moment, but I dare say you can guess them, and if not, invent others for them which will do quite as well.

The children went on undressing the dolls very carefully, and making every arrangement for putting them snugly to bed. Gertrude got a bason, and Mary fetched a jug, which she said was for the hot water. Then Emily took a little make-believe warming-pan, and pretended to warm the bed, and all this time the children were as happy as possible—no unkind word ever passed between them, but they seemed to be all fond of each other, and to be enjoying their play together as contentedly and merrily as little brothers and sisters ought always to do, if they want to be happy whilst they are children, and in after years to have nothing but sweet, cheerful, happy thoughts to cast back upon the days of the early childhood which they have left behind.

The mouse thought it was very pleasant to see this loving little family at play, and he would have liked well enough to have joined them, or at least to have stayed a little longer and listened to them as they prattled away so merrily. But as he cast his bright black eyes round the room, he espied a large tortoise-shell cat, fast asleep upon the hearth-rug in front of the fire-place, and at this terrible sight he shivered all over, crept back into the wainscot, and continued his travels. As he passed into the next house, loud and angry voices met his ears.

'Give me that doll, I say! give it me quick!'

'No, I sha'n't ; it's mine, and I won't let you have it !'

Such were the words which met his ears, and the little mouse peeped through a hole in the wall with great curiosity and amazement. Two little girls were quarrelling about a doll, which one held in her hands, and which the other wanted, whilst their baby brother was seated on the floor, staring at thèm in silent astonishment. Their little eyes flashed with rage, and they looked quite ugly in their passion, as children always do look, and other people too, when they let their evil tempers get the better of them.

The mouse only stayed here for a moment, for no sensible creature, mouse or man, likes quarrelsome children ; and our little friend crept slowly away, thinking to himself how odd it was that big creatures like boys and girls, who have so much to be thankful for and to make them happy, should be so foolish as to fly into passions, and be cross, and quarrel with each other for really nothing at all. 'I am glad,' thought he to himself, 'that this is not the custom with us mice; and if it is so with many children, I really think that it is much better to be a mouse than a child.'

Then he pursued his journey to the next house, and crept into a room where all was very still and quiet, so still and so quiet, that he came out of the wainscot and on to the soft carpet of the room. The blinds were drawn down and there was but little light from the windows, but the rays of the moon crept in just sufficiently to shed a soft tender light into the room, by which the visitor could perceive a child's cot, placed near to a larger bed. There, in the cot, lay a little child whose spirit the good God had taken to Himself, so that it was only the body which lay there, cold and dead. The little eyes were closed to the sights of this world ; the small ears would no more hear the loving voices to which they had so often listened with childish interest and pleasure; the baby hands were cold and stiff as wax and there was only the casket which had held the jewel which the Father had taken to His own home in heaven. And as the little mouse softly advanced over the floor, he saw a lady dressed all in white with dark hair falling over her shoulders, and large eyes that were red with crying, come gently into the room and sit down upon the large bed and gaze earnestly upon the dead child. And her tears flowed again as she looked upon the little face which she had loved so well, and upon which never more for her might beam the light of life, never more be seen the sweet smile of trusting love, never more the tender, touching glance of confidence and safety which twines the little ones round the hearts of those to whom God has given them.

'Oh, my baby, my baby ! ' sobbed the poor mother, 'it is so hard to lose you, it is so hard to think of what you were to me, and what I am without you; your pretty playful ways, your loving little heart. Oh, when shall I forget you, and how can I bear this sorrow ?' And the poor mother wept again, and she kissed the pale, cold face, and then again she spoke and said, 'But I know that *you* are happy, my angel child. The good God who gave you to me has taken you back to Himself according to His own will and for His own good purpose, and He will give me strength to bear your loss, for only He can do so.' And still the poor mother wept, but softly and silently, and the little mouse was sad to see her sorrow. And as slowly and quietly he returned to the hole from which he had come out into the room, he thought in his heart that if even men and women had so much unhappiness to go through, he must not complain if to him and his fellow-mice the ways of the world were not always easy and comfortable.

On he went, with soft and stealthy tread, into the next house, and he peeped in upon a scene of a different character.

There was a mother, too, but she was not in sorrow. She was sitting up in her bed, and a sweet smile was upon her face, as her young children sat around her, some on the bed, and some in little chairs close to it, whilst she gave them their early reading of the Holy Book. She spoke to them of the great and good God who had made and who preserved them; she told them of the Saviour, who was once a child like themselves, upon His blessed mother's knee, who bade His apostles to 'suffer little children to come unto Him,' and who loves them still, and will love them to the end of time. And the dear little eyes looked up with quiet solemn interest into the mother's loving face, and the little ears drank in eagerly every word she spoke, and the little hearts received the good seed which the earthly parent sowed, in humble hope that the Heavenly blessing would water it and keep it alive in those hearts, to the children's eternal happiness.

And the mouse looked and listened; and though he could not understand all that he heard, yet he knew that it was something which it was well for the children to hear, and that to hear and know it was one of those privileges which raised human beings above creatures of his own kind. And he wondered what it could all mean, and wished he could know and understand it all;

and because he could not do so, he felt sad and sorrowful as he passed along to the next house and into another
room.

Here was something altogether different from anything which he had seen before. A large table was set
in the middle of the room, on which were lots of cups
and saucers, plates of bread and butter, and slices—large
slices, too—of cake, and a number of children all sitting
round just ready to begin. The mouse opened his eyes
wide at the sight, and felt as if he should like to be going
to begin too, for he was rather hungry, and the food
looked uncommonly good. It was a children's feast, that
was plain enough; and, to tell the truth, it was a birthday feast, and one little girl sat at the head of the table
with a crown of flowers on her head, to show that she
was the queen of the feast, for it was her birthday which
the other children had met to celebrate.

Happy faces were there to be seen, and cheerful
voices to be heard, and the mouse cast a wistful glance
upon all the good things which the little ones now
began to devour. Oh, it was a pleasant party, indeed,
and the sound of the children's merry laughter made
the mouse wish more than ever that he was a child instead of a mouse. As this, however, was impossible,
he had nothing for it but to make the best of matters
as they were, and accordingly determined to watch his
opportunity and try to get some small share of the feast
which the young ones seemed to be enjoying so much.
There was little chance for him for some time, for there
were several maids hurrying and bustling about, and
handing the tea and cake and bread and butter to the
children; and even if they had not seen the mouse, they
might possibly have stamped upon him by accident,

which would have been remarkably unpleasant.   So he
waited on and on, and presently the maids had finished
moving about, and the children had done eating, and
they got up from the table, after they had said their
grace, and some one proposed that they should have a
good game of play, and so they all began to get ready
for it.   Then the little mouse peeped out again, and put
his head and half his body out of the hole; and then,
as he saw that everybody was thinking of their own
business and not minding him (which was very natural,
inasmuch as none of them had seen him), he came
quite out, and sat still upon the carpet.   By this time
the children had all sat down in a circle, and began to
play at 'Hunt the slipper,' which took all their attention
away from everything else; and what was more, the
maids, instead of taking away the tea-things, which they
had just been about to do, stood watching the game, and
chatting and laughing as they did so.   Therefore the
table was left just as it was, and as all the people, big
and little, were at the side of it furthest from the mouse,
he thought he might as well steal out and try to get his
share of the good things.   So, very softly and slyly he
crept over the carpet till he reached the table, and seeing
a crumb of bread, commenced his dinner with that, and
ate it up in a moment.   Then, casting his eyes forward,
he saw, a little in front of him, a nice little bit of plum-
cake, which one of the children had dropped.   He lost
no time in approaching this, and found it so sweet and
good, that he began to nibble away as happily as possible, and thought of nothing else than the meal which
he really wanted so much.   Nibble, nibble, nibble went
the little mouse, enjoying himself quite as much as the
children had done, and in a very little while he would

have finished the cake as he had done the bread.   But, as ill luck would have it, before he had got above half through it, one of the maids turned away from the rest, and, coming back towards the table, prepared to take away some of the tea-cups.   As she came up, she happened to cast her eyes under the table and caught sight of our little friend at his feast.   She screamed out directly,—'A mouse, a mouse—ah! ah!' and seemed as if she was actually frightened at the sight, which was very foolish as well as unnecessary, for the little mouse had a great deal more reason to be frightened than she had, as she perfectly well knew, if she had given the matter a moment's thought.   However, she screamed out aloud, as I have already told you, and all the children jumped up directly and came running round, and the other maids came too, all in as much fuss and trouble as if it had been an alligator, or a camel-leopard, or a griffin, or a boa-constrictor, or a Red Indian, instead of a harmless, trembling little animal that could hurt nobody, and was frightened out of his wits at their noise and outcry.   So frightened, indeed, was the mouse that he quite forgot the way back to the hole from which he had come; and instead of running into it as fast as he could—which no doubt he would have done if he had remembered it—he darted up to the other end of the table at the top of his speed, and scurried along the wall, vainly searching for some hole in which to hide himself.

Meanwhile the maids and the children all kept saying first one thing and then another, as fast and as loud as they could speak, and such a noise as they made you never heard.   'Where's the cat?' said one of the maids.   'Where's the mouse?' said another.   'Oh, *do* catch the mouse for us!' said one child. 'Oh, yes,' said another, 'let us catch it quick before it gets into a hole.' 'Run and shut the door.' 'Look under the grate.' 'Ring for John.' 'Fetch Fido,' and all kind of remarks of a like nature they made; and two or three of the youngest children got together, and stood still, and opened their eyes as wide as ever they could, and asked each other what a mouse was like, and whether it was a beast or a bird, and whether it could bite or not?

The mouse, meanwhile, finding no hole or corner in which to hide, and being in a state of alarm, to imagine which one must fancy one's self in a wild animals' country, with all the wild animals running after one, and no place of escape open; the mouse, I say, began seriously to doubt whether he should ever come out of this business alive. There was, however, no time for doubting, for the maids and the children ran round, and came so close to him, that all he could do was to run under the fender, and crouch down, with his little heart beating as if it would burst.

'There he goes; I saw him,' cried one of the maids, and then the whole party gathered round the fender, and began to consult what was best to be done. One of the maids proposed that they should lift up the fender, and the others should stand round with the poker, shovel, and hearth-broom, so as all to make a dash at the enemy as soon as he should be seen. Another wanted everybody to be very quiet till the cat could be fetched, and another said that they had better all go away, and leave a trap with some toasted cheese, by which means the intruder might certainly be caught.

The mouse heard all these proposals as he lay

crouched down close under the fender, and hardly
knew which sounded the worst for his chance of escape.
At last some one of the party, in her eagerness, pushed
the fender, which disturbed and frightened our friend so
much, that he rushed out again, and ran along the wall
further on. Close up to the wall, but not so close as to
prevent the passage of a mouse, stood a black ebony
cabinet, not very big and not very heavy, and behind
this, between it and the wall, our mouse hid himself,
still trembling with excitement. Alas! it was no safe
hiding-place. Some of the people got on each side of
it, and found that they could see the mouse quite well,
and that he could not get out, either to the right or to
the left, without being in their sight and passing under
their very noses.

'Now we have got him!' they cried out, and
directly they popped down a napkin from the table
at each end of the cabinet, so that the poor mouse
could not possibly get out. Then they began to hold a
consultation as to what they should do next. One
maid said that if they tilted the cabinet back a little,
they could easily kill the mouse with a stick. Another
thought they could catch him in a napkin, and pop him
at once into a basin of water, whilst a third was for
bringing the cat up, and moving the cabinet so far as
to let her seize her victim easily. But while they discussed the matter in a manner which made the mouse's
blood run cold, one of the little girls came forward with
haste from among the rest, and spoke in an earnest
voice to the maids, whilst the tears stood in her blue
eyes.

'O 'Mima,' she said, 'you mustn't kill the mouse,
poor little fellow! I dare say he only wanted a teeny-

tiny share of the feast, because it was Eva's birthday. It would be a shame to kill him! Spare his little life, and let me have him to take care of.'

'Ah, I dare say!' answered another of the maids. That's just Miss Kate, all over. " Never kill the poor thing, but let me have it to make a pet of." No, no, my dear; nobody with sense in their heads ever makes a pet of a nasty little mouse. They're only meant to be killed; or if not, what's the use of having any cats?

But the other maid answered and said, ' And if it *is* just like Miss Kate, to my mind it's a very good thing to be like, and I don't see why she shouldn't have the mouse. For my part, I like to see young ladies kind to dumb animals, and why not a mouse as well as a bird or a cat, pray?'

Thus encouraged, Kate renewed her entreaties; and as all the children backed her up, and cried out with one voice, 'Kate shall have the mouse! Kate shall have the mouse!' the other maids had nothing for it but to give in, and so the matter was settled.

The next thing was, how to catch the little animal, but this was soon managed. Some one brought an old mouse-trap, and held up the lid, then they placed it at one end of the cabinet, close to the wall. They moved the cabinet a little, and pushed a stick gently from the further side until it touched the mouse, and when he darted to the other end, he ran straight into the trap, down they popped the lid, and there was the little captive safe and sound. The next few minutes were the most terrible of his life. There was a grating over his head and on each side, through which he could be seen; and all attempts to escape from the pry-

ing eyes which looked in upon him were vain. Up and
down, to and fro, he ran in his fright, and looked
about for a hole where no hole was to be found, expect-
ing he knew not what, and being quite bewildered.

Meanwhile all the children crowded round the trap,
which one of the maids held in her hand, and each
peered eagerly in, to see the little captive.

'Oh, look at his dear, bright little eyes!' said one.

'Just see how his tail keeps getting between the
bars of the trap!' cried another.

'What funny whiskers he has!' exclaimed a third,
and they all seemed delighted with their prize.

The maid held up the trap above their heads, when
she thought they had gazed sufficiently.

'Well,' she said, 'here we have him safe enough;
and now, Miss Kate, what are you going to do with
him? Your papa and mamma will never like you to
keep such a pet as this.'

'Oh yes,' answered the little girl, 'I think they
will, because they like me to be kind to animals; and,
then, I remember that Cousin Amy had a little pet of a
mouse once—two, I think there were—who used to
roll themselves up in cotton wool, which she put in their
box, and make a regular nest for themselves, and sleep
ever so long without waking.'

'Ah, yes,' answered another child, 'I remember
that, too; but I don't think Amy's mice were like this
one. They were of a lighter colour, and more sleepy-
looking.'

'La, Miss Eva,' said one of the maids, 'it is a dormouse Miss Kate means. Nice little quiet pets *they* are,
but this is quite a different sort of a creature. A little
restless, mischievous, common mouse is no more to

The Mouse Traveller.—P. 210.

compare with your dormouse than a crab apple with a china orange.'

'Never mind, 'Mima,' replied Kate; 'I'll risk it, anyhow, if mamma doesn't mind my trying.' And so, after a little more looking and wondering, the trap was put into Kate's hands, who carried it off in triumph to her mamma. The latter was rather astonished at the new pet which her little girl had found, and told her that she was afraid she would find it difficult to keep; however, as she had set her heart upon it, she would give her leave to try, and accordingly off marched Miss Kate, mouse in hand. The first thing to settle was, where the new pet should be kept. • The trap was very small and inconvenient, and Kate was sure he would never be happy there. She thought for a moment, and then, clapping her hands with joy, told the nurse-ry-maid that she should keep it in an old band-box which Chamberlain, her mamma's maid, had given her. But she was told that the sharp teeth of the mouse would very soon find their way through the band-box, and that some stronger place must be provided if she intended to keep the little prisoner safe. Kate was rather disappointed at finding that her plan would not do, but at once set to work thinking, and racked her brains to discover the best plan for securing her new pet. At last she hit upon a scheme which seemed to promise well. Her brother Ned had had given him a large box of tin soldiers: the box was thick and strong, with a sliding lid, on the top of which were painted the most extraordinary pictures of wonderful battles, full of cavalry and infantry soldiers charging, and firing, and fighting in a hand to hand manner, such as the world never saw. However, the lid fitted tight for all that, and there was plenty of room in the box for the mouse, which could have holes bored in the lid to give him air, and might be as happy as a king there if he could only make up his mind to be contented.

So into this box Mr Mouse was placed, and Kate put a quantity of bread crumbs in with him, so that there might be no chance of his starving. Then she went and told her papa, with great glee, all that had happened, and asked him what he thought of her plan. He listened to his little darling's story with interest, and told her how pleased he was that she had been kind and merciful, and had saved the poor mouse's life. But he also told her that he did not think that the little animal would thrive or be happy in that dark box, and that it was very doubtful whether he would eat anything whilst he was there. But whilst the father and daughter were talking over the matter, the poor little mouse was by no means happy.

On the contrary, he was as miserable a little wretch as had ever crept along inside a wainscot. He crawled round and round the box without finding a hole of any sort through which he might escape; he peeped up through the little air-holes which had been bored in the lid, but they were too small for him to be able to squeeze himself through, small as he was, and there was no other outlet whatever. He tried to gnaw the wood, but it was too hard—he only hurt his teeth; and, after looking about on every side, and finding that escape was impossible, he gave himself up to despair, and began to bemoan his sad fate in melancholy tones.

'Alas! alas!' he said to himself, for there was no one else to talk to, 'why was I beguiled, by the talk of those two gentlemen, to leave my quiet, happy home,

and go out on this unfortunate expedition? Why did I
want to travel? Why could not I be contented where
I was, instead of so foolishly going forth in search of
adventures? Oh my home, my home! there, at least, I
was always safe; and had I but been wise and sensible,
I might have lived on peaceably from day to day, and
died comfortably behind the wainscot when my time had
come. But now, what will become of me? I am in
the power of human beings, who are never to be trusted.
This little girl who spoke so kindly, and who was certainly the cause of my life being saved, may at any moment become tired of me; and, besides, how do I know
the reasons which make her keep me here? perhaps she
only keeps me—oh horrid idea!—to give me to some
favourite cat; perhaps she has put these crumbs in, that
I may eat and grow fat, so as to be plump and tender
when my poor little body is required for some mouse-
eating monster. Oh dear, oh dear! what shall I do?
what *will* become of me?'

And so the poor mouse went on, until he had not
the least bit of courage left in him, from the tip of his
nose to the end of his tail, and began really to feel that
it would be a mercy if some one would put him out of
his misery at once. What made it worse, too, was that,
being left on the floor of the nursery, he heard soft footsteps approaching, and presently a low purring sound,
which informed him of the presence of one of those terrible cats whom every well-conducted mouse hates, fears,
and abominates from the bottom of his heart.

Pussy came up to the box, smelt at it for a moment;
and having by this process discovered that there was a
mouse within, began to push the box about and to pat
the lid, as if she thought she could get him out, in which

case she would no doubt have very soon given a good
account of him.   But, fortunately for the mouse, the lid
was firm and did not move; and although the box
shook, and the voice of the cat frightened the little fellow so terribly that he thought he should have died then
and there, yet he was really quite safe; and after a little
while the cat discovered that this was the case, and accordingly moved off with an angry ' miaw,' and he heard
no more of her.   Eating, however, after this fright was
out of the question; and when Kate came to look, she
found the crumbs of bread untouched, and the mouse
crouching in a corner trembling all over and looking
utterly miserable.   She spoke kindly to him, but it
was of no use; she put a little water into the box in a
doll's teacup, but he would not touch it, and she did
not know what to do.   So she got a little toasted cheese
and put it in the box, and then she closed the lid again,
and left Mr Mouse for the night.   A long, sad, dreary
night it was for him; for while Katie was sleeping sound
as a top, and dreaming of her pony and her little white
dog, and all kinds of pleasant things, the poor new pet
never closed his eyes, but sat shivering and trembling,
thinking of his past and happy days, wishing himself
home again, and starting with fear at every sound he
heard.   So he was not very comfortable or happy, as
you may suppose; and when Kate came again early in
the morning, she found him looking utterly wretched,
with none of his food touched, and his eyes peering up
at her with a sad, wistful expression which went at once
to her heart.

    ' Poor little fellow!' she exclaimed, ' so you won't
eat and be tame.   I am afraid you will die if you don't
eat.   I wonder if I can tame you and make you take

some of your food? I wish I knew how.' And then she
went and asked the maids, but they didn't know any
more than she did; and then she went to her papa's
study, and asked him his advice upon the matter.

'Well, my darling,' he said, 'since you ask me, I
will tell you what I think at once. These wild animals
can hardly ever be made tame unless you catch them
when they are very, very young, which is difficult in the
case of a mouse. If you keep your pet in the box,
I am afraid you will find that nothing will make him
eat, and in a day or two he will starve himself to death.
If you want to be really kind to the poor little fellow,
the only way is to turn him loose in the room where
you caught him, and let him find his own way back to
his home and his friends!'

Kate's blue eyes filled with tears at first, for she had
set her heart on making the little mouse quite tame, and
she didn't like the thoughts of losing her new pet. But
she knew that her papa was sure to be right; and she
would have been very sorry if the poor little mouse had
starved itself, and died in the box, which would probably have been the case if he had been kept there
another day. So she gave a little sigh, and then determined that she would do what was most kind to the
prisoner. She took the box, and went with it to the
room where they had had the tea-party, with nobody
with her but her little sister. Then she said to the
mouse, 'You poor little fellow, I am determined that
you shall not die if I can help it. I am going to let you
loose, so that you may run back to all your mouse
friends and relations, and play about and be as happy
as ever.' Then Kate put the box down upon the floor,
and took off the lid. The mouse was too frightened

and weak to move at first; but presently he ran up the side of the box, and hopped on to the carpet. Meanwhile the children stood quite quiet, watching what would happen. The little mouse did not at first know where he was; but as nobody chased and confused him, he had time to collect his scattered ideas, and presently remembered all about it.

Casting his keen, black eyes about, he saw the corner of the room from which he had come into it through the hole in the wainscot, and he ran off in that direction as fast as his legs would carry him. The little girls clapped their hands with joy, as they saw him run off.

'There,' cried Kate, 'the little thing is quite safe and happy now!' and she ran off to tell her papa and mamma.

You may well imagine that Mr Mouse was right glad to be free again, and safe and sound behind the wainscot. He made the best of his way back to his old home without any delay; and squeaked with delight when he found himself once more in the house from which he had started.

'Well,' said he to himself, 'travelling may be all very well for those who can afford it; but for my part, I think the danger is greater than the pleasure. Besides, we all of us have duties to perform at home; and although it is doubtless a good thing to gain experience by going out into the world, still it is better and wiser not to neglect our duties, and home is the best place after all for a well-behaved mouse. So now that I know something of what goes on outside in the gay world, I will rest satisfied with the knowledge I have already gained, and remain where I know that I am well off,

as well as safe from the dangers which I have so fortunately escaped this time. Home for me henceforward,
and let those travel who like it.'

True to his word, the little mouse always stayed at
home after that famous journey. Nothing could tempt
him to leave the old house in which he had been born;
and although his travelled friends often laughed at him
for being such a 'stay-at-home' fellow, he only winked
his eye knowingly at them, and kept on in the usua!
habits of his every-day homely life, which he was still
living and enjoying when I last heard of him.

VI.

THE WITCH OF BROOKE HOLLOW.

PART I.

In the good old days—I don't know exactly their date, but it comes to the same thing—in the good old days, when there were no railroads, nor, for the matter of that, turnpike roads either, and when the best highways were but bad, and people moved about so little from place to place that any one who had been twenty miles away from home was thought to have seen a good deal of the world, and a person who had ever been to London was accounted a mighty traveller indeed; in those happy times when the penny post had never been dreamed of, and if it had been in full work, so very few people knew how to write, that there would have been light work indeed for the postman, witches and wizards flourished in great abundance, and the famous witch of Brooke Hollow was one of the foremost among them all.

Everybody knows Brooke Hollow, who has ever walked from Wye by the road under the hill which joins the old Stone-street road above Horton Park. A couple of miles or so from Wye the hill seems as if somebody had cut a huge slice out of it just like a thick wedge of bread cut out of a loaf by a very hungry school-boy. Exactly like the great hole which would thus be left in the loaf, a deep ravine runs back into the hill, which at the present time is entirely grass at the top, bottom, and sides—a pretty green valley forming a break in the otherwise uninterrupted line of chalk hills which are called the ' Backbone of Kent.'

But in these good old times of which we are now talking, this ravine was a rough, wild place,—rough with tangled brakes, briars, and brambles; wild with scraggy bushes and stunted trees, and only to be traversed by narrow little paths which seemed as if they had been made by wild animals creeping to their hiding-places, and perfectly impassable for any crinoline-wearing mortal, or indeed for any one at all who had much respect for his or her dress.

This was Brooke Hollow in the olden time, and never was there such a place for a witch to choose for her home ! In fact, any elderly lady who had taken up her abode in such a queer locality would have been set down for a witch at once, for no one who was not either a witch or stark staring mad would have dreamed of living there. Small blame to the good people, therefore, who declared that old Goody Stickels was a witch and nothing but a witch, and who never went nearer Brooke Hollow than they could help, but hurried past it as fast as possible whenever they had occasion to travel upon the road of which I have spoken.

And there were more reasons than the mere fact of her living in Brooke Hollow which proved old Goody Stickels to have something strange about her. Had not Tom Tickner, the crafty ' higgler' of Brabourne, been terrified out of his wits one Saturday evening when driving home over the Leese, by the sight of several old women on broomsticks flying through the air, in one of whom he declared that he distinctly recognized the features of old Goody Stickels? It was a very rough, windy night, and branches of trees, and straw, and leaves, and everything that the wind could get hold of, were whirling about in the keen blast which howled over the common, but Tom had fortified himself with several strong glasses of good stuff at the 'Five Bells,' so that he had his eyes open, and vowed that he could not have been mistaken. Then Sam Hankey had sneered at the old dame and threatened her with the stocks, and had not his lambs died in a most unaccountable manner that spring? Nothing seemed to suit them and nothing could save them, so it was plain enough that the witch had been at work, and that all this came of having offended her. True it is that Sam laid it all to the foxes, and revenged himself by trapping these animals whenever he had a chance, but he must have known better in reality.

Goody Stickels lived in a kind of mud cabin, hardly to be called a cottage, in Brooke Hollow. There was no road up to it, and nobody knew when or how it was built; you could only get to it by means of one of the narrow paths which I have already mentioned; and when you found it out with difficulty, it was harder still to find the door; and, in fact, such was the general terror of the place and its owner, that very few people ever tried to find either one or the other.

Of course Goody Stickels had a cat, or else she couldn't have been a witch; all witches have cats, which are generally black, and have larger eyes than ordinary cats. This particular cat fell short in nothing; she was, if possible, blacker, and her eyes larger, than common witch-cats, and she was generally seen with her mistress whenever the latter went out. You may well believe that the witch and her cat formed a frequent subject of conversation among the good people about that neighbourhood, and many an evening had they been talked over at the alehouse, till all the strong ale couldn't prevent the stoutest heart from trembling as the tales were told of the wonderful doings of Goody Stickels and her cat.

This was the state of things when, on one notable evening in May, Giles Butcher wended his way homeward to Brooke from his work in West wood. Giles had been engaged hedge-making, and as the distance from his home was long, he used to start on the Monday morning, and seldom return before Saturday afternoon, lodging meanwhile at the 'Half-way house' on the Stone-street road. This week, however, for some reason or another, he had left work on Thursday, and started for his cottage at Brooke. The evening was as windy an evening as Giles ever recollected. He managed well enough whilst he was in the lanes, with high banks and hedges on each side of him, but when he came out on Brabourne Down it was a difficult matter for him to keep his legs. The wind howled over the Down with great violence, and seemed determined to have its own way, and sweep everything before it. Heavy, black clouds followed one another in quick succession across the rapidly-darkening sky, and the moon seemed to struggle in vain to throw a ray of her softening light upon the dreary world below. Giles wrapped his gabardine tightly round him, and bore

himself bravely against the wind, until, breathless and
fatigued, he reached the edge of the Down, and descended the hill into the Wye road.   Here, though the
wind still whistled and raged around, it had less power
over him, and he pushed on towards Brooke with the
comfortable feeling that every moment was bringing
him nearer to his warm fireside, and the pleasant
greeting with which his worthy wife would certainly
receive him.   No doubt the kettle would be singing
merrily on the fire, and the table would be all ready
laid, and a good meal and a friendly pipe would soon
make him forget all the troubles of the road, and the
assaults of the windy weather.   With such thoughts in
his mind Giles trudged steadily forward, until he
reached the mouth of Brooke Hollow, which was barely
a quarter of a mile from the turning from the main
road which led to his own cottage.   Just as he came to
the mouth of the Hollow, a stronger and keener blast of
wind seemed to pierce through and through him, and
loosened the gabardine which he had folded so closely
around him.   He stopped for an instant to make it more
secure, and in so doing could not avoid casting his eyes
up the Hollow, when a sight greeted them which filled
him with mingled astonishment and alarm.   Seated
upon a large three-legged stool, such as dairy-maids are,
or were, wont to use in carrying on their profession,
with her legs tucked under her, Turkish-fashion, and
her arms crossed over her breast, sat no less a personage
than Goody Stickels.   She had an ordinary, or extraordinary, old bonnet upon her head, and a tattered red
cloak over her shoulders, but neither did the one blow
off nor did the other appear to be affected by the
weather, by which the old lady herself seemed to be

entirely undisturbed.   Indeed, for the matter of that, it might as well have been the warmest and most pleasant summer's evening, as far as she was concerned, for she had a short pipe in her mouth, and sat there smoking away, and enjoying it, too, as thoroughly as possible, whilst her black cat sat upright by her side, as comfortable and contented as if it had been dozing upon the hearth-rug opposite to a blazing fire.   And at the moment when Giles cast his eyes upon the old lady and her companion, she, too, cast her eyes upon him, and, taking her pipe out of her mouth, called out to him, in a voice deep as a man's and hoarse as a raven's—

'Giles Butcher!'

Now, Giles had heard many tales of the witch of Brooke Hollow; and being a steady, sober man, and withal first cousin to the parish clerk, had thought it best to keep his distance, and to avoid meeting one of whom so much evil was whispered.   So when he heard himself thus familiarly addressed by the old dame, his first thought and desire was to hurry on and take no notice of her greeting.   Being, however, naturally of a civil disposition, and, moreover, not feeling sure of the extent of her power to stop him if he made a run for it, he changed his first intention, and, keeping hat and gabardine on as well as he could, faced the Hollow boldly, and replied, 'Here I be, mum; did you speak to I?'

'Giles Butcher!' again exclaimed the old dame in the same tone of voice as before; 'whither away so fast on this pleasant eve?'

'Home, mum, home,' answered honest Giles, 'and that as fast as I can; but as to a pleasant eve, 'tis rather too windy for me, let alone the rain.'

'Not a bit of it, Giles,' responded the dame; ''tis a fine night for broomsticks. Did'st ever ride on a broomstick, Giles?'

'No, mum, no, and don't want to, thankye kindly,' said the now half-frightened Giles. 'Good-night to ye, Dame Stickels, good-night;' and began to make as though he would hurry on.

'Stay a bit, Giles Butcher; stay a bit, hasty man,' said the old woman. 'Thy kettle does not boil at home yet, for thy wife overset it half an hour ago, and had to fill it again. There is no hurry for thee, and I would fain have a chat. Come into the Hollow. Choose a broomstick, and go out with me to see the world, worthy Giles.' And as she spoke the old dame smiled a peculiar smile at Giles; and the cat seemed to him to swell to an unnatural size, and its eyes glared like red-hot coals. Giles felt his heart sinking down into his boots, and trembled violently. He feared to say yes, and he didn't dare to say no, and altogether he felt particularly uncomfortable. However, some power beyond his own seemed to compel him to take a step forward in the direction of the Hollow; and, sorely against his will, he found himself drawing nearer and nearer to the spot where sat the dreaded witch, if witch she was. Still she smiled upon him in a friendly manner until he had almost reached her seat, and then she drew from behind her several broomsticks which she had hitherto kept concealed. 'Here, worthy Giles,' said she, 'take your choice of these good steeds, and then we'll be off.'

Giles was never so frightened in his life, and rather puzzled, too, at hearing broomsticks called 'steeds;' but he couldn't help himself, and dared not offend the old lady by refusing or hesitating. So, without more ado, he held out his hand and took hold of one of the broom-sticks, shivering and shaking with fright as he did so.

'Get astride of it, good Giles, get astride of it,' said the witch, and clumsily and with difficulty (for Giles was no horseman) he followed her directions. Dame Stickels did the same upon another broomstick, and her cat leapt up and sat on her shoulder. Then occurred a strange and an alarming event. The witch—for that she *was* a witch it was impossible to doubt any longer—muttered some words which Giles could not exactly make out, but which his broomstick probably both heard and un-derstood, since they produced the same marvellous effect upon it as upon that which Goody Stickels bestrode. All of a sudden up into the air flew the broomsticks with their riders. Giles strove to cry out, but his tongue clove to the roof of his mouth with terror, and his voice failed him altogether. You would have thought that he *must* have tumbled off, but somehow or other he kept his balance in the most extraordinary manner, and was by no means so much troubled with giddiness as you might have supposed.

'Away, away!' shouted the old dame as they rushed through the air, mounting higher and higher each moment. 'Merry work to-night, Giles Butcher. Fine fun this, my man; better than trudging through the mud and wet. Forward we go!' and she gave a wild chuckle as she looked back at Giles's broomstick, which was apparently doing its best to keep up with her. Giles made no reply, for the reason that, as I have told you, he was unable to speak; but he certainly did not feel the same delight which appeared to possess his companion, inasmuch as he had the greatest doubt both as to the security of his present position and as to the

15

manner in which the business would end. On they
went, however, with the wind whistling round them,
and the rain beating wildly in their faces. Goody
Stickels' grey locks streamed out behind her, thin as
they were, and the hair of the cat appeared to Giles to
stand upon its back longer and stiffer than the hair of
mortal cat had ever stood before. At last, after a brisk
ride of twenty minutes or so, they descended upon the
top of a hill, which, when Giles had stared round him
for a minute and recovered his scattered senses, he made
out to be a part of the same Backbone of Kent, which I
have mentioned before, and as he looked a little closer
he found that it was part of the Downs which belonged
to the very Sam Hankey whom I have spoken of as a
particular enemy of the old witch. Here there was a
field of growing wheat upon the side hill, at the top of
which a stake and bind fence separated the field from a
large meadow in which a number of sheep were grazing.
There was a small hollow cleft in the midst of the aforesaid arable field, probably an old chalk-pit, in which
nothing grew save rough grass and brambles, between
which was a clear open space sufficiently large to admit
of a dozen or more people being gathered together in it.
Down into this hollow flew Goody Stickels, closely followed by her unwilling attendant, and in this open space
they both alighted. But they were not alone. Three more
old women were there before them, each of whom appeared
to Giles Butcher's terrified eyes more grim and horrible
than the other. One had only one eye, and winked
wickedly and incessantly with the other. Another had
an enormous nose, hooked like a falcon's beak, and
bright scarlet at the tip ; whilst the third had a mouth
big enough to swallow a moderate-sized baby, and teeth

the sight of which made you devoutly thankful that *you* were not a baby of moderate size.   It was by no means a pleasant or reassuring sight to Giles to see this select party awaiting his arrival.   They, however, seemed to take a different view of the case, for they burst out in a chorus of welcome as Goody Stickels and Giles lighted down in the midst of them.

'Here you are, dame,' said the one-eyed lady, with a fearful wink. 'Rather late, but ever welcome.'

'Ay, ay, here we are, croaking Jenny,' said Goody Stickels, 'me and my mate, you see, me and my mate.' And the whole party set up a shrill laugh, which made Giles's blood run cold.   He observed that three broomsticks, one for each of the other witches, were laid in a row behind them, and dame Stickels having deposited hers in the row also, Giles, seeing nothing better to do, did the same with his.   Down sat his companion, and, as she gave him a hearty push at the same time, down sat Giles, hardly knowing what he was about, and, as you may suppose, in about as big a fright as mortal man could be. Then he noticed for the first time a huge black pot or kettle in the circle round which the four witches were seated, and his mind instantly became filled with wonder as to what could be in it.   It was not long, however, before his curiosity was gratified, and that, too, in a manner more pleasant than he had anticipated.   For though honest Giles did not believe in all the curious and somewhat disagreeable stories of the food upon which witches love to feast, and in all probability had never turned his attention very seriously to the subject, still he had a kind of idea that they were very likely to eat something different from the food of which the meals of ordinary mortals are composed, and moreover he was not very con-

fident that there was any food at all in the pot.   Perhaps it was some mysterious and awful charm which
they were about to work; perhaps it was some strange
ceremony which they meant to perform; perhaps, even,
it might have something to do with himself and his
fate, and he might be called upon to play some extraordinary part, if indeed he escaped being himself cooked
and served up as a repast for his wonderful companions.
But all these visions were dispelled when Goody Stickels,
snatching off the lid of the pot, caused a most savoury
perfume to issue forth, which told Giles more plainly
than words could speak that meat—ay, and good meat
too—was contained therein.   Giles saw no fire, but the
pot was hot, and so was the meat; and to his dying
day he was ready to declare that the jugged hare (if
hare it was) of which he then and there partook, made
the most delicious dish which was ever set before him
in the whole course of his life.   With chuckles of joy
the old women fell upon the savoury mess, and dame
Stickels told Giles to take his share and welcome.   He
needed no second invitation, but attacked the pot like
a man; and when each old woman produced a wooden
plate and a knife and fork, he was by no means surprised that they handed over to him the like things, and
accordingly made the best of his opportunities then and
there.   When they had all eaten heartily for a few
minutes, the witch with the nose, whom the others
accosted as dame Lovelamb, pulled out a huge stone
pitcher, at which she took a long pull and handed it to
her neighbour, who in turn passed it on.   Nothing
loth, Giles took his share when his turn came, and to
his great delight found that the contents of the pitcher
were nothing more nor less than gin, ay, and strong

gin, too.   Little by little honest Giles lost all sense of
alarm; indeed, he began to feel warm and jolly, and to
fancy that the witches looked quite young and beautiful,
though in reality you might have looked long and far
before you would have met four such uncommonly ugly
old bodies as those four dames.   I had almost forgotten
to tell you that behind each dame, sober as a judge,
sat her own particular cat—black, white, tabby, and
tortoise-shell; there was one of each; and the only
odd thing that Giles remarked was that they kept their
large eyes very open all the time, and every now and
then burst out into a strange kind of laugh when any of
their mistresses said anything more funny than usual.
At last up jumped Goody Stickels and cried out, ' Now,
my sisters, the hour is come; don't let us forget our
business in pleasure.'

Giles did not know what was about to happen, but
backed a little out of the circle, thinking, perhaps, that
it didn't concern him.   But, to his surprise, Dame
Stickels seized tight hold of one of his hands, croaking
Jenny took the other; the two remaining witches also
joined hands, and very slowly they began to dance
round the circle, in the centre of which stood the pot.
And as they danced, Dame Stickels, in slow and
measured tone, sang the following weird words :—

> ' Sisters three of Brabourne Down,
>   When the storm-wind whistles shrill,
>   By the aid of simple clown
>   We can work our magic will.

> ' We will work as work we can,
>   By the potent spell and charm ;
>   But to injure mortal man
>   Seek we aid from mortal arm.

' On the storm and on the blast,
    With our broomsticks hither bound,
  Through the air we've hurried fast
    To th' appointed magic ground.

' Here is our appointed work,
    Here our new ally we know ;
  Let him not the office shirk,
    To annoy the witch's foe.'

And as she sung, the whole party moved faster and faster round the circle, till they all lost their balance, and came down in a heap together. Up again they were, however, in a moment, and then Giles found himself led up the hill between the same two who had previously held him by the hands, whilst the other two witches followed. But, strangest of all, each of the cats shouldered a broomstick. Dame Stickels' cat, being the largest and strongest of the lot, took two broomsticks, one on each shoulder ; and, thus armed, they all walked on their hind legs before their mistresses, until they came to the top of the hill, and to the fence which separated the two fields. When they came there the four witches surrounded Giles, and, looking earnestly into his face as they did so, all exclaimed, in one voice :—

' Butcher, Butcher, man of sense,
    Go, demolish Hankey's fence ;
  So shalt thou deal heavy blow
    To the witch's hateful foe.'

And as they spoke, Giles felt himself compelled to attack the stake and bind fence with all his might. He pulled up the stakes, he tore away the sides of the fence, and went at the work with such good will that

before long a considerable length of it was entirely
destroyed, and there was nothing to prevent the sheep
from getting into the arable field, trampling over the
crops, and eating the young wheat.   Nor was this the
only means which the witches took to carry out their
will.   Giles found time, during his labours, to observe
that the five broomsticks, having been placed upright
on the ground by the cats, moved off quickly by themselves into the grass-field, and, spreading themselves
widely over it, began to surround the sheep, and drive
the frightened animals through the broken fence into
the arable field, where they might do all the mischief
that was possible.   Meanwhile the witches and the
cats danced merrily around Giles, whilst he was engaged in his work, and chuckled and yelled with
laughter as they did so.   I cannot tell you—for Giles
never could tell—how long this strange scene lasted;
all Giles recollected afterwards was that, all of a sudden,
croaking Jenny exclaimed, in a hoarse voice,—'Time's
up, sisters; time's up; mount and scurry, mount and
scurry'—and that, within a moment or two afterwards,
he saw the four old hags, each on her broomstick,
rising into the air, waving their hands towards him in
a jeering manner; and that, to his great disgust, he
perceived that Dame Stickels held in her hand the
extra broomstick which had served him for a steed in
his wonderful ride.   He remembered nothing more
until he was awakened from a sound sleep by a thun-
dering kick in the side.   'Get up, you audacious
vagabond!' exclaimed a voice at the same time.   'You
drunken brute, you!   So it's you who have been breaking down my fence, and letting the sheep into the
wheat!   I'll have the law of you for it, though, I can

tell you! You shall smart for this, Master Butcher!'

Looking up, and rubbing his eyes with astonishment, Giles saw that he was in the hands of Sam Hankey the farmer, whose property had been so wantonly damaged; and what to say or do he didn't know, so he scrambled up as well as he could, and looked pretty foolish, as you may well imagine.

'Twarn't me, sir—' he began to say, but Hankey cut him short directly.

'Not you, you rascal!' he replied. 'Why, here you are caught in the act, as one may say—what's the good of denying of it?' and he shook his fist in a threatening manner at the trembling Giles, as he continued— 'Hanging's too good for such thieves as you, but you shall have a grind at the mill for this, never fear,' and seizing Butcher by the collar of his coat, he lugged him along in the direction of his house, which stood some half a mile beyond the fence, on the hill. When he arrived there, he ordered a horse to be put into his cart at once, and terrified Butcher out of his life by declaring that he should drive him down to Scott's Hall, and see what Sir Edward would say to him.

Now Sir Edward Scott was in the eyes of Giles a very mighty and much-to-be-dreaded personage. A great deal of the country belonged to him. His were the fair manors of Brabourne, Hall, Evegate, and many more; his vast estates comprised the parishes of Brabourne, Horton, Smeeth, Aldington, Bircholt, and other neighbouring parishes; his park was the largest in the county, and the name of the owner of Scott's Hall was known and respected far and wide. A wise and a just man was Sir Edward reputed, and withal no friend to witches and wizards, but would he believe Giles's story,

and understand that he was really blameless in the
matter of Hankey's hedge? There was the hedge destroyed and the mischief done, there was Giles caught
upon the spot, and Sir Edward was not the man to
pass over such an offence as the wanton, useless destruction of property. No! Giles felt perfectly sure
that the stocks, at least, if not imprisonment in the
county gaol, awaited him if he were once brought into
the awful presence of Sir Edward. Therefore he
begged Hankey to forgive him this once, and vowed
he would never be found upon his land again, witch or
no witch, if he would only do so.

But the angry farmer was not to be turned from his
purpose. 'Let you off!' he exclaimed. 'Just catch me
being such a flat as that! No, no, my man. I've
suffered too much before to-day. Don't talk to me
about witches! I'll witch you away to Sir Edward,
and you may persuade him if you can.'

So saying, the worthy farmer had his horse har-
nessed to the cart, ordered Giles into it, and drove off
towards Scott's Hall. Slowly they descended the rough
cart track which led down the hill, and reached the
road from Wye which, as has been before mentioned,
skirts the bottom of the hill. It is not a first-rate road
now-a-days, but it was worse at the time of which I am
writing, and Sam Hankey could only drive slowly. He
turned towards Wye, and after a hundred yards or so
reached the lane which leads down to Bull town farm,
which he had to pass, and then, following the road
which wound in a zigzag fashion through the pleasant
grass meadows of West Brabourne, he would come out
upon Brabourne Leese and pick his way across that
large and barren common until he reached the gates of

Scott's Hall. This was his way and this was his plan, but he little knew what was before him.

First of all, as he turned the corner down to Bull town, snap! one of the traces broke, and master Sam had to get out and splice it up as well as he could, muttering to himself all the time that the traces were lately new and 'hadn't ought to have broken that like.' He mounted again and drove steadily along until he came opposite Bull town house. Now, the farm-yard sloped down from the house to the road, from which it was divided by a low stone wall. Just as Farmer Hankey got opposite this wall, up upon it there suddenly leaped a large black cat, so close to the horse's head, and so unexpectedly, that no horse in the world could have stood it. Old Dobbin, as Hankey's horse was named, was as quiet, sober-minded, respectable an animal as any in the county of Kent, but this was a little too much even for *him*. He shied violently, and in spite of all his master's attempts, ran away down the road as fast as he could go. 'Wo-woah-wo-ah-wo!' shouted Hankey, tugging hard at the reins meanwhile, but the horse seemed mad with terror, and dashed on down the lane, throwing the mud on all sides, and jolting the travellers far more than was pleasant or agreeable. This state of things could not last long, of course, but it came to an end in a manner peculiarly disagreeable to Farmer Hankey. A few hundred yards down the road were a number of his own lambs, some of the survivors of the flock, which were being driven off to Ashford market. Now, lambs are not easy things to pass at the best of times where the lane is narrow and the road only fit to

travel on in the middle, but to pass them with a run-
away horse is next to impossible. Dobbin, however,
did not seem to think so, and he rushed bang into the
midst of the drove, scattering them here and there,
breaking limbs and bruising bodies, and doing his master as much mischief as he well could, until, a lamb
having fallen exactly under his nose, he stumbled over
the poor creature, came smack down on his knees, both
of which he broke in the fall upon the road (which had
been recently mended with sharp flints at that particular spot), and sent the Farmer and Giles both flying into
the air, from which they descended with some force
into the road.   Fortunately for both of them, the
crowd of lambs somewhat broke their fall, and the
worst personal consequences which they experienced
consisted in a few bruises and a good shaking. Up
jumped Farmer Hankey in a tremendous passion.
' Confound the cat ! ' he shouted, and proceeded to use
language more strong than polite towards the cat, the
horse, the lambs, the road, and Giles Butcher into the
bargain, when a low laugh very near to him caused
him to turn his head in the direction from whence it
appeared to come.

The accident had happened at the corner of Cadman wood, just opposite to the stile into Cadman
meadow, and upon that stile, with a wicked smile upon
her face, her old bonnet cocked in roguish fashion on
one side, and her red cloak over her shoulders, who
should be sitting but Goody Stickels !

' Ha, ha ! ' she laughed, as the angry farmer turned
round and faced her.   ' I never seed such a sight in my
life !   Sam Hankey driving over his own lambs and

throwing down his good horse! Merry deeds, Sam; merry deeds, Giles! Ha! ha!'

The farmer was made more furious than ever by her conduct, and burst out into exclamations by no means of a flattering nature towards the old lady.

'You wrinkled old wretch!' he said, 'I believe you are at the bottom of the whole business. Dash my wig if I don't! Such things as these don't happen of themselves. Pretty times these are, when an honest man is to be troubled by such as you! But if you *have* been the cause of my troubles, look out for yourself, Mrs Stickels. Take care of the horse-pond. We won't have no witches here, not if we know it. Let's see what Sir Edward will say to it'—and he only stopped because he was out of breath with rage.

But the old dame chuckled again, and then said in a very quiet tone. 'Never give way to temper, Sam.'

This enraged the man more, and he made a step towards the stile, when suddenly out of the corner of the wood sprang a huge black cat, suspiciously like that which had just been the ruin of Dobbin, and planted itself between him and Dame Stickels, setting up its back and spitting violently at the same time. Sam Hankey stepped back at once, and at that moment caught sight of Giles Butcher slinking away along the road-side hedge. For Giles, who had made no resistance at his first capture, nor during the drive down the hill, had now begun to think that he might as well be off, for he didn't see any fun in keeping in the farmer's company longer than he could help. So he was slipping away by the side of the hedge when Hankey saw him, and shouted loudly, 'Stop, you thief; stop, I tell

Flight of Dame Stickels with Giles Butcher.—P. 237.

you. You're not going to get off like that,' and leaving
the driver to look after the lambs, Dobbin, and the cart,
as well as he could, Farmer Hankey set off in pursuit of
Giles. The latter got as far as the gate into Cadman
meadow, some hundred yards from the stile by the
wood, and then turned in to take a short cut to Brooke
across the fields. But the farmer was so close to him
that I think he would scarcely have escaped if, all of a
sudden, assistance had not arrived. With a speed beyond her years, Dame Stickels ran up, and called loudly,
' Follow me, Giles Butcher ; come along, my man.'

Puzzled and frightened, but being upon the whole
more afraid of the farmer than of the old woman, Giles
followed, and the two rushed into the nine-acres hop-
garden, with Sam Hankey in hot pursuit. What was
Giles Butcher's surprise, however, as soon as he had
entered the hop-garden, to perceive two broomsticks
standing upright in the ground immediately before
him.

Dame Stickels seized one of these immediately, and
handed Giles the other, exclaiming as she did so, ' Now,
Giles, my boy, do as I do. Mount and scurry, mount
and scurry,' and before he knew where he was, Giles,
obeying her orders from very fear, and repeating the
words after her, flew up into the air not half-a-dozen
yards before the nose of the astounded farmer. He,
worthy man, rushed forward for a few yards, as he saw
his prey escaping, and the witch snapping her fingers at
him and laughing in a shrill tone as she went off. But
the late rains had made the hop-garden heavy, and the
farmer found himself sinking deeper at every step. So
he walked slowly and sulkily back to the road, his
astonishment being overcome by his rage at the loss

which he had suffered, and at the escape of his enemies. He found that thirteen of his lambs had been more or less seriously injured, some of which were past help, but some might recover with timely care and attention. He therefore resolved to return home with these at once, which he did, as Dobbin's broken knees did not prevent his drawing the cart back, and the poor horse was quiet enough now. Home went Farmer Hankey, therefore, and told to his family all the adventures of the morning.

' The matter shall not rest here,' he said. ' It is not to be endured that one's hedges should be broken, one's crops injured, and one's lambs hurt, because an old hag of a witch chooses to spite one. To Sir Edward Scott will I go, and that before the world is a day older.'

His wife could not oppose him, and, in fact, Sam was a man who liked to have his own way in his own household, but the next question was how to get to Scott's Hall. This, however, was soon settled. Dobbin could not go out again, that was clear, but Mildew the pony, on which Hankey usually rode about his farm, would carry him down to Smeeth safe enough, and to Smeeth he would go immediately after dinner. So he dined with such appetite as the morning's bad luck had left him, and then he mounted Mildew and off he went. He did not follow the same road as before, for there was a shorter way to ride, across the down where the fence had been destroyed on the previous night, and so into and across the Wye road, down Coombe Lane, past Coombe wood, and through the meadows away to Brabourne Leese. Fresh and green looked the hedges, and the beautiful timber of which Brabourne Coombe could then boast formed quite a feature in the country, as you left the chalk hills and rode through

the lanes towards the good land of the pleasant vale.
And the sun was shining brightly, and the birds were
singing merrily as Farmer Hankey rode down the lane
and through the meadows, and came out upon Brabourne Leese. It was a wild, dreary place in those
days. Drains were unknown and enclosures never
thought of. So, instead of square fields, and prim fences,
and hard roads, and everything turned to the best
account, so that corn might be grown and rent paid for
the land, you had the wide open commons over which
the free air of heaven blew unchecked, and gorse-bushes,
and broom, and fern, with here and there a wild thorn-
tree, and plenty of brambles and briars, met your eye
in every direction. Every poor man in the place might
turn his cow or his donkey out upon the common, and
some, who had no good substantial cottage of their
own to live in, had run up mud hovels on the Leese, and
dwelt there, making the best of matters, and feeling
free of all the world. I don't know that these people
were all of the very best description of character, and I
fancy these wild open tracts of country were a great
boon to the gipsies and other roving gentry, who pre-
ferred living upon what they could get of other people's
property to earning their own living by hard work.
But they were places pleasant to the eye, and made a
man feel that there was something free and wild in the
country, which was delightful by its very contrast to the
prim, formal life of more civilized places and people.
There was not much of a road across Brabourne Leese
at the time I speak of—deep ruts and rough ground
made it bad travelling, but Mildew was sure-footed, and
the farmer knew the country well, so he picked his way
across the Leese without much trouble on that fine day,

passed the warren-house, where the Scott's Hall warrener kept watch and guard over the rabbits which
abounded in the place, and rode up to the gate which
led into the park itself. The common came quite close
up to the park, and the lodge-house was but a little distance from the warren. Through the lodge-house gate
rode Farmer Hankey, and came to the edge of the hill
which overlooked the lovely park of Scott's Hall. The
sight which met his eyes was one well suited for the
subject of a painter's art. The green hill sloped down
to a sparkling trout-stream which wound through the
valley below, supplied from the spring which, rising in
the spacious shrubberies upon the right, filled first
several skilfully planned fish-ponds at the edge of the
said shrubberries, and then sent its fresh clear water
gliding into the stream, winding and twisting about in
the fertile meadow land of which that part of the park
was formed. You could see the shrubberies from the
hill—they were at some little distance from the house,
and very beautiful they were; grass walks being cut by
the side of the fish-ponds away through the shrubs, and
stretching away northwards in the direction of the warren and lodge-house; whilst a magnificent avenue of
oak, elm, ash, sycamore, and other trees mingled together, led from the shrubbery to the house. Here was
the favourite pleasure-ground of the ladies of the house,
and 'Lady Scott's walk' was well-known to all the
neighbourhood. But Farmer Hankey, though he could
see this shrubbery on his right hand, saw before him a
wider and more extensive view. Beyond the stream
the ground slightly rose, and some few hundred yards
up the slope stood the vast mansion and extensive
grounds of Scott's Hall. Beyond these, again, the

ground stretched away, all laid down in rich pasture land, until it reached a large wood. Park wood—beyond which the eye could not reach from the spot upon which the farmer stood, but on the left of the wood stretching away up to the old church of Aldington, was a further sight of green pastures sweet to a farmer's eye, and right pleasant to the eye of any one who loved to look upon a country view. Down the hill rode the farmer, intent upon his business, and ascending the slope, rode boldly up to the court-yard of the great house, and rang the bell. He was answered by a serving-man, who told him that Sir Edward was within, and would doubtless see him ere long. And before many minutes, the same man came to him and informed him that he could now be admitted to the presence of Sir Edward. The farmer followed the servant along a passage paved with large flag-stones, and was shown into Sir Edward's study, where sat the owner of Scott's Hall to transact business and receive the many visitors who came to him with some complaint to make or some grievance to be removed.

A much-respected man was Sir Edward Scott, not only on account of his wealth and station, two conditions of existence which are pretty certain to secure to their possessor a large portion of respect from his fellow-mortals, but because of his high character and reputation as a just, wise, and good man. For many generations his family had been settled at Scott's Hall, which indeed had been built by no less a person than that John de Baliol, who was ·Robert Bruce's rival for the Crown of Scotland, and who was the founder of the family which, from his beloved northern country, had taken and ever after held the name of Scott. They

16

had generally stood well with their neighbours and
with the public, and Sir Edward was in no degree a
loser by comparison with those who had gone before
him.　Crafty in council, fearless in the field, he guided
men with as much discretion in the one as courage in
the other; and whether as soldier or statesman few
names stood higher than that of Sir Edward Scott.
He was a tall and portly man, of dignified appearance,
but with a friendly smile on his face which betokened
a genial disposition, and those who were in trouble or
doubt never hesitated to come and ask advice in a
quarter from which it was sure to be both promptly
and wisely given.　The room in which Sir Edward sat
was of a square shape, with windows looking north-
ward to the hills.　Around the walls were hung
numerous old-fashioned weapons of different sorts and
sizes, such as an antiquary would prize now-a-days, and
many of which, though they bore a deadly appearance,
were even at that time more valuable as relics of the
past than for service at the present.　On one side, however, arms of a newer fashion were to be seen, and it
was well known that in case of need Sir Edward could
with little delay or difficulty turn out a goodly body of
retainers, well-armed and equipped.　He sat in a low
chair opposite a library-table of curious and ancient
shape, impossible to describe, since nothing is ever
made like it now-a-days.　It was composed of three
times as much wood as is used by our table-makers of
the present day, and as to table-turning, any set of
ladies and gentlemen who could turn Sir Edward's
table by sitting round and putting their hands upon it
would have been the most wonderful table-turners ever

heard of, and would have at once converted the un-
believing world to the certainty that they were assisted
by invisible hands.   Sir Edward was clad in a buff jerkin (a kind of garment with which of course my
readers are well acquainted, although I think a London
tailor would open his eyes remarkably wide if you
walked into his shop and ordered a buff jerkin to be
made for you), a large waistcoat of curious pattern, and
enormous jack boots which reached half way up his
legs.   Several books lay upon the table before him,
and on the wall immediately at his left hung a copy of
the celebrated roll of Magna Charta with the names
attached of the mighty barons who had wrung that
foundation of English liberties from the tyrant John.
The great man received his visitor with friendly condescension.

'What ho! Master Hankey,' said he, 'have you
come off the hill to bring news this fine morning, or
what has brought you down into our quiet vale?   I
trust you have buried your nose in a flagon of Scott's
Hall ale before coming in here for business?'

'Thank you, Sir Edward,' replied the farmer, 'I
have no heart for ale-drinking to-day, and so your Worship will think when I tell you what has brought me
here:' and without more ado he told his tale to Sir
Edward from first to last.

'By my halidome!' cried the lord of Scott's Hall,
'this must be seen to; these are not days when such
doings can be suffered: the knave must be punished and
the witches sought for and got rid of if their crimes can
be proved against them.'   And accordingly Sir Edward
sent off at once for a warrant, which he duly signed and

intrusted to Hankey, telling him that he must take the constable with him and apprehend Giles Butcher under this authority.

The farmer left Scott's Hall quite satisfied with the result of his visit, and made the best of his way to Brabourne-street in order to find the constable, and proceed to arrest the culprit without delay.

Meanwhile Giles Butcher and his companion flew forward over the nine acres hop-garden, across the Bulltown farm in the direction of Brooke, and before Giles knew where he was, he found himself lying on his back upon Brooke Green, quite alone, with neither witch, cat, or broomstick near him, but the bright sun shining down upon him, and the pleasant breeze blowing softly on his face. He sat upright, put his hand to his head, as if to clear his memory, and looked around in a state of utter bewilderment. From this position he was roused by a female voice which addressed him in accents which he had no difficulty in recognizing as those of his estimable wife.

' Well, Giles, my man, here's a pretty state for a poor woman to find her husband in. Never home to tea last night, and kept me a-waiting and a-waiting till my poor head was nigh ready to drop off my blessed shoulders, and then to turn up here at this time o' day, and in sich a state of mud and dirt as I never seed in all my born days. Oh, you bad man, that's what you are. 'Tis that drink what's done it. I'll be bound you've none of your wages to give your poor wife ; all gone on your own greedy self. There, get up and come along home, do!' So saying, she seized Giles by the shoulder and gave him a hearty shake, which somewhat roused him from his dreamy condition. He rose to his feet and followed his wife as meek as a lamb to their cottage, which was at a short distance from the green. What happened there I have no means of knowing, but there can be little doubt that Giles had to endure a pretty good ' setting to rights ; ' and whether he was successful in clearing himself in Mrs Butcher's eyes, or whether she either heard or believed his story and his excuses, is more than I dare to guess. At all events, I believe that his afternoon was not passed in a very agreeable manner, and that before it was over he heartily wished that he was well back at his faggot-work in Westwood. The afternoon was wearing fast away, and matters at home were becoming somewhat more quiet, when an unexpected interruption occurred. Mrs Butcher, who, whatever might have been her faults, was a good soul at bottom, had gradually calmed down, and all the more so when she found that Giles really had most of his week's wages in his breeches pocket. She had therefore come round a bit, and when the usual time arrived, began to busy herself about getting tea ready, and Giles looked forward to an evening of a less exciting description than he had passed the day before. No such good fortune, however, awaited him. The teapot was about to be placed upon the table, the fire was burning brightly, and the kettle hissing and steaming away merrily, and an air of comfort pervaded the whole scene, when on a sudden a loud knocking was heard at the cottage door, and a voice exclaimed in tones of authority, 'Open in the name of the law!' Mrs Butcher very nearly dropped the teapot in her surprise and fright, whilst Giles trembled visibly with agitation. His suspense, however, was not long, for in another moment the door was flung open, and upon the threshold there appeared no less a personage than Farmer Hankey himself, attended by big Billy Trice, the constable of Brabourne. The latter held Sir Edward Scott's warrant in his hand, and appeared fully conscious of his own position and dignity.

'Master Butcher,' he exclaimed in a pompous tone of voice, 'surrender to the law!' and he strode forward into the little room.

Mrs Butcher uttered a faint shriek and sank into the nearest chair. Poor Giles never thought of resistance, but heaved a deep sigh as he replied to the constable, 'Well, master Trice, here I be, ready to go along with you, if go I must. 'Tis precious hard, though, on a poor chap as hasn't done nothing to be collared and hauled off like this.'

'Not done nothing!' said the constable. 'Well, that's more nor I can tell; but there's Farmer Hankey says different, and come along to Sir Edward you must.'

Here the farmer chimed in, 'Yes, my man, you must learn that pulling people's fences down is not an amusement you can have for nothing, and it will be well for you if no worse charge is brought against you and your friends.'

At these words Mrs Butcher held up her head suddenly. 'What friends, Giles?' she said sharply. 'You never told me of no friends.'

'No, no, my good lady,' laughed the farmer, 'it wasn't very likely he would tell *you* of his going out walking and riding with other ladies. You must ask him when and where he saw old Goody Stickels last, if you want to know the whole truth.'

'Is this true, Giles?' asked his wife eagerly.

Giles hung his head and made no reply, upon which she began to upbraid him bitterly for his cruel and wicked conduct. Poor Giles vainly tried to excuse himself, but his wife would not hear a word, and there was nothing for it but to hold his tongue. Worse than all, the constable now produced a pair of handcuffs, with which he secured the prisoner's hands, and then led him from the door, and placing him between the farmer and himself, they all three walked off together. Giles humbly asked where they were going to take him, and was informed that as it was too late to go down to Scott's Hall again that evening, he would be lodged at Brabourne street for the night, and await Sir Edward's pleasure on the morrow. So he walked quietly along between his two companions; and as the Wye road, though it would have been by far the best way to travel, would have obliged the party to pass close to Brooke Hollow, Farmer Hankey advised the constable to follow the pathway across the fields, so that they might avoid the witch's quarters. Accordingly, they marched off from poor Giles's cottage in the direction of Hampton Farm, intending to pass through Beddleston and Bull-town, and so away by Taylor Farm and Brabourne Coombe to the street. But however clever Sam Hankey might have thought himself in planning the journey as he had done, there were those abroad who were still more clever, and who could not be so easily outwitted. The three men walked safely enough along the path until they reached Hampton, and then the path lay across a ploughed field, where the land was of a deep clay, never very agreeable to walk across at the best of times, but doubly difficult after the storm and rain of the night before. The men sank in over their boots; and walking was so tiresome

and heavy, that they all began to repent having taken
that way instead of keeping to the main road. They
crossed the field, however, and passing the farm, came
into the Beddleston lane, which led back to the Wye
road if you turned to the left, but which they had to
cross in order to proceed by the footpath through the
fields on the other side. There was an old ruined cottage close to the road where they had to cross, which
was not a favourite place with the people of those parts,
inasmuch as report said that strange noises had been
heard and strange sights seen by those who passed it
late at night on their way between Brabourne and
Brooke. However, as it was not yet eight o'clock, and the
sun still gave his light, though the shades of evening were
beginning to close in, the men felt no alarm, and at all
events thought it much safer than passing Brooke Hollow, which was now half a mile or more behind them
on the left. But as they neared the cottage the sound
of mirth and laughter greeted their astonished ears, and
they looked at one another in a doubtful and inquiring
manner, as if each thought the other could tell him
something about it. No word was uttered, however,
until they were close upon the old tumble-down wall of
the cottage, and then, through one of the old windows,
an unexpected sight met their eyes. Around a common deal table in the middle of that which had formerly
been the living-room of the cottage, but which was now
a mere open space, with flooring worn away, bare walls,
and a rickety roof overhead, with no ceiling left between
room and rafters, sat four old women, whom Giles recognized in a moment as his companions of the previous night. Yes, there they certainly were. Croaking
Jenny, with her fearful one-eyed wink; Mother Love-

lamb, with her nose; the dame with the mouth, whose
name Giles had not heard before, but whom he found
out afterwards to be known by the title of Mother Night-
hawk; and last, not least, the noted witch of Brooke
Hollow herself in all her glory.   There they were sure
enough, seated round the table, on which was an
enormous metal teapot and several cups.   Behind each
dame's chair stood her cat on its hind legs, whilst several
broomsticks were huddled together in a corner.   But
the appearance of these respectable old ladies was by no
means the same as they had worn on the previous evening.   Each was dressed in her best attire, each had her
cap upon her head and her cloak tidily arranged over
her shoulders, and it evidently appeared that they were
keeping holiday, and having a lively time of it, too.   As
the three men paused for an instant at the window, the
voice of dame Stickels was heard raised in shouts of
shrill laughter, and at the same moment all four of the
old crones sprang from the table and joined in the
chorus.

'Visitors, visitors!' said croaking Jenny; 'here come
our visitors!'   And before the astonished men knew
where they were, each of the three other dames rushed
out and seized her man, so that they were all brought
without further delay into the room, if room it might
be called, in which the merry female party had been
assembled, and in which dame Stickels had remained.

'Welcome, my masters, welcome all!' she exclaimed
as they entered.   'What, crony Giles, is it thou?   Art
in trouble again, or how is it that thy hands wear such
strange gloves?'   And she pointed at the handcuffs,
and leered wickedly at poor Giles as she did so.

Now, Trice was a bold, plain-spoken man, and had a

great respect for the law withal; so when this remark was made he thought it high time to speak, and accordingly he said in a voice intended to be firm and impressive, though it must be owned that it trembled somewhat, which was not surprising, 'Giles Butcher is my prisoner, Mrs Stickels, under a lawful warrant from the hand of the worshipful Sir Edward Scott; and when the law sends its officers for to take a man, it most times makes a man safe by means of such fastenings as those which you see on Butcher's wrists.'

'Stuff and nonsense with your Scotts and your law, Gaffer Trice,' rejoined the dame; 'we don't know anything about prisoners here. Come, crony Giles, hold out your hands and let us have a look at these fine law bracelets.'

Giles held out his hands as he was told, and the witch laid her fist upon the handcuffs, which, to the astonishment and indignation of the constable, fell to the ground and left the prisoner free.

Then out spoke Farmer Hankey, whose anger overcame his fear and prudence at the same time. 'How dare you interfere with the prisoner in this manner?' he cried. 'You may depend upon it that Sir Edward shall hear of it, you old witch, and your lean carcase shall be made acquainted with the horsepond before many days are over!'

Scarce were the words out of his mouth when all four of the old women burst out into a violent outcry, 'He calls names! he calls names!' they cried. 'Out upon the knave; let us show him what it is to abuse his betters.' And then joining hands, they commenced a slow dance round the table, at the same time chanting these words:

' Powers of evil, rise for ill,
　　Aid the servants whom ye know ;
　On the mortal work our will,
　　Persecute the witches' foe.'

And as they concluded the verse a wonderful and terrible
thing occurred.　The four broomsticks rushed out of
their corners across the room, and without saying a
word to any one (which, possibly, they might have
found it difficult to do), fell upon the farmer and the
constable, and began to belabour them with all their
might and main.　Now, it is not a pleasant thing to be
beaten by a broomstick in the hands of an angry man
or woman, but in such a case you have the owner of the
broomstick to attack or to calm down if you can, and
you at least understand what they mean.　But to be
assaulted and violently beaten by broomsticks on their
own account, with no visible hands holding them, and
no one to be seen directing their attack, is a state of
things so unusual, so remarkable, and so uncomfortably
embarrassing, that the two men were as much puzzled
as they were alarmed, and could indeed make no effect-
ual resistance.　The broomsticks rained blows, and by
no means soft blows, upon them incessantly, and it was
quite impossible to defend themselves.　They vainly
tried to do so at first, but finding it no use, sought for a
few moments to ward off the blows, and then took to their
heels and fairly ran for it, whilst the four old dames followed them as far as the cottage walls, and sent after
them peal upon peal of exulting and triumphant laughter.
Giles meanwhile, seeing his gaolers gone, stood doubting for a moment, when dame Stickels' cat suddenly
stept up to him, laid one of its forepaws upon the side
of its nose in a peculiar manner, pointed in the direc-

tion of Brooke with the other, and winked in a knowing style which it was impossible to mistake. Nor was this all, for the shrill voice of the mistress exclaimed at the same time, 'Run, cummer Giles, run an' you will, for your brave masters have set you the example.'

Giles needed no second hint. He was out of the cottage and off in a moment; nor do I believe he was above half the time in going back that he had been in coming from Brooke with his two companions. Mrs Butcher was so glad to get him back that she forgot the scolding she had been about to give him when he left, and I believe he satisfied her of the truth of his story before the evening was over. Hankey and Trice, however, had a less happy journey. The blows which they had received were many and severe, and they ran with less ease than they could have done before the attack of the broomsticks. Run they did, however, right up Beddlestone lane into the old Wye road, and several hundred yards along the same before they pulled up, panting and breathless, at the bottom of the green down belonging to St Thomas' Hospital, right above Bull-town Farm, and looked at each other with mingled doubt, fear, and rage.

'Well, constable Trice,' at length said the farmer, 'a pretty officer of the law *you* are, to be sure, to run away from a parcel of broomsticks and old women.'

Trice grumbled out a reply at once. 'I don't know about running away, Farmer Hankey. I think some one else has been pretty nigh as good as I have at that game to-night; and for the matter of that, I don't see why an officer of the law is to have his bones cracked by broomsticks any more than another man.'

Hankey could make no reply, and the two trudged

slowly along the road together, feeling rather ashamed of themselves, and much disappointed at the fruitless journey they had had after the hedge-breaker. They parted at Hankey's down, and each went home, but not before they had arranged to meet the next morning at Brabourne Manor Pound, and go up together to Scott's Hall to tell their story to Sir Edward.

VII.

THE WITCH OF BROOKE HOLLOW.

· PART II.

IT was a beautiful May morning: a real good old English morning, which is a form of expression which we modest English people frequently make use of when we want to describe something more than commonly excellent or beautiful. Talk to me of a French morning being beautiful—whisper a hint about the bright sky of Italy—speak of the warm Spanish sun— I don't care two-pence about any of them. Good in their way they may all be, but I am an Englishman, and such being the case, I wrap myself up in my cloak of wholesome prejudice, as thick and impenetrable as one of our dear old island fogs, and I declare at once, openly and without reserve, that the way to describe anything as perfectly charming and beautiful is to call it a 'good old English' thing, and nothing else. However, be this as it may, the Saturday morning after the events which I have lately chronicled was as delicious a morning as you could wish to see. Now-a-days we have cold winds and frosts in May, and we hardly feel ourselves safely landed in summer weather until we have passed half through June. It wasn't so in 'the good old times,' you know, at least no well-educated English boy or girl ever heard of such things. May was in those days a respectable, pleasant, genial month, when the thorns were in bloom, and the country was full of flowers, and the birds were warmed by the rays of the sun whilst they sat upon their eggs, and everybody knew that frost and snow were gone for the season, and that people might sit out-of-doors after dinner, and take pleasant walks in the green lanes and shady pathways, and begin to enjoy themselves without fear of being disturbed by cold or rain.

This particular May morning was perfectly delicious, and to no part of the country did it beam out more brightly than to the favoured region which our story concerns. Scott's Hall looked lovely indeed. The morning sun shone upon the old walls with a cheerful light, the birds were singing their sweet songs, and the flowers were filling the air with their fragrant perfume, and it was impossible to fancy any scene more exquisitely peaceful and charming. The dew was glistening upon the old bowling-green, trim and smooth as it was, as there tripped lightly across it a fairy form with which I have now to make my readers for the first time acquainted. Mortal she was, though there was something so airy in her appearance, something so weird in her beauty, that you would have been inclined to take her for some being from another world, and all the more when you heard the low, silvery tones of the sweetest voice which maiden ever owned.

Agnes Forrest was the niece of Sir Edward Scott, the orphan child of his dead sister, whom he had dearly loved, and to whose daughter he had transferred the affection with which he had always regarded the play-mate of his childhood.

Sir Edward had no children of his own, and Lady Scott was in delicate health, rarely able to leave the Hall, so that Agnes was the constant companion and comfort of Sir Edward during his rambles in the park and grounds. He loved her as the apple of his eye; and well did she deserve his affection, for the beauty of her features only reflected, as in a clear mirror, the loveliness of her soul. I wish I could paint her as she deserves to be painted! Among the birds and bees and flowers which she loved so well, she seemed herself to partake of some of the nature of each. A bird she might have been called for the clearness of her voice and the lightness of her step; a bee, for the useful manner in which her time was employed, as well as for the sweetness, as of honey, which dropped from her lips when she spoke; and a flower of flowers indeed she was in the tender, soft colour of her cheeks, and the pleasant freshness which pervaded her whole nature. She loved to tend her flowers and bees, and to listen to the warbling of the spring-tide songsters who filled the shrubberies around her home; but she had other tastes of even a higher character. Not a cottage in the neighbourhood where her footstep was unknown or unwelcome; not a sick or sorrowing person among the poor by whom the tender, soothing accents of that sweet young voice had not been blessed again and again; not a peasant for miles around who did not worship the very ground on which ' Saint Agnes' trod. 'Saint Agnes,' they called her, the simple people of that day, because they saw in her something so pure and good and chaste and holy, that she seemed to them a being to be distinguished from common mortals, and nearer than themselves to the Heaven they worshipped.

Oh, sweet 'Saint Agnes!' No wonder that your old uncle doted upon you as if you had been his own child, and that a sunny, joyous atmosphere seemed to surround you wherever you went. It was a pleasant sight to see you lightly tripping across the old bowling-green on that bright May morning, and I think of you and your happy smile and cheerful look as I walk over the same ground to-day, and I carry myself back in thought to those old days when your presence blessed the place. Alas! it is all changed now: the glory of the House of Scott has faded, as all mortal things fade, the memory of their power and pride has passed away from the minds of men, the old Hall itself exists no longer, and the curious searcher can with difficulty trace the spot where once it stood. I stand upon the very place where once those light feet merrily tripped, and as I muse upon the history of the Past, and strive to picture to myself the forms and faces of those to whom it was once the Present, visions steal over me which I would fain describe in words but that the words fail me, and I long to be carried back to those old times—if only for a brief space—that I might see those things and people as they really were, and teach my children how the changes from that time to this will be repeated in the Future before us; and how that the things we see around us, and the people we love to-day, will fade and change and pass away, like the things and people of whom I am telling them; and that other eyes will look upon these scenes, and other feet will tread these green fields here-after, all changing and passing away in their turn, but all tending towards the land where there will be no

fading away and no changing, because all will be cen-
tred in and around that Love of the Eternal God
which knows no change, and upon which alone change-
less and undying happiness can be founded.

I stand, I say, upon the old bowling-green: the
homely caw of the rooks in the rookery close by is ringing in my ears, and before me lie the pleasant pastures
and rich lands of Scott's Hall, and I seem to be wit-
nessing the very self-same scenes which I am describing
to you ; and pleasant scenes they were. A window on the
ground floor is thrown open ; one of those curiously
fashioned old windows with half a hundred little dia-
mond-shaped panes of glass set in lead, which look as
if they had been made to tantalize you by letting in
only just so much light as should show you how much
more you might have had if the panes had been larger
and of clearer glass. And from the window comes a
loud, cheerful, ringing voice—'Agnes, my darling,
early abroad, as usual ?' And the sweet, silvery tones
float back so pleasantly across the lawn—

'Yes, uncle dear; the morning air is so lovely !
Come out, and stroll in the shrubbery before breakfast.'

Then opens the door on to the lawn, and the manly
figure of the owner of Scott's Hall appears, as he steps
forth to join his child in her morning ramble. That
morning they walked for a longer time than usual, for
the weather was tempting, and they strolled beyond
the shrubberies and down to Park wood before they
returned to the house.

As they reached the east garden gate on their return, they perceived two persons approaching from the
direction of Brabourne Leese, whose strange appearance
at first puzzled them exceedingly. Both appeared to

be dripping wet, although not a drop of rain had fallen that morning; the face of each was as black as a coal, only varied by a red stain here and there as if from a severe scratch, whilst their clothes appeared as if they had recently emerged from a bottle of ink.

Sir Edward viewed the appearance of the new-comers with mingled surprise and amusement, and it was not until they had approached quite close to him that he began to think that he had seen them some-where before. He had not long to wait for an explanation.

'Is this a Christian country, Sir Edward, and are I constable of Brabourne? that's what I wants to know, your Worship?' said a melancholy voice, which proceeded from the tallest of the two.

'What, Trice, my man, is that you?' replied the astonished gentleman. 'And this—why, this surely can't be Sam Hankey, of Hastingleigh?'

'Sure enough it is, then, Sir Edward,' answered the latter. 'And here we are, as you see us, all along o' them wretched old witches, drat 'em!'

Sir Edward eagerly inquired what had happened, and the cause of the sorry condition of the two men. Their story was short, though curious. They had met, according to appointment, at the Manor Pound that morning, with the intention of proceeding forthwith to Scott's Hall, in order to lay before Sir Edward their account of the doings of the previous 'evening and the manner in which his warrant had been treated and his authority set at nought.

Fine, however, as was the morning, they had scarcely set foot upon Brabourne Leese before a curious and unnatural mist appeared to spring up around them, and before they had gone a couple of hundred yards they were as much lost, as if they had been in an American forest. To make matters worse, a voice which he took to be Hankey's (but the latter declared he had never said a word) called Trice to the right, and then somebody imitated Trice's voice, and called Hankey to the left, so that they got separated one from the other, and matters were worse than ever. Then they declared that they heard strange, shrill bursts of laughter around them, and now and then the unmistakeable ' miaw ' of a cat, which frightened them still more.

Presently Sam Hankey stumbled right into one of the pits which were by no means unfrequent on the Leese, and which, although not deep enough to drown a man, yet, being half full of water and fringed by brambles, wet him thoroughly and scratched his face into the bargain; much the same misfortune shortly afterwards befell Trice, and the pair were in the greatest distress imaginable.

To crown all, amidst renewed and redoubled shouts of laughter, some person or persons fell upon the two unhappy men and banged them again and again over face, head, and body with sacks full of some soft substance which they took to be flour, but which presently turned out to be soot; for, after about an hour's wandering in this agreeable manner, all of a sudden the mist or fog disappeared, the sun shone out clearly, and the two men found themselves standing in the very midst of Brabourne Leese, ' staring at each other like stuck pigs,' as Hankey remarked, and as wet and as black as need be from top to toe. They saw no one at first, and were so bewildered that they hardly knew what to do. Determined, however, to persevere in their walk to Scott's

Hall even in their sorry condition, they set their faces in that direction, and moved forward. Not many steps had they taken, however, before a low laugh attracted their attention ; and looking round, who should they see but croaking Jenny, the one-eyed dame of Brabourne Leese, seated at the foot of a huge gorse bush, with her tabby cat by her side, as grave and demure as possible !

'Whither away, my masters, whither away so early?' said the old dame in her hoarse voice. 'And oh ! in what a pickle ye both are ! Is that spruce Farmer Han-key from the hill ? indeed, I wonder you're not ashamed to come out in such trim ; and Gaffer Trice, the Bra-bourne constable ! Well, I never did,' and croaking Jenny burst out into a jeering laugh, which exceedingly provoked the objects of her mirth.

As, however, they had already experienced the power of the witch and her companions, they had sufficient prudence to restrain themselves from further provoking the wrath of the old dame, and hurried hastily forward upon their way without making any reply. She fol-lowed them with jeers and taunts for some little distance, and then left them to themselves, having apparently done them as much mischief as she could.

The worthy pair made the best of their way to Scott's Hall, where, as we have seen, they met Sir Edward and his niece returning from their morning walk. Great was the indignation of the worthy knight at the treat-ment which his warrant and its bearers had received. He declared at once that such doings could not and should not be tolerated, and that measures should be forthwith taken to put a stop to the practices of which complaint had been made.

He told the two men that they might rely upon it

that the law would, in the long run, be found too strong
for those who now sought to defy it, and that they need
not fear but that the matter should be followed up, and
that without delay. He then directed the farmer and
the constable to go round to the buttery and obtain
some refreshment, after which they might return home
and leave the matter in his hands.

You may well believe that the men were not slow
to take advantage of this permission; and having par-
taken of no small quantity of good Scott's Hall ale, they
went back to Brabourne. After their departure, long and
deeply pondered the Lord of Scott's Hall, and much he
mused and meditated upon the strange events of which
he had heard.

At last he made up his mind to ride over to Mersham
Hatch, and take counsel with his friend and neighbour,
Squire Knatchbull, who was a man of high repute for
book learning, and withal well versed in the ways of
the world, and keenly alive to the necessity of putting
down witches and all such evil creatures. The Knatchbull family had long been neighbours of the Scotts in
the adjoining parish of Lympne; and it was the grand-
father of the then owner of Mersham Hatch who had
purchased the latter property.

Although his estates were not equal in extent to
those of Sir Edward, they were still considerable, for
the Knatchbulls had for years past been gradually advancing in prosperity and taking their place in the front
ranks of the old country families.

There had always been friendship between the neighbours, and neither was accustomed to act in local matters without taking the other into counsel; it was natural, therefore, that in such a crisis as the present Sir

Edward should desire to act in concert with his friend, and to obtain the benefit of his advice. A crisis, indeed, it was, for if it were true that these wicked old women possessed such powers as those which were attributed to them by Hankey and Trice, there was no knowing what they might do next, or where they would stop; and if disrespect to the warrant of the magistrate and contempt for the majesty of the law were thus openly shown, neither magistrate nor law would any longer have that authority in the land which it was absolutely necessary that they should possess for the security of life and property. Pondering such thoughts deeply in his mind, Sir Edward mounted his well-known black horse, ' Mustafer,' and attended by two grooms, as became his rank and position, rode through his park in the direction of Mersham Hatch. He passed along the Ridgeway, as the road was called which skirted the Knatchbull territory at the point nearest Scott's Hall, turned into Barracks wood, and rode along a somewhat rough and uneven track, which brought him out into the park beyond. Wild and beautiful was Hatch Park, covered with fern and plentifully ornamented with thriving oak trees.

As Sir Edward rode gaily along, the deer started from their shady nooks in the fern, the rabbits scurried away, and hid themselves in the vast earths with which the park was undermined, and the pigeons darted out of their leafy homes above the rider's head, and mounted high in the air, in their circling flight. It was a beautiful scene—wilder than his own park—and one upon which it did one's heart good to gaze. On rode Sir Edward, beyond the wood, across the open plain skirting the foot of the hill on which now stands the comparatively modern mansion of the Knatchbulls,

and so away to the gates of the old house. A loud
peal of the bell summoned the household, and in a few
moments Sir Edward entered the room, in which sat
the neighbour whom he wished to consult.

Richard Knatchbull was a man somewhat advanced
in years, but hale and hearty; and as he rose from
his seat to welcome his visitor, strength, both of mind and
body, was sufficiently apparent both in his form and
face. He greeted Sir Edward warmly; and after that
preliminary conversation about the weather and the
crops, which the best and most enlightened of English
country gentlemen have never been able to avoid, they
began to discuss the subject which had really caused
their meeting. With great attention did Squire Knatchbull listen to the tale unfolded by Sir Edward, and expressed in strong terms his sense of the importance of
the crisis.

He gave it as his opinion that if witches were allowed
to carry on their wicked pranks without hindrance, there
would be no safety for any one, and the sooner some
decided steps were taken the better for the peace of the
neighbourhood and the welfare of the people. There were
several courses which might be pursued with advantage.
The Ashford bench of magistrates were pretty sure to
deal heavily with these creatures if brought before them,
and it might be worth while to do this. Again, the
idea had only to be set afloat, and there would soon be
collected a sufficient number of people from the neighbouring villages, who would duck the old women in the
horse-pond till the fact of their being witches or not
was made plain. Or, if it seemed more desirable, the
squire was ready to ride with his neighbour, and arrest
the culprits then and there, so that the common folk

might know that the power and authority of the law could not be set at nought, at the pleasure of witches.

After some consultation, the latter plan, or something akin to it, seemed to commend itself to the two neighbours. Accordingly, Richard Knatchbull mounted his dark grey charger, and, one of his grooms having joined those of Sir Edward, the party set off together, the intention of the two gentlemen being either to arrest the old women, or to make such full inquiries upon the spot as would discover the whole truth of the complaint against them, and perhaps prevent their misdoings for the future.

Down the Horse-park they rode, and through old Quarrington farm, and so away to Naccult. Here they got into bad roads and muddy lanes, through which they picked their way with no little difficulty. It was a beautiful day. The sun shone out with a mild, genial warmth, and a soft, westerly wind blew gently across the vale, and bore the sound of the pleasant Ashford chimes to the ears of the party, as they wended their way along the lanes. Old Naccult wood was left behind, and nearer and nearer they came to the hills, riding always in the direction of that Brooke Hollow, where dwelt the ancient dame, who is the subject of my story.

Now, among other habits of Richard Knatchbull, was one which the coming events of this truthful history compel me to mention here. He had a famous breed of deer-hounds, of which he was extremely fond, and seldom went abroad without being accompanied by some of these favourite animals. On the present occasion two beautiful specimens of the race, ' Venture ' and ' Welcome,' followed at his horse's heels, and it

was their presence which led to the following occurrence. The party had passed Naccult wood, when in
the middle of one of the green lanes which I have mentioned they suddenly perceived a white doe, standing
perfectly still, and staring them in the face.

'Ha!' cried Sir Edward Scott; 'another of my
deer has got over the park fence. We shall have our
neighbours complaining again of damaged crops and
broken fences. How tiresome this is!'

'Say not so,' replied his companion; 'for as I fortunately have my hounds here, your truant shall soon
be caught,' and with a shout to his favourites, he showed
them the animal, and in an instant they darted forward
in pursuit.

Throwing back her head as if in disdain, the pretty
doe gave two or three short, sharp springs up in the air,
and then darted down a lane to the right, the hounds
following. The two gentlemen clapped spurs to their
horses at once, and the chase began. Squire Knatchbull, proud of his hounds, and confident in their
strength and swiftness, never doubted that a run of
half-a-mile at most would be finished by the capture of
the doe. Not so, however, did matters turn out. The
graceful creature bounded forward at such a pace, that
her pursuers scarcely seemed to gain a foot upon her;
and as the horsemen leapt the low fence out of the lane,
and found themselves in the pasture fields between
Hampton and Naccult woods, they saw the doe some
two hundred yards in front of the hounds, all going at
best speed.

'Forward,' cried Sir Edward, and Richard Knatchbull re-echoed the cry as they rode along the pleasant
meadows, the green turf springing beneath their horses'

feet, and the sweet fresh air fanning their faces as they galloped through it—on, on, to Foreland wood, into which the doe gracefully bounded, and was lost to their sight. But both gentlemen were good horsemen; and the two stiles, one at each end of the footpath through the narrow neck of Foreland wood, at the south-west corner, formed no obstacle to their progress. Over they went, and landing in the green pasture field beyond, skirted the wood in time to see the hunted animal heading straight for Bircholt, the faithful hounds still following close.

'Strange!' shouted Richard, as he galloped side by side with his companion. 'Never did I know living deer which could so long keep ahead of "Welcome" and "Venture."'

'Ha! by my halidome, Master Richard,' laughed Sir Edward, 'if you have not over-rated your fine hounds, you have not given full credit to the swiftness of our Scott's Hall deer,' and on they pushed. Forward through the Bircholt pastures, and the little Bircholt wood, and away to the borders of Brabourne Leese, and out on to the common. Forward, still forward; but it was bad riding on the common, and the horsemen were obliged to draw rein, and slacken speed; still they pressed on, until they had reached the Warren-house, and then they were stopped by an unexpected sight. Both the hounds were standing near some gorse bushes hard by the large rabbit-warren, panting with exhaustion, and looking up and down at each other with a puzzled expression, which no doubt they would have explained in words if they had been able to do so. But where was the doe? nowhere; there was no doe or deer of any kind to be seen; and after chasing her for some three miles, she seemed to have as utterly disappeared as if she had never existed. The two gentlemen stared at the hounds and at each other, and Sir Edward was about to speak, when casting his eyes forward, he perceived the weather-beaten countenance of old Brooks, the warrener, peering up the other side of the gorse bushes.

'Ha! Brooks, my man!' exclaimed Sir Edward. 'Which way has the white doe gone? have you seen aught of her?'

'Nay, Sir Edward,' replied the old man. 'I have seen nought of no doe. I came out of the house, on account of seeing Squire Knatchbull's hounds racing like mad over the Leese, but what they were after I know not. There was a white rabbit ran into a hole just now, but that is the only white thing I have set eyes on to-day.'

Again the two gentlemen regarded one another with looks of astonishment. What could this mean? Was it possible that the doe had been a delusion? No, they certainly had seen her, as large as life, and so had the hounds, else why should they have chased her? The servants also bore witness to having seen the animal, and there could be no doubt about it. They could not all have been mistaken. That was impossible, and the only conclusion to which they were able to come, was that some trick had been played by the Witch of Brooke Hollow and her friends, in order to prevent the intended visit to her home. If so, the trick had certainly succeeded, for Sir Edward, finding himself close to his own Park gate, the day far advanced, and his horse heated with his sharp gallop, declared that he wouldn't ride back to Brooke that night for all the witches in Christendom, and Squire Knatchbull entirely agreed with his neighbour's view of the case. So they settled matters by riding up to Scott's Hall, and spending a friendly evening together, after which he of Mershan Hatch rode home, promising that on the following Monday he would be at Scott's Hall between nine and ten in the morning, ready to ride with Sir Edward, warrant in hand, to arrest these wicked persons, and put an end, if possible, to their evil doings.

Meanwhile, Hankey and Trice, having returned safely home, well fortified with the good ale of Scott's Hall, and satisfied that the matter was in better hands than theirs, told their friends, right and left, that Sir Edward Scott was going to put down the witches for good and all, and dropped many hints of ducking in the horse-pond, and other pleasant amusements, which were deemed in those days specially suitable to be employed with respect to old ladies who kept cats and lived in lonely places. I cannot tell whether or no these rumours reached the witches' ears, or whether they had private means of knowing what was going on without trusting to rumours. I think, however, from what I am about to tell, that somehow or other they *did* know all about it, and acted accordingly.

Bright and fair beamed Monday morning; and as Sir Edward Scott looked out of the window from his dressing-room on the north-west side of the house, he perceived his worthy neighbour Knatchbull spurring across Callan Plain, accompanied by his two trusty retainers, Blechynden and Cornell, and followed, as usual, by 'Venture' and 'Welcome.' But, casting his eye towards the northern entrance of the park, where the road led down the hill-side from Lodge House, a cavalcade of a somewhat different appearance met his eye.   Four donkeys were slowly descending the hill, on the back of each of which sat a respectable-looking matron, clad in a red cloak, and wearing a black straw bonnet.

Sir Edward was at a loss to know what this unusual spectacle could betoken: there was no thoroughfare there, and the good dames must therefore be bound for Scott's Hall, but who or what they were, or what might be their errand, he was quite at a loss to guess.   Slowly they descended, and gradually approached the house, the court-yard of which they reached just as Richard Knatchbull galloped in.

The two hounds were close at his heels, but as soon as they saw the donkeys and the red cloaks, their usual courage seemed to have deserted them, and with a low whine they slunk away into the shrubberies.

'Good-morrow to you, friend Knatchbull, good-morrow to you,' quoth Sir Edward, in a cheery voice. 'Thou art true to thy time, forsooth—"Punctual as a Knatchbull," was ever our saying in these parts.   But who hast thou in thy train?   Verily, times are changed when the squire rides abroad with matrons instead of grooms to follow!   Hast thou founded an alms-house, and are these the recipients of thy charity? or art thou about to take a housekeeper, and hast a mind to ask my advice respecting the same?'

'A truce to thy jesting, Sir Edward,' cried his neighbour.   'These be none of my people, though they entered the court-yard at the same time with me.   I know nought of them, and they may tell you their own business.'

By this time the four donkeys had approached close to where the lords of Scott's Hall and of Mersham

Hatch stood talking, and the rider of the foremost animal thus addressed the gentlemen :

'Sirs,' she said, 'we be poor wronged creatures, against whom evil tongues have wagged of late, and we be come to seek justice at your worshipful hands.'

'Say you so, dame?' replied Sir Edward. 'Justice shall not be sought here in vain. Who and whence are ye, and what is your complaint?

'Good sir,' answered the matron of the donkey, 'my name is Stickels, and I come from Brooke, and these my neighbours are from Brabourne and hereabouts.'

'Ha!' shouted Sir Edward, 'is this the case, indeed? Are you, then, the persons against whom so much has been laid before me?'

'Alas! sir, I know not, but so I fear it is,' returned the old dame. 'A poor lone woman has but a poor chance in this bad world, in which might and strength rule everything, and the weakest goes to the wall. But, in truth, it is I and my companions who should make complaint, for it is we who have been cruelly treated.'

'If this be true,' responded the stout knight, 'doubt not that ye shall be righted; but speak out boldly, and declare the matter which has brought ye hither.'

'Sir,' began Dame Stickels, 'I have much to tell—more, indeed, than I could venture to ask your worshipful ears to hear at this moment. Our story is long, but it is all of the same kind. Because we are old, and not so well-favoured as younger damsels; because we shun the busy world, and prefer the quiet of our lonely cottages; and, more than all, because we love to keep our innocent cats as some company to us in our solitary homes; therefore men look askance at us, and give us ill words, and for ever threaten us and put us in fear of our lives. If a cow dies, Dame Stickels has done it; if the sheep have the rot, Croaking Jenny must have had a hand in it; and, in fact, the most ordinary troubles which fall upon mankind are all attributed to us poor harmless old creatures.'

'But what is this I hear about Giles Butcher and Farmer Hankey's fence?' demanded Sir Edward.

'Alas and alack-a-day!' whined the old dame, 'how could a poor old creature like myself have had any hand in such a deed? the truth is easy to see. Worthy Giles had taken a drop too much on his way home from work on a stormy night, and, mistaking his road, came across the farmer's downs. Whether he broke the fence in getting over it, or whether it was the wind which did the damage I cannot say, but the poor man was overcome with fatigue and liquor, and sank down to sleep on the side hill, where the farmer found him, and at once accused him of the mischief. But ne'er a hand in it had any of us four, as how, indeed, should we? Glad enough were we to keep at home that night.'

'But,' said the master of Scott's Hall, 'if this be so, how about Hankey's horse falling down, and the escape of Giles upon a broomstick, with you upon another? How about the beating of Hankey and Constable Trice, and the little respect shown to my warrant? Ay, and how about the two men losing their way on Brabourne Leese, and coming here in so sorry a plight?

The dame shrugged her shoulders and put on a sad expression of face.

'How can I tell,' she said, 'what lies people invent

when they wish to excuse their own misdoings? As to the horse, the stingy old farmer has been often told that he wasn't safe, and that he should buy a new one. He has driven that same poor animal these fifteen years; and though I wonder he had strength enough left to run away, it is only a marvellous thing that he hadn't fallen down years ago. For the story of the broomsticks, I am sure Sir Edward Scott is too wise and clever a gentleman to believe such silly tales. The farmer must have invented it, because he was ashamed of his carelessness in letting the prisoner go, with which I had nothing whatever to do; and as for the Brabourne Leese tale, it is hard indeed if every drunken fellow that loses his way and tumbles into a pit is to lay his misfortune to the charge of poor, helpless old creatures like us.'

'Well,' said Sir Edward, 'your words sound reasonable, and I would not have wrong done;' and turning to Squire Knatchbull, 'What think you, neighbour?' he said; 'you are learned in book lore. Believe you that these old women can have done the things of which we have been told, or are these the idle tales of village gossips?'

Richard Knatchbull shook his head as he answered in a low tone, 'I like it not, neighbour Scott, I like it not. These dames look too innocent, and, to my mind, there is a queer appearance about their very donkeys. Moreover, I marvel that my bold hounds shrunk from them. There is something here more than meets the eye, and I would have thee be wary and cautious.'

Now, Dame Stickels saw the gentlemen whispering, and was sure that her story had made some impression upon Sir Edward, at least. She therefore continued to address him in plaintive tones.

'Sir,' she said, 'it is not only on account of these idle tales that my sisters and I have come to Scott's Hall to-day, but verily we are in fear of our lives. Farmer Hankey is a terrible man when roused, and he and Trice have vowed that they will not rest until we be driven away or killed. We know not what offence we have given, but we crave at your hands protection from these knaves.'

'But,' answered Sir Edward, 'you have not yet explained the beating of the two men and the treatment of my warrant in the ruined cottage.'

'I have nothing to explain,' replied the dame, 'for indeed I know nothing of the matter. The men are quarrelsome fellows, and, for aught I know, may have beaten each other; certainly I was not near the place, nor do I believe that any of these good women were there. But I pray you, Sir Edward, listen not to such idle tales against your poor neighbours.'

Sir Edward was about to reply, when a loud noise outside the court-yard attracted his attention; and turning hastily round, he perceived a crowd of some twenty or thirty people entering the place with loud shouts and cries of indignation.

Foremost among them were Farmer Hankey and Trice, and between them, held tightly by each arm, they dragged along no less a person than the now celebrated Giles Butcher. His coat had been torn from his back, his face was scratched, his shirt was torn, and he had evidently been subjected to rough usage. Behind him and his captors came a number of labourers and cottagers of Brabourne, yelling and hooting, and only half understanding what it was all about.

'Come on, Trice! bring him along!' shouted Han-

key, as they entered the court-yard. 'Let us see what
Sir Edward will say to this friend of the witches. Stick
tight to him, my man; come on!' and as Trice set his
teeth together with a fierce and determined look, there
seemed but little chance of escape for poor Butcher.

Into the court-yard came the people, and you may
fancy their astonishment on turning the corner, when
they found themselves in the presence not only of the two
gentlemen, but of the very four old women of whom
they stood in such fear.

For a moment they were silent, and then all burst
out into loud cries of, 'The witches, the witches! hang
'em, burn 'em, drown 'em!' and their exclamations were
scarcely stopped by the authoritative voice of Sir Edward
Scott demanding silence.

Then Hankey and Trice left hold of Butcher, whom
they had waylaid and caught as he was slipping off to
his work in West wood, and began directly to call
upon the lord of Scott's Hall for vengeance and justice upon the real criminals. After a short time silence
was obtained, and Sir Edward spoke to the excited people. He told them that certain accusations of witchcraft had been brought against the old women who
were before them, and that much mischief and damage
to property had been attributed to them. But he said
that all this was denied, that the helpless old creatures
had protested their innocence, and that he was quite
sure that no honest Englishman would wish to condemn
any one without clear proof against them, least of all
when the accused were old and weak persons, who
could not take their own part. Still, he remarked, he
could not refuse to hear anything which any one might
have to say against them, but he must insist that the

charge should be clear and precise, and that no empty
rumours or reports should be brought forward, as the
most innocent person in the world might be condemned
if such were permitted. Then he called upon Farmer
Hankey, who eagerly told his tale, and was supported by
Trice.

Goody Stickels shook her head sadly meanwhile,
and throwing her eyes upwards, declared that she never
expected to have lived to hear so many wicked falsehoods.
On hearing his word thus questioned, and the charges so
boldly denied, Farmer Hankey flew into a furious passion.

'Is this to be endured, Sir Edward?' he cried.
'Are the words of an honest man to go for nought,
when he is but relating what he has seen with his own
eyes?'

Then Dame Stickels, with another shake of her head,
and a sound very like a sob, spoke out in a melancholy
tone—

'Oh, sirs, for the wickedness of men! To think
that this cruel farmer should not only slander us poor
people, but bribe the wicked constable to back him up!
But justice will be done, never fear; justice will be
done!' and she sighed aloud.

Sir Edward Scott was for the moment fairly puzzled; and, turning to his neighbour of Mersham Hatch,
once more asked him his opinion.

'Methinks,' said old Richard, 'the way of proceeding is clear enough. Here stands the very man whom
they accuse of being friend and partner with the witches.
Let us ask *him* how the matter stands. Come forward,
Giles Butcher, and give your testimony.'

'Well thought of,' cried Sir Edward. 'Now, Giles,
speak out like a man, and tell the truth.'

Giles trembled like a leaf. What could he do, and what could he say? Should he be believed if he told the truth? And, if not, what probable tale could he invent to excuse the damage to Hankey's fence, and the escape from the constable? Never in the whole course of his life had he been in such doubt and difficulty. To make matters worse, out spoke the farmer of Hastingleigh in these words :

'Tell the truth, Giles, and shame the evil one. Never mind the fence, man. I'll forgive you all, and willingly, too, if you aid us in bringing these vile creatures to justice.'

And then in her softest tones spoke Dame Stickels.

'Good Giles, kind Giles, you'll never say a word against innocent neighbours, if I judge you rightly. Tell their worships what cruel lies are these which are told against us,' and she looked at Giles with eyes that seemed to pierce through and through him, and, to his surprise and terror, her donkey appeared to do just the same.

Placed in this painful position, Giles at first remained perfectly silent, but this by no means suited the rest of the party. Goody Stickels and Sam Hankey were equally anxious that he should speak in their favour, and the bystanders were waiting for his evidence with breathless impatience.

'Come, Butcher,' said Sir Edward, in a stern voice, 'there must be no nonsense now. Speak out like a man, and tell us all you know, or we shall be obliged to deem you guilty, and act accordingly.'

Thus addressed, Giles opened his mouth, and at first could only gape widely, as if trying to find words which would not come.

'Now,' said Sir Edward, angrily, 'tell us what you know of this matter without delay. Is it true that you have reason to believe that these women are witches or not?'

At this moment, just as Giles was on the very point of bursting forth with the whole truth, he cast a sidelong look at the four old women; and to his excited imagination their eyes, and the eyes of their four donkeys, appeared so extraordinarily bright and dazzling, and withal wore such a threatening expression, that his courage entirely failed him, his head swam, he lost his wits altogether; and, impelled by some power which he was quite unable to resist, he blurted out in an enormously loud voice, 'No, Sir Edward, I don't know nothing about it.'

'Oh, you lying villain!' shouted Hankey; but Sir Edward at once stopped him, with an air of authority.

'This will not do,' said he. 'Butcher must be neither abused nor frightened. He tells us that he knows nothing of the witchcraft of these old women. If you wish to ask him any questions, now is your time; but you must do so in a quiet and becoming manner.'

Upon this the farmer turned to Butcher, and demanded in a loud voice whether it wasn't true that he had found him asleep on his hill by the damaged fence? Gathering courage from the presence and protection of Sir Edward, Giles admitted that it was so.

Then Hankey hastily asked him whether he denied that he had escaped from him after the fall of his horse, and the overturning of the cart? This Giles also confessed.

'And didn't you go away over the hop-garden on

a broomstick, you thief?' asked the furious farmer.

'Oh dear, oh dear, he never saw no broomstick,' cried Dame Stickels at this moment; and Giles, as if saying a lesson, slowly repeated her words, "Never saw no broomstick."

'What!' shouted Hankey at the top of his voice, 'and Trice and I were never beaten at the old cottage, I suppose?'

'He don't know,' said Dame Stickels.

'I don't know,' repeated Giles, and the farmer stamped on the ground in his rage.

Then said croaking Jenny, in her hoarse, harsh voice, ''Tis hard upon us, good sirs, that this cruel farmer should have invented such false tales to get us into trouble. Butcher has surely said enough to show that there is nothing against us. But is such a man as this to go unpunished, who slanders his innocent neighbours?'

'Ah, sirs,' added Goody Stickels, 'we would pray you to stop these persecutions. Innocence is of no avail where malice is so powerful. A day in the stocks, or even a week in gaol, would not be too great a punishment for this wicked man.'

'Well,' said Sir Edward Scott, 'as far as the matter has gone, it would certainly seem that the case against you has broken down; but although this may be true, I cannot say but that Farmer Hankey has had losses, which may in some measure justify his determination to find out the authors if possible; and as to punishing a man who makes a mistake in such a matter as this, I cannot say that—'

What Sir Edward could not say was never known, for at that moment an interruption took place, which

gave an unexpected and extraordinary turn to the
whole affair. A little door which led into the bowling-
green from the side of the court-yard was suddenly
thrown open, and Agnes Forrest stepped lightly into
the yard. She stopped short as soon as she found herself in the presence of so many people ; whilst the men,
who had followed Hankey and Trice, all touched their
hats, or made their rustic bows, and several low mur-
murs of respectful but affectionate greeting were heard
amongst them.

Agnes stood for a moment, then she looked right
and left, and put her hand to her forehead.

'Uncle,' she said, 'what is this? All is not well.
There is something evil here. I cannot breathe freely,'
and as she spoke she turned round, and cast her eyes
upon the four old women and their donkeys. At the
same moment the eyes of all were turned in the same
direction, although their owners little guessed what was
about to follow.

Nought that was evil and unholy could live in that
pure young presence, and the powers which had been
able to resist and to deceive the wisdom of a Scott and
of a Knatchbull, to evade the majesty of the law, and
escape the pursuit of justice, trembled and owned their
weakness before the sweet innocence of the youthful
maiden.

As Agnes gazed upon the old women, a visible
shudder passed over their frames : their eyes fell, and
their countenances were overcast with a look of mingled
melancholy and fear. More extraordinary still was the
effect upon the animals which they bestrode,—they,
too, shook violently ; a strange, moaning sound of
anguish seemed to break from them ; and, turning

hastily round, they suddenly rushed out of the court-yard, away from the fair young presence, which had exercised so wonderful an influence upon them, and with shrill and alarming cries, carried off their riders at a speed never before witnessed in living donkeys.

For one instant everybody in the court-yard stood transfixed with astonishment. Then, with a mighty yell, they rushed off in hot pursuit. But there were present those who outstripped the crowd in speed.

As Agnes entered the court-yard, the two noble hounds, 'Venture' and 'Welcome,' had crept quietly out of the shrubbery, and nestled up to her side. On the head of each she laid her little hand; and, as if they had gathered fresh courage from the touch, their mien became more bold, their eyes sparkled and glared with anger, and a low growl betokened their rage and hatred of the evil things which they saw before them. And as the donkeys and their riders fled madly from the court-yard, the hounds cast one look at the maiden, as if her consent was necessary to their action; and then with a deep, loud bay of wrath, darted eagerly after the fugitives.

'Ho!' cried Sir Edward loudly, 'ho there! My horse, my horse!' and in an instant 'Mustafer,' who had been standing, saddled and ready for the expedition which the two gentlemen were about to take, was brought to his master. One moment they paused, for something seemed to speak to Agnes' heart, and tell her that her presence was necessary. Her beautiful Arab was made ready with as little delay as possible, and she followed the running and roaring crowd, which increased every moment as the cottagers came rushing out to see what was the occasion of so unusual a noise.

The witches and their donkeys had got such a start, that when the pursuing party reached Brabourne Leese tney could see the long tails of the flying animals disappearing down Bircholt lane ; whilst the deep bay of the hounds told that they were following close and true upon the track.

Onward pressed the party, and still the old women kept ahead, until they passed Broad Oak, entered the wide track in Chute's wood, and scurrying along it at best speed, came out upon the Beddleston pastures, and headed straight away for Brooke Hollow.

As Sir Edward Scott and Richard Knatchbull, with Agnes by their side, rode into Beddleston lane, the foot people, who had taken a shorter cut, came over the brow of the hill, and rushed on between Foreland and Cadman woods. From some cause or another, the strength of the donkeys appeared to be failing; and as they came in sight of the self-same ruined cottage which had proved so unlucky to Hankey and Trice, the gallant hounds came close upon them, and rushed open-mouthed upon their prey. Then, indeed, was witnessed such a sight as in these modern days has never been seen.

The old women jumped off their donkeys, and ran screaming and yelling right and left. But the most wonderful thing was that which happened to the donkeys. Their ears almost sank into their heads, their long tails quite changed in form and appearance, their heads and bodies suddenly grew smaller, and all that was to be seen of them was four enormous cats bounding and scurrying along in the green meadow, between the Beddleston lane and the great Fish-pond field. But they bounded and scurried in vain. The hounds rushed madly forward; and as Sir Edward and his party came up, they were worrying the last of the four victims, and with an unearthly scream, the great black cat of Brooke Hollow yielded· up her breath. Up came the eager crowd, shouting with rage, and frantic with excitement

'The witches, the witches!' they cried, and hurried forward to seize the unfortunate old creatures.

Sir Edward's authority was vain and useless to stop them. The stern look of Richard Knatchbull betokened that little of mercy was to be obtained through him; and in a few moments the old women would certainly have been torn to pieces, or drowned in the nearest horse-pond. But as they crouched and cowered on the ground in a terrible state of fear and trembling, deserted by the evil powers which had hitherto helped them, and apparently about to suffer the reward of their crimes in a speedy and degrading death, she who had been the cause of their detection came forward to be the guardian of their safety. Agnes rode boldly between the people and their intended victims, her sweet young face flushed with excitement, but her voice and manner soft, gentle, and soothing as ever.

'Do not this wrong, my friends,' she said; and at the sound of her voice the crowd stopped short, as if by magic. 'Do no harm to these old women; they may yet repent of their evil deeds, and their repentance will punish them more than your violence. You have suffered losses, you say; you will be more blessed in forgiving those from whom you have suffered than in taking vengeance upon them. Spare these poor miserable creatures for my sake, and you will never regret it hereafter.'

Was it a miracle that they all listened to and obeyed her words so readily? I cannot say; but purity and innocence combined with youth and beauty, can work miracles even in this wicked world of ours, and such was the effect which the maiden of Scott's Hall produced. Even Hankey and Trice were softened by her words, and felt a pity in their hearts towards the old women which they had never felt before..

My story is now nearly done. The old women came crawling and cringing to sweet Agnes' feet, humbled to the earth, and full of deadly terror. I cannot tell you all the good words she said to them, nor how she persuaded her uncle and the sterner Squire of Mersham Hatch to forbear punishing the wretched creatures. So, however, it was, and they were saved from the fate which had appeared so certain.

Doubtless you will ask what became of the old witches, and were they again let loose upon the world? Not so; but I am happy to say that they were witches no longer, the power and the will to do evil had gone from them, and regret for their misspent lives was now the principal feeling of their hearts.

Not far from that Brabourne Leese, which had been the scene of so many of their exploits, a line of red-brick cottages, built in homely style, but withal strong and comfortable, stood by the side of the road from Smeeth to Bircholt. These were the Scott's Hall almshouses, built by Sir Edward Scott, to please his favourite niece, and for years after the date of my story (if you had happened to live at that time) you might have seen four quiet, demure-looking old women, each spinning at her door, and looking as unlike a witch as anybody you ever saw. Yet these were the noted witches of that

day, and she who was the quietest and best-behaved of
all was the famous witch of Brooke Hollow.

As for the cats (and this proves the truth of the
whole story), some of the people buried them then and
there, when the hounds had killed them, and it is from
this event that the little green meadow where the
hounds overtook and slew them has been called by the
queer-sounding name of 'Cat's hole' from that day to
this.   Farmer Hankey returned home that day a happy
man.   He had no very heavy losses for the future, and
became more and more prosperous.   I regret to say,
however, that as he came to believe less and less in
witches and their evil-doings, he began to lay the blame
of any losses which *did* happen to him at the door of
the foxes, and he consequently entertained and handed
down to his descendants a foolish and unreasonable
hatred of foxes and fox-hunters, which was subsequently
the cause of much unpleasantness.   As for Trice, I never
heard much more of him, except that he lived to a good
old age, and often talked of the time when he had helped
put an end to the witches' frolics.   Giles Butcher became
a pattern labourer.   His wife read him a severe lesson
when she knew the whole truth, and never quite forgave
him that supper with the four witches.   For my part,
however, I think it was only her jealousy that made her
find fault, and I believe she would have very much liked
to have been one of the party.   She and Giles, however,
lived very happily, and their descendants are well-known
in that part of the country as honest and industrious
people.

And now I must take leave of my story, and all the
personages of whom I have told you.   I need not follow
the career of Sir Edward Scott, which may be gathered

from the history of those times.   Of Richard Knatchbull
I will not speak, inasmuch as the chronicles of his
family will tell you all you want to know.   I cannot
leave 'Saint Agnes' without regret, and a wish that I
could tell you more about her.   But I am unable to do
so.   'Whom the gods love, die young,' says some
wise person somewhere; and if this be true, perhaps our
Agnes' sweet spirit lingered not long upon the earth she
blessed by her goodness.   I cannot say, and I will not
guess.   Let us leave her as we found her; let us think
of her soft voice and gentle manner, her graceful fairy-
like form, her weird beauty, and all that made her so
precious to her uncle and so dear to the people among
whom she dwelt; above all, let us think of her purity of
heart and sweet innocence of thought and deed, and let
us ever bear in mind that such innocence and purity are
beloved of Him who reigns above and over all, that His
blessing will rest upon those who cherish and cultivate
these qualities in their inner hearts, and that to such
they will prove an endless source of peace, and rest, and
comfort, and happiness; sin and sorrow will flee before
them as the witches fled before 'Saint Agnes,' and they
will prove a sure safeguard against greater powers of evil
than even those which were possessed by the noted witch
of Brooke Hollow!

VIII.

THE MAN WITH A BEARD.

THERE was once a man who set his heart upon growing a very long beard. His friends endeavoured to persuade him not to do so, but all their entreaties were vain. They told him that he looked much better without a beard, that dust would get into it in summer, and rain in winter, so that it would always be either too dry or too damp, and that it was much better to keep his chin open to the air. They urged upon him, moreover, to consider how he would scratch his children, if he kissed them whilst his beard was growing, and how that his wife would shrink from him if he attempted the same thing with *her*. All this, however, was to no purpose; determined to have a beard, he persisted in the plan, resolutely refused to shave, merely smiled when people tried to reason with him, and was in due time rewarded by becoming the possessor of a beard of respectable length, breadth, and thickness. It hung down over his breast in quite an imposing manner, and none of those inconveniences which his friends had prophesied appeared likely to occur. With conscious

pride he dipped his ornament in the basin every morning, dried and combed it out with tender care, and
sprinkled 'eau. de cologne' upon it when he dressed for
dinner. Oftentimes his hand would steal naturally
towards his chin, and he would catch himself gently
stroking the hairy treasure in which he so much delighted. Nor were there wanting other friends who, taking
a different view of the case from those who had opposed
his wish, told him that, in their opinion, his personal
appearance was greatly improved by the beard, and advised him to follow up his success by cutting back his
whiskers from his face, so that the ornament might stand
out in bold relief. There were some who even suggested
the growth of a moustache, but for this he had not
sufficient courage, entertaining grave doubts upon the
question of soup, of which he was very fond, and with
his enjoyment of which he fancied a moustache might
interfere. He contented himself, therefore, with his beard,
which day by day became longer, and, in his opinion,
more beautiful, filling up all the space in his double-
breasted waistcoat which, in the case of beardless mortals, would have been devoted to a scarf—not that he
had no scarf, but that it was entirely concealed from
view by his enormous beard.

Now, I dare say that you will wonder how it was that
I ever came to write a story about this worthy man,
and what possible interest I can expect you to take in
his beard. But you will not wonder any longer when
you hear what I am going to tell you next. One day
the good gentleman had gone out on his lawn, and having sat down in an iron-chair easy arm-chair, where he
was wont to smoke his after-dinner cigar, fell fast asleep.
After a while he woke up suddenly, and felt a curious

sensation in his beard.   He could not understand it at
first, and put up his hand to feel what was the matter.
Hardly, however, had his fingers touched the beard,
when he received a smart peck on the top of his fore-
finger, and hastily withdrew it, exclaiming at the same
time, 'Why, what on earth is the matter with my
beard? there's somebody in it!'   And to his intense
surprise, a little voice answered him in a cheery, chirping tone, 'Yes, it's me, and here I mean to stay,' and
he instantly became aware of the fact that the speaker,
whoever it was, was certainly quietly and snugly established in his beard, and was making himself or herself
quite at home there.   Without a moment's hesitation,
he rose from his chair, strode into the study on the
ground-floor, close by which he had been sitting, and
went up to the looking-glass over the fire-place.   Then
he looked steadily and carefully at his beard, and very
soon became acquainted with the fact that a regular
little brown wren had taken up her quarters in his beloved treasure.

'Wren!' he exclaimed in a voice of thunder,
'this is really the height of impudence! who on
earth gave you leave to come here and settle in my
beard, as if it was your own? Get out of it, will
you?'

'Not a bit of it,' chirped the wren in cheerful accents.   'I haven't the least intention of moving from
where I am.   I find this a warm, airy, and pleasant
dwelling-place, and I have quite made up my mind to
stop here for a while.   Now, pray don't make a bother
about it; you will find me useful upon many occasions,
and I assure you that my intentions are not otherwise
than good, if you will only treat me with that respect

19

and consideration to which, as a lady, I am fairly entitled.'

The man stared very much at this speech of the wren's, and hardly knew what to make of it. He did not much fancy the idea of having to carry a wren about with him always, whether he would or no, and he thought it possible that she might disturb him very much at times. On the other hand, he did not like to be uncivil to a lady, and, after all, wrens were friendly, jovial little birds, and she might perhaps turn out to be something of a companion, when he came to know her better. Moreover, he did not know what power might be possessed by a wren who spoke such good English, and appeared so well to understand the ways of the world. So, after a short pause, he replied in a milder tone,

' Well, I hardly know what to say to this; but since you seem to come as a friend, and are evidently a lady, from your language and conversation, I will say no more, but trust that you will be as good as your word, and as useful as you promise.'

' All right,' rejoined the wren; ' trust me for that. You shall find no inconvenience from my living with you, and, in fact, it is the best thing for your interest that could possibly have happened. I may as well tell you, however, that you must let me do your future beard-combing for you in my own way. In fact, I have made my domestic arrangements within your beard in such a manner as to forbid the use of a common comb. I may mention, in passing, that I have just laid an egg; and that as I propose to follow this up by a number more, I shall be obliged to you if you will be careful, for some time to come, not to take your beard roughly into your hand, or to squeeze it, as some men do, as the consequences would probably be unpleasant to both of us.'

The man listened to the little bird with great surprise. Strange, indeed, it was that, without invitation, and, apparently, for the mere whim of the thing, a wren should come and take up her abode in a man's beard; but that she should justify her doing so, and announce her intention of laying eggs in his beard, and making her nest in it, was something surpassing all belief. Having formerly studied the habits of birds, our friend was well aware that wrens lay ten, twelve, fifteen, or even a larger number of eggs, and although the weight would not be great, still there was considerable delicacy and responsibility involved in the carrying about so many of these brittle things; and then, if any fair number of them should hatch out, the responsibility would be tenfold, and the annoyance possibly considerable, when he had to furnish a lodging for so many small birds, who could hardly be expected to remain either quiet or silent for any great length of time. However, he had now given his consent, and, in fact, he scarcely knew how he could have done anything else, so there was nothing for it but to make the best of his bargain, and hope that things would turn out pleasantly. Sundry little twinges and hair-pullings in his beard made him start from time to time during that afternoon, and once or twice he gently remonstrated with his little visitor. She replied, however, that although she should much regret to be the cause of any annoyance to him, it was absolutely necessary to make the resting-place of her eggs secure, and her nest tolerably comfortable; and that in order to effect these objects she was twisting and twining a few hairs in the interior of his beard, which, however, she trusted would only trouble him for a short time. With this explanation he was forced to be content, although he began to feel that his beard was no longer his own, but had become, for all practical purposes, the property of the wren.

Time went on, and although he could not ascertain the fact by combing out his beard or closely inspecting it—for both performances were strictly forbidden by his little tyrant—yet as she daily vouchsafed to him some information concerning herself and her proceedings, he became aware of the circumstance that each day added an egg to the collection for which he was obliged to furnish room, and this went on until the number positively reached seventeen. At this point the wren duly informed him that she thought she had laid enough, and should begin to set. He entirely agreed with her upon the first point, but was the victim of many doubts and fears as to the latter statement. What care the little bird might require, what attention she might expect, what liberty she would allow him during the process of setting upon her eggs, was a matter of serious speculation, and he much feared that he should find himself a greater slave than ever

But the business did not turn out so badly after all. The wren merely required that he should be more care-ful than usual not to use his beard roughly; and although she occasionally scolded him for shaking his head or nodding, and had, moreover, a disagreeable habit of chirping loudly in the middle of the night, to make the time pass pleasantly, as she said, but with the effect, if not the intention, of waking the unhappy man when he wanted to be asleep, yet upon the whole he had not much to complain of.

Day after day passed by in this manner, and he had got quite accustomed to his visitor and her ways, when about four o'clock one morning, just as it was getting light, he was awakened by a terrible racket and confusion, which caused him to start up in real alarm. A little voice, clear and sharp, was the first thing he heard.

'They're hatching, friend; they're hatching,' said the voice; and true enough, so they were. Chip, chip, one little egg broke after the other, until sixteen out of the seventeen produced a lively child to the little wren mother.

After this event there was no peace to the owner of the beard for days together. The little bits of egg-shell in his beard were bad enough, especially since combing them out was still forbidden, for fear of disturbing the little ones. Lucky he was, indeed, to get rid of the seventeenth egg, which turned out to be rotten; and the wren was rather inclined to attribute this misfortune to some fault in the beard, loudly declaring that she had never laid a rotten egg before. However, as it was rather in her own way, she consented to get rid of it, and pushed it out of the nest by herself, although the man was rather annoyed by her doing so at a moment when he was sitting down, dressed in his best evening clothes; and as the rotten egg fell upon his knee, and smashed instantly, mischief was done in the way of a stain, which might easily have been avoided. He bore it, however, with due patience, having long since made up his mind to submit to the yoke of the wren with humility.

Fortunately for him, the habits of the little bird were clean and lady-like, and her young family were brought up in the strictest rules of propriety. Their food was given them with care; and as the worthy wren demanded that they should be supplied with bread-crumbs during their early infancy, there was none of the unpleasantness which might have been caused by the introduction into the beard of those animals of the insect tribe, which form the usual food of an ordinary bird. But as the little nestlings grew bigger, day by day added to their weight, their voices became louder, and the victim whose beard was their home was occasionally hard put to it to secure a quiet hour's sleep. Other circumstances also occurred, which were by no means pleasant.

Calling one day upon an old maiden aunt, who was very rich, and from whom he entertained great expectations, her favourite cat suddenly sprang upon the man's knee, and began to raise herself up to his beard with loud purs of joy and expectant pleasure. Seeing, or by her natural instinct discovering, the young wrens, she made sure of a treat, and was evidently prepared to attack the fortress at once. A chorus of voices from the beard called the attention of its owner to the danger of his guests. Much as he respected his aunt and her money, he feared the wren more, nor was it possible for him to resist the cheery little voice, raised above the rest, which in bold accents chirped out in his ear,

'What are you about, sir? Don't you see that I and my children are in danger? Down with that cat directly!'

He had no time for doubt and hesitation. The paw

of the animal was actually raised to touch the beard, and he could only prevent the misfortune by a sudden but powerful movement of his arm, which sent poor pussy flying off his knee, right on to the top of a favourite lap-dog, who, fat, puffy, and generally disagreeable, as favourites are, was slumbering at the end of the rug, and, starting up, furious at the sudden and unexpected assault, overset a small, light table, on which were sundry valuable china cups and plates, several of which were smashed by the fall. The old aunt flew at once into a passion, which was quite inexcusable, as the man had fully confided to her the history of the wren.

'I never saw such a thing in all my life!' she angrily exclaimed. 'To treat a poor dumb animal in that abominably cruel way, and such a darling pet as my cat, too! A parcel of beggarly wrens to be made so much of! Why, the man must be little better than a fool!'

In vain did he try to make his excuses. The old lady would not be satisfied, but packed him off out of the house at once, and vowed that sooner than let such a cruel wretch touch one halfpenny of her money, she would leave it all to the newly-formed society for the relief of decayed cats, and so she did.

However, the more he suffered, the more faithful to his wren was the bearded man. In fact, he became quite attached to her; and none the less when, her little family having been happily fledged, and the beard put fully and completely to rights, she expressed her readiness to make it her permanent home. And now, having long since got over the first difficulties of her residence, when the novelty of the thing, and the

unusual twinges of his beard, coupled with the occasional tickling caused by the fluttering of its little
inmate, had all combined to render his position rather
unpleasant, the man really began to feel that he could
not part with his visitor without regret.

Many little acts of kindness did she do for him.
When he was asleep, she would creep out of the beard,
and keep flies and gnats away from him. But the most
extraordinary thing was her conduct at meals. She
seemed to know, as well as any doctor, what was good
and what was bad for her friend to eat. If she saw him
pitching into hot muffins at breakfast, drinking ale in
the heat of the day, devouring plates-full of fruit late at
night, or indulging too freely in lobster-salad just before
bed-time, she would bring him to his senses by a sharp
peck; and thus, as he usually followed her advice,
saved him from many an internal pain, and rendered
unnecessary many a dose of physic.

You must not suppose that our wren was for ever
in the beard. Oh no. She was never far off, it is true;
but she hopped out, and flew into the world whenever
she pleased, and there were many occasions when the
man felt her absence, missed her voice and advice, and
got into trouble, as he afterwards knew, for the want of
her. So altogether I think you will agree with me,
that the wren was a desirable companion, and that her
visit to the man was very fortunate for him.

One night—for I must hurry on to tell you some
more of this true but wonderful story—one night the
man was awakened by a strange sound of scuffling and
wrangling in his beard. Unable to discover what was
the cause, he got up and went to the looking-glass,
where he soon perceived what had occasioned the dis-

turbance.   A daring mouse had entered the beard, and attempted to dislodge the wren, who stoutly resisted his endeavours.

'It was *her* home,' she said, 'and he had no business there.'

To this the mouse replied, with a jaunty air, 'that there was plenty of room for both; that it seemed a comfortable place, and one in which a good, snug nest might be made; that a mouse was as good as a wren any day, and that come he would.' He added, I am sorry to say, several disrespectful observations about wrens generally, and this wren in particular, and seemed by no means disposed to give up the point.

In this state of things, the little bird appealed loudly to the man, and begged for his interference. The mouse, on the other hand, in soft and smooth accents (for the rogue had a silvery tongue of his own, and knew how to use it), argued his case. He said that he had at least as much right to the beard as his opponent, for it really belonged to the man himself. The wren had come there as an intruder, and it was only owing to the great kindness and generosity of the real owner that she had been suffered to remain. And now, forsooth, the tenant wanted to make herself out to have as much right to the property as the landlord. This was a pretty way of showing her gratitude to so good a friend! Besides, there was plenty of room in the beard for others besides one paltry wren, and it was at once rude and selfish of her to try to keep everybody else out.   Such a thing was really too bad, and he, the mouse, hoped that the man would not allow it, but by admitting him also into the beard, would secure to himself another trusty and true friend, and in fact shake off the tyranny to which he was subjected by the pride and conceit of this feathered creature.

These arguments made considerable impression upon our friend's mind. He could not deny that the wren had at first come there uninvited; and although he was now not only used to her, but actually regarded her as a friend, it was not to be forgotten that the beard was really his own property, and that if he intended it to remain so, it might be well to take this opportunity of asserting his rights of ownership, and exercising his authority by permitting the entrance of another guest. In spite, therefore, of the remonstrances of the poor wren, the man gave his decision in favour of the mouse, and declared that if he behaved well, he might share the hospitality which had been so long enjoyed by the bird. With a smile of triumph, the mouse crept into the beard, and established himself quite near enough to the wren to be excessively disagreeable. Henceforward whatever she did was wrong. He laughed at her cheerful chirping song as she went about her daily work, saying that he had a cousin who was a singing mouse, and could make much better melody. He kept as close to her nest as he could, so as to disturb and annoy her, and raised objections to everything she said or did. Worst of all, however, was his interference with her counsel and advice to the man. The mouse was always blaming her for being so strict and tight-laced. What business was it of HERS, he continually said, to tease her friend as she did. If he liked hot muffins for breakfast, why shouldn't he eat them? if he fancied fruit at night or ale in the middle of the day, why not let him enjoy himself? and what right had anybody to interfere with his lobster salad whenever he chose to indulge in it?

Not only did the mouse say this to the wren's face, but he took every opportunity of her being out of the beard, to poison the man's mind against her, and speak of her as a selfish, tyrannical little thing, who made his life a burden to him. Getting bolder by degrees, the mouse began to offer his own advice, in opposition to that of the wren, and to tempt the man to shake off her yoke, as he said, and to think and act for himself. Now, though the man knew in his heart that the mouse was wrong, I am sorry to say that he listened more and more to this bad advice, began to take less and less heed of the wren's counsel, and at last left off listening to it altogether. Her influence was gone, and that of the mouse prevailed. You may easily imagine the consequences which followed. No bird possessed of ordinary self-respect could remain in such an humiliating position. She must at once assert and claim her rights; and if these were denied to her, the beard was no longer her proper home. Accordingly she one morning made a formal complaint to the man of the conduct of the mouse, and pointed out to him that the state of things had really become unendurable. She upbraided him with his readiness to forget an old friend, and declared that whilst she had nothing to reproach herself with during the time of her residence in the beard, she could not help feeling that under existing circumstances she was rather a burden than a comfort to him.

The man listened to what she said with some attention, but having been warned by the mouse that she was about to make a great effort to regain her power over him, and that he must show firmness and courage if he wished to call his beard and his life his own, he gave her no very friendly answer. He told her that she had had everything pretty much her own way since she first came to live with him, that she had taken too much upon herself altogether, that her advice was often given when it was neither asked nor wanted, and that her desire to maintain her power without a rival was the real cause of her complaints against the mouse, and showed a selfish spirit, which was anything but creditable to her.

The wren rather ruffled up her feathers when she received this reply; but having made up her mind as to the course which she should pursue, she chirped out her regret in sorrowful tones, and told the man that, since he had made his choice in favour of the mouse, she could no longer remain and make her home in his beard, but that he must be content with his new friend, and be prepared to say good-bye to his old one. She had endeavoured to do her duty to the best of her power; and as he had not been satisfied and had failed to show her proper consideration, she must at once leave him to himself.

As soon as the wren had announced her determination of leaving the beard in which she had passed so many happy days, the joy and triumph of the mouse knew no bounds. He sneered at the little bird in discordant squeaks, and twitted her with her smallness of size, the dusky colour of her brown gown (though his own coat was no better), and her general plainness of appearance. He told her to her face that he had intended from the first to get rid of her; and that although she might fancy herself very clever, he hoped she would now own that she was no match for a mouse. There she had been established, quietly and comfortably, ruling the beard and its owner just as she pleased, but she had found that to oppose a mouse was the sure way to get herself turned out, and out she might go and welcome. He kept saying everything that was disagreeable a great many times over, and in such a tiresome teasing manner, that many birds would have been provoked to make an angry reply, if indeed they had not been tempted to peck at his eyes. But the wren treated his conduct and language with calm and lady-like contempt. In fact, she did not take the slightest notice of anything that he said or did, but occupied herself in her usual household arrangements until the time arrived which she had fixed for her departure. Then, with a sad look at her old home, and a reproachful glance at the ungrateful man, she flew chirping off to find some other place of refuge, and left the mouse in undisturbed possession of the beard.

Having now obtained his desire, and feeling himself secure, his first object was to congratulate the owner of the beard upon his freedom from the tyranny of the late occupier, and so he did. The man, however, was not quite contented with what he had done, and did not seem disposed to join in the rejoicings of the mouse, so that the latter was forced to be content with the result of his advice, and to await silently the march of events. At first the man certainly missed his little companion, and expected to hear her voice when he was about to do any of those things against which she had always set her face.

Little by little, however, he got used to her absence, and after a while began to feel rather glad that he could do whatever he pleased in the way of eating and drinking without being called to account by any one. And as the mouse never lost an opportunity of putting in a

word against his old enemy, the man began ere long to
fancy that he had really got rid of a troublesome customer; and that whilst the wren had been with him, he
had been subjected to a sort of tyranny and oppression
which were both disagreeable and unnecessary. With
this feeling, therefore, he launched out into all kinds of
excesses, and before very long forgot the sound of the
voice which had so often chirped good advice into his
ear; and if he ever thought of the little bird at all, ban-
ished the memory as soon as possible, just as one throws
aside a disagreeable subject whenever one is fortunate
enough to be able to do so.

But this entire change of system was not long in pro-
ducing its effects. However unpleasant the advice of
the wren might occasionally have been, the man soon
began to feel the loss of it. There was now no friendly
voice to warn him against muffins, he drank his strong
ale at mid-day without restraint, and went to considerable lengths in the matter of lobster salad and such
like delicacies at night. The mouse, indeed, rather encouraged him in these indulgences.

'Why shouldn't a fellow enjoy himself?' was his
frequent remark, and the man was only too well inclined to listen to it.

The consequences soon became apparent in the
altered state of our friend's health. Little by little he
became listless and inactive, less fit for exercise of either
mind or body, and more addicted to sloth and idleness.
He contracted a bad habit of going to sleep immediately
after dinner; he took to snoring so loudly that his
friends constantly remonstrated, and the mouse himself
frequently had recourse to scratching and pulling at the
beard in the dead of the night, when aroused by this

disagreeable noise. But the evil did not stop here.
Sundry pains and aches began to make their appearance, which had never troubled the man before. His
appetite failed him; his head was not so clear as of
old; he began to listen to suggestions about dinner
pills, and, to crown all, he grew quite short in his
temper; and then, after making himself unpleasant to
everybody, gave way to fits of melancholy, which made
him truly miserable.

In this state of things the mouse proved but a poor
comforter. He now considered himself as much the
owner of the beard as ever the wren had pretended to be.
He brought crumbs into it whenever he pleased, and
even went so far as to feast upon toasted cheese in his
home, without saying so much as 'by your leave,' or
'with your leave,' to the real owner. Besides this, he
was positively impertinent with regard to the man's
sufferings, telling him boldly that it 'served him right,'
that he 'had nobody to blame but himself,' and acting
altogether as if it was no concern of his.

The poor man, feeling that he really *was* to blame,
bore all this patiently for some time. Pride forbade
him to own that in turning out the wren he had only
procured for himself a worse tyrant, so he determined
to put up with it as best he could, and tried all the
while to believe that he was really pleasing himself.
But at last the trial becam really too great to be
borne. Enfeebled in health, and broken in spirit, he
obtained neither comfort nor assistance from the tenant
of his beard. The mouse kept very bad hours, too,
being constantly out late at night, and returning in the
small hours of the morning, not unfrequently dirty and
dusty, and smelling unpleasantly of strong cheese.

Once or twice the man spoke gently to him upon the subject, but without any effect; and he was really so much in the habit of giving way to the mouse, that, upon the failure of his remonstrances, he merely sighed, and said no more.

But the crisis came at last. He was awakened one night by a tumult and noise which, trying at any time when made immediately under your nose, are much worse when, as was the case with our friend, you happen to have gone to bed with a bad headache. He roused himself unwillingly, and in no very good temper; and on inquiring what was the matter, discovered that the mouse was giving a supper-party in his beard, at which a field-mouse, a dormouse, and worse than all, a lively young rat, were the guests, and the food was of no very savoury character. The noise was principally occasioned by the lively young rat 'chaffing' the dormouse, whose tail he had tied round with certain hairs out of the beard, and was playing sundry practical jokes upon him, to the great amusement of the other two.

The man spoke out at once, and told the mouse his mind plainly, upon which the latter quietly told him to 'shut up,' and not interfere with gentlemen, who were enjoying themselves as gentlemen should.

This was more than the man could bear. He told the mouse that he would stand it no longer; and upon the impudent little fellow telling him that in that case he had better 'sit it,' he jumped hastily up, and without another word, plunged his head, beard and all, into his hip-bath, which stood in the middle of the room. You may imagine the effect of this bold measure. The lively young rat nipped out of the beard like a shot, and bolted before the head touched the water. So he would have been all right if he hadn't happened to meet with a terrier puppy on the stairs, who played the practical joke upon *him* of biting his head off.

The three mice, however, were in a moment plunged into the water, and shrieked dreadfully. With a shake of his head which sent them all flying out of his beard into the tub, the man raised himself up, and looked down upon the little animals struggling in the water. Observing that one was a dormouse, he stretched out his hand and saved it, for he remembered that his little niece had expressed a wish to possess such an animal; and, as a matter of fact, she did possess and keep this self-same mouse for a long time afterwards. But the man looked calmly down upon the other two mice, and watched their vain efforts to escape.

In a shrill and feeble voice the mouse of the beard begged for mercy and aid, and asked what he had done that he should be treated like that?

'Done!' replied the angry man. 'Everything that you should not have done! You have been the cause of my banishing my best and truest friend; you have poisoned my ears and mind with bad advice (more fool I to take it), and have rendered my life miserable.'

'Alas!' replied the mouse in a voice which grew fainter and fainter, 'I did but seek to make my own life happy. Had you been patient with your "best friend," as you call the wren, she would never have left you, and I should never have troubled you or your beard. It was only because you were tired of her good advice, and dissatisfied with the restraint which she exercised upon your indulging in all kinds of pleasures that were bad for you, that you listened to me, and now you make

me suffer for that which was in reality your own fault.
I had no power over you but through your own will,
and you need never have received me as a guest if you
had been contented to let things remain as they were,
and to listen to your former tenant.'

As he heard these sad words the man hesitated for
a moment as to whether he should save the mouse or
not.   It was true enough that by his own act he had
admitted him into the beard, and, after all, he had given
him many pleasant words, and only advised and encouraged him to please and enjoy himself.   But, on the
other hand, his advice had always been bad, and he had
been the means of banishing the friendly wren, and the
cause of all his illness and misery.   So the mouse
pleaded in vain, and both he and his companion perished
then and there.

The man's next step was to wash his beard
thoroughly, comb and dry it afterwards, and then go
and think the whole matter over whilst he smoked a
quiet cigar, over which he not unnaturally fell asleep.

Next morning he awoke more refreshed than he had
been for many a long night, inasmuch as there had been
no noise in his beard to disturb his rest.   In fact, the
quiet seemed to him quite strange, and half a hundred
times during the day he listened, and put his hand up to
his beard, to make sure that there was really no one there.
So passed on the time for several days, and our worthy
friend positively began to find that he was rather lonely.
He could not, however, regret the mouse, who had
done him so much mischief, but he felt more and more
tenderness for the memory of the wren, and frequently
wished that he had never driven her away.   At last,
when seated one evening in that same iron-chain easy

chair of which I have already spoken, he sighed out aloud his sorrow and repentance.

'I feel,' he said, 'how great an error I committed in permitting my little friend to depart. Her kindly hints, her warning voice, saved me from many and many a mistake whilst she was with me; and now that I am without her, I value more than ever the blessing which I have lost.'

My children, the man was only saying that which children and grown up people very often are obliged to say to themselves. While the blessings which the good God has given us are with us still, too often we value them lightly and make but small account of them; then, when He sees fit that they should be taken from us, we begin to know how precious they were, and learn their value when it is too late. Our man, however, was more fortunate than many people in such-like positions. Whilst he was sighing and sorrowing as I tell you, he suddenly heard a little chirping, cheerful sound, and, lo and behold! up fluttered the dear little wren from a holly-bush hard by.

'Oh, my beauty, my pet,' cried the man, 'are you come back to me again?'

'Yes, dear friend,' replied the wren, 'I have heard what you have said; and since you have got rid of the mouse, and have become convinced that I only sought your good in all that I said and did whilst I lived with you, I am quite ready to let bygones be bygones, and to come back to my old home.'

I need scarcely tell you that the man was overjoyed at hearing this good news. He took the wren into his hands and gave her a gentle and affectionate kiss; he thanked her again and again for coming back; he offered to re-arrange his beard carefully according to her wishes, and promised faithfully that he would never again give her cause to leave him. Whether or no the man kept his promise I cannot tell you, because the old cock robin who told me the story did not know. He had it from a granddaughter of the wren's with whom he was on very friendly terms, and who routed it out when she was looking over some old letters and papers belonging to her departed grandmother. But I *do* know that for some time to come, at least, the man and the wren got on very well together; and I hope that our friend was too wise not to profit by the lesson he had already had, and that by paying proper attention to the advice of the little bird, he became restored to his former health of mind and body, and lived very happily all the rest of his life.

Now, I dare say you are all very much surprised and amused at the idea of a man having a bird to live in his beard. Of course this cannot happen to every one, partly because a great many people have not got beards, and partly because there wouldn't be enough wrens for all the people in the world. But every man, woman, and child that lives, has something inside them which acts the part of the dear little wren in giving them good advice, and warning them when they are going to do wrong. This is generally· called a conscience, and a very useful thing it is, if you will only attend to it. It is a true friend; and if you listen to it and encourage it to speak, it will guide you away from evil and lead you right. But if you try to stifle it—if you reason against it, or refuse to listen to it—after a while it will speak less and less, and will at last be silent. As the mouse drove the wren out of the beard,

so will your self-indulgence and the evil within you
hush the voice of conscience and undo all its good.
And if this once occurs to you, you will never be really
happy until you determine to conquer and drown the
evil, and not listen to its bad advice.   Then, if you
have not gone too far, your conscience may begin to
speak to you again ; and, if you are wise, you will encourage it, like the man welcomed back the wren, and
you will pray to the good Father of All that He will
keep your conscience tender for you, and incline you
always to listen to its voice, so that you may ever have
a sure guide and friend to warn you against the dangers and evil things which you must expect to meet
with in this world, but from which you will be preserved
and saved, if you make use of the means which our
merciful Father has provided for all His children.

THE END.

Bungay:

CLAY AND TAYLOR, PRINTERS

𝕸essrs. 𝕲eorge 𝕽outledge and 𝕾ons'
NEW BOOKS AND NEW EDITIONS.

PRICE.

£7 7s. THE KNEBWOTH EDITION OF LORD LYTTON'S WRITINGS. In 39 Volumes, crown 8vo, half-roan, gilt tops.

EDITION DE LUXE.

s. d. *Uniform with the India Proof Edition of* BIRKET FOSTER'S PICTURES OF ENGLISH LANDSCAPE.

ENGLISH RUSTIC PICTURES. Drawn by the late FREDERICK WALKER, A.R.A., and the late G. J. PINWELL, Engraved by the Brothers DALZIEL. (Only 250 copies printed.)

10 6 THE PLAYS AND POEMS OF SHAKSPERE. Edited by CHARLES KNIGHT. A New Large-Type Edition, with full-page Illustrations by Sir JOHN GILBERT, R.A. In Three Volumes, crown 8vo, cloth. (*Routledge's Standard Library.*)

7 6 PAN PIPES. Newly arranged, with Accompaniments by THEO. MARZIALS ; set to Pictures by WALTER CRANE, Engraved and Printed in Colours by EDMUND EVANS.

7 6 RANDOLPH CALDECOTT'S "GRAPHIC" PICTURES. A Collection of Mr. CALDECOTT's Contributions to *The Graphic*. Printed in Colours by EDMUND EVANS.

7 6 SIR JOHN GILBERT'S SHAKESPEARE. Edited by HOWARD STAUNTON. With Portrait and 511 Illustrations by Sir JOHN GILBERT, R.A. 680 pp., medium 4to, cloth, gilt tops. (And in boards, cloth back, 6s.)

7 6 THE MICROSCOPE : Its History, Construction, and Application. By JABEZ HOGG, F.L.S., F.R.M.S. With more than 500 Engravings and Coloured Illustrations. A New and Revised Edition.

6 0 ROUTLEDGE'S EVERY BOY'S ANNUAL FOR 1883. Edited by EDMUND ROUTLEDGE, F.R.G.S. With Illustrations, and Twelve full-page Coloured Plates. (*Twenty-first Year of Publication.*)

6 0 ROUTLEDGE'S EVERY GIRL'S ANNUAL FOR 1883. Edited by ALICIA AMY LEITH. With Illustrations, and Twelve full-page Plates printed in colours. (*Fifth Year of Publication.*)

6 0 LITTLE WIDE-AWAKE FOR 1883. By Mrs. SALE BARKER. With 132 Coloured Illustrations by M. E. EDWARDS, M. KERNS, F. A. FRASER, F. BARRAUD, GORDON BROWNE, CHARLOTTE WEEKES, L. HOPKINS, and A. C. CORBOULD. Cloth, gilt edges. (And in boards, 4s. 6d.)

6 0 WARRIOR KINGS, from CHARLEMAGNE to FREDERICK THE GREAT. By Lady LAMB. With numerous Woodcuts and full-page Plates.

5 0 KATE GREENAWAY'S NEW BOOK—LITTLE ANN. With 64 pages of Illustrations by KATE GREENAWAY, printed in Colours by EDMUND EVANS.

www.ingramcontent.com/pod-product-compliance
Lightning Source LLC
Chambersburg PA
CBHW020941030726
47496CB00005B/1297